W9-BZO-242

Praise for

The Courtesan's Secret

"Clever, smart, fresh, and passionate . . . [A] lively romp . . . Delightfully entertaining."

—Library Journal

"Highly amusing repartee and some wickedly attractive open ends round things out."

—Publishers Weekly

"Dain's clever tale of love and mayhem . . . Her talent for writing humor remains. That, plus her suggestive dialogue and a diverse set of characters, comes together in an enjoyable story."

—Romantic Times

The Courtesan's Daughter

"This cleverly orchestrated, unconventional romp through the glittering world of the Regency elite [is] graced with intriguing characters, laced with humor, and plotted with Machiavellian flair."

—Library Journal

"A witty Regency that sparkles and sizzles!"

—New York Times bestselling author Liz Carlyle

continued . . .

"[The author adds] a feel for the ton . . . well-written."

—*Midwest Book Review*

"Wonderful . . . great dialogue . . . Sophia the seasoned courtesan [is] so feisty and fun . . . Don't miss this fresh and extremely fun romp through romantic London. It is, as Sophia would say, 'simply too delicious to miss!'"

—*Night Owl Romance*

And more praise for
Claudia Dain's novels

"Dain deftly blends humor, adventure, suspense, and pathos."

—*Booklist*

"Claudia Dain writes with intelligence, sensuality, and heart, and the results are extraordinary!"

—*New York Times* bestselling author Connie Brockway

"Claudia Dain never fails to write a challenging and complex romance."

—*A Romance Review*

"Dain is a talented writer who knows her craft."

—*Romantic Times*

"[Claudia Dain writes] a red-hot romance."

—*Publishers Weekly*

How to Dazzle a Duke

Claudia Dain

BERKLEY SENSATION, NEW YORK

THE BERKLEY PUBLISHING GROUP
Published by the Penguin Group
Penguin Group (USA) Inc.
375 Hudson Street, New York, New York 10014, USA
Penguin Group (Canada), 90 Eglinton Avenue East, Suite 700, Toronto, Ontario M4P 2Y3, Canada (a division of Pearson Penguin Canada Inc.) • Penguin Books Ltd., 80 Strand, London WC2R 0RL, England • Penguin Group Ireland, 25 St. Stephen's Green, Dublin 2, Ireland (a division of Penguin Books Ltd.) • Penguin Group (Australia), 250 Camberwell Road, Camberwell, Victoria 3124, Australia (a division of Pearson Australia Group Pty. Ltd.) • Penguin Books India Pvt. Ltd., 11 Community Centre, Panchsheel Park, New Delhi—110 017, India • Penguin Group (NZ), 67 Apollo Drive, Rosedale, North Shore 0632, New Zealand (a division of Pearson New Zealand Ltd.) • Penguin Books (South Africa) (Pty.) Ltd., 24 Sturdee Avenue, Rosebank, Johannesburg 2196, South Africa

Penguin Books Ltd., Registered Offices: 80 Strand, London WC2R 0RL, England

This book is an original publication of The Berkley Publishing Group.

This is a work of fiction. Names, characters, places, and incidents either are the product of the author's imagination or are used fictitiously, and any resemblance to actual persons, living or dead, business establishments, events, or locales is entirely coincidental. The publisher does not have any control over and does not assume any responsibility for author or third-party websites or their content.

Copyright © 2009 by Claudia Welch.
Cover art by Jim Griffin.
Cover design by George Long.
Cover hand lettering by Ron Zinn.
Interior text design by Tiffany Estreicher.

All rights reserved.
No part of this book may be reproduced, scanned, or distributed in any printed or electronic form without permission. Please do not participate in or encourage piracy of copyrighted materials in violation of the author's rights. Purchase only authorized editions.
BERKLEY® SENSATION and the "B" design are trademarks of Penguin Group (USA) Inc.

PRINTING HISTORY
Berkley Sensation trade paperback edition / September 2009

Library of Congress Cataloging-in-Publication Data

Dain, Claudia.
How to dazzle a duke / Claudia Dain.
p.   cm.—(Berkley Sensation trade paperback ed.)
ISBN 978-0-425-22968-2
1. Courtesans—Fiction.   2. Aristocracy (Social class)—England—Fiction.   3. Marriage brokerage—Fiction.   I. Title.
PS3604.A348H69 2009
813'.6—dc22   2009020346

PRINTED IN THE UNITED STATES OF AMERICA

10 9 8 7 6 5 4 3 2 1

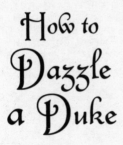

How to
Dazzle
a Duke

One

London 1802

Miss Penelope Prestwick stood in the middle of the conservatory of her father's Upper Brook Street home and stared at the roses. The roses were a disaster.

The roses, purchased to make a pleasing and, one hoped, impressive display of her horticultural talents to the marriage-able men of the ton, none of whom had any need to know she did not possess horticultural talents until one of their number was securely married to her, had not done the job at all. All her roses had done was to somehow become involved in getting Lady Amelia Caversham married to the Earl of Cranleigh.

Which, actually, was perfectly lovely as Lady Amelia had been rather obviously on the market for a duke. As Penelope was also on the market for a duke, it would certainly have become awkward very quickly. Her roses, ruined now, had done a good bit of work, now that she considered it.

Penelope Prestwick was a girl who considered everything, a trait she found quite admirable and certainly useful. Her future husband had no need to know that either. Men were so much more pleasant, which is to say, manageable, when they did not understand too much.

"What will you do to them now?" her brother, George, asked her, rather ironically, given the direction of her thoughts. "Throw them down some distant well?"

"Don't be absurd, George," Penelope said stiffly. "How can I get rid of the evidence of my spectacular talent with roses? I must save them, somehow. I can't simply get rid of them, can I?"

"They did serve their purpose. What point in keeping them, Pen?"

"George," she said with strained patience, "everyone at our ball, indeed, everyone in Town, knows that I keep roses and that they dwell in my conservatory. Having played a part in Lady Amelia's marriage, how can I ever be rid of them now? Besides, everyone thinks I'm rose mad. I shall have to continue on with it, shan't I?"

"I don't suppose you could simply inform people that they'd died of some malady. That would be too simple by half."

"Who would ever believe a word of that? These roses are famous. I can't be rid of them now. No, the thing to do, obviously, is to use them somehow. I wish I could think how."

"As to using things, there's that shawl."

Yes, there was *that* shawl. Of course, it was quite well-known that Lady Amelia, a duke's daughter, had behaved in quite questionable fashion and that a scandalous satire had been done of her, and of Penelope's roses. As a result of all of it, or a part of it, no one was quite certain, Lady Amelia had been promptly married to Cranleigh.

It was, to put it mildly, a scandal.

Penelope had the shawl, ripped, and the roses, ruined, and knew she had to do something with both, but was not at all sure what.

Lady Dalby would know.

Yes, that was undeniable. Something had to be done. And when something had to be done, particularly concerning men, Sophia Dalby was the precise person one should see. Of that, Penelope had no doubt whatsoever.

"George, we're going to see Lady Dalby," Penelope said firmly. "You, of course, will wait for me outside. I do not think this will be an appropriate conversation for a gentleman to hear."

"Going to talk marriage, are you?" George said wryly.

"Precisely," Penelope said as she walked away.

She was going to change her dress. She was not going to face Sophia looking even slightly less than perfect. That it was coming on five and the Duke of Edenham had an appointment with Lady Dalby for six o'clock was not a coincidence to be ignored. Indeed, Penelope did not believe in coincidence. All could and should be arranged to suit oneself beautifully. Relying on coincidence was for spoilt girls, and she was no such thing. She was a determined, logical, precise sort of girl, and she had determined to marry a duke, or an heir apparent at the very least. Logically, she had made it a point to overhear Edenham make his six o'clock appointment with Sophia. She planned to arrive at Dalby House at precisely half five. There was no need to look *too* precise about running into the duke, was there?

Of course not.

❧

DALBY House was quite lovely, though the Dalby House butler was not. He was a rugged-looking man, not at all what one sought in a butler as to physical appearance, and he was of somewhat irregular demeanor and perhaps just slightly indiscreet in his responses, which was also not at all desirable in a butler. Why, he very nearly grinned when he accepted her card. And then he was bold enough to stick his head out the door and twist his neck around until it was perfectly obvious he'd spotted

George loitering across the street, fussing with his waistcoat, most like.

What a perfectly horrid beginning to what was certain to be an awkward exchange once she put her request to Lady Dalby in the flesh.

In the flesh was not the sort of expression common to Penelope, but when one was dealing with Sophia Dalby, it was the expression that sprang most vigorously to mind. Sophia Dalby was, without question, the most famously seductive woman that anyone in two generations had occasion to know. Even Penelope's father, Viscount Prestwick, who did not know Sophia personally, knew nearly everything about her and found her fascinating. It was one of the main reasons that Lady Dalby had been included on the guest list for the ball. One of *his* main reasons. Penelope's sole purpose in wanting Sophia to attend was that if a woman was as famously seductive as Sophia was reputed to be, and indeed she was, then all the most interesting men in Town were certain to follow her about like cats after cream.

And so it was.

Very nearly everyone who had been invited, and her guest list had been aggressive and high reaching, had attended. Hence the horrid crush of people. Hence the attendance of two dukes and one heir apparent. She hadn't dared to even hope for that, but come they had, trailing in Sophia's wake. Penelope was far from being outraged or insulted or alarmed by Sophia's blatant allure, for what good would that do? Besides, Sophia had married well and had provided the proper heir to the Dalby earldom, what need had she for a husband now? No, Penelope was nothing so foolish as to be jealous of Sophia. What she intended was to make use of such a valuable lure. How could she not? With so many perfectly eligible men of the proper rank buzzing around Sophia like so many bees, it would make catching her own man so much easier, wouldn't it? It was a perfectly logical and, dare she admit it, nearly effortless way to get a man.

But naturally, she did not want just any man. She wanted a duke. And for that, she rather suspected she would require expert assistance. If any woman was an expert in getting a man, that woman was Sophia Dalby.

Penelope was no fool. She wanted the best, both in husbands and in aid. Sophia was the best. Penelope had absolutely no qualms at all about seeking the proper help.

Although, perhaps, just perhaps, she did have the slightest qualm about actually putting into words what she wanted when faced, well and truly, by Sophia's perceptive gaze.

Which was precisely the situation she found herself in when the Dalby House butler, with quite a bit of cheek, announced her to Lady Dalby and she entered the famous white salon.

It was a beautiful room, famously done up in white damasks and white velvets, pale blue braid here and there. An exquisite and clearly priceless Chinese porcelain vase in celadon green was the strongest spark of color in the pale room. Penelope, as diligent as anyone in listening to pertinent gossip, and surely it was *all* pertinent, had known of the famous porcelain in the famous white salon, though she had supposed the porcelain to be white, which only proved that gossip was not as reliable as it ought to be. Still, it was Chinese porcelain and it clearly was the centerpiece of the room, so she was not too disappointed in the reliability of casual gossip. According to the most popular report, the vase was a gift from Pitt the Younger for some aid she had done him in the Commons two decades past, but another version had it that it was a gift from the Prince of Wales for one night in her bed.

Penelope did not have an opinion on the matter one way or the other. Of course, there were many more speculations on the origin of the vase, which in some reports was a bowl or even a cup, but there was the porcelain and Sophia had done *something* to earn it, and that was quite enough information for Penelope.

She made her curtsey to Lady Dalby with the grace she had been tutored to display, sat prettily on the edge of her white upholstered seat, arranged her crimson shawl attractively over her arms, and proceeded to the task at hand.

"Lady Dalby, thank you for receiving me," she said, mentally commanding herself to hold Sophia's dark gaze. It was most peculiar, but she had the most uncomfortable sensation that Sophia not only knew why she had come, but found it utterly amusing.

"How lovely of you to call, Miss Prestwick," Sophia said. "You are quite recovered from hosting your wonderful ball? Truly, it may be remembered as the event of the Season."

As the Duke of Aldreth's daughter, the inconvenient Amelia, had been nearly ruined at the Prestwick ball, Penelope should not be a bit surprised. Of course, it would be remembered as the most *disastrous* event of the Season, but Sophia was too experienced at conversation to make such a bald statement.

"Yes, that would be lovely," Penelope said absently.

There was simply no point in discussing the ball. It had not yielded the desired fruit: no duke or heir apparent had considered her as a prospective wife. She knew enough of men to know that, at least. Men got a certain look when they were considering a woman, for anything. No man had looked at her in any fashion beyond the bare necessity of civil conversation. It was very nearly insulting.

Oh, very well, it had been completely insulting, and she was such a handsome-looking girl, too.

"And how are your marvelous roses doing?" Sophia asked. "Not damaged in any way when poor Lady Amelia became entangled in them? Roses are fragile, are they not?"

Oh, bother; this is just the sort of nuisance that the roses were clearly going to become in Society. Everyone now would expect her to practically give horticultural lectures on the peculiarities of roses. And what was she to say? That she was fairly certain they required watering on some sort of regular basis? That she thought the blooms quite pretty, when they could be bothered to appear? All the roses were to have been was a point of interest laid at her very petite feet; she was not supposed to be required to actually discuss them upon command. This was all Lady Amelia's doing, without question.

"Even with their thorns?" Lady Dalby continued, a certain malicious light in her dark eyes. "Of course, the very reason roses have thorns is because they are so fragile, or so I have surmised. Would you agree?"

"I would, Lady Dalby," Penelope answered. Anything to end the flow of words, and pointed questions, about roses. She very nearly regretted buying the stupid things in the first place.

"Then your roses have quite recovered?" Sophia asked, displaying a rather bold streak of cruelty, as it was perfectly plain that Penelope had no wish to speak of her annoying roses.

"They give every appearance of being so," Penelope said tartly, quite unable to stop herself and nearly unapologetic about it.

Sophia gave her a considering look, her eyes twinkling, and then asked, "How do you take your tea, Miss Prestwick?"

Bother. Now, if the pattern held, Sophia would engage her in a perfectly pointless discussion about various teas for the next quarter hour. The Duke of Edenham was due to arrive at Dalby House in less than thirty minutes, but if Penelope did not have Sophia firmly in her corner by then, Edenham would prove useless. She knew that as well as she knew her own name. Unless aided by Sophia, there was not a duke in Town who would fall into her very deserving lap. They hadn't yet done, had they? Without the proper aid, they clearly never would. Sophia, as annoying as she could clearly be, was the proper aid, indeed the *only* aid. That was more than clear.

"Lady Dalby," Penelope said, ignoring the subject of tea entirely. "I am quite aware, indeed, all of Society is quite aware, that you have a particular talent, one could even say a passion, for matchmaking." Penelope paused briefly to study the look on Sophia's face. She looked not one whit alarmed, or even surprised. She did look entertained. Penelope was perfectly willing to be the source of humor for Sophia, as long as she got her duke in the end. "You have done so, quite obviously, with three women of gentle birth in the past month, one of them your own daughter."

"But of course with my own daughter, Miss Prestwick," Sophia interrupted, needlessly. "How else was she to marry without my guidance and permission?"

Penelope shook her head in annoyance and continued. "Clearly true, Lady Dalby, I was only recounting my observations. If I may continue?" She was not asking permission, which was perfectly obvious to both of them.

"Please do," Sophia said with a smile, leaning back against the cushions.

"If one includes Mrs. Warren, which I feel I must as she is a close family friend, then the number jumps to four. Four women within a month. Four women who have made stellar, if not to say unexpected, matches with respectable and honorable men. Is that an accurate recounting of events, Lady Dalby?"

There. She had got it all out without further interruption. Penelope was aware that she was holding her breath, her spine very straight as she held Sophia's gaze. It was, surprisingly, not a particularly awkward moment. Sophia made it so, of that she was certain. No huffs of outrage or looks of offended dignity; no, she was completely at ease, calm as a shallow pond. Strangely, Penelope realized she had expected nothing less.

"I am completely charmed," Sophia said softly, "that you've taken such trouble, Miss Prestwick. I do think, however, that if your accounting is to be precise, the true number is four women in not quite three weeks. You seem to be a woman who values precision."

And indeed she was. How unusual and how pleasant for someone to have noticed that about her. But then, she was under the rather firm impression that Sophia noticed everything about nearly everyone.

"I do, Lady Dalby," Penelope said. "I also value results, which I suspect you do as well."

To which Sophia Dalby nodded and smiled in clear delight. Perfect. Things were going so well and so very quickly, which is just as things ought to go. Penelope plunged in to the full; whatever hesitation, and indeed she had nearly none to start with, cast away in the pure pleasure of such plain speaking.

"Then, Lady Dalby," she continued, "I have come to ask if you will help me as you've helped the others. Will you make it five, Lady Dalby? I should like a husband. I have only one requirement, and having met that, he can be whomever you think best." A gamble, certainly, but the events of the past three weeks had proven sufficiently to Penelope that Sophia was a woman to gamble upon. "I am quite convinced that you know what you're about. The women who have sought your aid seem to me to be entirely delighted by, if not the chain of events, their conclusion. Will you help me, Lady Dalby?"

There was no taking the words back now. No, nor the wish. She wanted a duke. She didn't see any reason at all why she shouldn't have one. Having come to Sophia for aid, it would have been a ridiculous bit of foolishness to not be forthcoming about what she wanted, wouldn't it? Penelope had decided her course and she would hold to it, with Sophia's help or not. But she did so want Sophia's help as her own efforts had produced not a solitary duke or heir apparent. Surely, she could do no worse with Sophia on her side.

Sophia, far from looking shocked, such a relief, leaned forward and stared in some fascination at Penelope.

"And what is your one requirement, Miss Prestwick? I confess to being curious."

Penelope suspected rather strongly that there was no mystery as to her one requirement, but she played along, not a bit put off by plain speaking, as should be perfectly obvious to the most obtuse of persons, which Sophia Dalby clearly was not.

Penelope leaned forward upon her seat, matching Sophia's pose nearly completely. "I want a duke, Lady Dalby," she said calmly and clearly.

Sophia did not so much as blink. "Many girls want dukes, Miss Prestwick. Indeed, I should say all girls would like one. Why should you get your duke?"

Penelope smiled and tilting her head playfully, said with the utmost earnestness, "Because I can afford one, Lady Dalby."

Sophia blinked. "Darling," she said with a smile, "we are going to get along famously."

Oh, she did hope so. She did so very much want her duke, or heir apparent; she was not unreasonable, after all.

Two

"As you can afford a duke," Sophia said, leaning back against the milk blue damask sofa and studying the lovely young girl before her, "you can almost certainly afford me."

"I beg your pardon?" Miss Prestwick said. She did not stammer, that could be said in her favor, but she did look more than a bit surprised. Small wonder, really. These young things, they did seem to think that life ever should fall their way with such very little effort on their part. It was most unfortunate, to be sure, that life was not nearly so accommodating. "Afford you, Lady Dalby? I do not comprehend you."

"Then allow me to clarify," Sophia said. "I have, or have not, aided the women you have observed; we shall not be so crass as to name them, shall we? Their privacy is as important to them as yours is to you. Being indiscreet is so rarely good form, though sometimes . . . but never mind that now, Miss Prestwick. The point must be that, while I did or did not aid certain women in attaining the men they desired, or at least deserved, my interests were also served. How am I to be served if I choose to aid you,

Miss Prestwick, that is the question. I do nothing for . . . nothing. Or had you heard otherwise?"

Sophia knew very well that Miss Prestwick had not. Of all the rumors that had ever been circulated about Sophia Dalby, being free and easy with her favors was not one of them.

To her immense credit, Miss Prestwick recovered her composure quickly. She blinked hard, stared directly into Sophia's eyes, and said, "What would you like, Lady Dalby?"

Sophia was more than a little impressed, which happened so very rarely that she took a moment to savor the sensation. What a truly remarkable girl. Miss Prestwick would do quite nicely as a duchess.

"What is it in your power to offer, Miss Prestwick?" Sophia responded.

Miss Prestwick blinked once more, took an audible breath, and said, "I am afraid I can think of nothing, Lady Dalby."

"You have reached your majority?"

"I have. I was twenty-one in February."

"You will wish your father's consent, however, will you not?"

"I would," Miss Prestwick said softly. "I confess to have given no thought to an elopement."

"And I should not think it will come to that, so give no thought to it now," Sophia said. Truly a remarkable girl, quite the most composed and straightforward girl of the Season. "Your father, Viscount Prestwick, should be involved in this, do you not agree? It is very much to be desired to have one's parent fully engaged in the marital dance. He wants you to marry well, I assume, so he can have no qualms about your seeking aid from someone reliably able to induce events to take the required turn, can he?"

"Can't he?" Miss Prestwick asked in answer, her dark eyes-glittering in suspicion. "Do you want something of my father, Lady Dalby? I can assure you that he has nothing you might want."

Charming. This was going to be a pure delight.

"But, darling," Sophia cooed, "that is flatly untrue. I've yet to meet a man who has *nothing* I might want. I want so very many things, you see, and yet not a one of them a duke, at least for a husband, so we shall not be in any competition on any item that truly matters. A most important point for allies in arms, wouldn't you agree?"

"In arms, Lady Dalby?" Miss Prestwick said with a sharp smile. "Shall it come to that?"

"Dukes do not come easily, Miss Prestwick, and very rarely do they come willingly."

"Perhaps I will surprise you and be the exception, Lady Dalby."

"Darling, you are already the exception, and perfectly delightful because of it. Now, shall we not trade your exceptional qualities for a dukedom? Is that not a fair trade?"

"And what shall we trade for your aid, Lady Dalby? What does Prestwick have that you could want?"

"He's a man, darling. He must have *something*."

"He has no wife, Lady Dalby," Miss Prestwick said stiffly, rearranging herself slightly.

Sophia laughed lightly, nearly mockingly. "Darling, can you possibly be insinuating that I am in need of a husband? And your father that fortunate man?"

Miss Prestwick said nothing. She did not look pleased, though neither did she look entirely insulted. Such a remarkably composed girl. Would it even take a week to see her married to her duke? How to get the bet on White's book was the question. She had quite used up the Marquis of Penrith's usefulness there. Oh well, there was always some man or other to do whatever a woman required of him, which was really so pleasant of them.

"I merely made an observation, Lady Dalby, not an insinuation. You do not wish to marry?"

"I have married, Miss Prestwick. Once is sufficient."

"I daresay I do agree with you there, Lady Dalby. Done well, once should be more than sufficient."

A heart like a diamond, had Miss Prestwick. Quite a rarity in any woman possessed of less than thirty years, and not even common in women above forty. Of men and the softness of their hearts, it was nearly impossible not to be crass and observe that they were entirely both more romantic and more self-serving than should have been possible. Which brought her thoughts round to the Viscount Prestwick again.

"Miss Prestwick, I hope I shall not embarrass you by remarking that you are quite the most sophisticated woman of your years and station that I have had occasion to meet. It is such a relief to know that some women are still capable of being both reasonable and well-informed about the state of things in general and men in particular."

"Thank you, Lady Dalby," Miss Prestwick replied cordially. "I have observed that there is far too much emotional disturbance and far too little intellectual calculation in Society. I fear that makes me unusual to an unpleasant degree."

"By being unique? Hardly. But who has implied this is an unpleasant condition? Not the viscount."

"Not precisely the viscount," Miss Prestwick said, squirming just a bit on her seat. "More a general impression from those I converse with."

"Such as dukes and heirs apparent?" Sophia asked.

"Such as, Lady Dalby," Miss Prestwick admitted with a solemn expression.

"On the occasion of your remarkable ball during which your remarkable roses were damaged?"

"On that occasion, yes," Miss Prestwick said. "But this does not bring us round to what you want of my father, Lady Dalby. I can't think that he would have anything you could want."

"You would likely be surprised at what I can want, Miss Prestwick. I am nearly certain your father can satisfy me."

If she said it with a certain suggestive overtone, she must be excused for it. Teasing Miss Prestwick was entirely too delightful as the girl was so artfully composed. One could not but wonder what, or whom, it would take to rattle her.

"Lady Dalby, if you could find satisfaction from Prestwick and if it were in my power, I would place him entirely at your disposal."

Well. How very interesting.

"A gracious offer, Miss Prestwick. Have Lord Prestwick drop round tomorrow, will you? I shall certainly be at home for him." Miss Prestwick lifted her head, took a shallow breath, and nodded. Such a completely remarkable girl. Sophia had not the smallest doubt that she'd make a duchess who would be remembered for a full century, at the very minimum. "Now then, as you so kindly offered Lady Amelia your shawl at your memorable ball, and as it has become something of a talisman for scandal, which is absurd as any method required to bring a man to heel is bound to require some small particle of scandal, it would be such a lovely display of friendship and concern if you should decide to give Lady Amelia your shawl, torn so violently upon your roses at your ball, so that it not fall into other, less generous hands and increase the scandal. Though, I do admit to some small bias as to the size of a scandal. Can a scandal ever be too large? Not in my opinion. They can, however, be too small to do anyone any good at all. Would you not agree, Miss Prestwick?"

Miss Prestwick smiled and said, "I confess to have not given scandal, its breadth or scope, very much thought at all, Lady Dalby. As you have done so, I will take your instruction upon its merits to heart."

"Miss Prestwick, you are entirely remarkable, and I am not in the habit of making such pronouncements. You will do exceedingly well and, I daresay, have all your plans and wishes bear the desired fruit."

Penelope Prestwick's dark eyes gleamed with suppressed joy, and she said, "I expected nothing less, Lady Dalby, having come to you for aid. Now, you wish me to deliver my torn shawl to Lady Amelia? I shall do so. Indeed, I had attempted to do so during the Duke of Aldreth's At Home, but could not find the opportunity."

"No, I should think not, what with the Earl of Cranleigh dragging darling Amelia into the mews and having his delicious way with her. Such an unexpected display, was it not?"

"Was it?" Miss Prestwick countered, holding Sophia's gaze. "The Duke of Aldreth did not seem either exceptionally surprised or displeased, which must also be said of Cranleigh's parents, the Duke and Duchess of Hyde. Quite remarkable behavior for parents to display when their children are behaving so scandalously. But you are friends with both the Hydes and with Aldreth, are you not? That was my impression."

"Your impressions, Miss Prestwick, are quite on the mark, which does commend you. There is very little that a woman needs beyond the ability to observe very carefully what occurs before her very eyes. It is a continual surprise to me that so few women, and indeed men, are able to see what is right in front of them. Now, in that vein, you certainly have observed the men whom must make up your list of potential husbands. Whom do you prefer?"

"Lady Dalby, I have no preference. I do not know the gentlemen well enough to have formed one."

Sophia raised her brows and considered Penelope. "Is that possible, Miss Prestwick? Surely a woman is able to form a preference for the simplest item almost instantly. How not with a man?"

"I may form an instant preference for a hat, Lady Dalby, but a husband is a far more serious acquisition. I am not in favor of either haste or carelessness."

"And of course, one always does try the hat on. Not every hat suits every face, does it, Miss Prestwick?"

Penelope Prestwick raised her own dark brows and said, "I have very many hats, Lady Dalby. I am quite adept at finding ones which flatter me. And if they do not, I adjust them until they do."

"I'm certain you do, Miss Prestwick," Sophia said, smiling. "Shall I take you at your word, then? Any man? The choice to lie completely with me?"

"If he is a duke or an heir apparent, Lady Dalby, I should think myself very much a fool not to leave the choice with you. You shall, I have been convinced by observation, make the choice for me in any regard. Why not dispense with the folly that I am in control of this? Having come to you, I leave all the details in your capable hands."

"Miss Prestwick, if England produced even one hundred women of your caliber, it would be an entirely different country indeed, and much the better for it, I assure you. Now," Sophia said, rising to her feet, "you will want to make your way to Hyde House to deliver that badly torn shawl to Lady Amelia. It will do much to recommend you to her and to the men of that house. If you do not tarry, you can arrive in good time."

"The men of that house?" Miss Prestwick said in a slightly raised tone. "Are you recommending Lord Iveston, Lady Dalby?"

"He is an heir apparent, is he not?"

Miss Prestwick, having stood in response to Sophia's rise to her feet and unable to keep herself from following Sophia's obvious lead in directing her to the door into the hall, was nevertheless obviously reluctant to leave before the Duke of Edenham's arrival. The darling girl, quite uncommonly practical, was still disposed to seek her own way, which was also quite practical of her. Sophia didn't fault her in the least.

"Yes," Penelope said slowly.

"And you would prefer a duke in the full and luxurious possession of his title? Such as the lovely Duke of Edenham?" Sophia asked.

Miss Prestwick blushed lightly. It looked most becoming on her.

"He is most eligible, is he not?" Penelope asked in response.

"You are not afraid of his reputation? He has had three wives previously, which has resulted in some perfectly ridiculous rumors about his tendency to kill off the women who share his bed."

"*Ridiculous* is the word," Penelope sniffed, pulling at her left glove. "Women die in childbed every day. I hardly see that the duke should be held accountable for ill health and a weak constitution."

"You are formed of hardier stuff?"

"Most certainly," Penelope Prestwick huffed.

"Miss Prestwick," Sophia said with a smile, "I do believe you. However, I do think that a visit to Hyde House is the thing to do at this moment." Miss Prestwick hesitated, even though Fredericks had opened the door and every physical indication was that the entire staff of Dalby House was encouraging her to the door onto Upper Brook Street.

"*At this moment?* Is this a ploy of sorts, Lady Dalby? Something to intrigue the Duke of Edenham?"

Sophia smiled and drew a deep breath before answering. "Darling, most men require ploys of various sorts. Even dukes. In point of fact, dukes more than any other sort of man. They are so very accustomed to achieving their every desire at every conceivable opportunity and not a few inconceivable ones. Do you not think it would intrigue them to be made to pause, even to stumble, if only for a moment?"

"I confess to have given it no thought," Penelope said. "But I suppose it makes sense, in a rather peculiar fashion. The lure of the unique, Lady Dalby? Is that what you're suggesting?"

"I am, darling, and you are the ideal woman to carry it off to perfection. Wouldn't you agree?"

"I would," she said, lifting her delightful little chin. "Then I shall make for Hyde House, engage Lord Iveston's attention if at all possible, whilst you meet with the Duke of Edenham and . . . what are you to do with the Duke of Edenham, Lady Dalby?"

"Why, entertain him, darling, as innocently as I possibly can. You truly have no preference? No hidden longing for Edenham over, say, Calbourne, or the intriguing Lord Iveston?"

Miss Prestwick fixed Sophia with a very direct look and answered, "Lady Dalby, I shall fix my longing upon the man you can best arrange, have no doubt about it. Good day."

"Good day, Miss Prestwick," Sophia said with a bemused smile.

Three

PENELOPE exited Dalby House as slowly as she could without looking ridiculous. Even so, she still managed to miss the arrival of the Duke of Edenham. No matter what she had told Sophia Dalby, she knew what she wanted, and what she wanted was Edenham.

He was nearly fatally handsome.

If she were going to marry a duke, why not marry the most handsome one available to her? And he was available. He had had his three wives and he had his two heirs, but could not a duke in the prime of life do with another fetching wife? And she was fetching; she knew she was. She had a mirror, didn't she?

She was a fine-looking woman and she had a fine, fat settlement upon her, her father being no dullard and understanding very well that a rich purse was a nearly irresistible inducement to marry, even for a duke with a fat purse of his own. Was not having more wealth to be preferred in every circumstance?

Of course it was. Surely a duke knew that better than anyone.

Penelope gripped her shawl firmly and waved crisply at George, who was loitering across Park Lane, ambling with evident cheer along the northernmost rim of Hyde Park. George was often wasting time in Hyde Park; he did love a good stretch of the leg, as he put it, and walked when any other man would have ridden. Any other man who was deeply and fully accustomed to being in the upper branches of the ton, that is. She was quite certain that the Duke of Edenham or even the rather odd Duke of Calbourne did not waste time walking to no purpose.

She did want Edenham.

She did not want Calbourne at all. He was rather too tall, a point which Lady Amelia had made all too publicly very recently. Calbourne had not taken Amelia's point very well at all, which was a puzzle. Didn't he *know* he was too tall to be considered elegantly proportioned? Not only was he taller than was entirely appropriate, he had the most peculiar sense of humor. And, truth be told, she had not made the most stellar impression upon him at her ball, a point she was still somewhat befuddled over. Calbourne was of that particular type who did not appreciate a logical, well-informed, reasonable woman. There were, sad to say, quite a few men of similar disposition in the ton, which did make it terribly inconvenient for a woman of her particular traits, being well-informed first and foremost among them.

What opinion the Marquis of Iveston had about women she had no idea, nor little interest. Lord Iveston was, in a word, *peculiar.* Or that was the rumor of him, and she paid particular attention to every rumor regarding every member of the ton. She had to. How else to know how to negotiate the twists and turns of Society? It was because of her bold observation of who was who and who did what that she had known to seek out Sophia Dalby for aid. While she was a bit uncertain what it was Sophia actually *did*, she was not at all uncertain that Sophia was very good at doing it.

Why Iveston should have been the man Sophia preferred for her was a puzzle, but she thought it might be because Sophia Dalby was on very close terms with the Hydes and thought rather more highly of the Hydes than was entirely deserved. She had, after all, seen two of their sons married in less than a week. That was not information which could be ignored.

But just because Sophia Dalby had some notion that it might be entertaining to see all of Hyde's sons married in the same Season, there were five marriageable sons as of last month and two had already been whisked off the marriage mart by Sophia's sure hand and ruthless gaze, Penelope felt no obligation at all to be the fodder for marriage number three.

Iveston was handsome, to be sure, but all the Hydes were handsome in their tall, blond way. It was only that Iveston, while only being an heir apparent and not an actual duke in the full force of his title, which was the point, after all, was so remarkably odd.

It was a well-known fact that he was very nearly incapable of speech, which might not be a bad trait to have in a husband, but it did put him out for ridicule and she had no desire to spend her life with a ridiculous husband. Not if she could avoid it. Because of Edenham and his wifeless state, she thought she should be able to avoid it.

At least Edenham could talk, and was quite charming about it, too.

"What are you looking so flushed about?" George said by way of greeting. "Did Lady Dalby fluster you with her bold ways?"

"Hardly," she huffed, reaching out to straighten his collar. He looked pleasantly rumpled, which was perfectly fine if one were in the country but not at all the thing when one was in Town. "We have made plans, she and I, and I am about putting them into play."

"Plans? What plans?" George said, reaching out to knock her bonnet askew in response to her very practical and necessary straightening of his collar.

"Plans to get my duke, George, which would go far better with a properly arranged bonnet!" she said primly. Trust George to get playful at the most important moment of her life, the moment when she began her assault on some duke or other, preferably Edenham. Iveston in a pinch. Calbourne as a last gasp necessity. They were so nicely and neatly arranged in her thoughts; one did hope that they would line up in an equally orderly fashion when she got round to them in person.

"Which one, Pen?" George asked pleasantly. "You've just missed Edenham it seems."

Penelope turned and there, of course, went Edenham in all his gorgeous splendor right up to Dalby House where he was admitted without pause. He didn't cast so much as a glance in her direction. Her timing had been *that* far off with him in this instance. She resolved to do better next time.

"We're off to Hyde House, George, where I will present Amelia with the famous tattered shawl, thereby proving myself to be a most stellar friend to her reputation," Penelope said, marching off down Upper Brook Street to their house at the end opposite Dalby House. "If we time this well, I might be introduced to Lord Iveston."

"You fancy Lord Iveston, Pen?" George asked.

"Not particularly," Penelope said, "but I shall make do with him, if I must."

George grinned and gripped his jacket lapels with both hands, ambling alongside her to their house. He looked near to whistling, silly old fool. "I'm relieved to hear it. I had not liked to think I'd misread you as badly as all that. It's Edenham you fancy. Am I right?"

"He's a duke, George. Of course I fancy him. Don't think yourself as wise as all that."

"Oh, not as all that," George said with a grin. "But wise enough, surely."

And then he did begin to whistle.

❧

THE Marquis of Iveston walked into the music room of Hyde House whistling. Everything was just as it should be. Blakes was married to Louisa, the woman he'd trotted after throughout the salons of London for two years, and Cranleigh was married to Amelia, the woman he'd either kissed or avoided for the past two years, depending on his mood of the day. All good and well, things settled as they ought to have been two years ago when his brothers had first set eyes on the women of their hearts, but which hadn't been settled easily at all, and certainly not quickly, which had made a bloody mess of everything.

Still, spilt milk and all that. Things were as they were and were well settled now. That was all that mattered, all that should matter. Indeed, just because he had spent the past two years very nearly hiding in his house, trying to avoid Amelia, who he was quite certain had expected to marry *him*, well, why shouldn't he whistle? He was free now to go about Town as much as he liked.

He didn't like to all that much, truth be told, but he liked it more than he had let on. He'd had to protect Cranleigh, hadn't he? Of course he had. It wouldn't have done at all for him to have somehow wound up being leg-shackled to Amelia. And he could have done. Men found themselves married at alarming rates, truly alarming. A man had to be quite on his best game to avoid the net.

Iveston, with quite justified pride, was always on his best game.

Two brothers married within the month and he still free. It was a good day, quite worthy of a hearty whistle. His mother must be satisfied now; two sons married to very respectable women. She could and should nearly forget that her eldest and Hyde's heir was still running free upon the earth.

Yes, that is how he thought of himself, first and always, as Hyde's heir. What else? It was his duty, his birthright, his place in the scheme of the things. He didn't quite know if he liked his place or not. Hadn't given it any thought, actually, as there was nothing to be done about it.

There were worse things, certainly.

He could be married, for one.

Iveston chuckled under his breath and whistled a tune he'd heard just that morning from a street vendor on Piccadilly, just beyond his window glass. Jaunty little tune. He quite liked it. Suited his mood to perfection.

"What are you so cheerful about?" Cranleigh said, coming upon him, some parcel shoved under his arm.

"I'm cheerful for the same reason you're not. I'm not married. You are," Iveston said, and then he laughed, quite fully in his younger brother's face. Cranleigh, not the most cordial of men, did not laugh with him. Well, Iveston hadn't truly expected him to.

Cranleigh, as second born of Hyde's five living sons, was not often of a cheerful bent. Probably a direct result of being second born and, thereby, feeling some ill-placed notion that he had to protect and support Iveston in every blessed thing. It was quite nice of him, naturally, but entirely unnecessary. Iveston required no support and no protection, though Cranleigh, a bit of a dockside dog, would hardly have agreed, not that Iveston was at all inclined to put it up for a vote.

"Ridiculous," Cranleigh snarled under his breath, a smile half tugging at his mouth. "You've got it entirely wrong, Iveston. I am merely out of sorts because I am on my way to Dalby House. Delivering a gift of sorts to Lady Dalby. Which would put anyone of any sense into an ill temper."

"A gift?" Iveston said, sitting himself in front of the pianoforte and beginning to play. "How very unlike you. Whatever for?"

Cranleigh grimaced fractionally and sat down on a small chair opposite the pianoforte, the parcel balanced on his right knee. "It seems I must, Iveston. Blakes gave her something, some bit of expensive frippery in thanks for getting hold of Louisa. What can I do but the same? It's perfectly obvious that Sophia had a hand in managing to direct Amelia in my direction, which is what Amelia states emphatically even when I expressly forbid her from talking about Sophia."

"She doesn't sound obedient or compliant in the least, Cranleigh," Iveston interrupted. "I do begin to wonder what you see in your lovely wife."

Cranleigh's ice blue eyes shone in the pale light of the music room. "Let's keep it a mystery, shall we? Lock your eyes upon your own wife, Iveston."

"Haven't got one," Iveston said with a flourish of the keys, the light notes rising to the impressive height of the room. "Hence, my innate good cheer, rising up to enchant all near me."

"Oh, yes, I'm enchanted," Cranleigh said sarcastically, moving the bundle to his left knee. "But, as I was saying, as Blakes has set the precedent, I feel I must match him, and so it's to Dalby House, gift in hand. She'll likely grab it out of my hands before I can explain myself," he grumbled.

"Hardly likely as I'm perfectly certain that Sophia Dalby has been the recipient of many gifts and is therefore quite adept at the protocol in receiving them. You shall be unscathed, Cranleigh, have no fear. But what did you get her?"

"Something I picked up whilst in China."

"Didn't Blakes give her some porcelain from China?"

"He might have done," Cranleigh said casually, tapping the parcel.

"And you are giving her . . . something infinitely finer?" Iveston guessed, his fingers moving over the keys effortlessly. He liked to play the pianoforte; music had entertained him during his long hours hiding in the house.

"Perhaps not infinitely," Cranleigh said with a smirk, "but it is a fine piece. I shan't be outdone by Blakes. His marrying Louisa was no better an acquisition than my marrying Amy."

"And the porcelains will prove that," Iveston said with a smile. "Does Amelia know?"

"Know? She helped me choose the item."

"What is it? Something costly? But of course it would be."

"I shan't show you. If you want to see it, you'll have to traipse over to Dalby House to see it," Cranleigh said. Iveston rose to his feet, looking imminently ready to go.

Cranleigh sighed. "Wait ten minutes, will you? I don't require an escort, which is surely what she will conclude."

"Why should you care what Sophia Dalby thinks?"

Cranleigh snorted and stared up at him. "Not Sophia. Amy. I can't have my wife thinking I didn't go willingly, can I? If it doesn't seem my idea, she'll get the notion that she can compel me to do anything."

Iveston, who knew very nearly everything as it pertained to the courtship of Amelia and Cranleigh, found it almost impossible not to laugh outright. He did chuckle, but that was to be expected, wasn't it?

"And she doesn't have that notion already?" Iveston said.

If Cranleigh hadn't been holding a very costly Chinese some-thing-or-other, he was quite sure Cranleigh would have given him a black eye. Or tried to, anyway.

"You're determined to come, aren't you? Just dying to find a laugh at my expense," Cranleigh said as they walked across the music room side by side.

"Well," Iveston said slowly, "yes, actually. I can't see how you'd disappoint me in that, can you? A gift for Sophia," Iveston said, grinning. "I quite think she must deserve one."

"I'm quite certain she would agree with you," Cranleigh grumbled.

Iveston could see the gleam of humor in Cranleigh's eyes; he was not fooled. It was as they were walking into the blue recep-tion room that Mr. George and Miss Penelope Prestwick were admitted to Hyde House by Ponsonby.

"Ten minutes, Iveston," Cranleigh murmured as they walked across the spacious room. "After that, you must face Miss Prestwick on your own. I'll not be waylaid in my own home." Nevertheless, Cranleigh bowed crisply to Miss Prestwick's pretty curtsey, accepted Mr. Prestwick's felicitations on his marriage, and said most cordially, "And how are your roses today, Miss Prestwick? Quite as lovely as they were when I last viewed them?"

Miss Prestwick, her dark eyes glittering, said a bit stiffly, "Most assuredly, Lord Cranleigh. Give them not a moment's worry. Whatever befell them, they have made a full recovery."

"How stalwart of them," Cranleigh said, "or is it your sure hand with roses, Miss Prestwick?"

"I should say the credit should go to the roses, in this in-stance," Mr. Prestwick said, smiling cordially. His sister did not appear to think him cordial in the least, to judge by her chilly demeanor.

As Iveston had developed the habit of spending the better part of his days avoiding the rabble that was the ton, he had not met Miss Prestwick before the night of the ball her father, the viscount, had hosted. She was, either fortunately or unfortunately, not quite like the other women of his scant acquaintance. In concert with her bold coloring, there was something about her manner that was equally bold, very nearly masculine in force. It was quite intriguing. In point of fact, he had never been looked over by a woman with quite so appalling a lack of subtlety since reaching his majority. In some strange fashion, it was very nearly refreshing.

Iveston, who was by no measure a fool, knew he was the most eligible man in Town. He was of good house, good family, good fortune, good health, and good teeth. He was heir to a dukedom, and quite a nice one. He, without being obnoxious about it, had it all. Naturally, women being what they were and Society being what it was, nearly every unmarried woman below the age of forty and above the age of fifteen would be delighted if he showed them the slightest interest.

It was not to be supposed that Miss Prestwick was any different.

"As interesting as I find my roses to be," Miss Prestwick said, glancing coolly at her brother, "I'm quite aware that others don't share my passion for horticulture. I can see that you are on your way out. Please don't allow us to keep you. My brother and I had hoped to see Lady Amelia, to return the shawl that was . . . that I . . . that she . . ." Miss Prestwick looked quite at a loss. Iveston had a most difficult time not laughing outright.

"How very thoughtful, and indeed generous of you, Miss Prestwick," Iveston said into the stilted and sudden silence. "Quite as generous as when you made loan of your lovely shawl when Lady Amelia was so in need of it."

Cranleigh, it should be reported, looked quite red about the neck. As well he should, as he had been responsible for Amelia needing the shawl in the first place, her muslin gown quite torn to shreds, very nearly literally.

"The shawl belongs rightly to you, Miss Prestwick," Cranleigh said, shifting his package from hand to hand.

"I feel that, as things stand," Miss Prestwick replied, ignoring whatever attempts her brother made to enter the conversation, "the shawl should remain in her care. Permanently."

"Goodwill gesture, you might say," Mr. Prestwick said in slightly cheeky fashion. Iveston found it all rather amusing. Cranleigh, by his expression, not as much.

"However it is phrased," Miss Prestwick said firmly, "we shall not keep you. As you are so readily available, will you not take the shawl, Lord Cranleigh? I will feel so much more at ease knowing it is in the proper hands." Clutching her own red shawl about her shoulders, she looked nearly ready to sprint for the door.

Odd. Should she not be making some more determined effort to stay? And to win his attention? It was completely irregular. Here he was, caught out, one might say, an heir apparent who was known best for not being readily available to callers. Yet here he was, available, facing a quite attractive girl with dark hair and eyes and fashionably pale skin.

It was beyond question that she would be very delighted to marry him. They all were, weren't they? He had what every woman wanted in a man, and he was not such a dullard that he didn't know it.

Of course, she was a bit peculiar. That might explain it. Wasn't she just slightly too forceful? Too direct? It wasn't at all what a man looked for in a woman, not if he had any sense. His mother was entirely too direct and very nearly forbiddingly forceful, so he was very clear about what he wanted in a wife, when he bothered to think about it at all, which he rarely did. He wanted a wife he could manage without any effort, he knew that. Most women looked pleasant enough from a distance, but get to know them in any degree of polite familiarity and they became positive dragons. Not that he would ever call his mother, the duchess, a dragon; however, the duke did have a bit of a time with her, not that he ever complained. On the contrary, his father seemed remarkably content with his situation, but Iveston was nearly certain that it was possible to be even more content with a less energetic wife.

Miss Prestwick, now that he had got a good look at her, seemed to boil with energy.

Entirely unpleasant. He was completely put off.

He stood in a relaxed posture of attention and said not a word, shutting her out and showing her that he was not in the least interested in her. Of course, he watched for her response.

Proving that she was peculiar and not at all aware of how to behave, she barely glanced at him. And when she did, she was quite obviously dismissive.

In all his twenty-nine years, nearly ten of them being feted and pursued by every mama to every girl above the age of fourteen, he had never been dismissed so thoroughly. In fact, not at all. Not a bit of it. He'd been hotly pursued, as was entirely appropriate, if annoying. This chit, this little nothing of more money than breeding, was discounting *him*?

Gad, she was peculiar. Very nearly mad, by all appearances.

"We must be off, Cranleigh," he murmured, ducking his head slightly before looking at Ponsonby, communicating without words that the Prestwicks could be shown to Amelia or out the door, so long as they were shown away from his presence. Ponsonby, quite well trained in that sort of thing, understood completely. "Your pardon, Miss Prestwick. Mr. Prestwick. My brother and I have an appointment we must keep."

"I shall inform Lady Amelia that you are calling," Ponsonby said. "If you will just wait here?"

"Oh, not at all necessary," Miss Prestwick said, eyeing the tall clock against the wall. "The shawl is safely in your care, Lord Cranleigh, and that is all that can matter."

"You do not wish to stay?" Ponsonby asked.

Cranleigh and Iveston, against all sense, stood somewhat mesmerized at being so ruthlessly managed by this slip of a girl. Her brother looked entirely accustomed to it, proving Iveston's point neatly.

"I'm afraid we can't. We have an appointment of our own to keep," Miss Prestwick said.

"We do?" Mr. Prestwick said somewhat comically.

Miss Prestwick did not look at all amused, which was somewhat delightful. Such a stiff sort of girl. One could not but wonder what it would take to unbend her.

"Of course we do, George," she said tightly, rearranging her perfectly arranged shawl. Did Miss Prestwick fidget when her plans were questioned? "And we must hurry."

"Excuse us," Mr. Prestwick said amiably, "we must hurry."

And with only the barest of cordial formalities, the two were out the door and back onto Piccadilly. Cranleigh looked nearly as befuddled as Iveston felt.

"Remarkable girl," Cranleigh said. "I never thought to see one like her."

"Remarkable? How?" Iveston said as Ponsonby arranged for their coats to be brought down.

"She's the only unmarried woman I've yet to see who didn't fall all over herself in trying to gain your attention. She had it, by all appearances, and she threw it right back at your feet."

"She did not have my attention," Iveston said curtly, taking his hat from Ponsonby.

"No?" Cranleigh said, his hands full with his mysterious gift for Sophia Dalby. "Then I suppose it doesn't matter."

"No, I'm quite certain it doesn't," Iveston said as they walked out onto Piccadilly.

And it didn't. Though Cranleigh found it all very amusing, to judge by his laugh.

Four

THE Duke of Edenham entered Dalby House fully ten minutes before his appointed time. He was no fool. A man who wished to remain on Sophia Dalby's good side paid attention to details of that sort.

He was shown directly into the white salon, where the blanc de Chine cup that was the reason for the salon was missing. In its place was a celadon vase of quite exquisite design. Edenham knew the origin of the blanc de Chine cup; he did not know the origin of the celadon porcelain. He was not a man who endured being kept in the dark about important changes such as these, with a woman such as Sophia Dalby.

"You're early, darling," Sophia said as he took a seat opposite her on one of the matching sofas in the room. "There is nothing more charming than a man who so promptly pays off his wagers."

"In ready money, too," he said, handing her a small bundle of gold coins. "Count it, if you wish."

"Oh, I shall," she said with a twinkle in her dark eyes. "There is nothing quite so delicious as the feel of gold between my fingers."

They sat opposite each other. The celadon vase gleamed on a low table between them, a spark of color in a room nearly glowing white.

"I see you have a new bit of porcelain, Lady Dalby," he said. "Another payment for another wager?"

"Not at all," she said, putting the bundle down next to the vase, her bodice dipping slightly as she leaned forward. Edenham appreciated the effort, and indeed, enjoyed the view. "It was a gift."

"For services rendered?"

"Edenham, you are too coarse by half. Why, I do wonder where you get such ideas."

"Do you?"

Sophia smiled and leaned back against the cushions. "Darling Edenham, if you want to know something, why not simply ask? I have very few secrets."

"But the ones you do have are so very intriguing," he said, studying her face.

He'd known Sophia for years. They were close in age, though not at all close in experience, either shared or otherwise. He had never known the sweetness of lying betwixt her legs; indeed, he had no wish to. He was, perhaps, one of the few men who could say that, not that he would ever admit so publicly. No, he was not such a fool, for a fool is what would be thought of any man not eager to bed Sophia Dalby.

It was not that he did not find her beautiful, for she was and he was not blind to beauty in any form. It was that he had so very few friends and he counted Sophia as one of them, though he could not think why. They shared no intimacies of any sort. He did not know her secrets, nor did she know his. It was, perhaps, that she did not hold him in either awe or fear, and that was worth more to him than he would have thought possible ten years past.

Perhaps, studying her now, her expression curious, clearly waiting for him to entertain her and even delight her, if he could manage it, she valued the same things in him. He respected her, who she was and what she had accomplished, but he did not fear her. Very many people did. And they were right to do so.

"There is very little point to having a dull secret, Edenham. It defeats the point entirely," she said with a smile. "Shall I guess it?"

Edenham left off his musings and chuckled, enjoying his exchanges with Sophia as he did with few others. "Guess? I've all but told you. The blanc de Chine cup is missing. Another priceless porcelain from China in its place. Did Westlin give you this one, too?"

Sophia grinned and said, "Darling, why should Lord Westlin give me anything more? He has given me his son, by way of my daughter. That is more than enough to satisfy me."

"You returned the porcelain to him then? It was worth a small fortune. I had no idea you were so generous. Certainly there isn't a single rumor to that effect."

"It was worth a very large fortune, darling," she said, taking a sip of her tea. "Let's be honest about it. It was quite generous of me to return it, true, but then, the need for it had disappeared entirely. Caroline is to be the next Countess of Westlin, once dreary Lord Westlin dies. What need have I for a small cup? He was more than welcome to it, though I must confess he did seem surprised that I returned it to him. Perhaps he is the one who started the rumor that I am not generous? I certainly think it sounds like something he would do."

"You could have kept it. I'm quite surprised you didn't," he said, taking a swallow of tea, studying her across the rim of his cup.

"Everything has its uses, darling, and when its use is fulfilled," she said softly, gazing serenely into his eyes, "why not be rid of it? I do enjoy a simple solution, don't you?"

Edenham smiled mildly and shook his head at her. "There is nothing simple about you, Sophia, and it is far too late to pretend so now. Are you going to tell me about this celadon vase or shall I be forced to place a wager on White's book as to its origin?"

"Why, it's Chinese, Edenham, as you can plainly see," Sophia teased. "As to who gave it to me, I don't think I shall tell you. Keeping this a mystery to you is far more entertaining than telling you could possibly be. See what happens when you push too hard? All is denied you."

"Dear Sophia," Edenham said, grinning like a boy, he was certain, "I can assure you that never in my life have I pushed too hard and been denied. Quite the contrary."

And it was on that rather ribald note that Sophia's butler, Fredericks, entered the room and informed Sophia that she had a caller.

Mr. George and Miss Penelope Prestwick were admitted nearly immediately. By the startled look on Fredericks's face, they stood upon his very heels.

"Miss Prestwick," Sophia said serenely, "what a surprise to see you again so soon, but how lovely of you to have brought your darling brother along. Mr. Prestwick, you are looking marvelous. Quite recovered from the ball you hosted, obviously."

"I find myself hardly taxed at all, Lady Dalby," Mr. Prestwick said cordially. "But then, I do think it is a woman's domain to be overtaxed by social tides and streams, wouldn't you agree?"

"I most certainly would not," Miss Prestwick said, flashing a dark look at her brother as she sat upon an elegantly proportioned chair. Mr. Prestwick smiled cordially and sat in a matching chair next to her. "I can't think how you came to such a conclusion, George, as I am not so fragile as that a ball would overwhelm me. Wouldn't *you* agree, Lady Dalby?"

Sophia smiled as she poured out two more cups of tea and passed them gracefully to Mr. George and Miss Penelope Prestwick. "Miss Prestwick, I can't think how anyone would ever conclude that you are the least bit fragile. Brothers, excluded, naturally. It is very nearly common knowledge that brothers are very nearly imbeciles when it comes to understanding their sisters, even if they understand all other women very well indeed. You have a sister, do you not, your grace?"

"As it happens, I do," Edenham answered pleasantly. Miss Prestwick did not look at all pleased by his admission, which was quite amusing.

"And do you find her fragile?"

"Not in the slightest," Edenham said, taking a slow swallow of his tea to seal the statement.

"Not highly emotional, perhaps a bit irrational?" Sophia continued.

"Well," Edenham hedged, shifting his weight upon the sofa, "perhaps occasionally, but certainly not as a matter of habit."

"And there you are," Sophia said, looking pointedly at Miss Prestwick, who was a quite attractive girl. "As I am cordially acquainted with Lady Richard, Edenham's sister, I can assure you that she is not irrational in the least particular. You, darling Edenham, are just the slightest bit deluded about your darling sister, which is perfectly normal. Don't bother about it in the least. You are quite astute in all other matters, I'm quite certain. Wouldn't you agree, Miss Prestwick?"

A most odd turn to the conversation, to be sure, but Edenham, quite relaxed, sat back against the cushions and waited to see what would happen next. It would have quite a bit to do with Miss Prestwick, of that he was certain. Sophia seemed to attract these young things like bees to honey.

Miss Prestwick, to her immense credit, did not blush, though perhaps her generally dark coloring was more to be credited than her composure. Her skin was quite a lovely shade of dark cream, from her throat to her forehead, with just a suggestion of rose pink in her cheeks. Quite a lovely looking girl, now that he took his time about studying her.

"I am sorry to admit that I don't know his grace well enough to have formed an opinion," Miss Prestwick said serenely. "I am more than happy to take your estimation of his general character as genuine and without fault, Lady Dalby. I hope that does not distress you, your grace?" she said, turning her gaze fully to his.

"As it has been decided that brothers are imbeciles where their sisters are concerned," Edenham said, "it does not. In fact, I think it highly logical and very nearly a compliment for a man to see his sister in an entirely different light than he sees all other women. Wouldn't you agree, Mr. Prestwick?"

George Prestwick, very nearly a mirror image of his sister with his dark hair and eyes and general arrangement of features, smiled and answered, "As this exercise in logic has resulted in a compliment to me, then I most heartily agree, your grace. Thank you, Lady Dalby. I had heard that you were most charming and now I can see why. I have never been called an imbecile with quite so much grace in my entire life. I can go quite contentedly on now, a happy imbecile, which is quite the way it should be, shouldn't it?"

It was at that rather oddly pleasant remark that Fredericks entered the white salon with slightly more force than was expected of a butler and informed Lady Dalby in the most amused fashion imaginable that she had two more callers and was she in?

She was most assuredly in.

Whereupon Fredericks allowed the Marquis of Iveston and the Earl of Cranleigh into the white salon. Miss Prestwick looked quite nearly shocked.

How perfectly amusing. Edenham hadn't been so entertained in a six month. He couldn't think why he'd been hiding away at Sutton Hall, his primary estate, when there was so much amusement to be had in Town. From the look which Sophia cast in his direction, it was more than obvious that she was of the same thought in the same instant. And was not above taking great pleasure in displaying that his seclusion, and his reasons for it, had been completely absurd.

And he was not above finding amusement in being very nearly publicly chided for what, in some circles, might be called *morbid mourning.* In point of fact, he had overheard his pastry chef say exactly that to his housekeeper. He had left for Town that very week.

"What a lovely surprise," Sophia said as they all stood to greet each other.

The men bowed.

The women curtseyed.

They sank back into their seats, Cranleigh and Iveston sitting side by side upon a settee done up in white velvet with pale blue braided trim. They looked uncomfortable, particularly as Cranleigh had an awkwardly shaped parcel that he was trying to hold as unobtrusively as possible. It was hardly possible.

"I had not thought to find you still in Town, Lord Cranleigh. No wedding trip? I shan't believe it. And Lord Iveston," Sophia continued, without waiting for Cranleigh to answer, which clearly annoyed him, which was dreadfully amusing, was it not? "I do believe that this is the first time you have ever visited Dalby House. I am most, *most* delighted that you have done so, though I cannot think what has spurred you to action now . . . although, do confess," Sophia said, smiling broadly, her dark eyes glittering, "can it be the lovely Miss Prestwick who has lured you out and about and into my salon? Can it be that she has done what no other woman has done before her? Are you smitten, Lord Iveston? Is it love?"

Well. What to say to that?

Iveston, clearly, did not know what to say. He looked, to be blunt, quite as chilly as November rain. Cranleigh looked hot to bursting, but he also said nothing.

Miss Prestwick was not so hampered.

"I do think, Lady Dalby," she said stiffly, "that as it is his first visit to you, you should not make Lord Iveston the butt of what is an obviously ill-conceived jest."

"Then," Sophia said innocently, a bit of acting far beyond her reach, "you did not come over from Hyde House together?"

Edenham snapped his gaze back to Miss Prestwick, as well as to Iveston. All at Hyde House? They did have a rather guilty look, now that the question had been put to them.

"Absolutely not," Iveston said, shifting his long legs, and then shifting them again. He could not seem to find a comfortable position, likely because Cranleigh was equally tall and the settee was not overly large.

"But why didn't you come together? How perfectly ridiculous," Sophia said crisply. "You were all at Hyde House not a half hour ago, were you not?"

She did not wait for a reply. It was clear that none was needed.

"And now you are here," Sophia said, driving home the point, which was perfectly unnecessary. But what had they all been doing there and what now were they all doing here? It was a question he should not mind an answer to. The fact that Sophia had known of Miss Prestwick's appointment at Hyde House . . . well, that did put a very particular spin on things, didn't it?

"I was merely returning–" Miss Prestwick began, then caught

herself at Sophia's raised brows. "An item of no particular interest to anyone here, to Lady Amelia."

"And did you?" Sophia prompted.

Miss Prestwick looked most uneager to answer. Cranleigh, Prestwick, and Iveston were all staring at her in a nearly accusatory fashion.

"I believe it was given to the butler. I am confident he will make certain she gets it," Miss Prestwick said primly.

"As to getting things," Cranleigh said, interjecting himself into the stilted and mysterious battle between Sophia and Penelope Prestwick, "I came for a similar reason, Lady Dalby, though I suppose I could have left this with *your* butler."

"But as it is a gift," Iveston said smoothly, "he was not at all disposed to do so."

Iveston looked askance at Penelope, his visage stony. Penelope looked stonily, and a bit dismissively, back at Iveston.

What on earth had happened at Hyde House in the past half hour? It looked not unlike some romantic entanglement was afoot between Lord Iveston and Miss Prestwick, which did make such sense as both were unmarried and at that point in life where marriage was a near certainty. On the other hand, it did not seem at all logical that three sons of the same father should find themselves married within the same Season. The odds were flagrantly against it.

Where odds were concerned, Edenham was well aware that Sophia Dalby was not to be discounted. Indeed, the odds, no matter how rigorously stacked against logic, invariably fell her way. *Toppled*, one might even say. Edenham crossed his legs and watched the entertainment currently under way in the white salon of Dalby House, wondering if there were a bet on White's book and what the odds were on an Iveston–Prestwick pairing.

By the frozen looks of complete indifference they were hurling at each other at the moment, he'd put them at eight to one.

"A gift?" Sophia exclaimed in obvious delight. "But I can't think why you should offer me a gift, Lord Cranleigh. I shouldn't have thought we were as intimate as all that."

Cranleigh, who did have the reputation for having the grimmest temperament, and who should have been expected to respond with some dismal and dismissive comment, chuckled. It was quite stunning. Marriage to Lady Amelia clearly agreed with him completely.

"It is," Cranleigh said, unwrapping the parcel with great care, "something of a family tradition, or shall be, I fear." Which made not a bit of sense to Edenham, nor to Mr. and Miss Prestwick to judge by their expressions, but which caused Sophia to grin fully and most, most delightedly. "I hope it pleases you, Lady Dalby. I trust you understand the reason behind the gift."

And upon those words, Cranleigh revealed the most exquisite Chinese vase in the most extraordinarily vivid shade of blue.

"Cranleigh, it is a most generous gift," Sophia said brightly, "and I would tell you that I am hardly worthy of it, but it is so lovely that I must and I will toss all civility onto the street. It is marvelous, darling. I don't feel I deserve it, but I will cherish it all my life. Thank you, Lord Cranleigh," she finished, her voice gone soft and, startlingly, quite sincere.

"It is quite beautiful, isn't it?" Lord Iveston said, his expression very nearly wistful. "That blue, it's very nearly the exact shade of Lady Amelia's eyes, is it not?"

"It is *not*," Cranleigh said stiffly as Sophia took the vase from his hands and admired it. "Amelia's eyes are the precise shade of the China Sea on a sun-drenched day. How peculiar that you didn't notice that, Iveston."

"As I have not seen the China Sea," Iveston remarked mildly, "I should perhaps be allowed some latitude."

"The color of the China Sea?" Miss Prestwick said slowly and not at all happily, perhaps because her own eyes were the precise shading of a lump of coal? Not unattractive, but still, not the China Sea either. "I had no idea you were so well traveled, Lord Cranleigh. Have you been to China often?"

"Only once, I'm afraid. I had thought to return, but–"

"He got himself married instead," Iveston interrupted cordially, ignoring the Prestwicks completely. It was most entertaining.

"Have you traveled widely, your grace?" Miss Prestwick asked him.

Before he could answer, Sophia said, still studying her rectangular-shaped vase, "How could he have done, Miss Prestwick, when he is forever getting married again and again?"

"And again," Edenham added with a smirk. "Thrice. I do think accuracy must be maintained, Lady Dalby. Have you traveled, Miss Prestwick?" he asked. What *was* Sophia about, to manhandle the girl so? It wasn't at all like her. Sophia was, as everyone knew, far more subtle.

"I'm afraid not, your grace, though I should think I would enjoy it," Miss Prestwick said, looking as eager and compliant as all proper girls should look. It did become somewhat tiresome as a steady diet.

"Perhaps on your wedding trip, Penelope," George Prestwick said brightly.

"Oh, are you planning your wedding trip already?" Sophia said. "Have the groom in mind, do you? Do I know him?"

"I should think so," Miss Prestwick replied sharply. "You know so very many men, don't you?"

Cranleigh coughed behind his hand. It was very likely he was hiding a smile.

"Only the ones worth knowing," Sophia answered calmly. "Why Edenham is the perfect example. We have known each other for years now. Quite a history we share, and such a cordial one, too."

Edenham knew very well how that sounded, but what did it matter? He knew the truth and that was more than enough to satisfy him.

"Except for a few odd exceptions," Edenham said, "I should think all your relationships are cordial ones."

"With men, certainly," Miss Prestwick said primly. Her brother moved his hand near her skirts; it was entirely possible that he pinched her. Miss Prestwick certainly gave every appearance of having been pinched.

"I, for one, find Lady Dalby completely cordial and most charming," Lord Iveston said softly, staring at Sophia, "and I have just recently met her. Yet even in so recent a history, I am nothing but delighted."

Miss Prestwick said nothing. Really, what was there for her to say at this point? She had made a muddle of it and now must be made to sit quietly until the conversation took a turn onto less fraught ground.

"It seems to me that a man who gets out as rarely as you do, Lord Iveston, might not be as discerning as others might be," Miss Prestwick said. Miss Penelope Prestwick, somewhat shockingly, might be the sort of woman who could not be made to sit quietly.

"It does not take an exceedingly great amount of exposure to bad manners and an uncharitable spirit to recognize it upon sight," Iveston responded a bit stiffly.

"Nor a great amount of exposure to recognize charity and generosity, either," Sophia said, "which are not in great supply no matter what the politicians might wish us to believe. Therefore, Lord Cranleigh, I again must thank you for giving me this vase. Do you have a preference as to where I should display it?"

"It looks very well in this room, I should say," Cranleigh said with a half smile. "Perhaps in place of the celadon?"

Sophia smiled and said, "And what would Lord Henry say to that slight? No, the celadon must stay. They look well together, do you not agree, Lord Iveston?"

Edenham admitted, if only to himself, to being slightly shocked. Henry Blakesley had given Sophia the celadon vase? For what? The only thing that he could think of was that Lord Henry was recently married. It could only be concluded that he credited Sophia for arranging for the wife he'd desired. And now Cranleigh, Henry's brother, was also giving Sophia a piece of rare porcelain . . . also in thanks for his newly acquired wife?

The puzzle piece of Miss Prestwick suddenly fit into place. She wanted a husband and she had come to Sophia for aid in acquiring one. A difficult piece to prove, but then, most things of interest could not be proved, they could only be observed, dimly at that.

Edenham opened his eyes wide and determined to give it his best effort.

∾

PENELOPE was giving it her very best effort, but the Duke of Edenham, who was even more handsome when observed in such an intimate setting, did not appear to find her captivating in the least. Of course, she was so annoyed at the Marquis of Iveston and the Earl of Cranleigh for intruding upon what she had *hoped* would be a small and cozy gathering of merely four persons, herself included, that she found it difficult to summon the will to be captivating.

She wasn't sure who to blame more, Iveston or Cranleigh. Of course, Cranleigh had the gift, and therefore the best excuse for ruining her plans to beard Edenham in Sophia's den, but Iveston seemed to take such joy in being loathsomely arrogant and dismissive that she was inclined to blame him entirely.

In fact, she would. He might not have known that she was coming to Dalby House to meet, in the most casual interpretation of that word, the Duke of Edenham, but he was certainly enjoying throwing his hammer into the works now. The look on his face declared all. She might have initially thought him mildly attractive in a very blond way, but as he now alternated between ignoring her completely and casting condescending glances her way, she thought him the most unattractive of men. It was going to be so difficult to make good use of him to make Edenham jealous, which had been Sophia's plan all along, as was perfectly obvious to her. Though what had gone amiss with her negotiations with Sophia of just an hour or so ago was completely beyond her.

They had made an agreement, a most cordial one, and now Sophia was treating her quite miserably. She had been forced by the most basic rules of survival and self-preservation to protect herself. And she had, though she did wonder, particularly after George had pinched her on the thigh, if protecting herself had been in quite good form.

She rather suspected not, which was decidedly unfair.

"Lady Dalby," Iveston said softly in response to Sophia's question—his voice seemed to have a particularly soft quality no matter what he said, which seemed perfectly ridiculous to her—"I think two such stellar examples of art must always look well together. Neither one eclipses the other."

"How perfectly true, and quite diplomatic," Sophia said with a nod.

Diplomatic? Weak at the knees, more likely. He looked the sort of man to blow over in a stiff wind, if he could be lured outdoors, that is.

It was going to be *so* difficult to pretend an interest in him. Would Edenham even believe it? How could a man who looked like Edenham, who behaved like Edenham, who had lived like Edenham ever believe that he was to run second in any race, particularly against a man like Iveston?

Oh, Iveston was not a bad-looking sort, not at all, if one liked the type.

At the moment, she could not think of anyone who could possibly like his type.

Iveston was so very blond, his eyes so brilliantly blue, his form so attenuated, his manner so chilly, and his clear determination to speak as little as possible . . . why, it put one in mind of a particularly odd boy who had somehow stumbled in upon the adults. Certainly Edenham put no one in mind of a boy, odd or not.

"It is quite lovely," Penelope said. "I don't pretend to know the reason for the gift, Lord Cranleigh, but you certainly have the knack for choosing beauty."

Iveston's gaze swung toward her briefly. She kept a pleasant look upon her face and ignored him.

"I must agree with you, Miss Prestwick," Cranleigh said.

"Indeed, for who would argue that you have the most lovely of wives, Lord Cranleigh," Sophia said. "I do wonder that you are not already on your wedding trip."

"My wife is packing, Lady Dalby, or so she claims. I have never found it to take more than an hour to have packed all I shall need for a twelve month," Cranleigh said with a brief smile. For all that he was a formidable man, quite unlike his tepid brother, he did appear quite taken with his wife. How admirable, though not entirely ordinary. She certainly didn't expect any such thing.

"You shall soon learn differently, if you haven't yet," Edenham said. "A woman likes to squirrel away a myriad of things she can't possibly need. It gives her an odd sort of pleasure. You are quite wise to indulge her."

"Is it an indulgence to pack for a trip?" Sophia remarked languidly. "A most peculiar perspective. Of course, I do suppose she could buy whatever she needs when she arrives. Where are you bound, Lord Cranleigh?"

As annoyed as she was with Sophia at the moment, Penelope did find she agreed with her completely. Who ever heard of packing being an indulgence? Edenham, for all his glorious looks, might be a bit trying on occasion. She might well need to begin packing for their wedding trip now, to save him the annoyance of her doing it under his own roof. Yes, that seemed a stellar plan; she'd begin as soon as she returned home.

"I am not completely certain, Lady Dalby," Cranleigh said, looking slightly less forbidding than usual. In fact, he looked very nearly embarrassed. "As you may or may not be aware, I have spent time abroad ship in the China Trade."

"Lord Cranleigh, I am aware of it," Sophia answered. "Indeed, you have quite the look of a seaman about you, which is nearly fatally dashing, as I'm sure you must know."

Cranleigh, remarkably, looked almost flushed. Why, was he *blushing*?

"Amelia has said something very much like," Cranleigh said in a hoarse undertone.

"Have you met our uncle Timothy?" Iveston asked Sophia. "He runs his four ships out of New York. We see him rarely, for obvious reasons, first and foremost being that he is so often upon the sea."

"How gracious you are, Lord Iveston, for surely you could have argued that the most obvious reason was that he was an American colonial in revolt against his king," Sophia said pleasantly. "It is so refreshing to see the bonds of family hold, even against the backdrop of war. But, to answer your question, I met Mr. Timothy Elliot only once, in New York, as it happens, and his lovely wife, Sally, was kindness itself. Is she well, do you know? I imagine the duchess must miss her profoundly."

Of course, Penelope was eating it all up with a spoon. Their Upper Brook Street house was on let from the Elliots, who had it from the Hydes, which was hardly a coincidence. If one were going to lease a house, certainly it was wise to do so with a house that belonged to a duke. Sally Elliot and Molly Hyde were sisters, that much she had just learned. She knew the families were somehow related, but until now, had not puzzled out how.

"If she does, she does not speak of it," Cranleigh said. He did have the habit of speaking for Iveston, which was clearly something of a necessity. Iveston might be a bit slow in the head; it would certainly explain why he was so rarely out in Society and why he rarely spoke when he was. "There is an Elliot ship due any day now, and quite unexpectedly, Amelia has declared that she is for a sea voyage. I can but oblige her."

Sophia smiled at Cranleigh in considerable warmth and said, "Unexpectedly? You are too modest, Lord Cranleigh. I do applaud you, however. Any man who obliges his wife only rises in my estimation."

"I should think so," Edenham said with a good-natured smirk. "What sort of woman would you be to not react so? But it is not always in a woman's best interest to be obliged. I have been instructed that following such a course, over too long a stretch of ground, leads to coddling, which is never to be desired."

Oh, Lord, but he was going to be a torment to her good nature.

Sophia laughed in Edenham's face. Penelope was secretly and enormously delighted. Oh, to be married and widowed so that she could then do whatever she wanted!

"Instructed? By whom, I should like to know?" Sophia demanded.

"By my mother," Edenham said solemnly, though his brown eyes were twinkling suspiciously.

"Oh, very well then. I'm certain your mother had her own

good reasons for instructing her son so," Sophia said brightly. "And has the Duchess of Hyde instructed her sons in like manner?" she asked Cranleigh and Iveston.

Penelope, as was perfectly logical, expected Cranleigh to answer. They had the same mother, and Iveston was the elder and the heir apparent, but Cranleigh was the bolder of the two. Quite obviously. She wasn't supposed to know about such things, but it was nearly common knowledge that Cranleigh had *breached* decorum, and by that she meant Amelia, in the mews behind Aldreth House. They had been married the next day, but that didn't take the taint off, did it?

To lose one's virtue in a horse stall . . . that took the shine off what everyone was whispering was a love match.

Penelope indulged in some minor head shaking. This is what happened to girls who lost their heads, something she was entirely certain she was incapable of doing. It was why she was going to be a duchess. She was simply too clear about her goals and too logical to be sidestepped.

A horse stall, indeed. The smell alone would have stopped her from making such a foolish decision within the first minute.

"The duchess," Iveston said *firmly*, which was shock enough, "has instructed her sons that it is a woman's duty to oblige a man upon the hour, if he so desires it, and so she instructs the duke upon the half hour where and when his desire is to be fixed. The duke, obliging her in increments, which she may well endure, finds no fault with the arrangement."

Well. How perfectly odious. The man gave every appearance of being barely able to speak and then when he let loose with a proper bit of conversation it proved to be highly improper.

She glanced in disapproval in his direction.

He glanced back in bald-faced delight.

She scowled.

He smirked.

Sighing, she turned her gaze to Sophia, who was smiling somewhat deviously at her. It did nothing to appease her, which of course it wasn't meant to.

"But naturally," Sophia said. "Who would? Now what of your father, Mr. Prestwick? Any pearls of wisdom dropped into your willing ear regarding the management of a woman? Should she be obliged? Or should she be boldly managed?"

"Lady Dalby, does any man possess a willing ear when listening to his father?" George said, which was rather clever of him. Penelope cast a casual glance to Edenham to see if he were offended. He didn't look to be.

"Now Mr. Prestwick," Sophia said, leaning forward and propping her chin up with her hand, "don't try and tell me that when a man speaks of women, another man is not instantly intrigued, even if that man be his father. Certainly he must have told you *something.*"

"He did, Lady Dalby," George said, smiling, his dark eyes shining in mirth. George was often mirthful. It was usually quite nice, but sometimes could be a bit tedious. Penelope was dreadfully afraid that now was going to be one of the tedious times. "Just before I left for school, he called me into his study and told me that, no matter what occurred, no matter the inconvenience to me or the relative amiability of the party or even the inevitable costs, I must be an obliging fellow. And so I was then. And so I am to this day. As I trust is plainly evident."

"But, Mr. Prestwick," Sophia said, very nearly laughing out loud, which only encouraged George, and he really should not be encouraged in such things, "you mention nothing of women."

"And neither, Lady Dalby," George replied with great cheek, "did my father. It was a full year before I realized that, but once I did, being a student of great diligence, I endeavored to make my own study of the matter. Being amiable, I am not in the habit of boasting; however, I am nearly forced to confess that my knowledge of women is as dismally inadequate now as it was then. I fear I am in want of tutoring. Are you taking applications?"

To which Sophia laughed outright, and right merrily, too. It was hardly to the point, the point being to get Edenham to fall in love with her, but it was also in horrid taste. Perfectly obviously so.

"Mr. Prestwick," Sophia said, still grinning, "I can teach you nothing. But your father has done marvelously well by you. You are, indeed, entirely obliging. I am certain some woman some day will cherish you for it."

"As it is not to be today, I find I have little interest," George said, "and indeed, no impatience."

"An entire year, Mr. Prestwick?" Edenham said. "At what age were you sent down to school?"

"I was a mere boy of thirteen years, your grace," George said, "and from what I can remember, barely able to manage spoon to mouth."

"You must forgive my brother, your grace," Penelope said. "I fear he makes himself sound quite backward, but he, spoon or otherwise, has always been amiable. Perhaps to a fault."

The lighthearted quality, indeed the smirks enjoyed by all present, excluding her, died upon the utterance of her words. Unfortunately, this sort of thing happened to her quite often. She could not think why. She was only trying to be precise and logical. Of course, it was this trait of hers that had sent the Duke of Calbourne nearly running from her, which was why he was not remotely a possible candidate, not that Sophia had to be informed of the peculiar details.

She had reviewed their single encounter and it had been peculiar, though she could think of no way to either unmake his initial bad impression of her or understand why she had made a bad impression. Calbourne clearly disliked logical, educated females, and had said so to her face, at her own ball. If he were not a duke, his behavior would have been nearly inexcusable. As he was a duke, his behavior became a trifle eccentric, but nothing more.

Being a duchess was going to be such a nice change. She could say whatever she wanted and no one would be able to find fault with it. At least not to her face, and that was all that mattered in any regard.

"If we are to list our faults, certainly amiability is the one to possess," Sophia said.

"If we are to list our faults," Iveston said, "perhaps we should list the faults we see in others."

He'd said that to *her*, she could just feel it.

"If we are to list our faults," Edenham said, "then I am certain to think of a pressing appointment for which I am a quarter hour late already."

Penelope looked at Edenham and felt her heart sink. She hadn't made the slightest impression upon him yet! He couldn't leave.

"If we are to list our faults," George said, "then I think they should be listed alphabetically, which would put my fault of amiability at the top of the list, and hence out of play. I shall watch, amiably, free of all anxiety."

"If we are to list our faults," Sophia said with a smile, "then mine is surely in being accommodating, which puts me quite at the top of the list, Mr. Prestwick. Being amiable, you would not, I am convinced, seek to supplant me."

George bowed his head at Sophia and smiled in acquiescence.

Acquiescence . . . was there not some way she could turn acquiescence into a fault and enter this odd game near the top? She was abysmal at games and hated these turn of phrase ones. Oh! *Abysmal*. Perhaps she could claim that as her fault.

"Your turn, Cranleigh," Iveston said softly. It was obvious that Lord Cranleigh hated games of this sort as well, which was simply lovely of him.

"If we are to list our faults," Cranleigh said, looking askance at his brother, "then mine must be an aversion to being instructed when to speak and what to do."

"What word is that?" Iveston said.

"I leave you to determine it, though if the word is *aversion*, that puts me third," Cranleigh said upon a half smile.

"Then the word must not be *aversion*," Edenham said, "as I am quite certain I must be found quite high upon the list. I leave you to choose my word for me, Lady Dalby."

"*Arrogant* it is," Sophia said with a chuckle.

"No, not arrogant," Penelope said impulsively, "for that would change the game, wouldn't it? Are we not supposed to choose our own faults, not note the faults of others?"

For what could she do? She had to defend the duke's honor, did she not? Particularly as he was to be her husband. And, as a small aside, she did not think they should follow Lord Iveston's suggestion, a small matter of spite. He was quite eager to throw a fault upon her, without doubt.

To judge by the general reaction of the room, it was quite possible she should have taken the time to consider another choice of action. The mood shifted downward, rather like a tile falling from the roof.

"If we are to list the faults of others," George said into the horrid silence, "then I am compelled to name *logic* as Penelope's greatest fault. Hardly a fault in normal circumstances, I know, but then, when are circumstances ever normal?"

How completely sweet and entirely like George. He had a

knack for turning most everything into something quite pleasant, which just now seemed his greatest talent.

"In a woman? I would have said never," Iveston said. "How unexpected to find logic residing in female form."

Penelope turned and looked at Iveston, quite truly perplexed at how much he had found to say, most of it quite unappealing. Perhaps he was not the dullard she had thought him, though finding he was a boor instead was hardly a noteworthy improvement.

"How right you are, Lord Iveston," Sophia said. "Miss Prestwick is that rare thing: an original."

Why, the way Sophia said it, it didn't sound like a fault at all. How extraordinary.

Five

An original? Is that what she was? Iveston was more than certain she was the most ordinary of things: a woman looking for a husband. In this instance, the Duke of Edenham. It was more than obvious, wasn't it? She had that look about her. Putting on that pretty, smiling, insipid creature that all women became when a likely man was in the room.

Of course, Miss Prestwick was mauling the whole thing badly. She was forever saying the wrong thing, wasn't she? Couldn't seem to help herself, poor lamb, and if he were any sort of gentleman, he'd feel some sympathy for her, perhaps even help her along with a friendly word to soothe things over.

He'd do nothing of the sort.

She wanted Edenham? Well, let her fight to get Edenham, like they all fought . . . like they all usually fought to get him.

He was a bit disgruntled. He could admit it. Here he was, in the full flush of his manhood, so to speak, and there was Edenham, three wives behind him and buried, two children to take on, and this little wisp of a girl preferred Edenham to him?

And her brother claimed logic as her fault. Logic? There was nothing logical about it. Nothing logical about her either. In fact, she might be a bloody imbecile. She gave every appearance of it, didn't she? Here he was, available, completely desirable in every conceivable way, and she had nothing but disdain and scowls for him. Why, he'd never been so dismissed in his entire life.

What was worse, Cranleigh clearly saw the situation for what it was and was having the devil of a time not laughing out loud. In fact, he might give way at any moment.

"How very true," Cranleigh said, crossing his legs casually. "There is certainly no other woman I know of who is so adept at horticulture, and with roses, too, known to be so difficult. I saw quite a few varieties whilst in China, yet none eclipse the perfection of Miss Prestwick's roses. When do you think the weather will be mild enough to remove them from the house, Miss Prestwick? Or do you keep them in all year?"

Every eye in the room was fixated upon Miss Prestwick, who did not look at all pleased by the attention. Most peculiar girl.

Penelope Prestwick looked first at Cranleigh, then at her brother, giving him something of an accusatory glance, then looked stonily at Sophia Dalby. Sophia returned the look and made no effort to reply. Indeed, the entire party was waiting in near comical anticipation for her reply about the summer location of her roses.

They *were* very nice roses. He'd been in the conservatory during the Prestwick ball and seen them. Very nice. It was actually a point in her favor that she could tend them so well, a full bounty of them, too. The room nearly filled to bursting with red, pink, and blush white roses. One would think she'd be eager to display her talent for roses, but Miss Prestwick was decidedly unpredictable in her responses to the most straightforward of prompts, one being her romantic and marital inclinations.

He *was* in his absolute prime.

Miss Prestwick seemed to collect herself, gathering a rather firm breath, and then said in a rush, "I put them out on June the first, Lord Cranleigh, and then promptly back in on the fifteenth of September. I have them on a very strict schedule that is designed to both give them ample opportunity to flourish under the gentle summer sun and to protect them from an erratic wind. I have yet to lose a single bush."

Why she sounded so martial about it, he had no idea.

Her brother coughed and straightened himself on his chair, keeping his gaze on his feet.

Cranleigh recrossed his legs and nodded amiably. Cranleigh never did *anything* amiably. Iveston knew in that instant that something was very amiss regarding Miss Prestwick and the Prestwick roses. Given that he was in his prime and she appeared blind to that fact, he decided to probe the wound, even if lightly.

"And your lovely roses weren't damaged the night of your ball, Miss Prestwick? I believe that many of your guests enjoyed the beauties of your conservatory that night, myself included."

Miss Prestwick fixed him with a glittering glare. Her eyes were quite dark, nearly black, and glittered quite spectacularly. "Roses have thorns, Lord Iveston, and therefore protect themselves most efficiently."

Which, naturally, brought the subject round to Amelia's torn gown and the haggard mess of Miss Prestwick's shawl. Most stupid of her to mention thorns, unless she wanted to muddy Amelia's name. But with Cranleigh in the room? She couldn't be that backward, could she?

It did seem possible.

"But not from an erratic wind, it would seem," Sophia said into the somewhat brittle silence. Miss Prestwick did seem to do that to a conversation. Could it possibly be intentional on her part?

Ridiculous notion.

Iveston glanced at Edenham. Edenham, far from looking put off or even bored, looked very nearly jolly. Was it possible . . . could it be that Edenham and little Miss Prestwick had formed an attachment of sorts? But when? And more to the point, why?

Iveston looked at her again. Yes, yes, she was pretty enough, the shape of her face quite nice and her brow a thing of true greatness, but her nose . . . it was a bit small and wasn't it a bit like a dairymaid's in pertness? Not at all the thing. Still, her mouth wasn't at all bad and her bodice filled out more than respectably.

But Edenham's latest duchess?

Impossible.

Fredericks, Sophia's butler, entered at that moment to announce another caller.

"Viscount Tannington is calling, Lady Dalby," Fredericks said, surveying the room with a nearly amused gaze. How odd, but then, Fredericks had that reputation.

"At this hour?" Sophia said. "It's half six. But he does owe me money, so let him enter, Freddy. A man with coin is always welcome."

"It's how I got in," Edenham said cheerfully.

"I brought the vase," Cranleigh said, looking at Iveston.

"I brought the man with the vase," Iveston said. "An escort, you might say, to ensure safe delivery of the vase."

"I brought Penelope for the very same reason," George Prestwick said, looking at Penelope. "An escort, ensuring safety."

Oh, dear, another impromptu game and Miss Prestwick quite out of her shallow element.

"I'm afraid I've only brought myself," Penelope said, looking quite miserable. Iveston could almost feel some pity for her. And then he looked at Edenham and the thought passed.

"Which was quite more than enough," Sophia said. "Men

must bring gifts. A woman need only bring herself, for her companionship is worth at least a small stack of gold coins."

"Is it?" Edenham asked.

"It is to me," Sophia said. "Oh, Tannington, how good of you to come," she said, rising to her feet to greet him. They all rose with her to greet the Viscount Tannington.

He was a tallish, leanish, sharkish-looking fellow with either a slightly sinister or slightly dangerous aspect, depending on the lighting. At the moment, he was looking more dangerous than sinister, but it was the sort of dangerous look that women seemed to find compelling more often than not. Iveston glanced at Penelope. She did not look compelled in the slightest. He found it strangely gratifying.

"I beg your pardon," Tannington said softly. "I had anticipated finding you alone."

"But of course you did, darling," Sophia said smoothly, "and of course, I am just as surprised as you are, but here we all find ourselves." Sophia shrugged. "Yet isn't it always pleasant to find oneself in such company, so unexpectedly? The unexpected does add such a thrill to what could have been merely a drizzly, quiet May afternoon."

Tannington sat. They all sat. Sophia smiled seductively at Tannington. Edenham looked on and smiled tolerantly. The look on Edenham's face put any thoughts of Edenham being amorously connected to Sophia Dalby out of Iveston's head, not that he'd had any thoughts of that nature to begin with, but one did hear so many rumors about Sophia that nothing, and no one, could be discounted.

Mr. Prestwick was watching his sister.

His sister, the peculiar Miss Prestwick, was watching Sophia.

Cranleigh cleared his throat and uncrossed his legs. Cranleigh was preparing to leave, his gift delivered. Iveston, quite unexpectedly and completely out of character, did not want to leave. He could hardly stay if Cranleigh left; that would look most odd. But he did want to stay, though he couldn't have said why.

Miss Prestwick had turned her gaze from Sophia, who appeared unreasonably amused by Tannington, to look at Edenham, who did not look at her.

It was a most peculiar form of entertainment, yet Iveston found himself strangely amused. It was clearly high time he got out of Hyde House more often; he was becoming quite eccentric in his amusements.

"We had a bit of an amusement going," Edenham said to Tannington, "just before you arrived. In the spirit of the game, and not to intrude, but are you here to give something to Lady Dalby?"

Tannington's pale-eyed gaze went from Edenham, circled the room, and back to Sophia. He was in the process of going from dangerous to sinister in his aspect, which did not speak well of his sense of fair play and pleasant dealings, did it?

"As you do owe me on a wager of some days past, I do hope so," Sophia said.

Tannington looked at Sophia, nodded, and said, "As it will please you, then I shall freely admit so, Lady Dalby. I have come to pay my debt to you."

"And never was anyone welcomed with more joy than upon those words," Sophia said with a smile.

Tannington, by every appearance, did not look the sort to be amused at being a part of a jest that had begun before he arrived. As to that, Iveston was not entirely certain Tannington was capable of enjoying a jest no matter when it began. He was that sort of man. He was not so very many years older than Iveston, perhaps five, and perhaps five years younger than Edenham, and a man who kept to himself more than was usual, though the same could be said of Iveston. Still, Iveston had done it for Cranleigh, not that anyone knew that, Cranleigh included. Why did Tannington keep such solemn and solitary company?

Tannington was a hard-featured man, though not an unattractive one. Quite the sort of wolfish, rakish type that women liked to giggle over.

Iveston stole a quick glance at Miss Prestwick again. She was looking at Edenham again. Edenham was ignoring her completely. It was quite strange but Iveston almost felt like chuckling, which was something he never did outside of the bounds of Hyde House. He simply wasn't the chuckling sort, never had been. Until now, apparently.

"Another wager, Sophia?" Edenham drawled. "You are not intemperate in that regard, are you?"

"Unless it is considered intemperate to win, which I am certain it must not be," Sophia replied.

"You do seem to make a habit of winning," Cranleigh said.

"A lucky habit to have," Mr. Prestwick said.

"Not so much a habit, Mr. Prestwick, as a vocation," Sophia replied with a smile.

"I don't suppose you lost much," Edenham asked of Tannington.

"Not more than I can afford to lose," Tannington answered, which was not at all friendly as replies went.

"A small wager," Sophia said, "concerning Caroline and Ashdon. I do confess to having an advantage, though Lord Tannington was willing to take the risk."

"More than willing," Tannington offered with a bit more warmth that he had as yet displayed.

That was to be expected, wasn't it? It was Sophia, after all, and men did react in certainly a very well-documented fashion toward her. Which could hardly be comfortable for Miss Prestwick, could it? Iveston looked again at Miss Prestwick. She was not looking at Edenham, which was a bit of a surprise; she was looking at him. That was actually nearly a shock and he did find it almost impossible not to sit a bit straighter, though Cranleigh hogging the settee did make sitting elegantly nearly impossible. Iveston, as discreetly as possible, elbowed Cranleigh in the ribs. Cranleigh, which was quite like him, refused to give an inch. He did twist his hips so that Iveston was very nearly pushed off the end of the settee. Iveston put both feet flat on the floor and leaned toward Cranleigh.

"Fredericks," Sophia said sweetly, "do bring another chair forward for darling Lord Iveston. He appears quite miserably uncomfortable."

"I beg your pardon, Lady Dalby," Iveston said stiffly.

"Don't be absurd. It's perfectly understandable, Lord Iveston. I've yet to meet siblings who can comfortably share anything so personal as seating. I should never have put you in this awkward position."

Which of course prompted him to glance at Miss Prestwick again, for when the word *awkward* was used, whom else to think of?

Miss Prestwick was looking at him most strangely. Not exactly daggers. No, hardly that, but rather in a sort of tepid and lethargic disbelief. In fact, she was looking at him in something quite close to boredom.

The Marquis of Iveston, heir to the Duke of Hyde, was in no way accustomed to inspiring boredom in eligible young women. Or old women, for that matter, eligible or not.

Fredericks offered him a chair. Iveston, by merely a look, indicated that Cranleigh should take it. He was keeping the settee, precedence and all that. Cranleigh, grinning, left the settee and took the chair.

A small victory, but he did feel he deserved it.

"Perhaps I should return another time?" Tannington said quietly to Sophia.

"If you'd like," Sophia answered pleasantly, keeping her gaze not on Tannington, but on Iveston. Iveston could plainly see that Tannington did not like it in the least.

Fredericks, who had not got fully out of the white salon, stuck his head back in, a truly abysmal bit of butlering, and said, "Are you in for the Marquis of Ruan, Lady Dalby?"

"I do believe I am," Sophia said, her dark gaze flicking over Lord Tannington, who was looking more sharkish by the second. He did seem a most volatile sort. Not the calm eye of reason in a storm of lunacy that Iveston knew himself to be.

The Marquis of Ruan entered the room with an elegant stride that halted fractionally when he saw that Lady Dalby was not alone in the white salon. Indeed, the room was becoming very nearly cozy with people.

They all rose, Tannington the most slowly.

Bows and curtseys were exchanged, Miss Prestwick looking very nearly annoyed as she dipped her dark head. Iveston found that mildly amusing somehow.

"Lord Ruan," Sophia purred. "What a surprise to see you."

"Not a delight, Lady Dalby?" he countered, his own voice a husky purr. "I'm devastated."

"Have you brought money or goods, Lord Ruan?" Sophia said, sitting down upon her sofa and arranging her muslin skirts. "Everyone else has done, Miss Prestwick excluded, and I find it so much easier to rise to delight when I have something of value in my hands."

"I'm quite certain I can accommodate you there, Lady Dalby," Ruan purred, his green eyes twinkling devilishly. "I rise to delight most regularly and can nearly effortlessly induce it in others."

Yes, well, that bit was obvious, wasn't it? Iveston glanced over to Miss Prestwick. Not a blush marred her cheek. She didn't drop her gaze or look discomfited in the least particular. No. In fact, Miss Penelope Prestwick looked intrigued.

Most peculiar behavior for a virgin to display. Which did beg the question, didn't it?

Mr. Prestwick stood, as was most appropriate of him, and said, "I do believe we should be off, Pen. Lady Dalby, a pleasure."

Miss Prestwick did not rise. Miss Prestwick did not look at all inclined to leave. Mr. Prestwick did seem to have his plate full with his unusual sister.

"I've a bit of a headache, George," Penelope said. "I do think it best if I sit here until it passes."

"It wouldn't pass at home, I don't suppose?" George said. As they lived just down the street, it was a most logical question.

"I shouldn't think so," Penelope Prestwick answered in a clipped tone.

George sighed, smiled, and sat.

"Are we hosting an event? And here I stand, with mud-spattered shoes."

They all rose at the entry of the Earl of Dalby, Sophia's son.

"Darling, if we are hosting an event, it is most awkward to remark on the condition of your shoes," Sophia said, offering her son her cheek to kiss. Dalby kissed it most warmly. "And if we are not, then it is most awkward to make any remark at all."

This time, it was Cranleigh who stood.

"No event, Dalby, simply a happy confluence of well-wishers and gift-bringers," Cranleigh said.

"Lord Cranleigh was of the gift-bringer variety," Sophia said, looking pleasantly at Iveston. Iveston had yet to stand. He did not care to leave at present. Certainly there was no rush? "As was Lord Tannington and the Duke of Edenham, both concerning minor wagers."

"Wagers, Mother?" Dalby asked, sitting down next to her on the sofa. They fitted quite nicely together, looking comfortable in each other's sphere, as was so unusual in Society as to bear taking note. "Is it possible that you wager too much?"

"I don't think so," she answered pleasantly. "Particularly as I win so often."

"Which would explain why some would come to the conclusion that you wager too often," Ruan said.

"The losers, you mean?" Sophia asked.

"Precisely," Ruan answered. "Lord Dalby, do you wager against your mother?"

"Not recently, Lord Ruan," Dalby answered. He was a handsome man of brown hair and eyes, quite tall and fit-looking. Still quite young, though fully in possession of his title. "My father warned me against taking on my mother; I thought I knew better, and lost two quid as a result."

"You don't mean literally," Penelope Prestwick said. "You can't mean that your mother actually took money from you, your own money."

"He who wagers must be prepared to pay his losses," Sophia said, looking directly at Miss Prestwick. "I do demand that once an agreement has been reached, even one bearing the structure of a wager, all parties play within the fences, so to speak. I'm quite firm about it, which I can't think is a surprise to anyone in this room."

Iveston did not know Sophia Dalby well at all, but he was quite aware in that moment that she was speaking very nearly directly to Penelope Prestwick. One had only to observe the slightly alarmed look on Miss Prestwick's face to see that. But about what?

He had no idea.

Suddenly and quite decidedly, he was determined to know all.

"Shall we leave, Iveston?" Cranleigh said softly.

"I should prefer to stay, if you don't mind," Iveston answered, studying Miss Prestwick's face.

"I never thought to hear it," Cranleigh murmured.

Cranleigh sat back down with great reluctance. Iveston didn't care if Cranleigh were reluctant or not; he wasn't leaving.

"What did you wager, Lord Dalby?" Iveston asked. "Can you remember?"

"Can I remember? I can hardly think it possible that I should forget, Lord Iveston," Dalby answered. "I wagered that the Duke of Aldreth's best hound would whelp less than six pups. My mother wagered that it would be more. The bitch delivered seven."

"A woman has an advantage in wagers of that sort," Sophia said mildly.

"Regarding bitches?" Ruan asked, also mildly.

"Precisely," Sophia answered with a languid smile.

It was quite obvious that Ruan was in the process of seducing Sophia. It was also quite obvious that Tannington was not happy about it. Edenham, on the other hand, seemed to find the entire thing amusing.

Miss Prestwick did not. Not amusing at any rate, but fascinating. It was most peculiar, but the girl did not seem to find any of this behavior, and surely much of it was not proper for her, an assault upon her sensibilities.

What to do but wonder why?

∽

IT was perfectly obvious to Penelope that Lord Ruan was very near to seducing Sophia Dalby completely. One was left to wonder, knowing what was common knowledge about Sophia, why it was taking so long. The sooner the better, certainly.

Penelope's greatest fear, well, perhaps not her greatest but definitely ranked within the top ten, was that Sophia would scoop

Edenham up before Penelope had a proper go at him. That wasn't going to happen. She would not have put it beyond Sophia's plans to actually have decided that marrying Edenham would only enhance her, but it was plain now, seeing them together, that they didn't have the slightest interest in each other that way. Which, truthfully, was absurd as they were a most glorious-looking pair.

One never could predict the way these things would fall, more's the pity. There was no logic at all to coupling that she could see, which was why she was approaching it from a truly logical foundation: that of social prestige and monetary gain. What other measure was as constant and precise? *Love. Passion.* Ridiculous, ephemeral notions that served playwrights and poets and no one else.

Still, Sophia clearly being no threat to her plans, Edenham appeared not at all interested in her. Worse, by returning to Dalby House at a time when Sophia had expressly not wished her to come, she had made a quick enemy of a barely made ally.

Bad bit of planning, that. Though, to be honest with herself, and she did make it a point to be honest with herself at least, it had not been so much of a plan as an impulse. Horribly untidy and unproductive, giving in to impulses. She'd known that for years and here she was, paying the price for impulse.

She'd simply have to make it up to Sophia, that's all. It couldn't be all that difficult, could it? She did seem to like getting gifts, and apparently had a passion for Chinese porcelain. She didn't suppose it could be that difficult to find a pretty enough, expensive enough vase and present it, groveling if necessary, into Sophia's lap.

Groveling was the least she was prepared to do to attain her duke.

The very *least.*

Penelope was quite well aware that Lady Caroline, Sophia's daughter, and Lady Louisa, Sophia's something or other, not to mention Lady Amelia and the episode in the mews, had each achieved perfectly respectable husbands in a matter of days, if not hours, by getting themselves well and truly ruined.

How difficult could it be to arrange for Edenham to ruin her? With Sophia's aid, it should be simplicity itself.

Oh, most girls of good family, and even those of questionable family, would look at ruination as being the worst fate that could befall a girl. Ridiculous. The worst fate to befall a girl was not getting what she wanted, and in her case, what she wanted was a proper duke. If she had to get him improperly, well then. What of it? Once she'd got him, she'd got him. What could he do about it then?

The thing to do, naturally, was to arrange for Edenham to ruin her before every man in the ton became aware that ruination had become the new betrothal. Once they had done so, and she was not so naïve as to believe they could be kept in the dark about it forever, it would become nearly impossible to lure a man into anything even resembling a compromising situation, which surely would turn Society on its head.

How to get him to do it, that was the question facing her now. Getting him alone was essential. Penelope surveyed the room. It was so very difficult not to give in to dismay. Was every man in Town going to be admitted to Dalby House today? It certainly appeared so.

Fredericks appeared at the door again and Penelope very nearly groaned, but he was only bringing in more tea things, so all was saved, or at least not any worse than it had been. The thing to do was to try and encourage some of these people to leave. Lord Tannington most definitely. She had never before met Tannington, but she could discern with no trouble whatsoever that he was a complete rogue, just the sort to ruin a girl for the fun of it. At the moment, he was staring insolently and with overt hostility at Lord Ruan, who was ignoring him completely to concentrate on Sophia. Lord Ruan must be got rid of as well.

He was, she could plainly see, a most experienced, indeed, perhaps even a dangerous rakehell. The type of man who did not seduce girls for fun, but, worse, did so without actually trying to at all. What was more dangerous than that?

Lords Iveston and Cranleigh should have left long ago. What were they lingering about for? Cranleigh had delivered his gift. Iveston had stumbled over some completely ridiculous remarks that were in the poorest taste and without a jot of wit. What more could they hope to accomplish in a single visit?

That left Edenham, George, Sophia, and she. It was going to be difficult enough to get Edenham to ruin her with having to dispose of George and Sophia. She did not think she had it in her to manage it with more than that clogging the corners of the room, figuratively speaking. She did know that she'd have to get him alone and arrange for him, or at the very least encourage him, to do something scandalous to her or her clothing.

Now, how to get Edenham to rip her dress? It would be so simple if she could get him to escort her into her conservatory somehow, putting those roses to good purpose, to *her* good purpose. How Amelia had mangled her chances on those thorns, well, it was very nearly disgraceful. Of course, when she'd arranged for the roses to crowd her conservatory, announcing without words her adept skill at rose horticulture to the world, she hadn't given a thought to using them to aid in ruining herself. Far from it. But with Lady Amelia so boldly leading the way, albeit that she appeared to have lost her way from the very moment she had found it, Penelope knew just what she wanted to happen.

She would get Edenham into her house.

She would get Edenham into her conservatory.

She would get Edenham into her clothing.

She would get Edenham.

So very simple. As to her list, it could all be rearranged, items dropped or added or repositioned. All but the last. She would get

Edenham. He was simply ideal. He would make such a lovely husband, she was completely certain of it. Why, the fact that he'd had three wives already spoke volumes as to his eligibility and appeal. Certainly a man who had married well thrice was a man worth marrying. As to his killing off his wives by his . . . *um*, prowess. Ridiculous bit of superstition. Women died in childbed every day and certainly Edenham could not be blamed for all of them, could he?

No, Edenham was the perfect choice. Now, how to get him into her clothes?

Six

IVESTON had no idea what thoughts were scurrying through Penelope Prestwick's head, but the look she was giving the Duke of Edenham was very nearly indecent. Actually, it did quite interesting things to her face. She looked, though she could hardly know it, quite seductive, nearly sultry. He had not thought she had it in her. It was becoming more than obvious that Miss Prestwick wore her thoughts and emotions on her very pretty face, and that she had no idea she was quite transparent.

Iveston smiled and ducked his head to hide it, just in case she was more cognizant of other people's expressions than she was of her own.

What an astounding blend of blatant intent and devious cunning she was, for he could read both on her face. In the next instant, her expression changed completely, becoming one of complete exasperation. Iveston supposed the change must be credited to the arrival of Sophia's brother and his three sons into the white salon.

Sophia Dalby, the dowager countess of Dalby, had a brother who was an Iroquois warrior. As Sophia and her brother John were full and complete siblings, it was therefore true that So-phia was an Iroquois.

This, it must be supposed, was a most extraordinary bit of news. No, not quite news, for Iveston was becoming aware that his par-ents, and indeed many of their generation, of which Sophia must be ranked among their number, had known of Sophia's Iroquois heritage from the start. The fact that it had become hidden, likely upon her marriage to the Earl of Dalby, was to be expected. Perhaps. Still, it did seem the worst sort of foul play for one gen-eration to be so familiar with a fact and keep it to themselves.

Actually, from what he could gather, Sophia and John were the children of an Englishwoman and an Iroquois, the result ap-parently being that Sophia was the more English of the two and John the more Indian.

Apparently being.

Iveston, who had truly not fully met Sophia before last week and who found her as delightful as every man of maturity did, was not at all certain that Sophia was who she seemed to be. He did not overmuch care, and certainly who she was or who she wasn't couldn't possibly affect him, but it was interesting, a sort of a puzzle to be worked. He did enjoy a puzzle.

Upon the thought, and rising to greet Lady Dalby's relatives, Iveston's gaze swung again to Miss Prestwick. She looked posi-tively incensed. It was quite amusing.

As they all stood, bowing and curtseying to each other, the introductions made as quickly as possible, Cranleigh whispered, "It's the perfect opportunity to leave. I'm certain there can't be enough chairs."

Whereupon four footmen brought in four Chippendale chairs with yellow silk damask seats. Iveston shook his head, grinning, and sat back down. The Indians sat. They *all* sat. Miss Prestwick looked nearly as dejected about it as Cranleigh did.

"Markham has informed me that you intend to stay in Town,"

Sophia said to her brother, John. John didn't quite nod, but did make a slight motion of assent. "I confess to being surprised. I didn't think the joys of Town were quite your thing, John. Don't tell me you have been seduced by its many pleasures."

"I have not been seduced," John said. He was quite a rugged, frightening-looking fellow, which Iveston suspected was entirely intentional. "I have been convinced."

"Convinced? Of what? And by whom?" Sophia glanced at her son, Dalby, who apparently was called Markham by family intimates. Most confusing.

"By me, Sophia," the elder son said.

George Grey was of an indeterminate age; he looked younger than Iveston, and likely was, but he had such an air about him of ruthless intent and abounding humor that he seemed very much more experienced than George Prestwick, who was in all probability the same age. George Grey, Iroquois, had dark curling hair and dark gleaming eyes and the curious anomaly of a single dimple in his left cheek. Coupled with his stature and obvious physical strength, it gave him the appalling appearance of being a gleeful murderer.

Iveston was not at all uncertain that the impression wasn't precisely on the mark.

"Of course by you," Sophia said with a slight grin. "Not possible at all for it to have been by Young."

Young, another private name which should have surely been kept private, was truly called John. As his father was also called John, the appellation was explained. He was the middle brother of the Iroquois in the white salon, which clearly was an odd conjoining of disparate words, for who could ever have anticipated Indians in a London town house? In any regard, Iveston understood from the way in which Young held himself, his posture and bearing, that he had no desire to be in Town and, indeed, no desire to speak a word if he could help it.

He could help it.

In response to Sophia's comment, Young simply looked at his aunt, made some pleasant motion of his eyes, and then looked down at the floor between his very large feet.

Matthew Grey, the youngest of them, was a startling-looking young man of dark hair and complexion and piercing blue eyes. As the Greys were cousins to Lord Dalby, they did bear a strong resemblance to each other, though Dalby looked completely English and the Greys looked nothing like. Although, perhaps it was not so much their physical appearance as their demeanor. They were very nearly pugilistic in their aspect, though almost silently so. Certainly they did not talk a great deal, though they appeared comfortable enough in their surroundings.

But of course they would. Sophia was their aunt.

Iveston could not quite wrap his thoughts around it.

Tannington appeared to be having the same trouble, though the same could not be said of Miss Prestwick. Miss Prestwick, as Iveston should have expected, was giving her complete attention to Edenham. Even Edenham seemed to sense it now, not that he looked at all delighted by the fact.

And who would? It was entirely too obvious of her. She really ought to at least put on an appearance of being demure and reticent. All the girls did, those who were not yet married. Once married, they behaved any way they liked, which was one of the problems of marriage, as he saw it.

Of course, he knew he would marry. It was his duty. He *must* marry. And he would. One day. There was certainly no rush about it, was there? He had years left to him. What he would do with those years left to him of freedom he wasn't entirely certain. He clearly hadn't done much by way of excitement with his un-married years so far, but the future looked as bright as it ever had done and he was prepared to enjoy himself, in whatever fashion suited him.

At some point, he did realize, he had to find something which suited him.

And, surely reduced to being a habit by now, he glanced again at Miss Prestwick.

"Convinced of what, I should very much like to know," Sophia asked of her brother, smiling at George Grey.

"Convinced that having a London Season," George said, "is good fun. You've convinced me, Sophia, and I convinced my father of the same. Why not stay?"

"Why not stay?" Miss Prestwick said abruptly, which was most peculiar as no one was speaking to her. "Why not go? I can't think what you would gain by a London Season, Mr. Grey."

"A wife, Miss Prestwick?" George Grey countered, smiling at her. A girl would have to be very unusual not to be disarmed by that single, deep dimple. Iveston watched Miss Prestwick. She did not look disarmed in the slightest, no, nor charmed. It was slightly gratifying, though he could not think why. "A man, just as a woman, wants to marry."

"Not all men, Mr. Grey," Lord Tannington said.

"You do not intend to marry, Lord Tannington?" Sophia asked.

"I will marry when I can avoid it no longer," Lord Tannington said, "but the point I believe your nephew was making is that all men *want* to marry. I would say that while all men may marry, very few of them actually want to."

"That sounds very nearly tragic," Sophia said, looking not at all tragic, but rather flagrantly amused. "I think a poll must settle it. Now, do answer honestly, which I know is very difficult for a man to do."

It was at this juncture that Miss Prestwick snorted in what had to be assumed was suppressed laughter.

"Now, how shall we organize it? Just around the room then?" Sophia mused.

"Alphabetically?" Edenham said pleasantly, his brown eyes shining with mirth.

"Far too difficult for me to manage," Sophia answered, smiling at Edenham.

"By age? Oldest to youngest?" Miss Prestwick blurted out.

"Oh, I think not," Sophia said. "Someone could well find himself insulted." And she looked at Edenham again and chuckled.

Was Edenham the oldest man in the room? Perhaps Ruan and certainly John Grey were of the same approximate age. Ruan didn't look insulted in the slightest, in fact, he was watching Sophia flirt with Edenham with a very nearly bored expression. *Very nearly bored.* He was watching, after all. And John Grey, well, his expression was impossible to read. He simply had no expression whatsoever.

The same could not be said of Miss Prestwick. She was watching Sophia dangle charm and gaiety like a ripe plum in front of Edenham's face and looked completely outraged by the prospect. Poor girl. She clearly didn't have a particle of charm to fight with. Of course, *he* was watching her and she *could* have turned some effort upon him, but she was clearly too simpleminded to know any better.

"By either age or alphabet, I shall not be first," Iveston said. "Shall it be a simple test of bravery then? Shall I not prove my courage and stout heart by declaring that I, for one, want to marry?"

Miss Prestwick looked struck dumb. It was a look which suited her.

"Do you, Lord Iveston? How charming of you," Sophia exclaimed. He felt the distinct urge to preen under her praise. He did not, however. "And when did the urge to mate first come upon you?"

"I believe the subject was marriage, Lady Dalby?" Iveston countered smoothly, his brows raised in mock admonition.

Sophia smiled and did not look the least contrite. Miss Prestwick looked appalled. Iveston felt the stirrings of a smile tease the corners of his mouth. "But as to marriage, knowing it was to be forced upon me at some distant point, I have not anticipated it eagerly. Until recently. Having seen two of my brothers so blissfully wed, I can now begin to imagine wanting a bit of bliss of my own."

Oddly, most oddly, the moment the words were out of his mouth he felt the truth of them. He'd been avoiding marriage for almost as long as he could remember. But Blakes and Cranleigh were so nauseatingly blissful that it did make the whole concept of marriage slightly more bearable. Indeed, even attractive.

But of course, both Blakes and Cranleigh had married for love. As the heir to a dukedom, he didn't suppose he'd have that luxury. In truth, he hadn't ever considered it. His entire idea concerning marriage, and he did have just the single idea, was to avoid it for as long as he possibly could, which surely was a most reasonable position and very much as Tannington had stated it. Though it did sound rather harsh when expressed, merely proving the point that some things should never be expressed. An idea Miss Prestwick was clearly a stranger to. She seemed unable to keep herself from expressing all over the room.

"How beautifully phrased," Sophia said.

"If nonsensical," Tannington said.

"Perhaps not so much nonsensical," Penelope Prestwick said with all the studiousness of a Latin tutor, "as highly emotional. I do believe, indeed it seems quite obvious, that the best marriages are made without undue emotion. Emotion makes everything so very cloudy."

"If one dislikes clouds, that is a disadvantage," Edenham said.

Little Miss Prestwick sat back on her chair and closed her mouth into a firm and very sultry pout. It was quite charmingly done, which was quite odd of her, wasn't it? She wasn't the charming sort at all, quite the opposite.

"I thought everyone preferred a day without clouds," Mr. Prestwick said, very nicely coming to the aid of his sister.

"Cloudy nights can be quite romantic," Edenham said, "though I don't presume to think there is a universality of opinion on that. Perhaps it is an acquired taste."

"As so much is," Sophia said mildly.

"And the longer one lives, the more tastes one acquires," Ruan said. "Or perhaps it is only that one learns to be adept at pretending to have wide and varied tastes."

It wasn't so much that Ruan was staring at Sophia, but that Sophia reacted so unusually to his remark. She came quite close to bristling. It was a fact well established that Sophia did not bristle.

"To what purpose, Lord Ruan?"

"To please a man, Lady Dalby," Ruan answered promptly. "A woman will do much to please a man."

"Only if a man has already done much to please her," she countered.

"My mother often gets into these sorts of conversations," Dalby said casually, looking about the room. "I learned early on to only listen to every third word. I kept my innocence until nearly the age of ten."

Sophia laughed and broke the brittle spell that had risen up between herself and Ruan, patting Dalby on the knee. "At every third word, you would have formed very strange ideas indeed. I know for a fact, Markham, that you are still very much the innocent about very particular things."

"But not in regard to pleasing a woman," Dalby replied, his dark eyes alight with humor, "because I learned that from Father."

"A most adept teacher," Sophia said.

"Most," Dalby agreed. "Father made certain I understood that the way to please a woman is to give her what she wants."

"And so we are back to where we started," Edenham said.

"But what is it that a woman wants?" Iveston asked. "Very often I am not convinced they know themselves."

"Do you think we all want the same thing?" Penelope asked sharply.

She looked at him directly and he returned her look, suddenly aware that very few women of marriageable age ever looked at him directly and certainly not with the sort of impassioned, determined, studious look that Penelope Prestwick was in the habit of displaying over the most inconsequential of topics. Yet this was not one of those, was it? This was a topic near to her heart and he found he could not much blame her.

"No, Miss Prestwick, not precisely the same thing," he answered, looking into her dark eyes. "But close enough, yes? Do you know what you want?"

"Of course I do," she answered instantly, her eyes flaring.

"And you can explain it? Put it into a single sentence?" he prodded, wondering what her eyes would do next.

"Naturally. I have given it a great deal of thought, as you can well imagine," she said. Her eyes did the oddest thing then, they got very wide and soft, like a cloudless summer night.

"And?" he prompted, his voice gone quite soft, to match her eyes, actually.

"I want to get married, Lord Iveston," she said, her own voice as soft as his.

The moment stretched out between them like a silken cord, until Sophia said, "Of course she wants to get married, Iveston, but why shouldn't she? Yet best not to ask whom she wants to marry as that would be in extremely poor taste."

Iveston did not ask. But Penelope, who did have the worst aptitude for this sort of thing, looked instantly at Edenham. And then she flushed.

And that was answer enough.

Seven

As a matter of courtesy, the party, while not departing Dalby House, did split into various groups. It was an awkward time of day for callers as it was well past time for the preparations to begin for their various evenings out. Still, they did not leave, not a one of them, and Sophia was hardly in the habit of throwing people out onto the street. Or that was the rumor. Even Sophia might be pushed to throwing if the circumstances required it.

"We should leave," George Prestwick whispered to Penelope, after he had dragged her to one of the front windows of the white salon.

"I'm not leaving!" she whispered in response. What could George be thinking? Edenham was here, now, and not another woman in sight, if one discounted Sophia, which she would and did. When would a chance like this ever come again?

"It would look better if you did, Pen," George said with a bit more force than was usual for him. What on earth had gotten into him? Was it possible that he was distressed at the thought of her imminent marriage? It had better be imminent. "We have quite outstayed our welcome, I am certain. Lady Dalby can't have expected half of London to pop into her salon, particularly at this time of day."

It *was* late. It was past seven and everyone was at home preparing for their evenings out. Everyone who wasn't in Dalby House, that is. If Edenham wasn't leaving now, then she wasn't leaving now. It was as simple as that. What was wrong with George that he couldn't see the obvious?

"Why should we be the first to leave?" she snapped under her breath, eyeing Edenham from across the room. He was talking to Sophia's brother, Mr. John Grey, about what she couldn't imagine. "No one else is leaving."

"True," George conceded, turning away from her to look across the room. "Do you think this happens often to her? That people come and refuse to leave her?"

"Her? You mean Lady Dalby?" Penelope said on a huff of disbelief. "I shouldn't think so. Why ever would you suppose that, George?"

"They're staying for some reason, Pen, and I don't think it's because of us, do you?"

Well. Actually, she had hoped so.

⁂

"Dare I hope that we may leave now?" Cranleigh said to Iveston.

"You need to learn to enjoy life more, Cranleigh," Iveston replied, looking about the room. "Relax."

"I have a new wife at home, Iveston. Relaxing is the farthest thing from my mind," Cranleigh said, shifting his weight slightly.

They were all standing now, even Lady Dalby, the afternoon visit having turned into something more resembling a formal At Home. Iveston glanced around the room again. Miss Prestwick looked somewhat agitated. He thought he could deduce the reason why. Very difficult to catch a man's eye when the room was simply clogged. He ought to know as women had been trying to catch his eye for years. All except this one, this little Miss Prestwick who obviously had more money than breeding. Certainly, for wouldn't a woman of careful breeding make it a point to chat him up? Wasn't he the most desirable, that is to say, most eligible man in the room?

He most certainly was.

Peculiar little thing not to act upon that fact. One did wonder how badly addled she was, to have missed the mark so. It had not escaped his notice that her brother was very nearly her keeper, smoothing the way for her as best he could. Given that she was so odd, he clearly had a time of it. Iveston didn't envy the man his task. Penelope Prestwick would exhaust and exasperate the most devoted of men, which George Prestwick certainly appeared to be.

"Peculiar, isn't it?" Cranleigh said softly at his side. As they were both looking at Miss Prestwick, Iveston thought the question remarkably apt. "She may be the first unmarried woman to ignore you completely. How does it feel, Iveston? I should think you'd be relieved."

Iveston looked askance at Cranleigh. Marriage had done something to him, something quite unappealing. Why, his brother now had a sense of humor. Most inconvenient, particularly at the moment.

"I am."

Cranleigh grinned. "You look it. Truly."

Iveston lifted his chin and said, "She's obviously some sort of imbecile. Why, she can barely hold her own in Society."

"You think so?" Cranleigh replied casually. "I had a nice conversation with her at the Prestwick ball and found her very entertaining."

"Trained bears are entertaining."

"Oh, come now. She's not anything like a trained bear. You're just being vicious, likely because you're not accustomed to being ignored by a likely female."

"Which is my entire point," Iveston said in a low rumble of annoyance, "she's not a likely female. She's the most unlikely female I've ever encountered."

"Get her talking about her roses," Cranleigh suggested, a perfectly lovely smile on his lips. As Cranleigh was not in the habit of putting on perfectly lovely smiles, Iveston, naturally, was instantly on his guard. "She delights in them. I should think you'll be as entertained by her as I was."

"I don't care to talk to her about anything. She appears quite preoccupied at the moment in any regard," Iveston said stiffly.

"Oh, well, if you're going to wait for her to stop twittering about Edenham, you'll never find your chance. Of course, that may very well be just what you intended. Is it?"

Cranleigh, really, was the most obstinate, most . . . well, his wife had named it best when she'd called him a bully. Normally Iveston was not bothered by it for the obvious reason that Cranleigh's bullying had never before been so forcefully focused on him. It was quite a nuisance now, and he wasn't enjoying it in the slightest.

"I have no intentions at all regarding Miss Prestwick."

"And she has none regarding you," Cranleigh countered. "It's quite remarkable, isn't it? Usually they fall all over you and now . . ." Cranleigh shrugged in the most insulting manner imaginable. "I suppose you're afraid to approach a woman who hasn't got her children by you already named. Lack of practice and all that."

"Are you implying that I can't manage women?"

Iveston was not at all amused, which he assumed was more than apparent by his frozen expression. Cranleigh, more than any of his brothers, with the possible exception of Blakes, who really was too observant for anyone's good, was quite adept at reading him. Why, Cranleigh had very nearly made it his life's work to protect Iveston from all sorts of trouble, usually of the female sort, and Iveston had got quite used to it. Perhaps too used to it?

"I think you manage them very well," Cranleigh replied softly, eyeing Miss Prestwick from where they stood. They were very near the door into the front hall, which Iveston suspected was not at all accidental. "As long as by managing you mean avoiding them entirely. Now that I think upon it, you haven't managed very many, have you, if by managing you mean actually interacting with them."

"I suppose you're trying to be funny? You're failing miserably."

"I suppose you think I can't add? How many, Iveston? How many women have you . . . managed?"

"More than enough. More than you, certainly. You've been at sea rather a lot in the past few years, haven't you?"

"But Iveston, all ships do eventually heave anchor. I've enjoyed more than a few ports of call."

"A metaphor, Cranleigh?"

"Not entirely," Cranleigh answered with a brief smile.

"What are you suggesting?" Iveston asked, for he knew Cranleigh as well as Cranleigh knew him. In discussions of this sort, a wager was the inevitable outcome.

"Nothing at all tawdry, I assure you." To which Iveston snorted in disbelief, which caused John Grey and his three sons to look at him in sudden interest. Iveston nodded curtly and refocused his attention back to his brother. "Miss Prestwick seems a lovely enough woman." And here Iveston came very nearly close to snorting again. He did manage to refrain. "I would not see her ill used for our entertainment."

"*Your* entertainment, Cranleigh. Don't forget, I think her a trained bear."

"As to that, Iveston," Cranleigh said with that same, small smile, "I should think that, what with your self-proclaimed skill at managing women you should be able to coax something from Miss Prestwick, particularly as you state she is already trained to respond to either encouragement or direction. Which, would you say?"

"A lump of sugar, would be my guess," Iveston said stiffly, avoiding looking at Miss Prestwick, whom he was certain, was staring at Edenham with all the subtlety of a cannon blast.

"Now, now, you shan't get far with her with that attitude," Cranleigh said, grinning, the sot.

"I haven't agreed to anything, you realize," Iveston said, "and I can't think how you'd induce me to. I have nothing to prove to either you or myself, and certainly not upon the very peculiar Miss Prestwick."

"Don't you?" Cranleigh asked. "Not even to Miss Prestwick? I do think that is where the heart of the matter lies. Why not prove to Miss Prestwick that you are not a man to be discarded without a second glance?"

"Come, come, I don't want even a first glance from her," Iveston said stoutly.

"Of course you don't," Cranleigh said. He sounded distinctly sarcastic. "But she doesn't know that, does she? Shall we not wager that you cannot attain her interest for, say, a week?"

Iveston looked at Miss Prestwick. She was, as to be expected, arguing with her brother while staring at Edenham. Edenham, also fulfilling expectation, was ignoring her. One could almost feel some pity for the odd little thing. Almost.

"A week? I should go mad. Say a day instead."

"A day? But how can anything of that sort be measured in a day?" Cranleigh countered. "Unless you expect to shadow her every moment of that single day."

"Hardly," Iveston said coldly. Iveston, when the occasion

required it, could be quite as stiffly formal as any marquis could be. He found, in this instance, that the occasion required it fully. "I should go barking mad. What say you to three days?"

"Three days," Cranleigh mused, rocking a bit on his heels. "I should think three days ought to work out nicely. How are we to measure it and who is to be the arbiter?"

"Oh, come now," Iveston said. "It shall be as perfectly obvious as it's always been. She'll behave as they all do, all simpering looks and sweet smiles and dipping bodices. It will be obvious to all."

"Perhaps, but I would feel better about it if we had a disinterested third party."

"Edenham?" Iveston said, grinning.

Cranleigh gave him a look and then said, "What about Mr. Grey?"

"Lady Dalby's brother?"

"No, he's too disinterested to even agree to take part. I was thinking of Mr. George Grey."

They both turned to consider the Indian, oldest of the three sons and Sophia's nephew. It was a strange coincidence indeed that he was staring back at them. That seemed enough to settle it.

"Done," Iveston said. "Three days, starting now, Mr. Grey to pronounce. Shall I broach the subject to him or shall you?"

"I shall. You have enough to do with Miss Prestwick, don't you? Best get to it, before she carries Edenham out of the room over her shoulder," Cranleigh said with a grin.

"I thought that was your duty," Iveston said mockingly, as it was now and forevermore a well-known fact that Cranleigh had carried his wife over his shoulder before she was his wife. Just look how well it had all turned out, if one wanted to be married, that is.

"Miss Prestwick looks at you like a woman who wants to be married," Tannington said.

Edenham glanced at Tannington and did something with his mouth that was nearly a smile, but wasn't. "Most women have that look. I used to believe they were born with it. Until I had my daughter. I now know it is a learned response that envelops a woman at a certain age," Edenham said, setting his cup down upon the table nearest him. "At what age I cannot say."

"Shall I offer an opinion?" Sophia said. "It depends entirely upon the woman. Some women never reach it."

"Never?" Tannington said. "I've yet to meet a woman who hasn't."

"You've met me," Sophia said with the slightest degree of chill to her voice.

"Yet you married," Tannington said.

"Yet without the requisite look, Lord Tannington, which is what I believe we were discussing."

"What look did you wear, Lady Dalby?" Lord Ruan asked.

"I should think a most satisfied one," she answered, "as is my habit."

"A most delightful habit," Ruan said softly, standing between her and Tannington, Edenham at her side. Ruan did not mind Edenham's presence as it was plain that he and Sophia were friends and only that. Tannington, however, was a threat, a predator to Sophia's affections that he was not prepared to tolerate. It was supremely helpful that Sophia clearly had no use for Tannington, not that Tannington seemed to appreciate that fact.

Lord Tannington was, by every description of him, a determined man to an almost ruthless degree. He wanted Sophia, that was plain and perfectly natural of him. He could not have her. If Sophia had not already decided that, and he would be shocked if she hadn't, then Ruan had. Lord Ruan had danced around Sophia Dalby for nearly a month now and seen very little in the way of results. He was not going to allow Tannington to slow his momentum now, however paltry it was.

"It was Dalby who wore the look then, if I remember," Edenham said. "He was most determined to have you, wasn't he?"

Sophia turned so that Tannington was slightly behind her and out of her line of sight. She smiled at Edenham with all the warmth of an old friend. Ruan felt himself relax, slightly. Regarding Sophia, one was a fool to relax fully.

"He said as much," Sophia said.

"How very peculiar," Tannington said softly. "I was told he had you already, repeatedly."

Edenham didn't have the chance to respond, no, nor Ruan either, though his mouth was already open to call the man out.

"But darling," Sophia said smoothly, her dark eyes shining in what could only be termed malicious joy, "there is such a difference between having what a woman parcels out to a man, drip by beggarly drip, and having all she is, never-endingly. But it's quite obvious that you have no way of knowing that. And likely never shall. It was so good of you to drop by and pay your debt. I do so appreciate a man who knows how to lose."

Ruan wasn't certain how it was arranged, but Fredericks and two footmen appeared to nearly surround Tannington, silently encouraging him to leave without making a fuss. He did. Both leave and not make a fuss. But he looked far from pleased about it. Who would?

"There goes my best chance," Ruan said under his breath, taking a step nearer to Sophia. She lifted her dark lashes and gave him an inquisitive look. "I was completely prepared to call him out and engage him in a nasty duel, which I would have won. You would have been most impressed. It was to have been my finest, most romantic gesture of the year. Now I shall have to wait for another opportunity to dazzle you. Can you wait, Lady Dalby?"

"It seems I must, Lord Ruan," she said, a smile playing around the corners of her mouth. "But I do confess some curiosity. What was your finest gesture of the previous year?"

"I hate to boast," he said.

"Is that the gesture? How odd," Sophia said, smiling fully now.

He loved to see her smile. She was not miserly with her smiles, far from it, but this sort of smile, the sort that took her unawares and took her over, those were rare. He wanted that from her. He wanted nothing of the careful sophistication that the rest of the world saw from her. He wanted what no other man, or damned few, had seen. He wanted her joy.

"I sang," he said. "Under a window. In the rain."

"Did she let you in?" Sophia asked, grinning.

"Immediately and completely," Ruan answered. "I made quite a dashing figure."

"Even wet," she said.

"Especially wet," he countered. "The wetter the better, has been my experience."

"Darling Lord Ruan, are you in the habit of making romantic gestures? How exhausting for you."

"I have nothing if not stamina," he said. "Determination as well."

"Lord Ruan," she said sweetly, "I do think you'll need both."

"You are a severe taskmaster, Sophia," Edenham said. "What would you have of him? Song?"

"Oh, no, not song. I would not steal another woman's victory," Sophia said. "Which brings me round to Miss Prestwick, Edenham. You are, as you must certainly know, every woman's dream of the ideal husband. It is entirely natural for Miss Prestwick to have formed a certain fascination for you, and indeed, it is quite obvious to even the most disinterested observer, though who that could be I have no idea, that she would very much like to attract your notice."

"I don't like to boast," Edenham said with a small shrug for Ruan. "Yet, I had noticed some small bit of something on her part."

"She's a charming girl, a bit unusual, but that's only to her advantage, wouldn't you agree?"

"I might," Edenham said slowly, studying Sophia.

"Well then, what more is there to say? If you want her to be your fourth wife, she's entirely at your disposal. The decision is entirely yours, Edenham. Do you want her or not?"

⁂

"You want me to judge if she wants you or not?" George Grey asked. "Can't you tell?"

"Of course I can tell," Iveston said. "It's only that, for the purposes of the wager, an entirely innocent wager—"

"Not entirely innocent," Dalby interjected.

"No harm will come to the girl," Iveston said. "Surely you can't think that simply talking to her at a few events would lead to her ruin?"

"I've seen very little more lead to a girl's ruin," Dalby said. "My own sister, for one."

"As you were not in Town, and yet as I would say nothing to offend you or your family," Cranleigh said, "there was slightly more to your sister's situation than talking."

Dalby, a decade younger than Cranleigh and a full stone lighter in weight, did not look put off by either fact. Dalby took a half step nearer to Cranleigh and said stiffly, "How much more, Lord Cranleigh?"

"Only slightly, Lord Dalby," Cranleigh said softly. "As I have my own history with my wife to hobble me, I am hardly likely to cast a single stone at any woman, particularly a woman who is so blissfully wed as your sister gives every appearance of being."

"My sister is not in Town," Dalby said.

"Hence, my conclusion," Cranleigh said with a small smile. "As soon as an Elliot ship arrives in port, I will also escape Town with my bride."

"The *Plain Jane* should arrive within the month," George Grey said.

Cranleigh looked sharply at George Grey. "You know of the Elliots, and their ships?"

"You're surprised?" George countered. "How did you think Sophia got to England the first time? An Elliot ship took her."

"A merchant ship?" Cranleigh said. "Why?"

"As a gift," John Grey said, his dark eyes flat and hard. "At Sally's insistence."

"*My* Aunt Sally?" Iveston said. How was it that this sort of information, information his mother and certainly his aunt had possessed for twenty or more years, had never been discussed with him?

"Why would my aunt give Sophia a gift?" Cranleigh said on the heels of Iveston's question.

"Since no one has told you, it must be none of your concern," John said.

He was an Indian. He had no status, no position, no title. Yet Iveston knew without question that the matter was closed, at least as far as John was concerned and that there would be no opening of it. Of course, that didn't mean that he couldn't, or wouldn't, ask his mother.

Dalby cleared his throat, clearly amused. The Indians did not look amused in the slightest, not even George, who looked amused more often than not. What the devil was so amusing about the British aristocracy?

"But how do you know which Elliot ship is on its way?" Cranleigh asked, clearly disturbed by the knowledge that these Indians knew more on any subject than he did. A perfectly understandable reaction.

"We saw her in New York Harbor, Lord Cranleigh," George Grey answered. "We talked to her captain. We know the Elliots."

Iveston was at a complete loss for words. So, it was readily apparent, was Cranleigh. Sophia's Indians knew their American cousins? How was it possible?

"But about that wager," George continued, "as it will suit me to spend as much time as I can with you English, I will arbitrate the bet. How long must I"—and here George Grey, Indian, paused to look at Miss Prestwick in what could only be termed the most horridly interested fashion—"watch her?"

"Three days," Iveston snapped.

"Only three?" George said slowly, still staring at Miss Prestwick. Miss Prestwick must have felt his leer, for that's what it clearly was, because she turned from talking to her brother, another George, which really was so very inconvenient, to glare at Mr. Grey. Good for her. Showed such pluck. "I guess I'll have to make do with that."

"Make do?" Iveston said. "I don't think you have the gist of the thing at all, Mr. Grey. You are to observe, not interact. I assume that's most clear to you?"

"You can assume whatever you want, Lord Iveston," George said without a smidgen of shame. Well, he was an Iroquois. One should never expect shame from one of their number. Actually, as he was a blood relative of Sophia Dalby, his lack of shame made even more sense. "You have your task before you. I have mine."

Lord Dalby very nearly chuckled. Oh, he tried to smother it, but Iveston heard it all the same.

"You must not interfere or you will spoil the wager," Iveston said.

"I understand," George Grey said, grinning like the very devil.

"'Tis three days from now, Iveston," Cranleigh said, grabbing him by the elbow. Whatever for? He wasn't going to thrash the grinning Indian, was he? Or was he? He hadn't felt this annoyed in years, and perhaps not *this* annoyed even then. "Best get to it and not waste any more time here. He'll be impartial, that's certain."

Hardly certain, what with all the leering at Miss Prestwick. Not that he actually cared in any personal sense, but as Miss Prestwick was an innocent English girl of good family, he did feel some general sense of responsibility, something along the lines of national pride or blanket patriotism. Or something like that.

Eight

"GEORGE," Penelope whispered to her brother, "one of those Indians is staring at me."

George looked around the room in the most casual manner imaginable, his glance sliding over the group of Indians with no sense of alarm whatsoever. "You are the only female in the room, Pen. That must account for it."

"Now they're *all* looking," she said, staring back at them. Nothing so tepid as a stare was going to intimidate her. "And I do think I have some charm beyond being the only female available! How insulting. If I didn't need you to chaperone me I'd dispense with you immediately."

"I'd best behave or I shall find that I have all my time to myself," George said with a very cheeky grin.

"Once I am married, you shall be free of me. Let the thought inspire you," Penelope said with a cheeky grin of her own.

She did love George. He was quite a lovely companion and so rarely disagreed with her, which was the nicest thing that could be said of a person, particularly a male. They were so regularly difficult and so very nearly irrational. One was left to wonder how they managed anything at all. Certainly they had somehow got the advantage of women in laws and the general assignment of power, and she could only surmise that they had arranged all that when the world had been simply taken over by swords and battle-axes and things. Of course, it was still a very bloodthirsty world, but certainly any educated person could see that a woman was far more self-controlled than a man.

"I am inspired," George said. "Now, may we leave? It's rather late and we have to dress for . . . where are we off to tonight?"

"A soiree at the Countess of Lanreath's," Penelope said softly. "I heard a rumor that Edenham was to attend. I do hope so."

"Then he should leave Dalby House as well," George said. "I don't know how we shall all get ready with only two hours left to do so."

Penelope looked at George. George winked. "I'll leave Dalby House when Edenham leaves Dalby House. I should think that was perfectly obvious, George."

"I believe, Pen, that it's perfectly obvious to everyone in the room."

She did look about her and they did all, all now including Edenham, appear to be staring at her. She smiled blandly, set down her cup, and adjusted her shawl. But she did not leave. What she did do, which she did think was most bold of her, was to walk over to the Indians, as well as the Lords Dalby, Cranleigh, and Iveston as they were all clustered together in a most uncordial grouping, which did take her very near to where Sophia, Edenham, and Ruan were talking, and say just loud enough for Edenham to hear her, "I noticed you looking at me, Mr. Grey. It has caused me to wonder if you have little familiarity with English women. I would be happy to answer any questions you might have, to ease your way in our Society, as it were. Are you staying long in England?"

Mr. Grey, the elder brother, the one who had been staring at her with the most inappropriately direct look, which she was certain had negatively affected the rest of them into doing the same, smiled at her, his rather disarming dimple . . . well, disarming her. He was, it was a shock to note, quite ruthlessly handsome in a perfectly primitive sort of way. She would not have thought that either being ruthless or primitive would have been in any way compelling. As it happened, she was entirely wrong about that.

"Miss Prestwick," Mr. Grey answered, "if I do have any questions, I will come directly to you. What is it you think I should know about English women?"

"That they don't like being stared at?" Lord Iveston said. *Really*. Had anyone been talking to him?

"Is that true, Miss Prestwick?" Mr. Grey countered, taking a step nearer to her. He was very nearly looming over her. He clearly didn't know the first thing about civilized discourse, but then, how was he to have learned that in the forests of New York or New Jersey or wherever his particular forest haunts were? "English women don't like being looked at? Sophia is English enough and she doesn't seem bothered by it."

"Sophia Dalby is quite unique," Penelope said, very diplomatically, if she did say so herself, "and I certainly would make no claim to be anything like her."

"Yet," George said in a playful tone. As if anyone wanted playfulness *now*. George, for all that she loved him, did have the most odd sense of humor.

"I'm certain that if Lady Dalby's relatives have any questions, they can ask Lord Dalby, wouldn't you think, Miss Prestwick? They are related, after all, and the Greys are hardly strangers to England," Lord Iveston said rather crisply.

"But hardly familiars either," Mr. George Grey answered, slightly less pleasantly than he had been doing. Apparently he found Lord Iveston as annoying as she did.

"*Familiars* is not a word we use, Mr. Grey," Penelope said, breaking the tension between Lord Iveston, who was behaving more peculiarly than usual, and George Grey, who seemed, quite up to whatever scant rumors she had heard about Indians, to be quite prickly. "It has an entirely different connotation."

"Of witches, Miss Prestwick?" Mr. Grey said with a saucy grin, his dimple positively winking at her. "Of the cats that wind round their legs and sleep on their beds in the dark of night?"

Why, if she didn't know better, she'd think George Grey was trying to be very forward with her. As he was an Indian, she was quite prepared to believe he didn't know any better. Perhaps because he was Sophia's nephew, she was more than willing to believe it.

"Now, George," Lord Dalby said, "you know perfectly well there are no witches in England. Not anymore."

"No, they all ended up in Massachusetts," Mr. Grey said, grinning fully, and then the rogue actually winked at her. *Winked!*

"The Iroquois don't have witches, Mr. Grey?" Iveston asked. Oh, bother, didn't he know enough to let the conversation die a peaceful death?

"Not as pretty as English ones," Mr. Grey said, looking down at her.

It was at moments such as this, and very many others as well, that she wished she were taller. It would be so very satisfying to stare an unruly man in the eye and give him what for. Of course, she managed quite well, but it had taken years of practice, mostly on George.

"I am no witch, Mr. Grey," she said. "England has quite done with witches. We have none."

"Or none we will admit to," her brother said cheerfully.

"And I do believe we've come to pronounce it differently,"

Iveston said, looking at *her*, of all people. Whatever was *that* supposed to mean? As Lord Dalby was grinning awkwardly and as Lord Cranleigh was shaking his head in mild admonishment, she could only suppose it was something entirely dreadful.

"We should go," Lord Cranleigh said to his distinctly peculiar brother. "It's gone quite late."

Penelope perked up at the words. Two less men in the room would make it so much easier to corner Edenham, who was still talking to Sophia and Lord Ruan. Whatever could they have to talk about for so long?

"It is, isn't it?" Lord Iveston said, looking at her in a most intent and highly unwelcome fashion. "I don't suppose you have any interest in Chinese porcelain, Miss Prestwick? My brother knows quite a bit about it, having traveled to China once or twice."

"Once," Lord Cranleigh said.

"I think it very pretty, of course, Lord Iveston," she said. "If I have any further need for information, I shall certainly find my way to Lord Cranleigh and have all my questions answered. But don't let me keep you. I have no pressing questions about Chinese porcelain at the moment."

"You know a good deal about Chinese porcelain, Cranleigh?" Edenham asked, leaving Sophia and Ruan by the fire and coming over to their rather large circle. Penelope straightened her shoulders a bit and stiffened her spine. She had quite a nice bosom, quite full and without any droop at all. Men, by every account available, did enjoy a nice bosom on a woman. "Quite a lovely piece here. Intriguing shade of green."

"Celadon," Cranleigh answered. "A gift from my brother, Henry. I have just gifted Lady Dalby this blue vase."

"It's quite exceptional," Edenham said, admiring it. "Is there some reason the Blakesleys are giving Lady Dalby expensive porcelain? I haven't forgotten an important anniversary, have I?"

As they were talking, Penelope, still shoulders back and bosom nicely lifted, felt Lord Iveston's eyes upon her. It was most distracting. Couldn't he see that he was blocking her view of the Duke of Edenham?

"No, I shouldn't think so," Cranleigh answered.

The Indians and Lord Dalby had moved off a bit, talking amongst themselves, which was a relief. She was down to four men, if she included George, which she did not. If only she could urge Iveston and Cranleigh out of Dalby House she might be able to manage five minutes of near solitude with Edenham. They wouldn't be actually alone, because that would be too forward by half, but if she could just speak to him and impress him with her pleasant demeanor and her cleavage, and she did not care a whit which impressed him more, then this entire afternoon would have been worth every inconvenience, even the dreary Lord Iveston.

"It's only that we've each just got married, you see," Cranleigh continued.

"And you're giving Sophia a wedding gift?" Edenham asked.

Actually, that was a bit odd, wasn't it? Why were men giving Sophia gifts, beyond the fact that she was Sophia Dalby and she required gifts, which was perfectly lovely as habits went and certainly Penelope was not at all put off by it. Once she was a duchess, she would think of some very good reason why she should be given perfectly extravagant gifts all the time.

George moved closer to Cranleigh and Edenham as they examined the vases, and Lord Iveston, before Penelope could do a thing about it, distracted as she was in planning all her future gifts, found herself in a corner of the white salon with him by a door leading to she knew not where.

The candles had been lit, but not well in this corner, and because of the rain, it had gone quite dark even if the room was done up entirely in white. That was the least of it, however. The worst of it was that it was Lord Iveston who had got her into this little corner and not Edenham, and that was just the sort of thing that Lord Iveston, whom she barely knew, but knew enough to know that she found him entirely peculiar, would do. Why, if she knew him any better, she'd think he was ruining whatever small chance she had at Edenham on purpose.

"It is very difficult to see the vases from here, Lord Iveston," she said, trying to peer round his shoulder, which was flatly impossible as he simply towered over her.

"You don't truly care about the vases, Miss Prestwick," he said, which was completely like him as he was so very contrary.

"I can't think why you should say such a perfectly ridiculous thing, Lord Iveston," she said, giving up peering and trying to gracefully accept being trapped within the least interesting corner of the room.

"Because they were prominently displayed in the center of the room for your entire visit and you did no more than glance at them."

"Was I supposed to inspect them? I didn't want to appear rude."

"I don't believe you, Miss Prestwick. I don't think you mind appearing rude at all."

"What a perfectly horrid thing to say!" she snapped, staring up at him. "And how perfectly like you to say it."

"I don't believe you know me well enough to say that, Miss Prestwick," he said, giving her the most strange of looks, which made sense as he was a very strange man.

"Apparently I know you well enough, Lord Iveston. You are not the most cordial of men, which I'm certain you will excuse me from saying because I am equally certain that your disposition can be no surprise to you."

Lord Iveston looked very much like he was developing a twitch near his left eye.

"My disposition . . . but perhaps I am merely modest, a most private man," he said.

"If you were a modest, private man, you would hardly tell me that, would you?"

"You are probably correct in that," he said with very obvious reluctance.

Penelope snorted, delicately. Most assuredly delicately.

"But I don't believe," he continued, "that you can possibly know me well enough to dislike me, Miss Prestwick. I am most unaccustomed to being disliked."

"I should think so," she said. "As you rarely leave your home, it is equally true that no one can know you well enough to dislike you and that no one whom you do see would dislike you. It's a very safe existence you've made for yourself, Lord Iveston. I don't say it's unattractive, but it is unusual."

There. How much more conciliatory could she be?

"But are you not also unusual, Miss Prestwick?" he said, proving most neatly her premise. What sort of man made a comment of that sort? "I don't say it's unattractive of you to be outspoken and given to making awkward remarks, but it is unusual."

"Awkward remarks?" she said in quite a curt manner, which he would likely think proved her outspoken nature, as if that were a flaw. "I do not make awkward remarks, Lord Iveston. It is only that I am unusually observant and proceed logically when all others stumble into emotional hedgerows."

"Emotional hedgerows?" Lord Iveston said softly, his mouth softening into a tepid smile. "That's quite good."

"Thank you," she said with rather more sarcasm than was

likely wise. "Is that all you wished to discuss? Your private nature and my forthright manner? The topic has been adequately covered, don't you think?"

"Miss Prestwick," he said softly, taking a half step nearer to her when he was already quite close enough. More than quite close. Very nearly hovering, if she wanted to be outspoken about it, which she did. "Miss Prestwick," he said again, very nearly whispering. His voice, and his nearness, sent a most unwelcome shiver down her spine. "I do think we've started on the wrong foot somehow. Can we not start again, this time with more courtesy and warm civility between us?"

It was a thought. Surely, if she were to follow Sophia's counsel at all, and she would be a fool if she did not, she was supposed to be using Iveston as a prompt to get Edenham to notice her. She'd not done at all well at that, though she couldn't quite reason out why. It must have something to do with Lord Iveston. He wasn't at all what she expected and her reaction to him wasn't at all convenient, which quite naturally resulted in her somewhat, but only somewhat, unpleasantly warm responses to him. She couldn't think why he should annoy her more than say, George, but he did. He was just so very peculiar. That was likely it. She had never been comfortable around peculiar people who behaved in ways she did not either approve of or understand.

And she did not understand Lord Iveston at all.

But far worse, she did not understand her reaction to him, which was reason enough to be uncomfortable in his presence, wasn't it? Of course it was.

There now. Having reasoned it all out and having determined that their initial wrong-footedness, surely a most apt word, was due to his peculiarity and her most reasonable reaction to it, she would and could proceed on better, firmer footing. Edenham was the goal, after all, and if Iveston could serve her purposes there, well then, he should be encouraged to do so.

"I find I agree with you, Lord Iveston, which I do fear will shock you," she said, looking him straight in the eye. He did have the most brilliantly blue eyes. "I am more than delighted to begin again. How shall we accomplish it?"

Iveston smiled softly. It did quite nice things to his face. She found herself smiling in return when she had had no plan to do so. How perfectly extraordinary.

"Miss Prestwick, I think the wisest course and the most time tested is the surest policy in diplomatic negotiations such as ours."

"And the wisest course, Lord Iveston?"

"Compliments, Miss Prestwick. Every ambassador of every nation begins with compliments, which are quickly followed by gifts."

"Which are less quickly followed by one nation or the other giving something up which they had no plan to give up," she said, smiling again.

"Ah, but you stray too far ahead, Miss Prestwick. Let us begin with compliments and see where that takes us."

"I must warn you, Lord Iveston," she said, still staring boldly into his eyes, which might have been a mistake as she could feel a thread of heat wrap itself around her throat, "that I cannot be complimented into giving anything up that I have determined I want."

"How can you know, Miss Prestwick? I have yet to tender even the first compliment. Perhaps it is possible to have what you want altered."

"By compliments? Impossible."

"By gifts?"

"What sort of gifts?"

"What sort of gifts would tempt you?"

"No, Lord Iveston, if you seek to tempt me, you must find your own way. I will not aid you in this hostile negotiation."

"Not hostile, Miss Prestwick, merely heated," Iveston said, his blue eyes looking quite as hot as flame. The thread of heat around her throat thickened into a cord and tightened, sending waves of awareness up her spine and down beneath her bodice ties.

How completely and perfectly extraordinary.

Nine

"Your work, I assume?" Lord Ruan asked Sophia.

He had not followed the Duke of Edenham over to inspect the porcelain, as indeed she had not expected he would. No, the Marquis of Ruan had not come to Dalby House to look at anything other than its mistress, which was so lovely of him, truly, and she did enjoy it, deeply, but there always seemed to be so much going on and, worse, Lord Ruan always seemed to be so aware of it.

If there was one trait a man should absolutely not possess, it was being observant. Being clever and observant was even worse. Lord Ruan, as much as she wished otherwise, was both.

"I beg your pardon?" she asked, staring up at him. He had quite rugged features and very green eyes. He was, not to put too fine a point on it, a very handsome man. And he knew it. There was that bit about being both clever and observant again. Such a strain, really, to keep a man like Ruan on such a tight rein. One could not but wonder what he would do, what he was capable of, if given even a nod of encouragement.

Of course, it was folly to even think such a thought with

Markham in the room. She was his mother and she did try to keep things comfortable for him, darling boy, and truly, she rarely had any trouble at all. Ruan was something else again. Ruan, she was very much afraid, was going to prove hard to resist.

"That," Ruan said with a shift of his head, indicating the very shadowy corner where Penelope and Iveston stood in what looked to be very pleasant conversation. How nice. Things were going quite well there and with hardly any effort at all on her part.

"I can't think what you mean, Lord Ruan," she said. "As you must be perfectly aware, I have not actually invited any of my guests today. You all just appeared from out of the mist and seem quite determined never to leave my house again. Of course, that might be due more to the rain than my charms."

"Which not even you believe," he said with a lopsided smile. It looked quite devilish on him.

"But one is required to make such remarks, Lord Ruan," she said, moving toward the front windows, Ruan trailing her like a trained hound.

"I can't believe that you answer to any requirements but your own, Lady Dalby," he said, "which is why you have, from your first day in London to this, turned the Town on its head."

"What do you know of my first day in London, Lord Ruan?" she asked, all thoughts of flirtation buried in suspicion. Too clever, too observant, that was this man's entire problem. Or at least it was a problem for her. "I'm certain I should remember you if you were here. Where were you if not in Town?"

"Out and about in the world, Lady Dalby," he answered. "Having the sorts of adventures that are very nearly required of a man at that particular age. Your own son is soon to be on an adventure, isn't he?"

"Where did you hear that?"

"From his own mouth, Lady Dalby, whilst we were chatting at Aldreth House on that delightful day that Lord Cranleigh finally claimed Lady Amelia for his own. The day of the satire."

There was something so very purposeful about the way Ruan had said the word *satire* that Sophia knew without question he was going to do something very awkward, something like prowl into the shadows of her very shadowy past. Oh, most people in London of a certain age were quite convinced they knew everything there was to know, of interest, that is, about her, but there was much she did not want known and Lord Ruan was just the sort to want to know those precise things. If he continued on in such manner, she would be required to drop him before she had even picked him up.

And she had decided to pick him up, just yesterday, in fact.

She was slightly bored, what with Caro married and Markham leaving with John and the boys for a lengthy visit to America. A lover was such pleasant way to pass the time, but only if the lover were pleasant and not given to looking in places he had no need to look.

"The day of the satire, Lord Ruan? Satires come out nearly every day."

"But so rarely to such quick effect."

"Only if they are not very good. Good satires create a very quick response."

"How are satires judged to be good, Lady Dalby? By their art? By their timeliness? By their cleverness?"

"By the response they provoke, Lord Ruan. I thought I had made that clear."

Lord Ruan smiled fractionally, his green eyes studying her most carefully. Let him study her. She could withstand a bit of study and not wilt. No, quite the opposite in fact.

"You have had a satire done of you, I suppose?" he asked.

"You suppose? You are not certain?" she prodded.

He smiled and then nodded, "All right. I am certain. You have had a satire done of you. It was not a pleasant experience for you."

"Is that a question, Lord Ruan? I think it must be because I always find satires to be enjoyable, particularly when they are done of me. Doesn't everyone? But darling," she said, laying a hand upon his arm, "haven't you ever had a satire done of you? How could a man of such esteem and . . . adventure been so overlooked?"

"I've been slighted, have I?" he said, very nearly grinning.

"Only you can decide that," she said, "but do something wonderful, something scandalous, something just beyond the pale and you shall have your satire, I assure you."

She was playing with him and he liked it, as well he should, but then his gaze strayed across the room to where Markham and John and the boys were standing, looking quite serious, she was sure, and Ruan's gaze slid back to her and all the playfulness had been bled out of him. Pity.

"He knows of it, Sophia. Did you know?"

"Yes," she said, staring into his eyes, showing him that she was not bothered, that nothing in her world had gone wrong.

Ruan nodded and looked down at the floor between them, wooden planks stained almost black and shining like a moonlit pond. "I saw it. The satire of you, of Westlin, of Dutton, of Melverley." His lashes lifted, dark lashes, thick and short beneath straight dark brows. "I saw what was done to you by them. It is an old satire. You were very young."

Was it . . . why, it was pity in his eyes. *Pity?* She needed no man's pity.

"It is an old satire, Lord Ruan, and I was old enough then and am young enough now, wouldn't you agree?" She held his gaze, smiling into his pity, refusing it, rejecting him if he forced it. She had outgrown the need for pity, indeed, she was nearly certain she had never needed it.

"What they did to you—"

"Darling Ruan," she interrupted, "what we did, we did together."

"You don't want my pity, do you?" he said softly.

"Not yours. Not anyone's," she replied instantly, though nearly in a whisper. She did not know why, and then she did. She whispered because this thing, this conversation, was the most intimate act they had between them and it deserved the delicacy of a whisper.

"Very well, Sophia," he said gently. "No pity."

They stared into each other's eyes, a soft look, a quiet look, a kind of look she had not shared with either man or woman for year upon year. And then she smiled, and broke it. Intentionally. *Very* intentionally.

"It was your doing, wasn't it?" he said after the moment was broken. "You did it. You punished them with it."

She could not seem to help herself. It was most disgraceful of her, to be sure, but she could not help it. She laughed. "It was a very good satire, my lord. It provoked such a vivid response." And then, because she truly could not help herself, she winked.

Ruan, because he was just that kind of a man, laughed with her. It was most charming of him.

"Did they suffer?" he asked.

"Darling," she said with a smile, "they suffer to this very day, though the second Marquis of Dutton is dead now, of course, so he can provide me with no more entertainment of that particular brand."

"His son, the third Marquis of Dutton, has not stood in for him?" Ruan asked. "You seem to have a special talent for making his life quite miserable."

"Poor man," she said gently. "I'm afraid he does that all by himself. I take no credit for it and, indeed, do not wish him ill." Which was not precisely the truth, but which was close enough to serve as truth.

"You know, Sophia, seeing you here with your brother, the light dancing in your dark eyes as you recount the joy of punishing those who have slighted you, you seem very much an Iroquois, very unlike the countess of Upper Brook Street, taking her tea, ordering her life around her pleasures."

Yes, very observant. The problem was, of course, that she was beginning to appreciate that in him, to treasure it for the rarity it was. Most men saw what they were prepared to see. The Marquis of Ruan simply *saw.*

"Ruan," she said, taking a step nearer to him, her breasts dangerously close to his chest, "I am very much an Iroquois. And I do order my life around my pleasures. The only thing left for you to ask is what my particular pleasures are. If you dare."

"If I dare? Will you punish me, Sophia? For what offense?"

"For not providing me with my pleasure? That would suit, wouldn't it?" She smiled up at him, enjoying this dance of war and seduction, of danger and satisfaction. It had been too, too long since a man had entertained her mind as well as her body. This one looked entirely capable of both. "You are a man of adventure. Will you not dare to ask me how you may pleasure me? Will you not risk my answer?"

"What am I risking, Sophia? For you, I would risk much."

"How much?"

It had all gone serious again, dark and deep, and she didn't care. More shockingly, she loved it. How much would she let him see of her and how much would he still want her, seeing more? She let very few see any part of her beyond the mask. Ruan sought adventure? Let him find it in her.

"My own satisfaction," he said. "I would see the men in the satire punished for what happened that night."

"That satisfies you. How does that satisfy me? It is an old story, long forgotten."

"You have not forgotten it. You have made certain that it was recorded, in the satire."

"Darling, you are too gallant. My daughter married Westlin's heir. Do you think I am not satisfied by that?"

"What of Dutton?"

"What of him? You think more of Lord Dutton than I do. I thought we were speaking of me and of what I want. And what you would risk to get it for me."

"Is this the Iroquois speaking or the countess?" he asked softly.

"Does it matter?" she countered.

Ruan smiled and shook his head. "No."

Sophia chuckled.

"Will I come out of this alive?" he asked her.

Sophia smiled. "Does it matter?"

"No," he said, his green eyes gleaming with humor and with stark intent.

❦

"No, Miss Prestwick, I don't know anything about Chinese porcelain beyond that it is expensive and therefore desirable," Iveston said.

"But if you knew something about it, perhaps that would explain why it is so dear," Miss Prestwick said.

"Miss Prestwick, it is perfectly logical, which you must admit as you are a logical sort, that if Chinese porcelain were ten for a penny, no one would want it to carry slops to the family pig. High price equals high desirability. It is the rule of the marketplace."

"You think I am a logical sort?" she asked quite earnestly, which was quite adorable of her. "That is most observant of you, Lord Iveston." Which took the shine off the adorable part of it. It would have been so much more effective for her to have told him he was kind or sweet or some such mildly chivalrous thing. But no, not Miss Penelope Prestwick. She thought him *observant* and praised him for it, much like a kind tutor with an earnest pupil.

What was worse, he found himself actually beginning to be charmed by it. It was just mildly adorable of her. He'd never encountered a woman anything like her before now. Of course, part of that was his very effective determination to avoid all marriage-minded women, but truly, even accounting that in, he had never met a woman anything at all like Penelope Prestwick.

Oh, she had all the female bits. The lustrous hair. The shining eyes. The stunning bosom. The rather charming heart-shaped face. But she wasn't at all *that* extraordinary. Until she opened her mouth and refused to charm him or compliment him or even attempt any effort at all to be noticed by him. In point of fact, she seemed rather often to be annoyed by him.

It was singularly unusual as experiences went. He feared, at least at present, that he was becoming increasingly fascinated by it. By her. By her lack of any sort of *normal* reaction to him.

He simply could not think of turning away from the delightful little oddity that was Penelope.

"But regarding the porcelain, even you must admit," she said, "that they are works of art and things of unique beauty, hence their dear price."

"Even I, Miss Prestwick?" he asked. "Because you have determined that I have no eye for beauty? That I would not recognize a work of art if it bit me on the chin?"

"Not at all, Lord Iveston," she said primly, looking at him

very disapprovingly, as if he were a complete dullard. "It is only that you clearly feel that for art to be precious it must be difficult to obtain. My belief is that beauty is what is being paid for, not rarity."

"Can something common be beautiful, Miss Prestwick?"

He said it to annoy her. He found it fascinating to watch her be exasperated by him. Why, he couldn't have said. Perhaps the rarity argument? Quite possibly.

"The glories of nature, Lord Iveston?" she counted.

"The simple magnificence of a rose?" he suggested, watching her swallow heavily and avert her gaze. Perhaps Cranleigh had something in suggesting he speak to Penelope about her roses. She did seem to have some sort of reaction to them every time they were mentioned. A most unusual and not at all positive reaction.

"Roses are beautiful, are they not?" she said.

"I would never argue against a rose, or the lady who grows them," he said.

She fussed with her shawl a bit and looked across the room, avoiding his gaze. What was amiss with her roses?

"I trust your roses are still beautiful after the events of the ball?" he asked.

"Everyone is so very concerned about my roses," she said, a bit sharply, too. "I had no idea that horticulture was such a common passion among the ton."

"Had you not, Miss Prestwick?" he said, trying to resist the urge to tease her, and failing at it badly. "The ton share many passions, common and otherwise."

She gave him a very scolding look, which suited her somehow, and said, "I have only to visit a shop and see a satire to know the truth of that, Lord Iveston."

A most awkward remark for her to have made as Cranleigh and his bride had been the subjects of a very lurid satire that had

had not a little to do with their getting married. But then, wasn't Miss Prestwick in the habit of making awkward remarks? And wasn't her brother in the habit of smoothing the way for her? Her brother was not at her side now. How would she do without him? As it was Iveston's brother who had been pricked, a most unintentional pun, by Miss Prestwick's remark about satires and common passions, he felt it was his duty, his right, and his pleasure to fight back against the most disapproving Penelope Prestwick. For the family honor, and all that. Oh, and for curiosity.

"Or visit your very bruised and broken roses? It was your conservatory, amidst your roses, that formed the backdrop of the satire regarding Cranleigh and Lady Amelia, was it not? Do you not bear some responsibility for what occurred at your own ball? Or did you perhaps inspire the creation of the satire by a whispered word to some fellow who would relay the information to Gillray?"

Penelope's mouth dropped open, snapped shut, opened again, and she said, very nearly standing on her tiptoes so that she could stare him down, "I would never do such a thing! Do you think I enjoyed having my ball ruined by that . . . that brawl that happened in my conservatory? Do you think that I wanted my roses to be the subject of speculation and lurid fame from now until I can't think when? And do you think that, if I had wanted such a thing to happen at my ball, that I wouldn't have gone to Gillray myself? I, Lord Iveston, am no such person as to require others to do my work for me, which I am quite certain must astonish you as you clearly have no experience in doing anything for yourself as it is well-known that you have required your very able younger brother to fight the females off of you in packs. I must express some pity for those who want to marry you as they are all clearly imbeciles." And here she stopped herself. Barely.

"For wanting to marry a man like me?" he finished, his voice as soft as eiderdown.

"I make no presumptions as to what sort of man you are or would be as a husband," she said, staring at the room behind him, clearly just now aware of how shrewish she had appeared. Miss Prestwick's voice carried quite well when she was impassioned. An interesting tidbit he filed away for later consideration. "I only remark upon my observations as to the man you appear to be today."

"Caustic observations," he said.

"As least mine were observations. Your remarks were accusations, and equally caustic," she said, taking a shallow breath and pressing her lips together. She had quite a lovely mouth, now that he thought about it. "I can't think how we came to near blows, Lord Iveston. I have no animosity toward you, but I think you must agree that I was provoked most unfairly."

"If I must, I must," he murmured.

Did she realize how often she made pronouncements and edicts? Likely not. Women never did realize those sorts of things, the very things that made them unattractive to men. The question now to be faced was why he didn't find her unattractive. With every impassioned word out of her lovely little mouth he found himself more and more intrigued. She wasn't the least bit in awe of him. The only other female he could think of who wasn't a bit intimidated by him was his mother. And Sophia, but he really couldn't put Sophia in the same class as a virginal young woman out in Society looking for a titled husband. And Penelope was looking for a husband, that much was obvious. She'd be a fool if she wasn't, and at least by her own definition, she was no fool.

"Would we really have come to blows, Miss Prestwick?" he asked. "I do suppose you would assume that I'd call Cranleigh in to fight for me, but in this instance, I do think I should like to fend for myself. A tussle, Miss Prestwick. To tussle with you. How do you think I'd fare?"

She smiled, which did show such a basically amiable nature

that he smiled in return. She was marvelous fun to tease. "I think, Lord Iveston, that I'd not disgrace myself."

"Miss Prestwick, do I hear a chiding note? Dare I think that you believe I would disgrace myself?"

"Lord Iveston, you are very much maligned, I think, to be so sensitive as to your abilities. For good cause, one must but wonder," she countered, smirking at him, "have you been often trounced? I find it difficult to fathom. You would outreach all your opponents, but perhaps it is your very nature which defeats you? Are you not a fighter, Lord Iveston? Perhaps it is that you lack not the experience but the need, for who would attempt Hyde's heir?"

"You are, aren't you, Miss Prestwick?" he countered. "I think you are brawling with me even now, using your very quick tongue as a sharp weapon when all I have is my long arms. What can I do with long arms in this instance, Miss Prestwick? I lack the swiftness of tongue you demonstrate so well. Propriety forbids me from explaining, let alone demonstrating, what tongues and arms may do when employed together."

He didn't know where that had come from. It was quite beyond the pale. It wasn't at all like him to taunt and tease a woman, and certainly not a virginal one, but there was something so very prim and superior and forthright about Penelope that he found he couldn't resist. What were her limits? How far could he go and how would she respond? All he knew without doubt was that she would respond unlike any other woman of his acquaintance. And that alone charmed him.

She didn't seem to want him. It was most peculiar of her, as well as being somewhat relaxing. His guard was down and he found it strangely refreshing. As well as more than a little insulting.

Of course there was the wager, but it was a paltry thing. He didn't care what Cranleigh, or anyone else, thought of him or her or the lack of interest on her part. What did it matter? In a week, at best, it would be forgotten forever.

But he knew even now that he would not forget. How could he? She was his first, rejection, that is, and a man didn't forget his first. No, not quite rejection, nothing so strong as that, but something almost infinitely worse. Little Miss Prestwick was not even bothering to look him over.

How utterly inexplicable.

He considered her as she considered him, his most inappropriate words hanging in the air between them. She didn't look especially alarmed, though she was looking at him more intently than she had yet done. He found he enjoyed it.

"Lord Iveston," she said, staring boldly into his eyes, "I do think your nature betrays you yet again. My initial impression was that you are not a fighter, and now I find myself adding that you are also not a lover. If a man is neither a lover nor a fighter, what is left for him to be?"

"A duke," he said, smiling at her response. Miss Prestwick was a fighter. What next but to wonder if she was also a lover?

What was wrong with him? He never behaved this way before today. Of course, he'd never met Penelope Prestwick before today.

"When a man is a duke, all else becomes inconsequential," she said, smiling. "I see you have your priorities well established and have nothing to fear and, indeed, no action or inaction to defend."

"You are not angry," he said, studying her. "I have not behaved as I ought, said things I've never before said, yet you are not angry. Why is that, Miss Prestwick? Is it because I am to be a duke?"

"I'm sure that's part of it," she said, with a brief smile. "I think it is only that you have surprised me, Lord Iveston. I have not had many conversations with men, aside from my brother of course, of such openness in both content and expression. I've enjoyed myself. I hope you have as well."

She was comparing him to her brother?

"I have, Miss Prestwick," he said softly.

Her brother?

"In the spirit of openness, and finding you not at all what I expected," she said, looking around the room behind him in the most careful manner, "I wonder if I may continue on in like manner, asking something of a minor favor of you."

"Minor favors often have very long strings," he said.

"Oh, no, not at all," she said with some firmness. "It is only that it would be so very convenient if you could, please, continue on being quite attentive to me."

He was puffing with pleasure before the word *convenient* pricked all pleasure of out him.

"Convenient, Miss Prestwick? I'm afraid I don't understand you."

"It is only that, I have found that the surest way to gain male attention is to have one male lead the way, as it were. I was only hoping that you might not find it inconvenient to lead the way, only for a time, until I gain the attention of the man I would not be at all displeased to marry. It would be the smallest of acts, Lord Iveston, and I do believe you have all the necessary skills to be convincing. If it would be no trouble?"

It took no effort at all to understand her words, obviously. No, the trouble was in believing them. Was this some ploy to haul him into marriage?

By the very earnest look in her dark eyes, it was not.

What was left was worse. She wanted him . . . no, no, that was the problem. She didn't want him at all. She wanted him to act as a lure to other, more desirable men. One man in particular, no doubt. A woman who had worked up a plan like this already had a man in mind. And it wasn't him.

By God, why wasn't it him?

He had no desire to marry her, obviously, why should he, but if she had the wit to entertain a single thought in her head, she should want to marry *him*. Perfectly obvious, wasn't it? It had been obvious all his life. He'd been outrunning and outmaneuvering mamas and their avid daughters for well over ten years. What was wrong with *this* woman? Certainly there was nothing wrong with him.

"I assure you, Lord Iveston," she said against the wall of his shock and silence, "there will be nearly nothing at all for you to do. A conversation here and there, a dance or two over the course of the Season, nothing much beyond normal discourse between two unmarried people enjoying their Season in Town."

"Nothing much beyond? Yet something beyond," he managed to say. "How else to work the trick, Miss Prestwick?"

"It is not a trick!" she flared. "It is nothing like. It is only that men behave in certain ways and respond to certain prompts."

"Like trained dogs," he said crisply.

"Rather like untrained dogs," she snapped back, her eyes flashing. "Even you must admit that men follow certain signals, particularly where women are concerned."

"Even I? Because even a dullard such as I must have experienced these signals? And what are these signals, Miss Prestwick? Half-wit that I am, I must have them spelled out for me."

"Oh, don't be cross. It is just like a man to be cross when his little mysteries are exposed."

"My mystery is not little," he said stiffly.

"I beg your pardon?"

"Never mind," he said, standing at his most rigid posture. "The signals, Miss Prestwick? I live to be enlightened."

"You know them, surely, Lord Iveston. I've come to think they are almost instinctual in a man, rather like the migration of geese in the autumn. Where one man of distinction goes, others will soon follow. Men do tend to cluster around objects of interest to them. I only ask, as a man of distinction, if you would mind very much clustering around me for a bit, to give the other men a chance to follow your lead?"

He knew very well that she did not truly think of him as a man of distinction. If she did, she wouldn't have discounted him in her husband hunt, would she? Of course she wouldn't. It was a sop to his pride, and a poorly executed one, too.

Still, she did have a point about men and clustering. It was only remarkable in that she hadn't understood the obvious point that it wasn't that they clustered to be in the same group, but that they each found the same things desirable. Did Miss Prestwick think of men as nothing better than sheep?

The answer was obvious, insultingly so.

When one had any sort of discourse with Penelope Prestwick, one was required to put away antiquated notions of what constituted an insult.

❧

"I think I ought to be insulted," the Duke of Edenham said to Sophia. The occupants of the room had shifted again, with the notable exception of Iveston and Penelope Prestwick, who remained nearly huddled in the far corner of the room next to the door to the dining room. Ruan was speaking with John, Markham was talking to George Prestwick, George Grey was talking to Cranleigh, Young and Matthew were standing together and talking to no one.

"If you have to think about it," Sophia said, "I don't think it possible that you are truly insulted. But, because I am, if nothing else, a courteous and gracious hostess, what, darling Edenham, has upset you?"

They were sitting on the matching sofas in front of the fire, the room gone quite dark now as it was past dusk and it was still raining. The candles struggled against the gloom, flickering seductively in the shadows, dancing against the darkness. It was a most unusual time of day to be entertaining, but what was she to do? Throw them all out upon the street? No, too much of interest was happening right now in her little salon. Such a surprise, really, as she had anticipated none of it. A London Season had a way of doing that, which was one reason why they all paid such a dear price to enjoy it.

"I thought you said Miss Prestwick was mine for the taking," Edenham said. He did not look at all upset, mind you, he merely looked slighted in that precise way men had of looking when every woman in the room did not fall into a dead faint at their feet. "She hardly looks it, does she? She's been nearly entwined with Iveston in the corner for fifteen minutes now."

"But, darling, does she look happy about it?"

"She hardly looks miserable."

Edenham, for all that he had already had three wives and had accomplished two children out of them, was, for a man of his mature years, a most insecure man. Of course, it was his three wives and two children who were most responsible for his feeling insecure. Certainly there could be no other cause. He was handsome to a nearly alarming degree, wealthy, titled, well propertied, and amiable. Women should be flocking to him.

Indeed, they had, when he had first entered Society and settled upon his first wife. Unfortunately for him, having three wives die as a direct result of bearing one's children did put a pall on the whole marriage matter. Edenham, spectacular in every way, was something of a legend now, the sort of whispered legend that had young girls crossing their legs and avoiding his gaze.

Of course, any woman who would let a few whispers put her off a man like Edenham didn't deserve to be a duchess in the first place.

"Darling Edenham, whoever would want a wife who couldn't

be graciously polite whenever the occasion demanded it? Miss Prestwick, forced into conversation with Lord Iveston, is merely showing him all the courtesy due him. Would you have less of her?"

"I suppose not."

"Then, by your protests, should I assume that you want to marry Miss Prestwick? I'm certain her father will be delighted."

Edenham looked at her from his lovely height, his brown eyes guarded. "I did not say I would marry her, Sophia. I only remarked that she did not seem especially interested in marrying me."

"These distinctions are so important, of course," Sophia said soothingly. "But, out of curiosity, what would you have her do to show her interest in you? Stand simpering at your elbow? Miss Prestwick, I can assure you, is not that sort of woman. I don't think she can even spell *simper*."

"I don't require simpering in a wife," Edenham said, a twinkle of amusement in his eyes.

"What do you require in a wife, Edenham? Beyond fecundity, naturally."

"Now, Sophia, pull in your claws," Edenham said pleasantly. "I only wondered what game is afoot between you and Miss Prestwick and how I became entangled in it."

"Darling, when did you become so suspicious? I have been perfectly honest with you from the first. Miss Prestwick, as is quite common, would like to marry. She would like to marry well, which does show such sense. She expressed a sincere, if tentative, interest in you."

"Tentative?"

"Well, Edenham, darling," Sophia said with a coy smile, "she barely knows you. What do you want of the poor girl? For her to carry you over her shoulder and drop you like a haunch of deer onto her father's desk?"

"Sophia, I *expect* nothing."

"Don't be absurd, darling," she said, shaking her head at him. "You expect what all men expect of a woman. But you shall not get it from Miss Prestwick. Not until you're properly married."

"That is not at all what I meant and you know it."

"Then I should like to know what you mean, Edenham. Do you want to marry the girl or not? I won't see you toy with her, as you men so enjoy doing to an innocent, earnest girl who only wants to do her family proud by making a good marriage."

"And marrying me would make a good marriage?"

"Edenham, do try not to be tiresome. There are only so many ways to be complimented and you have quite run to the limit on yours," Sophia scolded playfully. "If you're interested in Miss Prestwick, I would advise you to pursue her. I can state without qualm that your suit will be met joyfully and enthusiastically."

"I suppose I could talk to her," he said musingly, studying what he could see of her from across the room. "I don't suppose that could do any harm."

"Talking, even between men and women, has yet to do anyone any harm. But talking only, Edenham. A man as experienced with women and as devastatingly handsome as you are will sweep her up and away in mere moments. Have a care of her, I beg of you."

Sophia watched Edenham preen just slightly under the shadow of her praise and hid her smile in the depths of her teacup. Darling Edenham. This was going to be so good for him. And even better for Miss Prestwick.

Ten

"You would like me to cluster about you, Miss Prestwick?" Iveston asked. "I confess to having never been asked to perform such a service before. Are you quite certain it will be completely proper and not do an injury to your reputation?"

Penelope suppressed the urge to smile. She was not certain she was successful or not. This was such an important moment in her life that she could not truly be bothered to monitor every expression on her face, as she was wont to do. Not because she enjoyed doing so, but because Society so rigorously demanded it. Once she was a duchess, she would not have to be such a slave to Society. If one had to go about in Society, and who did not, being a duchess was the way to do it.

But truly, did Lord Iveston think that her reputation could be harmed by him? He was so utterly harmless. Why, it was very nearly like being with George. Except for the odd moment or two when he'd look at her a certain way or say a certain something that would cause the most unlikely sensation to ripple through her.

It was just as well that it passed, leaving her to concentrate more fully on Edenham, who she did fear was being dreadfully ignored by her. What must he think? With any luck at all, he would think that she was charming Lord Iveston and would wonder if she would charm him just as much, which she would, and then he would decide to marry her. Perfectly simple, if only she could get it all to work as it should, and by *it* she meant Lord Iveston being encouraged to show a more than tepid reaction to her and the Duke of Edenham being the sort of man who would notice and respond to such things.

"I feel completely safe in your care, Lord Iveston," she said. "I could not imagine myself even skirting along the edge of the bounds of propriety with you at my side. No, I am quite certain that I shall have nothing to fear."

Strangely, Lord Iveston did not look as complimented by her observation as he should have. There was that peculiar streak again. He did seem able to combat it at times, seeming almost normal, but then he would delve back into his odd little expressions that were apparently his response to a perfectly normal statement on her part. He was not a bad man, but he was most decidedly an odd one. It was very fortunate for him that he was going to inherit a dukedom. Who would have him otherwise?

"Miss Prestwick, I am flattered," Iveston said, his blue eyes looking quite dark in the shadows. They really should move out of the corner. She wasn't even certain Edenham could see her from this angle. "I would ask, at the risk of sounding quite ungentlemanly, what I am to get out of this little arrangement you have proposed?"

Penelope's gaze snapped fully onto Iveston, Edenham forgotten for the moment. "Why, do you require something, Lord Iveston? I assure you that it will hardly be an onerous duty."

"I believe, Miss Prestwick, that only I can decide what is onerous for me or not."

Well. That wasn't very polite, was it? He certainly knew how to be high-handed when he wanted to be, a sure sign of his inheritance. It was perhaps the first glimmer she had experienced that life with a duke might be a bit of a grapple. They did tend to be so autocratic, didn't they?

"I suppose that's true," she said, sounding very reasonable about it, if she did say so.

"I assure you it is quite true."

Pushy, too. Who would have thought the mild Lord Iveston had it in him?

"As you are so certain, then you should be able to name with ease what it is I can do for you in return," she said a bit stiffly. Bother, she was going to owe favors all over Town before this was finished. "Is it goods or services you need, Lord Iveston?"

He smiled. She could see that in the dim light of the corner, the white of his smile, the crinkling of his eyes. He had quite nice features, actually, quite refined, and his coloring truly was extraordinary. With his fair hair and pale skin, his vividly blue eyes shone like flowers in the snow.

"Perhaps a bit of both," he replied evasively.

"Well, when you decide, you just let me know. In the meantime, will you help me?"

"Help you snare the Duke of Edenham?"

"There's no need to be coarse about it."

"I thought I was merely being direct. My pardon."

He didn't look at all sorry, but she appreciated the effort, paltry as it was.

"The Duke of Edenham? What made you think it was he?" she asked.

If she was that obvious in her interest, did that not imply that Edenham could read her? And if so, why had he not responded? It was the clustering principle. Edenham needed encouragement. Iveston, mild as he was, would just have to be encouragement enough.

"Only that he seems to be exactly what a young woman would want in a man. True?" Iveston said, a bit stiffly, if she could judge.

She had noticed that men really did not enjoy making positive remarks about other men. She understood that entirely as she saw no need at all to praise other women. To what purpose?

"I, of course, would never presume to speak for other women," she said.

"Of course, but what of yourself?" Iveston pressed.

"I think," she said, trying to think of how to say what she wanted to say without saying too much. She didn't know if Iveston were truly trustworthy, did she? As to that, she didn't know if he were trustworthy in the slightest. "I think that the Duke of Edenham, having been happily wed three times, must be a most experienced husband and, therefore, would be very likely to make his next wife equally happy."

"Because of his experience."

"I should say so."

"And his wives were happy?"

"I have never heard they were not."

"And do you think you would have heard if they were not?"

"Certainly, I would have heard something."

"Because news of that sort gets round."

"It does."

"And you listen to the gossip that goes round about a duke and his family."

"I said no such thing! I can't think why you're choosing to be so contrary about this. It's a simple thing, a very pleasant thing I'm asking of you."

"Pleasant for whom?"

"Why, for . . . for . . ." Because, truly, it wasn't going to be pleasant at all for her and she really hadn't thought or cared if it would be pleasant or not for Iveston. But it wouldn't be unpleasant for him, would it?

Would it?

What kind of low insult was that?

"Are you saying that you would find it unpleasant to be in my company at a social gathering of your peers?" she asked, quite nearly breathless with outrage.

"I am saying nothing of the kind. I was merely wondering if you had given me any thought at all in this plan of yours. It's not much of a plan, by the way. By your own definition of male behavior, you need more than one man to cluster about you. I am only one man. There is only so much I can accomplish. If you want this to work, I should think you'd want at least four men to point the way for Edenham. There are four men in this room, if you're in a hurry. Or would you rather handpick them? I'm not sure how eager you are for Edenham's attention, so naturally I want to present you with choices in how you gather your cluster."

She was quite literally speechless.

This is what came of being open with a man, of being logical and forthright. Why, they fell completely apart and became nearly hysterical.

"All you have to do is refuse," she said with quite a bit of composure, considering.

"I am not refusing," he said, his own voice quite composed. She didn't believe it, not his words and not his feigned composure. He sounded just like her French tutor did when she provoked him with a question he could not answer. "I am only trying to arrange it to your best advantage."

"Why would you do that, Lord Iveston?" she said.

"For money, Miss Prestwick," he said mildly, as if he had not just said the most hideous thing. "It would be a simple matter to get a wager on the book at White's that you will marry the Duke of Edenham this Season; I do think I should leave it open as to the actual date, don't you? As I am an essential part of the hunt, I do think I should benefit somehow at the catch, wouldn't you agree?"

For a moment, just a moment, she again was struck speechless. There was so much that was so hideously wrong with Lord Iveston's little proclamation. And yet.

And yet.

If his involvement resulted in her being the Duchess of Edenham, did she really care if he made a wager about it?

"I never said I wanted to marry the Duke of Edenham," she said, still thinking it over furiously.

Iveston shrugged casually. "It was a logical deduction. And, if I may say so, you do look at him with all the subtlety of a hawk on the wing."

At that remark, she very intentionally looked at Iveston with all the subtlety of a hawk on the wing. Which apparently caused him considerable amusement as he came near to laughing. Yes, well, he could afford to laugh; he was going to be a duke, his future secured.

"If I may say so, Lord Iveston, you are more astute than the rumors indicate," she countered.

The look that appeared on his face at that was completely worth the breach of etiquette. With Lord Iveston, she had quickly moved past every boundary of decorum. And he appeared to enjoy pushing her beyond it. Strange to admit it, but she was having more fun with Iveston than she had yet done in Society. He was so easy to talk to, likely because he was so peculiar.

"If I have convinced you I'm not a complete lackwit, then I am satisfied, Miss Prestwick," he said, grinning.

"Not a *complete*? My, you do have lower standards than what I would have expected, Lord Iveston," she teased.

"As I am to be a duke, I have great freedom in my standards," he said.

"And in your behavior, clearly."

At which point, they stood grinning at each other. It was, oddly enough, very nearly comfortable to be talking to Lord Iveston, and she had never found anything at all comfortable about talking to a man. It was quite a surprise.

"Now, have we parried enough? What do you say to my suggestion?" he asked.

"I say, Lord Iveston, that it would look peculiar indeed if you were to wager that I will marry Edenham in this Season or any other," she answered. "First, it would alert Edenham to my intentions, which is never wise for a woman to do when dealing with a man. You may well be the exception, but they are very skittish as a general rule. Second, as you have spent a more than ordinary amount of time talking to me now, and then for the wager to appear on White's book, it would look very much as if I had asked you to place the bet, perhaps with the hope that it would force Edenham's hand somehow. Or worse, that you had found me very lacking indeed and were wagering on Edenham taking up the challenge. Or yet again," she said, growing quite breathless as the possible outcomes spun out before her, "that you and Edenham had some sort of wager as to whom would escape the net of Penelope Prestwick."

"Miss Prestwick," he said, laying his hand upon her arm. The strangest warmth, soothing and calm, flowed through her. "Stop. There is no need to drive yourself into a frenzy. I shall not wager such a simple thing if you feel so many ill responses could accrue to you."

"Thank you, Lord Iveston," she said, staring up at him. He

was a very attractive man, wasn't he? Quite tall and so very fit-looking.

"Perhaps the answer is to wager on something else entirely," he said, smiling gently down at her. "I could wager that it is I who will marry you this Season. That will throw the odds very much in my favor as we both know you and I will not marry. I could make quite a purse, once you break Edenham to the halter."

"Lord Iveston! That is such an odious way of putting it!" she said stiffly. "But it does make good sense," she added with a grin. "Of course, there is the question as to why anyone would believe I would prefer Edenham to you."

"You make a very poor liar, Miss Prestwick," he said. "Your very eyes proclaim your preference. You do remember the meta-phor of the hawk?"

"Lord Iveston, do not say I am so obvious in my interest. It strips me of every notion I have of myself as a proper woman."

"A proper woman is deceptive? Or is *devious* the word you meant?"

"*Discreet* was the word I meant, Lord Iveston, as I am quite certain you are aware," she said, smiling with more pure enjoy-ment than she had ever yet done with a man. What was it about Iveston that made her laugh? She wouldn't have thought it pos-sible for an heir apparent to provoke such a response in her.

"Then we have an agreement, Miss Prestwick?" he said, his eyes shining merrily.

She nodded. "You are to place your bet that you and I will wed. I am assuming that men, being men, will cluster about to see what you see in me and to perhaps beat you to the prize. It is to be hoped that one of those men is the Duke of Edenham."

"You shall not mind being . . . *clustered*, Miss Prestwick?" Iveston asked softly. He seemed to put undue emphasis on the word; she couldn't think why.

"I think I shall enjoy it completely, Lord Iveston," she said. "I have watched it happen to other women and I think I can manage it very well. After all, the gentlemen of the ton do know how to behave around a woman of refinement, don't they? I should think it will all be good fun."

"I do think I must remind you that you did just refer to yourself as a prize to be won. The rules of engagement are a bit different in situations of that kind. You might ask Lady Dalby for some help in learning how to handle yourself."

She puffed out her chest. "Lord Iveston, I know how to handle myself in any circumstance in which I find myself. I do not require instruction. From anyone."

Lord Iveston dipped his blond head down and looked at her from beneath his pale brows. "Then, Miss Prestwick, let the games begin."

⌘

"I don't care what you say. This game has gone on long enough. I want to get home to my wife and play a game of my own."

When Cranleigh snarled in that particular fashion, it truly was time to give in to him. Iveston was more than certain that Amelia knew that quite well by now.

"Would you say I'd won the bet?" Iveston asked him as they walked across the salon to Lady Dalby.

"All she did was talk to you. Once. She'll need to do more than that to convince me."

"Convince you? It's Mr. Grey I must convince, isn't it?" Iveston asked in a hushed undertone.

"You're not leaving?" Sophia said as they stood before her, making their bows. "So soon?"

"I'm afraid we must," Iveston said. "A new husband. A new bride. There are laws, I think, demanding adherence."

"Demanding something," Sophia said with a small smile.

She was standing alone near the front window, her white dress nearly glowing in the candlelight and reflected in the dark panes of glass. She looked very mysterious, very separate, though in a room full of people, Iveston couldn't think why.

"You have been most kind, to allow us all to overrun you," Iveston said.

"I don't feel overrun in the slightest, Lord Iveston. You and your brother, all your brothers, are welcome in my home, always."

"And our cousins?" Cranleigh said. "It seems you know our American cousins, Lady Dalby. How is that?"

"We shared a country?" Sophia countered, then laughed lightly. "No, I don't suppose that quite answers it. It's not a complicated story. Do you mean to say your mother never told you?"

A moment of uncomfortable silence followed. It was not possible that Sophia had not orchestrated it intentionally, a punishment of sorts. Iveston didn't know her at all well, but even he knew that Sophia was careful of her privacy and didn't allow intruders into the depths of her life. He hardly blamed her as he was much the same way himself.

"She did not," Cranleigh said.

"How odd," Sophia said, then shrugged. "It is only that I was in New York and needed passage to England. An Elliot ship was in the harbor, your aunt made the arrangements, and voila, I was on my way. Such a lovely woman, very much like your mother, but then, you know that."

It was perfectly plain that Sophia was not going to say another word on the subject, that she was aware that their mother had said nothing to them about it, that their aunt had said nothing to them about it, and therefore, she saw no reason to say anything more about it. Which of course only proved that there was some secret to the whole affair; and Iveston, for perhaps the first time in his life, was curious about things that had gone on before he was born. Oh, he was as interested as the next man about wars and kingdoms and all the important things that had fashioned nations and treaties, but this was a very small thing. He had never before been interested in very small things, such as those things that involved his parents. It was particularly odd, almost a revelation of sorts, to think of his parents as having a history that did not intimately involve him. He wasn't sure he liked it.

"You and Miss Prestwick seemed to get on quite well together, Lord Iveston," Sophia said, changing the subject and proving his point. "I had no idea you were so well acquainted."

"We're not, actually. She is a recent acquaintance," Iveston said.

"Kindred spirits, clearly," Sophia said.

"We really must be going," Cranleigh said, taking Iveston by the arm.

"I do thank you most sincerely for the vase, Lord Cranleigh," Sophia said. "You Blakesleys are so very generous. I am so appreciative."

She looked quite genuine about it, which was almost touching. Even Cranleigh looked somewhat emotional about it all, which was so unusual an occurrence as to be remarkable.

"You're very welcome, Lady Dalby," Cranleigh said, tugging on his arm again. It was most tiresome.

"You have plans for this evening, of course," Iveston said.

"How nice of you to inquire," Sophia said. "I do."

Of course, nothing so simple that she should offer up her destination so that Iveston could follow her there and perhaps run again into Miss Prestwick, Mr. George Grey somehow in tow.

This wager was becoming quite difficult to manage. He should never have agreed to it. How was he to win if he could never get all the participants in the same room? And he had to run over to White's tonight and get his wager there on the books. Small good making a pudding of Penelope Prestwick would be if he had no wager recorded on it.

"I find myself open," Iveston said as casually as possible.

"Really?" Sophia asked innocently. As Sophia was hardly an innocent, it was entirely comical of her. "But then, you do have the reputation for enjoying the quiet of Hyde House, feeding your solitude."

"I did think," he said, ignoring Cranleigh's rumbles of discontent, "that it was time I fed other needs, Lady Dalby. Perhaps acquired a new reputation for enjoying different things."

"Broadening your scope," she said, nodding approvingly. "How wise of you."

"I don't suppose you'd like to help me?"

"Lord Iveston! I am on quite close terms with your mother," Sophia said.

Iveston blushed. It was completely reprehensible of him, but he did. "I'm afraid that's not what I meant, Lady Dalby."

"I don't know whether to be relieved or not," she said with a half smile, teasing him mercilessly. "But what did you mean?"

"Iveston, we should leave now," Cranleigh said at his back.

"Don't worry, Lord Cranleigh," Sophia said. "I shan't harm your brother a bit. Not even if he asks it of me. Not even if he would enjoy every moment of it."

Iveston did not blush. He grinned. It was a vast improvement. It must have been that his mother was mentioned before; that was the reason for his unmanly blush at Sophia's first ribald remark. It stood to reason.

"Lady Dalby, may I confide in you?" Iveston asked. Cranleigh made a sound; it might have been a moan.

"Please do," she said. "I simply adore it when a handsome

man shares confidences with me. I am quite discreet. You may trust me completely."

Cranleigh definitely moaned. It was a most unpleasant sound. He should give up the habit immediately.

"I have a wager in play, two actually, though both are connected," Iveston said. "May I ask your help in arranging them?"

"I never like to get involved in a wager, Lord Iveston."

Cranleigh snorted. It was an improvement, but a slender one.

"I do think wagers ought to play out without any interference, don't you?" Sophia continued. "How else is a wager ever to be thought honorable if any sort of arrangements are connected to them?"

"Oh, please," Cranleigh said under his breath.

"You misunderstand me, Lady Dalby," Iveston said. "The crux of each wager is a woman."

"But naturally, darling. The most interesting wagers always are," she said.

"And the woman is—"

"Miss Prestwick, of course."

"But how did you know?"

"She is quite beautiful, quite available, and quite the most unique woman out this Season," Sophia said. "Whom else should you be tempted to wager over? I should be surprised if Miss Prestwick does not induce many men of discernment to seek her favor."

"By wagering about her?" Cranleigh said, rather snidely, too.

"But, Cranleigh, surely as a man of the world you know perfectly well that that is precisely how men behave. It is not how they *should* behave, at least as instructed by their mothers, but it is *how* they behave."

Unpleasant, but true. Even Cranleigh was forced to silence. Something of a relief to Iveston as this wasn't the most effortless conversation he found himself having. But what else to be done? He needed someone to make the arrangements to get the proper people in the proper room, and he knew without question that Sophia was the one to do it.

"Will you help me, Lady Dalby?" Iveston asked. "I am involved in a wager that I fear is quite beyond me to manage. A matter of gathering the principals into the same place at the same time, you see."

"And the principals are?"

"Your nephew, Mr. George Grey," Iveston said, "Miss Prestwick, Edenham, and myself."

"Ah, the matter becomes quite clear upon hearing the names of the principal players, Lord Iveston," Sophia said, smiling brightly up at him. She was quite a beautiful woman and so sparkling in her intelligence. "You and George have a wager as to how soon Edenham and Miss Prestwick will marry. I daresay, it will not be long before White's book is full of such wagers and counter wagers."

Perhaps not as intelligent as he had first hoped, but her beauty made up the lack somewhat.

Cranleigh chuckled. Iveston elbowed him in the ribs, discreetly, of course.

"Not precisely," Iveston said. "However, the particulars of the wager are really not the point. It is only that we all must be together as often as possible over the next few days. Can you think how to manage it, Lady Dalby? I must believe that you would know how, you have such skill at these things."

"Wagers, Lord Iveston, or managing?" she asked.

"Both, I should think," Iveston said with a hesitant smile. He had her. She was going to help him. He could see it in her eyes.

"How right you are, Iveston," she said. "I don't see a problem at all. Leave all to me."

"Happily," Iveston said.

"Fool," Cranleigh said under his breath, still rubbing his rib cage.

"You have received an invitation to the Countess of Lanreath's soiree tonight?" she asked. Iveston nodded. "Perfect. I'll see you there, Lord Iveston, as will all the principals."

"But Miss Prestwick," Iveston said, "you have no doubt that her presence is assured?"

"Lord Iveston, would you care to wager on it?" Sophia answered with a bright smile.

As it happened, he did not.

Eleven

ONCE Iveston and Cranleigh had departed, with obvious reluctance on Iveston's part and obvious eagerness on Cranleigh's, the others did not long linger. Of course, as it was long past the time for them all to prepare for the evening's revels and they did have to dress the part, lingering was not at all to be encouraged. Miss Prestwick and her darling brother stayed the longest, partly to stay near Edenham for as long as possible, but also because Sophia had by a most quelling look encouraged her to stay for a private moment between them.

She had very much to say to Penelope and very little time in which to say it. Things were moving at a furious rate, which was sometimes enjoyable, but only if one were prepared. She very much doubted Miss Prestwick was properly prepared and equally certain Miss Prestwick thought she was.

"Mr. Prestwick," Sophia said, sliding her hand around his arm, "do make it a point to drag Lord Ruan with you as you leave. I shall never be able to perform the necessary steps in my toilette if he cannot be encouraged out upon the street. I think it must take a man of your affability and charm to accomplish the deed. I shall just have a small moment with your sister whilst you engage him in some topic that will compel him to follow you out, shall I?"

Of course it was absurd to think that a young man of Mr. Prestwick's experience and disposition could compel Ruan to do anything, but it was just as true that a man of Prestwick's disposition and youth would be delighted to perform an act of apparent chivalry. What was left to conjecture was how Ruan would react. Sophia couldn't help but be curious. She didn't think Prestwick would come to any harm. She was very nearly certain of it. Certainly Ruan had better manners than that.

"I should be delighted to assist you in any way I may," Prestwick said. "Do you know what his interests are?"

"I believe he enjoys the hunt," Sophia said, meaning something else entirely, something that did not involve dogs or foxes but perfume and stays.

While Prestwick walked over to the door to the white salon, where Ruan was most definitely lingering, Sophia took Penelope by the elbow and led her firmly to the other side of the room, to the precise spot where she had been engaged with Iveston for the better part of a quarter hour.

"We had an agreement, Miss Prestwick," Sophia said. "I don't enjoy having a firm arrangement change under my very feet, and certainly not under my very roof."

Penelope looked at her with her dark eyes wide and said, "I desire no change to our agreement, Lady Dalby. Not at all. I only sought to hurry things along. I am very eager to have it all settled, which I'm certain I made clear to you."

"And I'm certain I made clear to you that I do nothing for nothing. I have yet to meet your father, yet to state my price, yet to have that price met. Of course, I am not unreasonable. The promise of the price is enough to satisfy me, if the person be someone of honor. You, Miss Prestwick, have not behaved honorably. You have acted precipitously and without due consideration of all the particulars."

"I only wanted to properly meet the Duke of Edenham. Surely the sooner the better, Lady Dalby."

"I thought that you were leaving it to me to decide which man is best for you?"

Penelope lowered her gaze for a moment and then stared boldly into Sophia's eyes. "I assumed you had Edenham in mind. He's quite eligible. I do think he was favorably impressed by me. It's a good beginning, don't you think?"

Sophia shook her head at Penelope and said, "It might have been a good beginning, if you had let me arrange things. It did you little good to meet him in a room full of people, all of them men."

"I thought that was to my advantage," Penelope argued, lifting her delightful little chin.

"It was not," Sophia said. "Men are very different when grouped into a throng. They are nearly desperate to behave in ways which are not at all flattering to them, and they are wise enough in the ways of women to know it. By being the sole woman in the room, your presence made them uncomfortable. Is that how you wanted to impress Edenham? By making him uncomfortable?"

"I was not the sole woman. You were there as well," Penelope said stoutly.

"Darling, I am very able to manage myself in a room full of men because I am very well able to manage the men. I assume that's why you came to me in the first place?"

"No, I–"

"Miss Prestwick, things have indeed, by your very wish, proceeded at a nearly alarming rate," Sophia interrupted. "The

Duke of Edenham is indeed interested in you, in so far that he has noticed you, for what cause I am not certain, but he has noticed you. He is not adverse to marrying again. He noted your extended and highly cordial conversation with Lord Iveston, which was very clever of you, I daresay. There is no good reason for Edenham to be encouraged to think you will jump into his bed if he but snaps his fingers."

"Lady Dalby, I would never—"

"Darling, don't say what you would never do until you are actually faced with the opportunity," Sophia said, tapping her fan against her thigh in clear agitation. "I am going to do you the great honor of being honest with you, Miss Prestwick. I do hope you have a stalwart nature and can bear up under something so uncomfortable as the truth." Naturally, she did not pause for either permission or approval and continued on, Miss Prestwick's lovely face showing her alarm most clearly. "The Marquis of Iveston has a wager going as to whom you shall marry. This sort of thing, managed well, can be a complete boon in situations of this sort. What I propose is that you get your brother to place a wager on White's book that you will marry Edenham."

"But, Lady Dalby, I have—"

"You do understand that the wager is a spur, darling. Men respond so well to the spur, it simply is foolish not to use one when they appear to require it so completely."

Penelope got a very focused look on her face, her gaze quite penetrating as she stared at the drapes at the front windows.

"Edenham will feel the need to compete," she said softly, stroking the edge of her crimson shawl. "He will feel slighted and will make every effort to . . . marry me to win a wager? No," Penelope said firmly, looking directly into Sophia's eyes again. "That's ridiculous. No man marries to win a wager. Especially not a duke."

"The wager is the spur, darling, that is all."

"It doesn't seem logical in the slightest."

"Of course it's not logical, but we're dealing with men. Had you forgotten that?"

Penelope nodded and said, "That's true. They can be very difficult, can't they?"

"I'm convinced they make a study of it," Sophia said. "Now, tonight you and your darling brother are going to attend the Countess of Lanreath's soiree."

"We have been invited, and I will admit that I was hoping to engage the Duke of Edenham in conversation whilst there," Penelope said.

"I shall manage everything, including the arrival of Lord Iveston, who is most essential to our plans, is he not? As to plans, I believe it would greatly simplify things if we all arrived together. You will attend with your darling brother, and I shall go on George's arm."

"George? You mean, your nephew?" Penelope did not look at all pleased.

"Yes," Sophia said. "He's most eager to see more of London Society and this should be an ideal opportunity for him. You can certainly have no objections."

"Of course not," Penelope said with alacrity, stiffening her shoulders.

"You can manage your brother?"

"Of course," Penelope said, nearly offended by the suggestion that she couldn't manage something as ordinary as a brother. Delightful girl.

"I shall arrange all else," Sophia said, "but I want it understood, your father must appear at my door tomorrow. I will aid you tonight only because I am choosing to believe you are an honorable girl. At heart."

"I am," Penelope said stiffly. "Have no qualms about that. You shall be paid in whatever manner you name, Lady Dalby. All I ask is that I get the man I want."

"Darling, I am quite convinced that nothing will keep him from you."

❧

Of course it didn't take any effort on Penelope's part at all to convince George to drop in at White's. The difficult bit was in convincing him make a wager that she would marry the Duke of Edenham during the present Season. His reasoning, and it was a bit logical, was that he had to make the wager *with* someone, and just whom did she suggest he do that with?

Typical. She had to think of everything.

In the end, she had declared that all he had to do was find someone in the mood to wager, and when was a man not in that frame of mind, and simply compel them into wagering against him. How difficult could it be? Anyone, just anyone would do. As long as the wager appeared on White's book, well then, she'd done exactly as advised by Sophia.

Penelope didn't give another thought to it. She had to dress for Lady Lanreath's soiree, as did George, so he'd best be quick about it.

With that admonition hanging over his head, George, slightly befuddled, made his way to White's.

❧

As it was just past eight o'clock, White's was filled with well-dressed gentlemen of the best families looking to start their evening with a drink, a hand of cards, an *on dit*, a wager. When that palled, they would find their way into salons and theaters across Town. And when that palled, they would find their way back to White's, to bring up the dawn with a dram of whiskey.

It was a lovely, predictable, comfortable life. Or it had been.

The Marquis of Dutton was miserable, and he knew why. He had been made a laughingstock by a woman. By two women, quite possibly. Make that most assuredly. Sophia Dalby and her pet project, Anne Warren, had, between them, made him look a fool. It hadn't helped his cause that he'd been struck a blow, a literal blow, twice in this very room, by two different members of the club, regarding two entirely different women, and that he'd been involved in a rather famous public brawl outside of Aldreth House. He had not, as was to be expected, come out looking the better for such activities. Oh, it was perfectly fine to engage in a fight or two or three, but not when one was continually found to be the loser.

He had failed to find his way beneath Anne Warren's skirts, though why that should be so was still a vast mystery to him. He was a marquis of some reputation, true, but not an entirely bad reputation, and she was a widow of reduced circumstances and highly unsavory pedigree who had nothing on the balance sheet besides Sophia Dalby. Having Lady Dalby as a protector of sorts had tipped every scale against him in his pursuit of Mrs. Warren. He had been foiled. He had been reduced to ridicule. He knew how to rectify all.

He would find another woman.

Which woman?

He had yet to decide. Certainly there were more than enough widows to keep a man busy. He did prefer widows; so much less complicated, really. No husband hunt involved. No husband banging at the door. A lonely, experienced widow was exactly what he preferred in women. All he had to do was find another woman, willing and eager to share his bed, and his reputation was restored to its former luster.

It was as Dutton was pondering women in general and widows in particular that he happened to glance up from his whiskey and see Mr. Prestwick enter the room, looking about with a mild degree of urgency. Upon seeing the Marquis of Penrith lounging in a corner, legs stretched out before him, Prestwick walked over to him and sat down. As Dutton was nearly certain that Penrith had placed a bet or two on White's book at Sophia Dalby's instruction, Dutton felt no great affection for Penrith, not that he was well acquainted with the man, but any man who would stoop to being a tool for a very devious woman was not a man he cared to know intimately, nor even cordially.

Penrith leaned his dark blond head forward to catch Prestwick's words. Prestwick shook his dark head once, gave a negligible shrug, smiled, and then shook his head again. Upon which Penrith laughed without noticeable sound, and the two men got to their feet as one and made their way to White's betting book.

At that, Dutton stood and followed them. What wager was currently afoot? And was there a way to salvage his reputation upon its back? Certainly, there must be. A wager and a widow to his credit? He'd erase the events of the past few weeks from all memory.

On the book was the wager. Ten pounds that the Duke of Edenham would propose marriage to Miss Penelope Prestwick, only daughter of the Viscount Prestwick, by the end of the current Season. The wager had been taken up by the Marquis of Penrith.

Did Edenham even know Miss Prestwick?

Why had Prestwick sought Penrith out?

To make the wager, almost certainly.

Penrith, Sophia Dalby, another girl on the market for a husband, and a wager. All the same pieces, though he could not quite piece them together into a coherent pattern. But he would.

Twelve

ANTOINETTE, the dowager Countess of Lanreath, was hosting a soiree. She was doing it not to please herself, though it would not displease her exactly, but to please her sister, Bernadette, the dowager Countess of Paignton. Yes, rather a lot of dowager countesses going on, but who would have thought that they should each have lost their husbands so early in life? Of course, Antoinette's husband had been old, a friend of her father's actually, so it was not unexpected that he find himself dead one morning in his kippers, but Bernadette's husband had been in the prime of life and killed in a duel, which as he was given to dueling, was not as unexpected an end as it might have been.

As Antoinette's husband had died in the normal way and Bernadette's had died in a scandalous way, Bernadette was looked at askance by many if not most of Society and Antoinette felt it was her duty to try and repair fences for Bernadette. Mostly because Bernadette told her it was her duty. Since Antoinette did not actually disagree, she did her duty.

She was giving a soiree. She had invited Bernadette. She had also invited Camille, her next younger sister, who had yet to marry and, therefore, yet to become a widow. She had not invited Delphine as Delphine had not had her come out, much to Delphine's annoyance. At seventeen, Delphine felt she was well old enough to mix and mingle with the men of Society. Antoinette had married at seventeen and married well, in most lights, a man thirty-two years her senior. Delphine could sit at Sheviock, their father's Cornwall estate, for another year. It would do her no harm at all.

"Toni, what do you think of the Marquis of Penrith?" Bernadette said, coming up softly behind her.

"I think he's too young for you, Bernie," Antoinette answered without turning her head. The soiree was slightly dull, the guests milling about almost tediously, fully half her list not yet arrived. Where was everyone?

"In years? Ridiculous," Bernadette said, twitching the hem of her white muslin skirt.

"In experience, dear," Antoinette answered.

They were a family given to pet names, as girls are wont to do. As there were four of them and as their mother, the Countess of Helston, was rarely at Sheviock and their father, the sixth Earl of Helston, didn't care if he saw his wife or children beyond the odd holiday, they had formed their own small family of four. The results of such emotional independence had not been entirely pleasant.

"I'm a widow, Toni, not an abbess," Bernadette answered. "Where are all the lovely men tonight? I had thought Penrith to make an appearance. He did show such promise at the Prestwick ball."

"Before the conservatory, certainly," Antoinette said. "After the rose incident, every rumor states that everyone was so busy gossiping and making wagers that the orchestra only served to get in the way of the gossip."

"Very true," Bernadette said, twitching her skirts again. Bernie had developed the habit sometime in her youth of doing little things to gather attention unto herself. As she was only twenty-three now, the habit might have been broken with some effort. Bernadette saw no reason to make the effort. She liked attention. Why not get it any way possible? "But who told you that? You weren't there, though I begged you to attend with me."

"You've never begged for anything in your life."

Bernadette smiled. "Oh, yes I have. Got it, too."

Bernie was, without qualification, a woman of exotic good looks and a definite erotic inclination. She had been a normal enough girl throughout her unremarkable childhood, but upon her marriage to a complete rake, who also happened to be an earl, she had learned she liked men very much indeed. Her husband first and foremost, but as he had not stopped being a rake upon marriage, she had found her own entertainment elsewhere upon occasion. She and Paignton had lived recklessly, loved brutally, and he had died predictably. The Paignton estate and title had passed laterally, that short phase of her life over. Not the men, obviously, but the house.

It was hardly possible for Antoinette to have experienced marriage, and indeed widowhood, more differently.

"I heard it from Lady Richard, actually," Antoinette said, watching the door for more guests, who did not appear.

"What? She wasn't there," Bernadette said sharply. "I'm sure of it."

And well she should say it sharply. Bernadette had indulged in a not very discreet affair with Lady Richard's husband. As Katherine, Lady Richard, had loved her husband very much, it had not been at all pleasant for her to share him.

"She heard it from her brother," Toni supplied. Which ought to have been obvious as Katherine's brother was none other than the Duke of Edenham and he had seen the whole thing, or very nearly.

"Oh, very well then," Bernie said, looking about the room. There was no one to interest her at present. Toni quite agreed with her. All the most remarkable men, no matter their age or experience, had yet to arrive. "Is Edenham coming tonight?"

"He was invited," Toni answered. "As was Lady Richard."

She cast her sister a sideways glance. Bernie liked her men well enough, but she did not like any entanglements they dragged into bed with them, such as wives. As for Toni, she had not quite decided yet how she felt about men. Certainly her husband, while not odious in the extreme, had not been remarkable in the extreme either. She was cautiously undecided and intended to remain so until experience taught her otherwise.

"Oh, bother, Toni," Bernie said. "Why? I thought you gave this soiree for me. I have such trouble getting invited anyplace anymore."

"You were invited to the Prestwick ball."

"Only because they invited everyone."

"As did I. You don't need to make it sound such an insult. Who knows whom you might meet tonight? Perhaps you shall even marry again."

"Why ever should I do that?" Bernadette said with a lovely pout.

A man across the room dropped his glass. As he was not quite as young as a woman preferred, it might have been due to palsy and not the pout. But it wasn't likely. Bernadette was that sort of woman, blatant, and not at all apologetic about it either. Half the time Antoinette envied her, and the other half, she pitied her. Paignton had done something to her sister, though she couldn't think what. Whatever it was, Bernie was not as happy as she ought to have been. There was a restlessness to her that seemed almost dangerous.

"Companionship? Children?" Antoinette said.

"Perhaps later," she answered. "When I'm tired."

That roused a laugh from Toni and from Bernie. It was not to be helped.

"Is Lady Richard truly coming tonight?" Bernadette asked.

"I hope so," Antoinette answered. "She needs to get out into Society more. I don't know how she fills her days, living with Edenham as she does. The two of them, widow and widower, alone in that house. Hiding away, is what it looks like. It can't be healthy."

"Edenham may have been hiding before, but he's not now," Bernadette said. "I think it's something to do with Lady Dalby. He appears to enjoy her very much."

"That sounds rather sordid."

"I know."

"Perhaps he'll marry again. Perhaps Lady Dalby will be the next Duchess of Edenham," Antoinette said.

"I can't think why she'd want to marry Edenham. Her life is perfectly ordered and well settled."

"But you can see why Edenham would want to marry again?"

Bernadette shrugged. "He's a man. And he's been married so often now that it must feel very peculiar to him not to be married. Why don't you marry him, Toni? You enjoy his sister so much, it would be quite nice for you."

"You're not afraid he'd kill me?" Toni asked with a grin.

"Not at all. Are you afraid he'd kill you?"

"I can't think how. I can't have children."

Bernie made a most unattractive sound with her mouth; it was very nearly comical. "You can't possibly be certain of that. Lanreath was nearly an old man. I would say I'm surprised the marriage was even consummated, but I know what men are capable of doing when they are inspired. I've no doubt you inspired him beyond his normal capacity."

"Bernie, you are grown coarse."

"I notice you don't deny it."

"I could say the same of you."

It was at that moment that, quite abruptly, the doors to the Countess of Lanreath's salon nearly burst in upon them and very many of the most interesting, most attractive, most unattached men who had been invited entered the room. Lady Dalby entered on the arm of one of those American Indian relatives of hers everyone was talking about.

And that is when the soiree at the dowager Countess of Lanreath's home on the corner of Berkeley Square truly began.

❧

LANREATH House had large rooms done up in the French style of perhaps ten to fifteen years ago. The walls of each of the main rooms, defined as the reception room, the drawing room, and the dining room, were painted in white paint that had gone to cream and ivory with time, and gilded trim everywhere, from the ceiling to the skirting boards. The floors were lightly stained parquet in a very pleasing geometric design and the furnishings were all French, from the gilded chairs with their rose-hued silk upholstery to the chandeliers hovering massively above them.

The rooms, it was perfectly obvious, set off a woman's beauty to perfection. It was such a pity that the dowager Countess of Lanreath did not entertain more often as very many women in Society would have benefited from appearing to their best advantage in such delicately hued rooms lit by gentle candlelight. As the current Earl of Lanreath, the son of the late Earl's first wife, was not married and was more interested in his hunting dogs than in the ton, he had happily allowed Antoinette to live in the family house in Town. He had not, nor had his father, allowed her to redo the rooms in the more current fashion.

Well, that was a man for you.

But, as the rooms looked quite well on Antoinette, Sophia supposed it wasn't such a bad state of affairs.

"Lady Dalby," Lady Lanreath said, greeting her, "it is a pleasure to see you again. Our paths seem never to cross with any regularity at all, which is most distressing."

"Lady Lanreath," Sophia said, her hand on George's arm, "what an entirely cordial remark. It is so like you. I don't believe you've met my nephew, Mr. George Grey."

George, with a very wicked grin, dipped his head in a very appreciative manner. He did not bow, though he knew he should, which was very like him.

"Lady Lanreath," he murmured.

Poor Antoinette looked very much like she was about to melt, which Sophia suspected she would enjoy fully. Her Lord Lanreath had been very old and Antoinette did not seek out her own amusements as often as she could have done. A very foolish choice for a woman with no husband, no children, and no debts to pay. Quite inexplicable, really.

"Lady Dalby. Mr. Grey," Lady Paignton said in a throaty murmur, eyeing George with blatant appreciation. "I am delighted."

"But of course," Sophia said. When Bernadette's gaze swung to hers, she added, "It is always good to see you Lady Paignton."

The sisters, widows both, and the two eldest of the Earl of Helston's four daughters, looked nothing alike, yet looked like sisters for all that. All four girls, by every rumor, as Sophia had not yet met the youngest girl, shared the same coloring and were quite stunning beauties because of it. They would have been beautiful women in any regard, but as each had dark hair and green eyes, they were truly remarkable. Antoinette was a refined beauty with features leaning toward the classical, while

Bernadette, which surely suited her nature, was a lush siren of blatant and carnal beauty.

George, as well he should be, was clearly delighted.

"Lady Paignton," George said, his dark eyes gleaming in that very specific way men had of gleaming at a woman. "A pleasure." He clearly meant it.

"Mr. Grey," Lady Paignton answered, "you are new to London and its various and myriad pleasures?"

"Not that new," Sophia interjected. "Come, George. I simply must introduce you to . . ."

"To?" Bernadette prompted.

"Everyone," Sophia said. "George does love to get out and about. He simply wants to meet everyone and know everything."

"And experience everything?" Bernadette said, giving George the most obvious look.

George appeared to enjoy it immensely. He appeared to have completely forgotten the reason he was escorting Sophia this evening.

Things were helped considerably by the arrival of Lord Penrith. Penrith had such a habit of doing a good turn that he was becoming quite invaluable to her, darling man. The greetings were made, the bows and curtseys exchanged in a graceful display of breeding and etiquette, and then Lady Lanreath said, "I am so glad you have come, Lord Penrith. We were expecting you and did begin to wonder if you were detained somehow."

As Bernadette, Lady Paignton, had just spent the Prestwick ball trying to seduce Penrith, who looked quite willing to be seduced, and since Antoinette had not been at the Prestwick ball, it was perfectly plain who had wanted Penrith to attend tonight.

They all, George included, gazed at Bernadette.

Bernadette smiled, not a bit repentant.

George smiled, as charmed by an unrepentant female as the next man.

Penrith smiled with just as much seductive force as Bernadette could manage, which was considerable, and said, "I did arrive later than planned, but then, I suspect I am not the only one?"

"As a matter of fact, you are not," Antoinette said evenly.

"I shouldn't be at all surprised," Penrith said. He did have the most enticing voice. Bernadette licked her lips and blinked in languid invitation. "It's the latest wager on White's book. Everyone wants to get their name down before the evening's events. I'm not sure I've ever seen such interest in a wager before, not on such short notice. Of course, that may explain it. It came out of nowhere, and of course, those are the best wagers of all."

"Does it concern you, Lord Penrith?" Bernadette asked in a sultry murmur. "Is a woman named?"

"I should say so," he said. "But I am not involved, at least not directly, Lady Paignton."

"Pity," Bernadette responded.

"What is the wager, Lord Penrith?" Lady Lanreath asked, making every effort not to look over their shoulders at her next arrivals.

"I shall tell you since there will be no keeping it from you, or indeed, from anyone. It shall be all over Town by tomorrow noon, I should think."

"Does it involve a marriage or an affair?" Bernadette asked. "Wagers about affairs are so much more exciting, don't you think?"

"I suppose that must depend upon the participants," Sophia said. "Yes, I'm quite certain it does. But do go on, Penrith. We simply must know."

George, to his immense credit, showed a fortitude of silence that was quite unlike him and said nothing. He even kept his face shorn of all emotion.

"It involves me," Penelope Prestwick said, having come up behind them with her brother at her side. "The wager is that I shall marry the Duke of Edenham by the end of the Season. My brother George made the wager, which was quite lovely of him as it does indicate such confidence in me, and Lord Penrith took it up, which I can't think what it says of him. Or of me. What do you say, Lord Penrith? Is it true you don't think I can induce the Duke of Edenham to offer for me?"

Sophia sighed and smiled in pure pleasure. Lovely, darling Miss Prestwick. She did like to play her own game. It was quite enchanting of her.

She looked wonderful, which was so clever of her. Penelope was draped in white silk, her bodice cut tastefully low and the train a graceful sweep at her feet. The gown was elegance at its most pure; there was no ornamentation beyond that offered by the sheen of the silk, but at Penelope's throat and ears were diamonds. She was glittering in diamonds set beautifully in the most modern of settings. She looked like a Greek goddess, her black hair pulled up and away from her face into a thick pile, her black eyes glittering much like her diamonds.

This was a woman who deserved a duke. And that could not be said of every woman, surely.

"Miss Prestwick," Penrith answered, looking quite as beguiling as he was in the habit of appearing, "nothing so bold as that. It is not that I don't think the Duke of Edenham should be entranced by you, or indeed, that he is not already entranced, but that as the Season is half over, that he may not offer for you, the details agreed upon, the license signed, the deed done, by the end of the current Season. You will notice that I make no wagers on what may occur between you and Edenham next Season."

Penrith was such a playful man. It was such an unusual trait in a man that it was worth valuing as the rare commodity it was.

"Then it is not the fact of my allure that is in dispute, but the power of it?" Penelope said, staring boldly into Penrith's cat green eyes. Not many women were so confident, or was it foolhardy, as to be so bold as to engage in any sort of verbal discourse with Penrith. The seductive power of his velvety voice was becoming legendary. "Is that the basis of your wager, George?" she asked her brother, turning her gaze away from Penrith's. Proving, if proof were needed, that she was not a stupid girl at all. Many a young thing had come close to ruination by staring too long into Penrith's eyes, spellbound by his voice.

His mother, traveling in Italy with Penrith's sister, certainly had a beguiling son. And knew it, too. It might have been the reason she traveled without him.

"Pen, it isn't at all the thing for a woman to inquire as to what appears on White's book," George Prestwick said, staring in a somewhat accusatory fashion at Penrith, who had the dash not to look at all abashed.

"Even if the wager is about her?" George Grey asked.

"Most especially then," Lord Iveston said, having come up behind Penelope. He towered over her. He so tall and fair, she so small and dark. Quite a stunningly unique couple, if one cared to make such judgments. Which Sophia most certainly did.

"Good evening, Lord Iveston," Lady Lanreath said with a smile of welcome.

Lady Paignton merely curtseyed her greeting; her gaze was still all for George Grey. As previously her attention had been completely consumed by Penrith, and as Penrith was now being devotedly ignored, it did bespeak some rather pointed effort to annoy Penrith. Penrith, younger and less experienced than Bernadette, did look somewhat put out.

Ah, youth.

Though, Sophia was quite certain she had never been quite that young, and certainly not in that precise way.

At Iveston's side was his brother, George Blakesley. Three Georges. Well, that was what happened when the King of England was a George. As to that, her own Dalby had wanted to name their son George. She had convinced him, slowly and quite pleasurably, that John was a far better choice. After her brother, naturally, whom she hadn't seen in years by then and, truthfully, could easily have been dead. How could she have known, separated as they were by a very large ocean? Of course, then John had found her and everything became then as it still was now. She lived in England as a countess and he lived . . . as he pleased.

Sophia smiled. It was precisely the way to live, wasn't it?

"Good evening, Lord George," Lady Lanreath said. "It is always a pleasure to see you."

Always?

Was something afoot between George Blakesley and Antoinette? It would show such good judgment on Antoinette's part if there were. George was quite a remarkable-looking man, and from such a lovely family, too.

The gentlemen bowed, the ladies discreetly looked them over, and then all eyes turned toward Miss Prestwick, which did not appear to alarm her in the least. Such a clever, resourceful girl. Now, if she would only say the right thing to get things moving along in the proper direction. If any young woman was up to the challenge, it was certainly Penelope Prestwick.

"Lord Iveston," Penelope said, gazing at him with her composure intact, "we were just discussing, improperly or not, the wager that has appeared on White's book. I presume you know of it?"

"Is it an improper sort of wager?" Iveston asked mildly, looking down at her with a definite twinkle in his eyes.

"I'm quite certain it must be, as all wagers involving a man and a woman must be improper somehow," she answered.

Lord George Blakesley lowered his gaze and appeared to be chewing his lower lip, likely against a laugh. It was indeed a most noble effort on his part not to call attention to this highly unusual conversation. Of course, it would be all over the room in a quarter hour, but the effort, the nicety of it, was a thing worth noting.

"That sounds a most logical conclusion, Miss Prestwick," Iveston said, "but I do wonder if you have the required experience to make it."

"Required experience? What can that mean, Lord Iveston?" she said, moving her truly lovely ivory-bladed fan a bit more briskly. "What sort of experience could possibly be required of a properly reared, unmarried woman?"

"If you'll excuse me," Lady Lanreath said, taking her sister, Lady Paignton, who did look quite ready to respond to Miss Prestwick's question with what was certain to have been a most entertaining reply, by the arm, quite firmly, too. "I must introduce Bernadette to an old acquaintance of mine."

Bernadette did not look at all eager to leave either George Grey or Lord Penrith, but off she went, with a sultry look for both of them, or it might have been all of them as George Blakesley did not appear to be completely immune to sultry looks that happened upon him. Sophia watched for Antoinette's response to George Blakeley's response, and could not see any response at all. Which did not mean everything, but surely must mean something.

"As you are clearly a properly reared, unmarried woman," Sophia said, "it is quite impossible to explain it more fully, Miss Prestwick. You simply, and most appealingly, lack the requisite experience."

Penelope did not look at all pleased at Sophia's insertion into the conversation. And who could blame the girl? She, like any reasonable woman, wanted to keep all male attention firmly on herself and was clearly prepared to do or say anything, or nearly anything, to make that happen.

Eyeing Penelope more closely, and truly studying the gleam in her dark eyes, Sophia amended her position. Penelope Prestwick looked prepared to do anything at all to attain her goal, which was quite clever of her, wasn't it?

"Yet as you have asked about the wagers," Penrith continued, looking askance at Sophia in what was to be assumed was a conspiratorial effort, "I must tell you, Miss Prestwick, that not only is there a wager that you will marry the Duke of Edenham, but also one that you shall soon marry the Marquis of Iveston. I presume you know of it, Lord Iveston?"

Iveston, to his immense credit, did not so much as blink. "As I am the author of the wager, I most definitely know of it," he said calmly. "I had, however, not anticipated making my suit to Miss Prestwick here, now, and under such unusual conditions. I will, however, not allow unusual conditions to hinder me. Miss Prestwick," he said, looking down at her from his very attractive height, "shall we take a turn about the room?"

Penelope looked at Iveston quite brightly; indeed, her cheeks looked nearly flushed. "To what purpose, Lord Iveston?"

"To win my wager, Miss Prestwick, what else?"

What else? Why to seduce her, if he had any skill at all. Sophia smiled just thinking of it.

Thirteen

PENELOPE barely kept her grin in check. George, her George, looked quite prepared to make a fuss of some sort, as if being a bit daring were not required to snare her duke for life, and by her duke, she obviously was thinking of Edenham. Iveston might be looking down at her quite jovially and she might be smiling up at him quite demurely, but it was all for Edenham. Who had not yet arrived. Still, he couldn't fail to hear about the wagers and Iveston's clear fascination with her.

How remarkably duplicitous he was; she wouldn't have thought Iveston had it in him. He certainly gave every appearance of being nearly captivated by her, which was perfection itself, if only Edenham were here to witness it. The question now remaining was whether Iveston could keep his performance in top form for the rest of the evening. As to that, the question was also whether she could keep herself looking at Iveston in anything approaching fascination.

Although, strangely, she wasn't finding it as difficult as she had anticipated.

He was not an unattractive man, not physically. He was quite well put together, actually, and his eyes were truly an intriguing shade of blue. Even his manner was becoming less irksome the more time she spent in his company. Wouldn't Edenham be pleased that she had a friend in the future Duke of Hyde? Alliances of that sort, the most innocent and socially appropriate sort, were always to be desired, were they not? Wasn't it very clever of her to have knitted the Hyde dukedom and the Edenham dukedom into a pleasant bond of even the most casual sort?

Of course, having it on White's book for all posterity that she had been wagered to marry one or the other of them wasn't precisely a casual sort of bond. And, by the look glimmering beneath Iveston's placid demeanor, he was thinking something along those very same lines.

He had to be told the reason for the Edenham wager, and she was the only one to do it. It would not be a pleasant duty, but as Iveston was a relatively pleasant, if odd, man, she was fully prepared to face him. In fact, the sooner he understood everything, the better.

It was for that reason alone that she said, "Why, Lord Iveston, in the spirit of fair play, I do think you and I may walk about the room. I would hate to deprive you of the opportunity to win your wager."

Iveston's blond eyebrows raised quizzically. George, her George, sighed heavily, which sounded nearly like a moan. George, Sophia's George, grinned, which did nothing for her composure. George, Iveston's George, pressed his lips together and studied her with rather more attention than was warranted. It wasn't warranted, was it?

What had she said? That she was trying to help Iveston win his wager, that's all. What was wrong with that? It was a very reasonable, very fair-minded position, wasn't it? Of course, she was going to marry Edenham, but shouldn't she at least give the appearance of being open to being wooed? How else to get Edenham into the halter? As to that, what other men had Iveston arranged for her? She needed at least three to give a good clustering effect, though five would be ideal. Anything more than five and she knew she couldn't manage it. Six or more men at once were quite beyond her abilities, and she was practical enough to admit it. She needed to make that clear to Lord Iveston as well. Really, she had so much to discuss with him. They needed to make a circuit of the room immediately.

"In the spirit of winning, I shall agree with you, Miss Prestwick. You are most gracious," Iveston said, with a casually delivered bow.

Avoiding looking into Sophia's clearly amused gaze, Penelope smiled with as much innocence as she could manage and began her circuit of the room, Lord Iveston at her side.

They were watched, obviously. But, in the spirit of London Society and the ton's intense curiosity over anything even remotely scandalous, they were not approached. Who wanted to stop the drama? Not a one of them.

Penelope understood them completely. She was one of them, after all, and as attuned to a good scandal as the next person. Perhaps more. She was very observant, after all.

"Imagine my surprise, Miss Prestwick," Iveston said just as she was opening her mouth to tell him all she expected of him in the next few days, "to discover a wager on the book that you would marry Edenham this Season. I thought it was your express wish to not taunt the duke in that precise way, given that it could reflect so poorly on you."

"Poorly on me? That is not at all what I said, Lord Iveston," she said, lifting her chin and smiling distractedly at Lady Paignton, who was watching them most avidly. Such a disagreeable woman. Why, she was nearly falling out of her dress.

"Isn't it? That's what I heard you to say," Iveston said, taking her rather firmly by the arm and nearly pulling her about the room. She cast a glance at his face.

He did not look any different than he normally did, though perhaps a bit more contained. As he was rather known for being contained, she was not at all certain how she was able to make the distinction in degree, but she was. Iveston was annoyed. Perhaps more than annoyed. Enraged?

Ridiculous. A man of his retiring nature didn't have the necessary spirit to engage in anything as energetic as rage.

Or passion.

Where had that thought come from? It was most inappropriate and entirely off the point. She cared nothing for Iveston's passion or rage, or more truly said, lack of either, or both. Very likely both.

She looked at him again, this time with more force, and was nearly astonished to see that the area just below his earlobe and just above the folds of his snowy cravat was chalk white. She had discovered that men, when annoyed or enraged or anything in between, had the tendency to go either red or white in their physical responses. Iveston was clearly a white. Her father was a red. Her brother was also a red. She, being a woman of remarkable composure and therefore with no occasion to be either annoyed or enraged, did neither. Her complexion was as constant as her composure.

But just looking at that tiny splash of white on his pale skin did arouse the smallest degree of curiosity. How far down did that miniscule display of broken composure descend? To his neck? To his throat? As a matter of scientific discovery, surely it was a logical question. Did Iveston even know that he was sporting a telltale mark of white? Would he care that she had seen it?

Of course he would.

And that, for entirely inexplicable reasons, made her smile.

"Find this all very amusing, do you?" he said under his breath.

"Not at all. I merely have a cordial nature. Unlike others I could name."

"Go ahead. Name them," he said. "I should like very much to hear your entire list."

"My entire list of what?"

"Whom, Miss Prestwick. List of whom. I should like to know precisely which men you intend to cajole into offering for you, by way of White's book, of course. That does seem to be your method, doesn't it?"

"I've never cajoled anyone into doing anything in my life," she said on a huff of outrage. Of all the insults! As if she would stoop to such asinine behavior. Did he think her no better than a shopkeeper's assistant, trying to cajole the baker's boy into marriage?

Iveston looked down at her with a very superior air and said, "Trust you to be insulted by being accused of cajolery."

"I can see that no one has ever accused you of it. It's demeaning in the extreme, Lord Iveston. As if, why, as if I cannot form a logical thought and see it to fruition."

"Thoughts do not come to fruition, Miss Prestwick. Actions, however, do," he said, tugging her around the room. They looked perfectly ridiculous; she was certain of it. "You have set many actions into play. How do you propose to pick all the fruit that shall surely come of it? And by fruit, of course I mean husbands."

"I only require one husband, Lord Iveston, as must be perfectly obvious, even to you."

She winced slightly as the words left her mouth. Bother it, but if one wanted to be very particular about it, and she was quite certain that Iveston was in a very particular frame of mind at the moment, one could take her remark as being slightly, but only slightly, insulting. She glanced up at him.

The white spot below his ear had grown slightly and was now very definitely trailing down below his cravat.

It was utterly fascinating. And what else to think but that she was making progress of a sort? She did enjoy making progress, in any endeavor. She wasn't at all fussy about that.

"As to that, Miss Prestwick, I should say it's not obvious to me or to anyone else," Iveston gritted out, nodding politely at Mrs. Anne Warren, who was standing next to her betrothed, Lord Staverton. Staverton and Mrs. Warren nodded in reply, but said nothing. How could they? Iveston was nearly dragging her around the room. "As there are two wagers on White's book, and as there are two names which appear, and as the odds are currently running in Edenham's favor, I should think the only thing that is perfectly obvious is that you have a penchant for making a spectacle of yourself and that you have arranged for me to be made a spectacle right alongside you. I, Miss Prestwick, have no such inclinations."

"Oh, now really, Lord Iveston," she said, digging in her heels. Iveston did not appear to notice. "I think you are far too—"

Iveston stopped so abruptly that she nearly tripped. "I am far too what, Miss Prestwick?" he breathed, and not at all nicely, either. Why, he looked nearly enraged.

It was most inappropriate of her, but she did feel the urge to giggle, which would have been a terrible breach of etiquette and in the worst possible form. So she didn't. But it was a struggle.

"Far too long of limb, Lord Iveston," she said. "You've run me to ground. I can't keep pace with you at all." And she put her hand to her heart, to illustrate. That her heart happened to be buried beneath her very fine bosom was none of her doing, was it? That Iveston's vivid blue gaze followed the movement of her hand and lingered was none of her doing either.

"Miss Prestwick," he said quietly, "I think 'tis you who have set the pace."

"I shall take that as a compliment, Lord Iveston," she said, staring up at him.

He was a fine-looking man, white spot and all. Did he have a white spot of frustration on the other side? She'd just have to arrange for him to turn his head, wouldn't she? Or perhaps to work his cravat down a bit so that she could see farther down his neck. That would take considerable doing, but she was quite certain she was up to the challenge. He was only a man, after all, and not even a duke yet. How much resistance could he offer her?

"I thought you would," he said. "But as you are fatigued, certainly by the heat of the room, and as we have so much to discuss, I shall escort you out of the room, shall I?"

Naturally, he wasn't asking at all and proceeded, under the false banner of concern for her welfare, to whisk her out of the room before she could say a word otherwise. And she was quite certain she would have, if given any chance at all. Quite certain.

❧

"I'm back to White's," Lord George Blakesley said the moment Iveston swept Penelope Prestwick out of the room. "I need to get my name on that wager. He's doing quite well, which I'm certain will surprise some, but not I."

"Some?" Sophia said. "By which you mean Edenham? A man does tend to put more emphasis on a woman's cordial nature and pleasant aspect than perhaps he should. Just because a woman smiles at a man is no reason to think that she'll take him for a husband. If that were so, I'd have been married scores of times."

George Grey looked at her and said, "And she'd hardly take him for a lover. Not a woman with her ideas."

"Ideas?" Lord George asked, looking Grey over. Grey returned the look.

"Marriage ideas," Grey answered. "It's after marriage that women of your country take lovers, isn't it?"

Lord George Blakesley, who was truly a remarkable-looking man, looked with rather a chilly demeanor at George Grey, who had only pointed out the obvious, after all, and was also not a man to be intimidated by something as inconsequential as a cool stare. Really, one would almost suppose that Lord George had forgotten with whom he was conversing.

"Not all women," Lord George responded. "Certainly no wife of Iveston's would ever find the need."

"They do it for need? Not want?" Grey asked.

Sophia very nearly laughed, but as it would have made matters much worse than they currently were, and as this evening had just begun, things being worse, or better, depending upon one's perspective, would have to wait until later. And she was quite certain there would be a later and that things, as defined by Penelope Prestwick, would most definitely get much, much worse. Or better. Very likely both.

"Were we discussing Lord Iveston?" she asked. "Is he to soon marry, Lord George? All part of a wager, I daresay. Didn't you have a wager of your own to put down? Something about White's?"

Casting a final, or one hoped it was final, dim and coldly forbidding look at Grey, who rebuffed it completely, Lord George Blakesley made his excuses, casting a final look at Lady Lanreath before he made his way through the reception room and out onto the street. He would be back, of that she was certain. Lady Lanreath's pointed stare at his back all but declared it.

"What is a London Season, Sophia?" George Grey asked her, staring at Lady Lanreath, his gaze moving casually to her sister,

Lady Paignton. Lady Paignton stared at him and smiled, a slow smile of pure invitation. "Beyond a dance between beds?"

"Politics, darling George," she answered him, "which can happen in the space between one bed and another. Do not imagine that the English cannot indulge their passions while fueling their ambitions. They are quite adept at it, I'm afraid."

George turned his black-eyed gaze upon her. He was quite tall and looked quite well in his English tailoring and his fine cravat. He looked like every other man in the room in his dress, and nothing like them in his deportment. Which was just as it should have been.

"If I climb into a woman's bed, it won't be for politics," he said.

"If you climb into a bed, it will serve someone's purpose, political or not, George. Have a care. The lion is the totem of the English. It is apt."

"And I am of the Wolf Clan, Sophia, as are you," he answered with the sliver of a smile. "I am not afraid of lions, as you are not."

Sophia smiled and nodded softly. "I am not, but have a care, George. Even a wolf is wary of the lion."

"Or the lioness?"

"Especially the lioness."

George looked again at Lady Paignton. Bernadette looked quite as seductive as she normally did, which was quite a lot. Small wonder that George was tempted.

As to temptations, what *was* Miss Prestwick doing to poor Lord Iveston behind that door?

Fourteen

THE reception room at Lanreath House was done up in ivory and rose. The drawing room was also a confection of ivory and gilding, the major difference between the two rooms being the design of the plasterwork and the amount of gilding. The drawing room had less gilding on the walls, but the chairs were gilded and upholstered in dark cream damask.

Lord Iveston, with his pale complexion and light blond hair should have disappeared against the drawing room walls, but he didn't. He didn't disappear in the least regard. It might have been his eyes. His eyes, so blue, so hot, looked nearly to burn a hole of outrage right through her.

Who would have thought he had it in him?

Of course, they were hardly alone. There were servants aplenty and the dining room was just beyond the door, which was also abuzz with activity. A soiree was many things in that many avenues of entertainment were offered. The three rooms which comprised the main rooms of this floor would be full of guests until dawn, once all the guests arrived, of course. They hadn't yet. And, according to Iveston, it was all because of that tiny little wager George had made for her.

He was going on about it now, on and on, while she stared at him, not bothering to listen to his words, because she had deduced what he was going on about after the first sentence or two, but he had clearly felt the need to go on and on about the same thing, as men so often did, and so she found herself studying his face and reminding herself that he couldn't possibly ruin her as they were not even remotely alone.

She was not entirely certain she was happy about that. Oh, she knew she ought to be happy, but she was not truly certain that she was.

How perfectly odd.

She found herself thinking that rather a lot. She'd never thought it before meeting Lord Iveston. And that caused her to ponder. She liked to ponder. She did not believe anything was ever gained by an impulsive display of emotion or raw reaction. No, the thing to do when caught unawares by a situation was to ponder it, considering all the elements.

Lord Iveston was a most unexpected element.

"I do appreciate it when I am listened to, Miss Prestwick," Iveston said crisply, practically looming over her.

She shook her head briskly, shaking herself back into the conversation, as it were, and said, "But of course you do, Lord Iveston. I'm quite positive that could be said of anyone. I myself come perilously close to demanding it. I can't abide being ignored."

Iveston looked quite near to grinning. Then he seemed to get hold of himself and suppress the urge. Quite rightly, too. As he was giving a good show of being angry with her, smiling would have ruined the effect completely.

Which, naturally, made her smile, and not at all hesitantly either.

"I do think you should look at least slightly abashed, if not flatly ashamed," he said. "I look the worst fool for having placed that wager. It was not at all what we agreed to, Miss Prestwick."

"I am aware of that, Lord Iveston, but I found myself in a position which would allow me no other course."

"And what position was that?" he said. As he was standing quite close to her, his head dipped down to speak very nearly into her ear, all for the servants, she was certain. He was trying to be discreet, which was very thoughtful of him, indeed.

Indeed.

The skin on the back of her neck tingled and her knees felt a bit watery. She couldn't think why. It was only the Marquis of Iveston, and he was no man to cause watery tingles.

"Position?" she said, her voice coming out quite soft. For the servants, obviously. There were still servants in the room. Weren't there? She couldn't see around Iveston to find out. It had gone quiet, hadn't it?

"Yes," he breathed, leaning closer. "Position. Prone, were you? Unable to fight back?"

She took a firm breath, shaking her head at him in admonishment, shaking away the tingles. "I am always able to fight back, Lord Iveston, prone or not. And I was certainly not prone. How inappropriate that would have been."

"And you never do anything inappropriate," he said, tracing his finger down the seam in her glove.

Now her elbows felt a bit watery. Most distracting.

"I do not make a habit of it," she said.

"But you do make an occasion of it."

"An occasion? No, of course not," she said.

"An exception then?" he said, slipping his finger inside the top of her glove and pulling it down an inch, then two, then three. Stupid glover, to make her gloves so ineffectual. She couldn't take her eyes off his finger in her glove. And she couldn't think why not.

"An exception?" she said softly. "That doesn't make any sense, Lord Iveston. Does it?"

And then she made the mistake, the wild miscalculation, of raising her glance to look into his eyes. She floundered in a blazing blue ocean of such quiet intensity that it quite took her breath away.

"But of course it does, Penelope," he breathed. "And I am the exception. The inappropriate exception."

He kissed her then, having given her all the warning in the world that he would.

She let him. Worse, she participated. Not much, not to any sort of disgraceful, distasteful degree, but still. She did participate.

In fact, she raised herself up on her tiptoes and, it was horrid to admit, actually leaned in to his kiss.

He appeared to like it very well.

He placed his hands on her waist and pulled her into him. She liked it. She didn't suppose there was anything wrong with enjoying a man's kiss, was there? He was, something of a shock, quite good at it.

Quite good at it.

His mouth was . . . oh, why be poetical about it? It was wonderful. His hands felt so large on her, quite encompassing her ribs. She felt nearly delicate.

And she felt very definitely watery. Simply and completely watery.

He lifted his mouth, nibbling at her lips, and then, every gesture declaring that he was having the most difficult time stopping completely, which was slightly charming of him, murmured, "You've been kissed before."

"Which is why I do it so well," she said, dropping back down from her toes to her heels. She felt a bit wobbly, which was completely unexpected. Watery and now wobbly. What worse could befall her?

Lord Iveston looked neither amused nor pleased by her revelation. Again, peculiar. What man of logic and efficiency would want a skittish and ignorant bride? Of course she knew very well that there were hardly any men at all who were logical and efficient in their thinking, and she was therefore almost certain not to marry one, but as she was not going to marry Iveston she did him the honor of speaking plainly to him. It was simply so like a man not to see honesty as honorable.

"What else do you do well?" he asked, looking down at her quite sternly.

This is what came of honesty with a man: stern rebuke. 'Twas no wonder that no one of any intelligence enjoyed talking to a man for any length of time.

"I could ask the same of you," she said, sounding a bit stern herself. She did not have to answer to him. Did he suppose otherwise?

"But you won't," he said.

"Only because I have better manners."

"Yet not manners enough not to go about kissing men."

"I suppose you would prefer it if I went about kissing women?"

She'd got him there. Iveston looked thunderstruck. He was even going a bit white around the corners of his mouth. If she kept at it, she might reduce him to a pillar of salt, and wouldn't he just deserve it? He'd been the one to kiss her, after all. She hadn't run him into a deserted room and kissed him for no reason.

As to reasons, why had he kissed her?

Then again, why had he stopped?

"You are in the habit, Miss Prestwick, of making the most awkward remarks. I can't think that it suits a future duchess."

"And I, Lord Iveston, can't think that dragging innocent young women into quiet rooms to kiss them can possibly suit a future duke."

Iveston blinked. The white smudges of outrage around his mouth faded away and his expression once again veered toward being pleasant and even amused.

"Only one woman, Miss Prestwick. As to her innocence, I believe that is something of a mystery."

"It is no mystery to me, Lord Iveston," she said, pulling her glove up firmly. Iveston noted the movement and grinned. Typical. "And it is no concern of yours."

"I fear that is untrue," he said. "I cannot possibly endorse a match with the Duke of Edenham if your innocence is in question."

"It is not in question!"

"It is if I say it is," he said, smiling pleasantly, as if he had not just said the most hideous thing imaginable.

"What are you implying, Lord Iveston?"

"Only that as I am conspiring with you to snare Edenham on the wrong side of the altar, that it would be good form for you to be honest about your innocence."

"I am being honest!"

"I'm afraid I require the particulars, Miss Prestwick. I must, for my own honor, make my own judgment upon what might be the meandering quality of your innocence."

He was enjoying this. It was perfectly obvious from the very lurid gleam twinkling from his very blue eyes. She smiled with all the stiff formality of a duchess and sat down upon a gilded chair. Iveston sat in a matching chair with a most amused expression.

Amused, was he? Well, if he wanted particulars, perhaps he would not be amused for very much longer.

There was a strange satisfaction to be found in that. She was going to enjoy this. Meandering quality, indeed. She was certainly more innocent than he was.

"As you require particulars," she said, "I will most cordially provide them, under the stipulation that our agreement is intact."

"Did I say otherwise?"

"You threatened otherwise."

"I am certain I did not."

"Are we to argue about this as well, Lord Iveston? Such a row over a simple affirmation does look so suspicious."

Iveston stared her down. She stared him down in return. She had a brother. She knew how this game of male domination was played, and she was quite accustomed to winning it. George was no Iveston, true, being far more amiable in general and more specifically inclined to want her happiness. Iveston only wanted *particulars.*

"I never engage in rows, Miss Prestwick," he said, studying her from beneath his golden brows.

"How lovely for your duchess. Your marriage will be most convivial."

His golden brows rose fractionally. "I am not at all certain that is what I desire most in a marriage, Miss Prestwick. I think I may prefer a more spirited relationship."

"I can't think why this is any of my concern, Lord Iveston."

"I think you can, Miss Prestwick."

And then, quite beyond all decency, Iveston reached out and took her hand in his. She allowed it. She was merely being convivial, that's all.

Looking with some curiosity at her arm, she watched as his hand slid up it by slow degrees. It sent a shiver across her breasts and up the back of her neck. She suppressed it admirably. Iveston's gaze was also on her arm, his blond lashes sparkling gold against the deep azure of his downcast eyes. And then his hand slid down her arm, slipping her glove down, down, over her wrist and to the midpoint of her hand, her fingers and thumb still trapped within.

She shivered again. She did not suppress it, not admirably. Not at all.

He lowered his gleaming blond head and kissed the base of her thumb. With an open mouth. With heat and teeth. And then his eyes lifted to hers, bold blue and burning like a cloudless summer day.

She gasped.

He smiled.

She pulled her hand from his mouth, from his heat, from his assault.

He released her.

"Another innocence breached," he said softly, studying her face. "You look none the worse for it."

"I shall judge what is the worse for me, Lord Iveston, not you. You are very casual about robbing women of their innocence, I must say. At this pace, you will find yourself married very soon."

"Do you think so?" he asked, smiling. "I cannot see it. I am very careful, you see, as to how and where I capture an innocence."

"But not upon whom, I gather," she snapped. "As I have no interest in marrying you and you have none in marrying me, your . . . activities seem very misplaced. I can't think why assaulting me is so very entertaining for you."

"Can't you?" he said in a low voice, his gaze quite intense of a sudden.

He was such an unpredictable man. His poor future wife would be positively exhausted in trying to keep abreast of him and on top of his many moods.

That unfortunate confluence of words, entirely unintentional on her part, caused a most violent fluttering deep within her.

"You are a most illogical man, Lord Iveston. I don't suppose you realize that, do you? You ask for one thing and do another. You are angry and suspicious, demanding proofs and explanations, and then without a word of warning become most peculiarly . . . playful."

"Playful," he repeated, pulling her glove from off her hand and wrapping it up into a very sloppy ball of fabric. "You think me playful?"

"Very," she said. "George gets like this sometimes, often when the weather has been wet for days and he is feeling cloistered. He behaves much as you are now. My conclusion, which I'm certain you must agree with, is that it is important for a man to get out, to walk about, to stretch both his legs and his mind. I am certain you will feel the better for it. George always does."

"You're comparing me to your brother," Iveston said. He seemed rather put out by the comparison.

"Of course," she said placidly. The look on his face was delightful. He looked nearly miserable.

"I am supposed to believe that your brother does to you what I have done?"

He looked perfectly dejected. As well he should, playing about when she had a duke to catch. Really, Iveston had become so distracted and it didn't do her a bit of good. Of course, as he had become distracted by *her*, she wasn't as annoyed as she ought to have been, but there was no reason to tell him that, was there?

"Lord Iveston, can you be such an innocent? Is kissing the hand of a woman a mark of something dire and dangerous? I am more sophisticated than that."

It was truly something to behold. Iveston looked quite fully angered. His jaw clenched. His mouth flattened into a grim line. His eyes blazed hot and then shuttered against her.

She could hardly keep from smiling at him. He was such fun to bedevil, and naturally, being a man, he had no idea how entertaining he was, particularly if she discounted the effect upon her of his kisses, which she should, and did, and would purge from her memory until she was married to Edenham and could safely indulge in a proper nostalgic appreciation for a kiss that was so seductive and compelling as to cause her heart to flutter and her pulse to skip. But that was for the future. For now, she kept her fluttering to herself.

"I believe you, Miss Prestwick. You are entirely sophisticated. Perhaps to an unflattering degree," he said, his hands lying against his thighs, looking relaxed when he had no business looking relaxed. Hadn't he just insulted her? "Why don't you tell me how thoroughly sophisticated you are?"

"I shall do just that, Lord Iveston. My innocence and my sophistication are in question. I shall defend them both."

"I don't see how you can effectively defend them both."

"You shall," she said smoothly, putting a finger into the hem of her remaining glove and toying with it. Iveston's eyes blazed, his look riveted to her arm. Delightful fun. "On the occasion of my twentieth birthday, I decided with extreme forethought that it was time that I was kissed. Properly kissed by an improper man." Iveston sat forward on his chair. His hands did not look nearly as relaxed as they had done. Penelope resisted a sigh of pleasure and continued on. "At Timperley, the Prestwick estate, there was employed a certain groom of quite handsome appearance. I always found him to be extremely amiable and so it was that," she said, shrugging, "I arranged for him to kiss me."

Iveston's eyes had gone quite wide and his breathing appeared to have stopped. Oh. There. He seemed to have got hold of himself and gulped in a ragged breath.

"Arranged? How did you arrange?"

"Oh, Lord Iveston," she said, "you must know how simple it is to lure a man into a simple kiss. A look. A smile. A quiet stable. It took very little effort on my part at all."

And then she smiled and tugged on her glove.

Iveston looked ready to strike something. Since he couldn't strike her, it was all quite entertaining.

"As I have never kissed a man, I had no idea it was so simple. I take your word for it."

"Thank you," she said. "Shall I continue? You did say you wanted details."

"There's more?"

If she had a single merciful bone in her body, she'd stop the carnage right now. But she didn't. So she wouldn't. She hadn't had this much fun in years.

"Of course there's more, Lord Iveston. You can't think that I would be so slipshod as to arrange to be kissed and leave it at that. No, I wanted to be taught, to be tutored, to be inspired."

Iveston looked quite white about the gills. Both sides. A clear white spot had appeared just below each ear. Well now. Perhaps she could tell him enough so that his white-tinged anxiety wound into a snake of outrage. And all of it true, mind you. She was no deceiver. Far from it. She was the most forthright woman she knew, not that she knew any forthright women at all. It did seem to be a most telling failing of her sex.

"Inspired to do what?" Iveston asked softly.

"To be honest, I wasn't quite certain at the time. But now, having been inspired, I am. I wanted to be inspired by passion so that I could inspire it in others, my future husband, to be precise. I am not certain I have mastered it, of course, but I did try, and I do think the duke should applaud my efforts to please him, don't you?"

Iveston was nodding, a most peculiar gleam in his eyes. He crossed his legs and leaned back upon the narrow confines of the gilded chair and said, "I can't wait to hear every detail, Miss Prestwick. I see that we are no longer alone, but I trust that won't keep you from continuing your tale?"

"My tale? You don't believe me?" she asked, noting as well that guests were drifting into the drawing room from the single door to the reception room. A cursory glance revealed the Lords Penrith and Raithby, Lady Paignton, and her brother George, among others.

"I believe you have been kissed. By whom, I dare not guess."

"There's no need to guess. I've told you plainly. It was a groom at Timperley."

"And his name?"

"I have no idea. If I ever knew, I've forgotten it completely. We weren't cordial, Lord Iveston. We merely kissed, among other things."

Iveston uncrossed his legs. "Among other things?"

The room was a bit noisier, the crowd growing. But that was to be expected at a soiree and she was doing nothing at all scandalous, merely having a pleasant and entirely public conversation with the Marquis of Iveston. It was the perfect setting in which to torment him, though why she should want to was a bit of a mystery to her. As he was so available and as it was so simple a thing to do, she did it. And not a bit of her story was a tale, either. No, it was a history. Her history. Let him choke on it if it suited him. She almost hoped it did.

"I think the best thing is to start at the beginning, don't you? So much less confusion that way. And as you did ask for details as to both my innocence and my obvious sophistication, I think proceeding logically and thoroughly through every essential moment is to be preferred. Now then," she said, without waiting for his approval of her plan, though given the look on his face, she did wonder if he could form a coherent word at all, "I was approaching my twentieth birthday and truly do believe that something special, some remarkable moment should mark the passage. Call it a rite, if you will."

"I suppose a rite is precisely what it was," he said. "Very nearly clinical, I should think."

She leaned forward in her chair and said with some animation, "That's it precisely. I did think exactly that. Of course, once he began kissing me, I realized how foolish a thought that was."

Iveston, from looking almost benign, looked properly alarmed again. She preferred him that way. Agitation suited him. His agitation suited her. Why, she could not have said.

"I can't think why you're telling me this, Miss Prestwick," he said, his eyes glittering.

"How absurd. I'm telling you because you asked for details, Lord Iveston. I am providing you with details. Actually, I find it enjoyable. I haven't, for obvious reasons, been able to tell anyone about it. I should like another person's perspective, and as you are a man, your perspective will be most interesting to me. I wonder," she said softly, staring at him, "if we shall see things in the same light."

"I hardly think so. As I am a man."

"Yes," she said slowly. "You are a man."

Something turned over, a wet flopping in her knee joints. Not that wet, wobbly feeling again. Not now. She had him very much where she wanted him. Though where she would want him in a quarter hour was far from certain. But she did, indeed she was nearly certain, want him somehow.

"He was very nicely tall, as you are," she said, putting them back on the track. They had fallen off it somehow, hadn't they? "His hair was brown, though, and his eyes a very unremarkable shade of blue. Nothing like yours. Your eyes, Lord Iveston, are quite . . ." *Remarkable? Arresting? Compelling?* No, no, that would not do.

"Blue?" he said softly, a smile working its way around his mouth.

He had a very nice mouth, quite elegant. Everything about Lord Iveston was elegant, from the shape of his head to his . . . to his . . . her eyes traveled down the length of him, past his shoulders to his lean waist and narrow hips, over his long legs to his well-defined ankles.

"Yes. Blue. Very," she said.

"Are you comparing this man to me?" he asked.

Her gaze jerked up from her contemplation of his legs.

"Naturally not. I'm comparing you to him," she said.

"And how do I compare?"

"I would hate to make a precipitous judgment, Lord Iveston. I've only kissed you once, haven't I?" she said.

To judge by the look on his face, it was exactly the right thing to say. He did not look the least bit pleased. Yet he did not excuse himself. And neither did she. They could have parted at any time. The room was filling. They were engaged in a perfectly inappropriate conversation in a perfectly appropriate fashion. To merge into the crowd and part would have been natural. And horrible. She did not want this to end, and so she stayed. And so did he. That meant . . . something.

"And he kissed you?" Iveston prompted.

"More than once," she said. "If you will allow me to tell it, you will discover all. I do find myself losing my way in this history with all these interruptions and objections."

"I would not have you lose your way, Miss Prestwick," he said quietly, looking deeply into her eyes, "unless you lose it with me."

"That sounds utterly scandalous, my lord."

"Perfect, then," he said, his very blue eyes twinkling with a very seductive gleam.

She responded first by slipping her bare finger into her glove and teasing it down her arm to her wrist. Iveston's eyes watched the action obsessively. And then she inched it back up. He could not seem to look away. She got a great deal of satisfaction from that.

"I first noticed the groom on a summer afternoon; I can't recall the month," she began. "He looked very much like any other groom, until he loosened his shirt. Upon seeing his throat exposed, a hint of curling brown hair on his chest, I wondered. When he saw me watching him and smiled, I ceased wondering. He was the perfect specimen upon which to conduct my practice of the amorous arts."

Iveston was staring hard at her, his breath quite shallow, his hands no longer relaxed upon his legs. Instead, he looked something very nearly enraged, but not quite enraged. Something else of a likely nature. Something hot-blooded.

"It wasn't until the autumn that I finally was able to arrange things between us."

"You initiated it?"

"But naturally. It was my idea, though he was very willing to accommodate me. Did you doubt it?"

"No."

Iveston looked quite savage suddenly. She would not have thought he had it in him. He was one surprise after another. She didn't enjoy surprises as a rule, but in this instance, it was most, most satisfying.

"It was the hunt, you see," she said, her voice lowered, her gaze holding his. "We had guests; they were out upon the field. The dogs were all out, the stables nearly deserted. Having the stables to ourselves, that decided it, of course. I approached him. He seemed to understand what I wanted of him."

"Yes," Iveston said, his eyes nearly glowing in their intensity.

"He led me into the hay and then, quite delicately and with exquisite gentleness, he kissed me."

"Once."

She shook her head. "All afternoon. The sunlight sparkled through the hay, dusting his skin. I untied his shirt and kissed his throat, the start of it all, really. His throat. There was something about it, some primitive grandeur."

Iveston lifted his chin and twisted his neck against the white restriction of his cravat.

"All afternoon? An afternoon of kisses with a groom on your father's estate," Iveston said. "Only kisses? Hours of only kisses?"

"He kissed very well. Much can be accomplished by kissing."

Iveston nodded once, his gaze flickering over her face. It was very nearly like a kiss, a string of kisses played out upon the air, not touching her skin, but touching her heart.

"Why did you do it?" he asked softly.

"It was my birthday. I wanted to mark it somehow. It was time for me to be kissed by a man. And so I arranged it."

Iveston leaned forward, and she resisted the urge to lean away from him. The groom she had been able to control, thoroughly. Lord Iveston was not a groom.

"You arrange for what you want, don't you, Penelope? For whatever you want? Even if what you want is a man?"

"Of course," she answered. "I like to get what I want. How am I supposed to get it if I don't arrange for it?"

"And do you know what you want?"

She did. Or she had. This contest, which had started from nothing and ended here, she knew not how or why, had changed things. She did not like things to change, especially if those things were her very carefully considered plans for herself.

"You, of all people, know that I do," she answered, avoiding the heart of the question. "I want to marry. Hardly surprising, is it?"

"No, not surprising," he agreed. "It seems nearly universal. All women want to marry."

"And all men want to avoid it, which makes things very challenging for a woman, wouldn't you agree?"

"I think, Miss Prestwick, that very little challenges you."

"Thank you, Lord Iveston."

"But I do wonder what else you learned from that groom, besides kissing. Hour upon hour of kissing does lead to—"

"It leads nowhere if the woman has other ideas. And I did. I can assure you of that. Besides, he was my father's groom. Was he going to step past the boundary I laid down for him? He was not. I chose my man very carefully, Lord Iveston. I do all things very carefully."

"I am quite certain of that, Miss Prestwick. I do wonder, however, if your boundary would stay quite so firm with a man who is perhaps better at kissing than a groom on a remote estate?"

"It's hardly remote," she snapped.

"*That* is the part of the question which offends you? How interesting," he said with a quirk of his lips. It was not a smile, but it bore the shadow of one. "Then you are amenable to my proposition? How cordial of you."

"What proposition? I don't know what you mean, Lord Iveston, which is hardly unusual, I must say."

"Why, I thought I made myself quite clear," he said pleasantly. His voice may have been pleasant, but his eyes were not pleasant at all. His eyes looked quite predatory. "I propose that you give yourself to me for an afternoon of kissing, just to see where it leads. I should like to find myself at least as good as a groom, no matter how remote the estate. Is he still there, at Timperley, by the by? I confess to some curiosity about him, seeing that I have made a wager to wed you and your brother made one that you would marry Edenham. We were going to discuss that, if you remember. I can't think but that I've been made to look a complete fool and I should like the chance to make it up somehow. Besting a groom, a small matter, I hope, would serve me well enough. You will agree, certainly. There is so much you would gain from it."

"Such as what?"

Truly, she was at a loss for words. She could barely think clearly. He had gone barking mad. She wasn't going to kiss him. Not anymore, anyway. And she wasn't going to feel at all guilty for the Edenham wager. It had been Sophia's idea and it had made perfect sense to her, at the time. Of course now, facing down Iveston, and who would have thought that he could look fierce in any degree, the double wager idea did seem a bit foolhardy and, worse, counterproductive.

"I beg your pardon?" he politely inquired, looking wildly innocent, as if he had not just proposed the most hideously awful thing.

For her to arrange an afternoon of kissing lessons was one thing, but to have a marquis suggest that he be allowed to kiss her was quite another. It was beyond obvious that he had missed the point entirely. She had done it for her future husband, hopefully Edenham. She hadn't done it for herself. Though it had been pleasant enough, in truth. She had quite surprised herself at how much she had enjoyed it. Which was why she had arranged for the groom to be sacked the very next day. It wouldn't do at all to have him underfoot after that, would it? Resisting temptation and all that. She didn't feel at all guilty about it, either. He had, at her suggestion and with a sack of coins to aid him, taken the Holyhead Road by coach to Shrewsbury, where he presumably had sought and gained employment. She was not one to do things without having thought it all out, and she had arranged it all very tidily, if she did say so herself. Certainly she must say so as there was no one else to say it. No one else knew of it, did they? Except Lord Iveston. But he wouldn't tell, would he?

Would he?

"Lord Iveston, I can't quite comprehend what it is you are suggesting. You are a gentleman of the first water. I am quite at a loss to explain your behavior. Perhaps the best thing to do would be to just forget this entire conversation, wouldn't you agree?"

"Miss Prestwick, I think you comprehend very well," he responded promptly, and without the courtesy hesitation would have implied either. No, he was straight to the point. Quite beyond his normal manner, she was sure. Everyone knew that Iveston wasn't straight to the point about anything. How could he be when he rarely left his house? "I want to kiss you. I want to kiss you for as long as I think necessary. I consider it a matter of honor, a duty to my class if nothing else. I do think I should have the opportunity to defend my class against the rigors of a mere groom. I also should very much like to test your theory about boundaries. I do think you may have overstated it. And I should like to do my best for your future husband, presuming he is of my class and not to be a groom?"

"Lord Iveston! I can—"

"Miss Prestwick, I know you can. I've kissed you myself. I should like more of the same, if you please. Then, and only then, shall I know if your innocence is true, as well as the proper depths of your sophistication. I shall have plumbed them, you see, which you can hardly object to as you're quite experienced at making calculated assignations and profiting from them."

"Profiting?" she said, pouncing on that last bit. The bits before were too horrible to contemplate at any length. "Hardly that."

"Then let's add profit to the mix, shall we? I have a wager that I am sure to lose, the wager that I will marry you is on the book at White's. The very least you could do is make it all as enjoyable as possible."

"I wasn't aware that losing could be made enjoyable," she gritted out.

"But you'll do your best, shan't you?"

She had heard, and indeed observed, that Lord Iveston was mild mannered in the extreme and could barely tolerate being noticed, let alone spoken to. He did not look mild in any fashion now. He looked, which was quite annoying of him, like a man about to go to war. And she was to be the battlefield.

Penelope found herself nodding, assessing Lord Iveston with new eyes.

"You have made your intentions plain, but how does this fit in to our original agreement, Lord Iveston? The wager has been made."

"Both of them."

"That was none of my doing."

"No? It is not Mr. George Prestwick who made the wager that you would marry Edenham this Season?"

She was not going to tell him about Sophia. He had absolutely no need to know that. In fact, he had no need to know anything. All he had to do was pretend an interest in her. Was that so difficult?

If she thought too long about that question, she would find herself seriously insulted. It was for that reason she pushed it from her thoughts.

"I cannot control my brother, as much as I would wish it," she said. "I'm certain you can appreciate that as it was displayed brilliantly at my ball that you cannot control your brother Cranleigh. He is as unmanageable as a young bull."

"That he is," Iveston said, "yet he did manage to marry."

"Many manage to marry. I choose to marry well."

"Are you implying that Cranleigh did not marry well by marrying Lady Amelia?"

"I'm implying no such thing. I am only stating in as many ways as I know how that George does what he wishes and I do not appreciate being held to account for his actions. Why, if that standard is used, then I should hold you responsible for the shameful events of the conservatory."

"Where your roses were put to such infamous use."

"I don't wish to discuss my roses at present, if you will excuse me."

"Oh? When do you wish to discuss your roses?"

Penelope didn't trust herself to answer him. She felt very close to screaming in frustration. How could everything have fallen into such disarray in only a few hours? Everything had appeared so well managed in Lady Dalby's white salon.

"By your silence," Iveston said, staring at her in flagrant amusement, "I would say that not at present, and perhaps not even in future."

"As I said, Lord Iveston, I would know how this kissing proposal of yours affects our previous agreement."

"Why, I should think not at all, Miss Prestwick," he said smoothly. "You wanted me to appear interested in you. I hardly think a few kisses will inhibit that impression, do you? Quite the contrary. I should have thought that was obvious. In fact, it seems ideal in the extreme. You shall get what you want. And I shall most definitely get what I want."

She was not comforted. Not even slightly.

Fifteen

"I'M going to wager on Iveston," said Lord Raithby. "I've already wagered five pounds on Edenham, but it's ten on Iveston. As soon as I can find my way back to White's."

The drawing room, as must be expected, was filling rapidly. As soon as Iveston had very nearly absconded with Miss Prestwick, and as she made no sounds of protest, and as there were servants in the drawing room, it was decided without a word being spoken about it, that it would be very interesting, indeed essential, to see Lord Iveston and Miss Prestwick together, interacting. And of course it was. Both interesting and illuminating.

There was something there. Something. It wasn't passion and it wasn't affection and it certainly wasn't animosity, but it was something.

"It should be a crush," Lord Penrith said softly, watching Miss Prestwick and Iveston do whatever it was they were doing. It wasn't exactly flirting, but it wasn't exactly anything else either. "I may have to amend my original wager that she would marry Edenham. They look not entirely uncivil, do they?"

"You can't bet against yourself."

"I'm not betting against myself. I wagered that she wouldn't marry Edenham. 'Twas George Prestwick who wagered that she would. I can certainly now wager that she will marry Iveston. It's entirely proper. And could be financially sound."

"That's true," Raithby said, nodding. "I'd forgotten that bit. You really think she'll choose Iveston over Edenham? Of course, her children by Iveston would be the heirs. Can't say that about Edenham. Doesn't he have three dribbling in the nursery now?"

"Two, I believe, though it could be three." Penrith shrugged. Did it matter? The point was that Iveston had yet to marry and girls seemed to like being first. As to that, so did men. "Did you happen to see if Sophia Dalby was chatting up Iveston?"

"I saw her with the ladies Lanreath and Paignton, the Indian, perhaps Iveston. Why?"

As Penrith had a quite cordial relationship with Sophia Dalby that had some little bit to do with his mother being friends with her, but more to do with the fact that he liked Sophia quite well on his own, and as Sophia had a way with women and men and a knack for making money on their amorous couplings, he had aided her more than once in the past weeks in placing wagers on White's book about certain most unexpected matrimonial unions.

After the marriage of her own daughter to Lord Ashdon had been wagered on, and he watched her win a fortune, Penrith had from that point on put his money where Sophia put hers, no matter how unlikely the situation might seem. He had made twenty-five pounds off the marriage of Lady Amelia and Lord Cranleigh, and was not adverse to making more. But off whom? Iveston or Edenham? Sophia had not asked him to place a wager for her, but he knew someone had. It was not like her at all to walk away from a profit, and this Season there was profit to be had nearly every evening. He had never seen such a Season for marriages. It almost made a man skittish to put on his evening clothes. He knew that if his name appeared on White's book, he was a doomed man and might find himself married by morning. By the look on Iveston's face now, it looked as if he might have realized the same thing.

"Edenham hasn't arrived, has he?" Penrith asked, looking about the room. "It would be much easier to know how to wager if one could only get all three of them together in the same room. Comparisons are invaluable in situations of this sort."

"You sound rather experienced at it," Raithby said.

"If you'd leave your stables more often, you'd be experienced as well," Penrith said. "It's been a whirlwind of sudden marriages this Season, and Sophia Dalby has been directly involved in each one of them."

"It's a common female pastime," Raithby said casually, looking at Iveston and Miss Prestwick with thinly veiled interest, as was more than half the room.

"With Sophia Dalby, nothing is common."

"You know her well?"

"Well enough. I can see by your calm in the face of what's certain to become a storm that you know her not at all."

"Only slightly, that's true. Still, she's only a woman, no matter the rumors of her supposed power over men and events."

"You really don't know her, do you?" Penrith said, grinning. "Perhaps you'd like to make a wager?"

"Concerning?" Raithby said, his dark blue eyes narrowed in skepticism.

"Sophia Dalby's success in getting Miss Prestwick married, of course. She is at the heart of this and she will see it done, I promise you. Five pounds? On the book?"

"As long as you're going to White's," Raithby said. "Five pounds it is."

❧

"I'd wager five pounds that Sophia is involved in this somehow," Anne Warren said, watching Penelope Prestwick in pointed conversation with Lord Iveston.

"In what?" Lord Staverton asked.

As Lord Staverton had been seeing to his affairs both in Town and out, and as he had not been out in Society for nearly a month since his proposal of marriage to Anne, and as he was a sweet, dear man who might not have noticed the rash of sudden marriages even if he had been in Town, Anne smiled tolerantly at him and slipped her arm through his.

"Miss Prestwick is very much marriage-minded, my lord," she answered. "I do think that Sophia is helping her make an ideal match."

Staverton, who was older than Sophia and a good deal older than Anne, and who had a long and intimate history with Sophia that was not at all lurid, smiled benevolently. "Quite nice of her, if true, and I should think it would be true. Sophia always has displayed the strongest interest in the welfare of young women. Why, even as a young thing herself, she was tooth and claw for a woman in need."

Anne, who knew only the barest details of Sophia's early years in London, was all ears. Certainly she could well believe it. Hadn't Sophia done the same for her? Taking her in off the streets when she was the destitute widow of a minor naval hero and delicately arranging for Staverton to propose to her? She was to be married in a fortnight and she couldn't have been more delighted, particularly as Lord Dutton was so clearly outraged by the idea. Being outraged, and drunk, suited him completely.

She did hope she had a fine heir to bestow upon Staverton so that Dutton would die of apoplexy.

"Did she help my mother?" Anne asked.

Staverton, his warm brown eyes shining in sympathy down upon her, even if one eye did wander erratically, patted her hand. "She did all she could, Mrs. Warren, and it was deemed quite enough at the time."

"Did you," Anne said, a sudden chill rushing over her skin, "did you know my mother?"

As Anne's mother had been a very unsuccessful courtesan, it was possible and highly unpleasant to contemplate. Staverton was wonderful, but if he had known her mother, then she couldn't possibly marry him. Though Sophia would not have arranged such a thing, would she?

No, assuredly not.

Still, she waited for Staverton to answer her.

"I'm afraid I did not have the pleasure," Staverton said, which was truly such a kind way of putting it as her mother had been just slightly better than a common lightskirt, and his consideration was precisely why Anne was so happy to marry him. He was such a kind man, and men were hardly known for being kind, were they?

❧

"THEY'RE not known for being kind, are they?" Katherine, Lady Richard, said to her brother, Hugh, the sixth Duke of Edenham.

"You're thinking of Lady Paignton," Edenham said mildly. "Lady Lanreath is not at all like her sister."

"You speak as if you know them very well."

"I know them as well as you, Kay, which is hardly at all," Edenham said. "Knowing of someone is not quite the same thing as knowing them, is it?"

"Isn't it?" Katherine answered. "How presumptuous of me."

Edenham looked down at his younger sister with a great deal of affection and toleration. They were very late to Lady Lanreath's soiree and the reason they were late was because Katherine had found one excuse after another to delay their departure. First she had to make certain his children, William and Sarah, aged five and three, were properly fed and bedded, a preposterous concern as they were properly cared for each night and Katherine was entirely responsible for that being so.

As a widow, a most unhappy one, she lived with them, a most happy circumstance. Edenham liked a woman in the house and he had always particularly liked Kay. She was his younger sister by eight years, having lost a middle sister, Sarah, to a riding accident when she just a child, and he was very protective of her. Perhaps too protective, but when one saw death as often as they had done, one was perhaps allowed a bit of laxity on degrees of protectiveness and, indeed, morbidity. Of course, when one kept company with Sophia Dalby, one was allowed neither of those things. And perhaps, no, indeed, that was for the best. He and Katherine had become entirely too morbid and utterly reclusive. It was no way to live, and he was going to do better. He was also, with a great deal of resistance on her part, insistent that Katherine also do better. Hence, this evening out. Hence, her delays.

As the event was at the Countess of Lanreath's home and as her sister the Countess of Paignton had engaged in a very poorly concealed affair with Katherine's husband, her delays were entirely logical. But they could delay no longer. If Katherine could face Lady Paignton, she could face anyone. And indeed, must be able to face anyone.

Life, for all its sorrows, must be lived.

He believed it. He just had the devil of a time convincing Katherine of it. She'd always been given to melancholy, even as a child. He had very likely indulged that side of her nature too freely. It hadn't done her a bit of good, and he was going to make amends for it by dragging her, if need be, to Lady Lanreath's doorstep. It might actually come to that.

"You need to get out of this house, Kay. It's swallowing you whole."

"I may need to get out of this house, but I don't need to go into that house," she said, fussing with the back of her hair. Katherine had warm brown hair with strands of gold, quite like Sarah's hair. In fact, his daughter and his sister looked much alike, which pleased him profoundly.

"I need you at my side," he said, taking her hand in his. "This is no easy thing for me, either."

"I don't believe you for an instant," she said, smiling reluctantly up at him. "Don't think I haven't heard the rumors, Hugh. Some pretty young thing wants to be the next Duchess of Edenham. What do you have to worry about?"

"That some young thing wants to be my next duchess?" he said, grinning. "Don't you think I've had enough wives?"

"No," she said, taking his arm as the door was held open for them. "And I don't believe you think so either. Some men love to be married and you, dear brother, are one of them. Oh, you're in scarce supply, I've no doubt of that, but you exist, you marrying men, and we women must hunt you down like the rare things you are."

"That sounds positively ghastly and quite utterly ruthless."

Katherine smiled as they walked out into the night. "And so it is."

❧

"AND so it is that I find myself here unfashionably late, Lady Lanreath," Lord Dutton said, his penetrating blue eyes trying very hard to pierce her civil and slightly distant exterior to the heart he must assume beat within. *Assume* because she gave no outward appearance of being at all interested in men in general or of Dutton in particular. Antoinette knew this to be true because she had made something of a practice of appearing completely proper and entirely inaccessible her whole adult life. It had made being married to a man as old as her father slightly more bearable than anyone could have supposed. She had never actually denied him anything, but she hadn't welcomed him either. A fine line and she walked it very well. "I do hope you can forgive me."

"Without hesitation," she said. "You are not alone, Lord Dutton. There seems much lingering at White's this evening. I suppose you were caught in the same net?"

Dutton smiled and shrugged. "I was. 'Tis wager upon wager tonight, quite entertaining."

"Isn't it always?" she said, being purposefully vague.

It was quite the most ridiculous thing, but she had never understood the fascination most of the ton had for wagering. It seemed a complete waste of time and capital. As she had married to secure a bit of capital, she was very concerned that her sacrifice not be dribbled away over a series of poor wagers. Wager upon wager, it was always the same and with the same result. Someone ruined. Someone desperate. Someone, briefly, victorious. Until the next wager.

"You may well find," Dutton said, looking particularly handsome, to be honest, "that your soiree is the most talked about entertainment of the Season."

"I do hope so, naturally," she said, "but hardly think it likely. I have been told by my cook that the oysters delivered today are not at all up to his standards. I can't think what my guests will say."

Dutton smiled. He was quite good-looking and fairly discreet, by all reports, which would have been an oxymoron in any town but London. "Lady Lanreath, I refuse to believe that any oysters you serve would be anything but perfection on the tongue." There was something about the way he said *on the tongue* that was very deliberately provocative.

She liked that.

"I was, of course," Dutton continued, leaning in closer to her, teasing her with the scent of him, "referring to the Duke of Edenham and Lord Iveston. They are the subjects of countless wagers, which I do hope will be decided tonight."

"A wager concerning . . . ?"

"A woman, naturally."

"Naturally. All the most contested wagers involve a woman."

"But this woman," Dutton began slowly, his eyes scanning the room, "is not the sort one usually wagers over. It is most remarkable and quite unusual, which surely speaks to something."

"To be remarkable and unusual is surely a point of considerable pride for her," Antoinette said, watching Dutton's gaze, noting when it halted upon Mrs. Warren and Lord Staverton, lingered, burned, and then moved on to where Sophia Dalby was passing through the doorway from the reception room to the drawing room, Mr. Grey at her side. Mr. Grey was quite remarkable and unique himself; she did hope Bernadette was not tempted to bite from that particular fruit. Mr. Grey was no London dandy, or even something so common as a rake. Her gaze drifted back to Lord Dutton. Rakes had their own charms and their own dangers, and certainly Bernadette had ample experience of them, but Mr. George Grey was nothing so simple as a rake. "I take it she has never been married?"

"I beg your pardon?" Dutton said, pulling his gaze away from Mrs. Warren. "Oh, yes, certainly. Never married, which makes the wager all the more titillating, naturally."

"Truly? I had heard that there was something of a rush on wagers concerning unmarried women of late. Starting with Sophia's daughter, wasn't it? Then moving to Lady Louisa Kirkland

and then, so very recently, Lady Amelia Caversham. It seems to have become the fashion to get a wager placed on White's book, though I do wonder how these girls manage it. It wasn't at all the thing when I married, but times and fashions do change so rapidly, don't they? I shouldn't think but that the new challenge will be for a woman of some experience of the world to work her way onto White's book. The trouble, surely, is that what could the wager possibly entail?"

Dutton smiled at her, a slow smile of seduction that she quite appreciated. She'd yet to take a lover, quite unlike Bernadette who took up lovers the way most women took up hats. She lived a careful life, but sometimes, on drizzly winter mornings or long summer evenings, she did wonder if being careful was quite the wisest course. Then she discarded the thought because being careful and precise was far more comfortable a habit than being the reverse. Yet, Dutton was a supremely seductive man, quite in the prime of his beauty. He would not be a bad choice to invite into her bed. Surely she could do worse.

"Lady Lanreath," Dutton said softly, "if you want your name to appear on White's book, you have only to ask it. I am quite certain I can think of something provocative to wager concerning you, something that will rouse the most avid speculation."

"Lord Dutton, I do believe you mean to flatter me."

"And are you flattered?"

"When you've placed the wager, tell me of it, and then I shall answer you," she said, looking again about the room. About half the party had drifted into the drawing room, following Lord Iveston and Miss Prestwick, one could only assume. "Until then, won't you tell me what the wager is and whom it concerns?"

"It is very unusual, I must say, even as these wagers are becoming something of a fashion, because it involves not one man and one woman, but two men and one woman."

"On White's book? Is that quite the thing?"

"No, no, you misunderstand me. I mean to say that it involves the question of which of two men will marry the girl. The men are, as you may have guessed, the Duke of Edenham and Lord Iveston. The girl—"

"Miss Penelope Prestwick," Antoinette said, cutting him off. She really did have to get into the drawing room. Dutton was amusing, but she did have a soiree to host.

"You'd heard?"

"Not precisely, Lord Dutton. It is only that Miss Prestwick was most enthusiastically escorted from this room by Lord Iveston upwards of a half hour ago. To see how he looked at her, well, the conclusion is inescapable."

"Truly? Inescapable?" Dutton said.

"I should say so," Antoinette answered. "You are certainly encouraged to see for yourself."

And so saying, they walked into the drawing room side by side. A sight not unnoticed by Mrs. Warren.

Sixteen

"I suppose you want to begin kissing me now," Penelope said stiffly. "The room is quite full and you would ruin me entirely, which I suspect would cause you no little amusement."

Iveston smiled and said, "You sound very much as if you want me to ruin you. Do you?"

"Of course not!" she said sharply.

Little Miss Prestwick was quite appealing when she was sharp, very nearly gleaming like a blade. He had never thought to find such behavior in a woman at all attractive, but on her, it was very nearly adorable. Of course, he didn't believe a word of her story about the groom. Oh, it was very obvious she'd been kissed before, briefly and perhaps pleasantly, but an afternoon in a stable with a groom? She'd likely heard the story as shared between two milkmaids. A milkmaid and a groom sharing an amorous moment was to be expected. Penelope with a groom, his dirty hands on her face, his roughly shaven chin rubbing against the skin of her jaw . . . he quivered in outrage just imagining it. No, she had kissed no groom. He was not going to entertain the thought for another moment. But he was going to kiss her. And he was going to teach her a lesson about kissing in the bargain.

How exactly he was going to do all that, he had no idea whatsoever, but he was convinced that he would do it and that he would do it well.

"Of course not, for then how could you induce Edenham to marry you? Foolish of me to have forgotten that."

"It certainly was, though I don't think you need to say it so often. It's not as if I'm going to forget my purpose. And someone might overhear you."

"The Duke of Edenham, for example."

"If he ever arrives," she said on a huff of annoyance, casting a glance about the room. "I can't think why you're wasting time with me now, when he's not yet arrived."

"Can't you? How peculiar. But then, you are in the habit of being peculiar."

Penelope flared like a match, her dark eyes glowing like coals against her flawless skin. "Perhaps only with you, Lord Iveston. Did you consider that?"

"No, actually, I did not."

"Perhaps you should."

"Now, now, Miss Prestwick," he said, grinning amiably, "is it quite wise of you to berate me? I thought we had made a bargain, and it is you who need my aid, not the reverse."

"Really?" she answered smoothly. "I had come to the conclusion that what you wanted from me was kisses, the more the better. The sooner the better as well, given your latest declaration. What to think but that you are a very inexperienced sort of rake who must bargain a woman into dallying with him."

He was no longer amused. Not even remotely.

"Have a care, Miss Prestwick, or I shall be moved to true anger. You would not enjoy that."

Penelope shrugged slightly and looked about the room. "You have no idea what I would enjoy, Lord Iveston."

"From your own lips, kissing hapless grooms, for one."

"He was far from hapless, which I think annoys you considerably."

"If I believed it, perhaps it would."

He did so enjoy taunting her. He couldn't think why, although the fact that she intended to use him to attract another man might have had a bit to do with it.

Penelope lowered her chin and stared hard into his eyes. "You think I would lie?"

"I think you, indeed any woman, would embellish the truth to get what she wants."

"And what do I want from you, Lord Iveston, that I do not already have? You have agreed to play a part. For money. I need not lie to you about anything. As to the groom and his sultry kisses, only my future husband need be kept in the dark about that. While I did it for him, I am not such a fool as to think he will appreciate my efforts to please him. No, I told you. Because what you think, Lord Iveston, does not matter. Can you possibly have believed otherwise?"

He could feel his blood roaring through his veins, pulsing like a drum through the chambers of his heart and belly. Lower, and lower still. Never had a woman treated him this way. Never had anyone sought to anger him when soothing and petting him would have been the better choice. All of his life, he suddenly realized, he had been petted and protected, sheltered and cozened. He was Hyde's heir, beloved son, esteemed brother, eligible bachelor. Until Penelope, who saw him only as a tool to be wielded to attain a better man.

There was no better man. And he would prove that to her on her very skin.

"You did it to please him?" he said in a hushed voice. "It

did not please you, then? You kissed a man and found no pleasure in it?"

"I did not say that."

"You almost said that," he taunted. "I think, Penelope, that you
may be the sort of woman who cannot find pleasure with a man.
With any man. How do you think Edenham will react to that?"

"As long as I am the Duchess of Edenham, I don't care."

"You don't care that he leaves you at his estate, alone, while
he stays in Town, finding his pleasure with a woman who can
share it?"

"I am not that sort of woman!"

"Prove it," he said softly. "Prove it upon me, with me, now."

She looked like a landed fish, all gaping mouth and staring
eyes. "What? You're mad."

Iveston shrugged as casually as he could manage. "I know
Edenham, and I like him. He has had troubles enough with his
various wives. I'll not send you into his life so that you may give
him trouble of a different sort."

"I am going to be the ideal wife! Anyone with any intelligence
can see that."

"Convince me of it. Convince me you will be a warm and
lively wife for Edenham."

"Good heavens, you really are pathetic, aren't you? Now
you're trying to bargain me into your bed. Is that the only way
you can get a woman?"

He swallowed his rage and said, "You flatter yourself,
Miss Prestwick. I do not want you in my bed. I only seek to protect Edenham, and to judge for myself how experienced you
truly are."

"Of course, you couldn't manage it the normal way, could
you? Seduction is far beyond your skills."

"Why should I trouble myself to seduce what I can merely
demand?"

"And I'm to deliver myself up to you? Honorable, aren't you?"

"It is still within the parameters of our bargain. I will not ruin you. I don't seek a wife. I only seek satisfaction."

Penelope laughed mirthlessly. "Yes, of course you do. You are a man, by all reports."

"By your report, very soon."

She eyed him carefully, the wheels of her mind turning furiously. Hardly any artifice at all, had Miss Prestwick. Perhaps she actually had kissed a groom. His mind spun just considering it.

"A few kisses," she said cautiously, "a sign of some warmth on my part, that is all you require? You shall not ruin me. You shall not ruin my chances with Edenham. That is the sum of our agreement?"

"The sum total."

"And you will stay true to it?"

"You doubt me?"

"Completely. You have shown yourself to be a man, which is bad enough, but a man of changeable temperament, which is the worst thing a man can be."

"Hardly the worst," he murmured. "It is comments like that which shout your innocence, Miss Prestwick, but then, there is the way you kiss which whispers otherwise."

"Yes, I understand you completely. You are confused. I am hardly surprised."

He could not understand why, but he found himself smiling again. She was such an odd, forthright little thing. It was quite charming, taken in certain lights.

"You agree to the slight amending of our bargain?" he asked.

"This is to be the last adjustment, Lord Iveston. I can't abide these ridiculous amendments made for no other purpose than your wandering attention and odd conclusions."

He nodded.

"Then, I will agree."

"Agreed, then."

"When would you like to commence? As soon as possible, I daresay," she said, looking him up and down. Yes, well, he did look interested just beneath his waistcoat. It was most bold of him, but she could just take the blame for that herself. "I would like to get this behind me so that I may concentrate on Edenham."

"Now?" he suggested. "Before Edenham arrives would seem wise."

"Oh, very well, then," she sighed. "Now."

❧

"Now what are they doing?" Lady Paignton asked Mr. George Grey.

"The same thing they've been doing," Grey said, staring at Penelope and Iveston as they walked with intense purpose out of the drawing room. He was not alone in staring. The whole room was staring. And placing wagers.

Bernadette looked up at Grey with a very considering gaze. Sophia knew that look well and knew what it boded. Not that her nephew would mind in the least, though John might. Women who used men like toys for their pleasure were not to John's taste. He was hardly alone in that. Most men, indeed perhaps all men, liked to be thought of as more substantial than playthings. Of course, they didn't mind in the least and certainly never noticed when a woman was treated so. Why should they? They had, in most every way, all the power. It was why stripping them of some of it was such a pleasant pastime.

However, George was her nephew and she wasn't going to allow him to become a pastime for a bored woman who distracted herself from unhappiness by romping from bed to bed.

"George, I'm certain Miss Prestwick's brother will want to know that she has left the drawing room with Lord Iveston. Will you find him and tell him just that, please?"

Without another word, George Grey left to find George Prestwick, which would not be at all difficult as Sophia was certain he was still in the reception room.

"You got rid of him quickly enough," Lady Paignton said. "Did you think I would devour him?"

"Lady Paignton," Sophia said, "what I think is that a woman with as carefully constructed a reputation as you have should choose a man who will add to her luster."

"And your nephew won't?"

Sophia looked at Lady Paignton almost studiously. She was a tall, well-formed woman of exotic good looks. She was a widow of questionable fortune. She was almost devotedly in pursuit of any man of likely age who happened to pass before her gaze. In short, she was a woman who was misusing every advantage she had and failing to gain advantages she didn't have, which was very nearly criminal of her.

"Darling, certainly there are more worthwhile men to entertain yourself upon. George is simply too primitive for your tastes, I assure you, and as he is leaving England shortly, how can he be made proper use of?"

Bernadette, Lady Paignton, looked somewhat surprised by Sophia's question, and then she smiled briefly. "You think my reputation has been carefully constructed, Lady Dalby?"

"But of course. Every woman's reputation, in fact. What else is a woman to do with her reputation but to manage it until it produces the desired result?"

"And my desired result?" Bernadette prompted, lifting her chin and staring with her remarkable green eyes into Sophia's.

"Darling, don't you know?" Sophia said gently. "To be desired.

Are you succeeding, Lady Paignton? Are you as desired as you want to be?"

Bernadette chuckled, a brief burst of air, and then shook her dark chestnut head at Sophia. "I'm afraid not, Lady Dalby, but then I am not done yet."

∽

"BUT I'm not done yet," George Prestwick said to George Grey, who stood at his elbow, looking quite as dark and dangerous as an Indian should look. That he looked it in such a refined environment as Lady Lanreath's pink and white reception room was something of a feat.

George Prestwick, who was as dark of hair and eye as George Grey, but who didn't look dangerous in the least, was playing cassino at a table that had been arranged for play in the corner of the reception room. Lord Dutton, Anne Warren, and Lady Lanreath played with him. It was a most interesting grouping of players as it was perfectly obvious to the most naïve of observers, which Anne Warren was not, that Lord Dutton was trying very obviously to seduce Lady Lanreath. He was doing it to annoy her, of that she was equally certain. That Lady Lanreath was considering succumbing to seduction by Dutton was almost certain. Lady Lanreath was a very cautious player, both at cards and at seduction, which Anne knew by both rumor and observation.

That Dutton was not a bit cautious at anything she knew by experience.

What George Prestwick knew of the situation as it was being played out before him, she had no idea whatsoever. If he had any intelligence at all, it should be perfectly obvious to him. Lord Dutton was punishing her for marrying Staverton by seducing within her sight, sound, and scent the completely lovely Lady Lanreath. That Lady Lanreath was a widow practically confirmed it. That Lady Lanreath had nothing to lose by an arrangement, however brief, with Lord Dutton made the whole thing a fait accompli. That Lord Dutton had been trying to seduce Anne for the past month made it very nearly intolerable.

But she would tolerate it and she would do so without any signs of distress to delight Lord Dutton. Because that's what he wanted, to distress her, obviously and perhaps noisily. He would laugh for a week if she displayed any sort of temper over his behavior. And she, she would lose Lord Staverton, whom she genuinely cared for and to whom she would devote her life.

Lord Staverton was an honorable man. He was good and kind and gentle. He was generous. He was willing to marry her, a poor and insignificant widow with a questionable past. Questionable because her mother had been a courtesan. On her better days she had been a courtesan; on her worse, she had been . . . desperate.

Anne was not going to live a life of desperation. No, she was going to be more clever and more sensible than her mother. She was going to marry well and she was going to be a contented wife to Staverton.

She would. No matter who Dutton seduced, no matter how his blue eyes twinkled, no matter what roguish blather fell from off his lips. No matter. She was going to marry Staverton, lovely Staverton, and if Antoinette, Lady Lanreath, wanted to tumble into Dutton's arms, lips, bed, then that was her choice to make. Anne had already made hers and Dutton had no place in it.

If only she could tell him that. If only she could get him alone, stare up into his handsome face and tell him that she didn't want him and didn't want him to want her.

She couldn't tell him, and she wouldn't. And so she told him the essence of her thoughts and plans by sitting down to table with him to play at cards and sat quietly and docilely by while he seduced another woman right in front of her.

She didn't care.

By every bone in her body, she didn't care.

Now, if only he would acknowledge it by breaking out in hives or something equally dramatic. He had been developing a strong tendency to drink since her rejection of him and acceptance of Staverton, but he seemed sober enough now.

Pity, that.

A drunken Dutton was quite, quite entertaining, purely as a subject of ridicule, you understand. Whatever had happened to turn him from that profitable path?

"Your sister needs you," George Grey said, pulling George Prestwick's chair practically out from under him. "Go to her. Now."

"Oh, bother it," George Prestwick said, rising to his feet. "I ask you to excuse me," he said to the players.

Dutton barely looked at him as he was so very busy staring heatedly into Antoinette's wide green eyes. She was a remarkably beautiful woman. Anne felt positively dowdy, and she was dressed most prettily in a modestly cut muslin gown with a simple silver cross at her throat. Lady Lanreath was spectacularly arrayed in a low cut gown of white silk with an absolute fountain of pinked topaz around her throat and dangling from her ears.

"It is a lovely thing you do, Mr. Prestwick," Anne said. "A woman does require so very often to be protected from men who are too casual in their address and too fervid in their manner. I can assure you that Miss Prestwick will be most glad of your assistance."

"Do you think so, Mrs. Warren?" Mr. Prestwick asked.

"I'm quite certain she does," Dutton answered in her place, vile man, "as Mrs. Warren feels very much put upon by the slightest attention paid to her."

"How very unusual," Lady Lanreath said softly. Lady Lanreath had a very soft, very calm demeanor that was quite exceptionally attractive. It was hardly possible for Lord Dutton to resist her. "I so very seldom meet a woman who is as shy of attention as I, Mrs. Warren. Perhaps you will come and visit me some afternoon so that we may discuss it?"

Lord Dutton looked ready to pop.

Anne felt better than she had in an hour. What a lovely woman Antoinette was, how astute and how supremely generous. Perhaps she would not tumble into Dutton's bed after all. Anne nearly sighed with satisfaction. But she didn't, for that would satisfy Dutton too readily and she had determined weeks ago that Dutton should, for as long as possible, be starved of satisfaction. Perhaps for as long as he lived. It was possible, wasn't it? He might even deserve it.

"I should love to, Lady Lanreath," Anne said, smiling.

"Your sister," George Grey said again, though he was staring at Dutton and looked very close to smiling.

It was rumored that George Grey had struck Dutton a blow to the belly not over a week ago. What delicious fun that must have been.

"Yes," George Prestwick said with a sigh. "If you'll excuse me?" and with a bow, he and Mr. Grey left them.

"May I join you?"

Anne looked up to see Lord Ruan standing with his hand upon the chair previously occupied by Mr. Prestwick. Dutton looked entirely comfortable with the notion. Lady Lanreath, on the other hand, did not. How very interesting.

Seventeen

"I think you should know that I'm not going to find this at all enjoyable," Penelope said as Iveston escorted her out of the drawing room and into the wide and well-lit stair hall, "but I might find it excessively interesting. As an experiment, you understand. A sort of comparison study. I do find it logical to assume that all men kiss very much alike, allowing for differences in the shape of the mouth, but once that is accounted for, how different can one man be from another?"

"I quite understand," Iveston said cheerfully. "I've come to quite the same conclusion about women, and given the fact that I've kissed more than a few, I can assure you that your suppositions are, in general, correct. One woman is very much like another. Nearly indistinguishable, actually."

"More than a few? How many?" she asked.

"I haven't counted."

"Why not? That lacks a certain precision, doesn't it?"

"I suppose it does. There simply have been too many."

Penelope felt the shock of that statement, which could certainly have been a lie and most likely was, penetrate her bones.

Too many? How on earth had Lord Iveston kissed even one girl? He never left the house!

He was peculiar in the extreme. Everyone thought so. There was not even any dispute about it. Every rumor of him, and she had listened to every one, naturally, as he had been on her very informal list of possible husbands, was firmly and resolutely clear that he was both odd and excessively retiring. How could he have kissed a girl?

Of course, if she were being honest, and she was always scrupulously honest with herself, he had kissed rather well. It did imply some small bit of practice on his part. Perhaps he had kissed a distant cousin once. Or a harlot. That made sense. He had more money than manners. He would have to pay to attain any female attention at all.

She felt immeasurably better.

And then felt profoundly worse.

A jade? He had paid to be kissed by a woman of the town? What had that been like? And could she do any better?

Of course she could. She was better than any strumpet. Every strumpet. She was completely certain of that.

But she eyed Iveston as he pulled her along, her hand clasped in his, barely taking notice of her as he decried the stair hall as too peopled, the servants hurrying up and down in their duties to the Lanreath guests, then pulled her without due care down the stairs and out a rear door to the small garden behind the house.

It was raining, lightly, but still raining.

Iveston was clearly an imbecile at this sort of thing. Her groom had been much better suited to an out of doors rendezvous; at least it had been warm and dry with a solid roof overhead. What sort of seduction was it to be in these conditions?

A very brutal one, apparently, for Iveston, without another word to ease her into it, or a gentle caress to announce his intentions to approach her, turned upon the flagstones, caught her in his arms, and kissed her with all the delicacy of a . . . of a . . . well, she couldn't think what. Couldn't think at all, actually, as his kiss quite swept her up and out of all thought.

How had that happened?

Before she knew what she was about, and she wasn't completely sure she'd ever know what she was about again, she'd lifted herself up onto her toes, clasped her hands to his head, and was returning his kiss in full measure.

Tongues were fully involved.

Heated breath.

Smooth lips.

Hands that held her against him with such force and such determination that she could do nothing but respond in kind. To be polite, most likely. Just meeting him halfway, really, that's all it was.

It was a kiss. She was supposed to be kissing him, showing some warmth about it. That had been the bargain.

And she was going to be found fully as accomplished at it as any common doxy.

Yes, that sounded ridiculous and completely off point, but it felt entirely on point and that's all she cared about at the moment, how she felt.

She felt glorious.

He was quite good at it, kissing, that is. Holding, too.

It was quite astounding.

She was responding quite . . . enthusiastically, and it might not have all been to do with their bargain, not that he needed to know that. The only thing she was determined that he know was how well she kissed.

This ought to do the trick nicely.

Just for a bit of variety, and to show him she knew her way around a man's mouth, she moved his head in the other direction with her hands, lifted him off her a bit, and nibbled his lower lip.

He made a noise very much like a growl, which was very nice indeed, and clasped her more firmly against him and kissed her very much more deeply than before.

It was very nice. She might have moaned. She did hope not.

The rain, a heavy mist of cool water, drifted over them. The droplets tangled in his golden hair, a shimmering veil of glistening beauty. His cheekbones stood out, his nose, the arching ridge of his brow, all illuminated in a silvery sheen. He looked nearly magical, otherworldly, and so very beautiful. His skin was cool beneath her fingertips, his hair slick beneath her palms. She felt hot and pulsing, a fire against his watery smoothness, her breasts aching, her breath ragged and thin, like upward flying embers struggling against a downpour.

He pulled away from her, slightly, only slightly, and whispered against her mouth, "You did not learn this from a groom."

She snickered lightly and licked her way down his throat, nibbling the pulse point on his neck, pushing aside his cravat with her nose. "Have you ever kissed a groom? Don't be so dismissive."

He let out his breath and pushed her down on her feet, stepping back a half step. Was any more proof needed that he was peculiar?

She grabbed his lapels and pulled him to her, staring at his mouth. "I insist on meeting the conditions of our bargain, Iveston. You shan't make me default."

And then, pulling at his coat, she made him kiss her.

In truth, it wasn't that difficult. She clearly had a knack for this sort of thing. One could only hope Iveston was intelligent enough to realize it.

He didn't have much strength to resist her to judge by his response. He grabbed her round the waist, pulled her against him, and kissed her quite savagely.

It was quite wonderful.

Her groom hadn't been savage in the least. Timid and curious would be the best words to describe his lessons. Iveston was quite utterly ruthless.

Who would have thought it?

Not only regarding Iveston and his apparently instantaneous transformation, but she would never have suspected that ruthless savagery would be at all appealing to her. Yet it was. Very.

"What else did you learn, Pen? Did you learn this?" and so saying, he ran his hand up the side of her body, the heel of his hand just brushing the side of her breast. It was most alarming. Her heart almost thudded right out of her ribs. She wanted more of it, immediately.

"Oh, naturally. He was very thorough. A natural tutor," she lied, her breath against his cheek, her mouth caressing his face, his jaw, his throat. He had such a lovely throat, so long and cool, his pulse pounding against her lips. It was quite extraordinary, what that did to her. She felt completely unlike herself. Certainly that must be a bad thing, yet it did not feel bad in the slightest. How very odd. She hadn't thought a thing about her groom's throat, once she'd seen it fully. Perhaps there had been something wrong with it. She ought to examine Iveston's more thoroughly, just to determine what it was that was so fascinating about it. "You aren't shocked, I hope."

She slipped her finger inside his cravat and pulled it down, exposing his throat more fully.

He slipped his hand over her breast, fully, and squeezed.

She thought she might faint, if fainting meant lurching into his hand and moaning in the most outrageous manner imaginable.

"Don't," she gasped. "Don't. Don't. Don't stop."

"Can't," he whispered, nibbling her lower lip, the heel of his hand rubbing over her throbbing nipple. "Won't."

The rain had turned to mist, weightless and cold, yet it did nothing to cool her. Her skin ached for his touch. Could he feel that in her? Had his doxy taught him how to feel a woman's longing?

His mouth captured hers again, open and wet, cool mist and hot breath, his lips sliding against hers, his tongue tangling with her own. His hands swept up her back, his fingertips grazing over her bodice ties, snagging them, pulling at them, pressing her to him in silent demand.

Silk had never before felt so thick. She might as well be wearing three layers of wool. She wanted his hands on her, skin to skin. She wanted more, everything, and she wanted it in the dark, with her eyes closed, with everything but the feel of his mouth and his hands washed from her thoughts. There was no thought to this, no reason, no explanation. There was only Iveston.

No, not Iveston. She'd ruined it. She'd broken the spell of his hands.

Not Iveston.

It was Edenham she wanted. Edenham was the right choice.

Edenham's name was a bell in her mind, dulling and distracting from the impact of Iveston and his wicked mouth.

And then Iveston grabbed her by the arms and pushed her away from him. She gaped, her mouth still reaching for him, her hands plucking at his shirt. He pushed her again, more forcefully, and turned his back to her.

It was everything she could do not to press herself against the long, straight line of his back.

It was as she was considering it that she heard voices. George's voice.

Of all the instances when a girl did not want to see her brother, now was a prime example.

Her hands went to her hair, which was a sodden mess, and then to her dress, which was twisted and damp and wrinkled far beyond anything seemly or even accidental, and then her eyes went to the door as it opened and both her brother George and Sophia's George stepped out onto the flags.

"Here you are," her brother said. "What are you doing out in the rain, Pen?"

George Grey looked at her, his face more than half hidden in shadow. His face was expressionless and a more frightening aspect she had never before seen. He looked, dare she say it, like a complete savage. How could George be so easy in his company?

"A wager, I'm afraid," Iveston said calmly, looking not the least discomfited by being interrupted by her brother when he had just been seducing her not a half minute before. If that wasn't just like the son of a duke. Quite above it all, wasn't he? Untouchable. Unflappable.

Unappealing toad.

"What sort of wager?" George asked, and quite rightly, too. He didn't look at all willing to overlook the situation, which was utterly astute of him. She didn't want to see them duel, naturally, but a good thrashing never killed anyone, did it?

"A quite simple one, actually," Iveston said, looking completely normal and at ease, which was the most annoying thing about him at the moment. Given a half an hour, she was quite confident she'd have a firm list of at least twelve annoying items arranged in alphabetical order. "Though, I must admit, seeing us now, a quite foolish one as well."

George was looking them over very carefully, as was the other George. What must they look like?

Ruined?

No, no, no. She was not going to allow herself to be ruined by Iveston. It was Edenham who was going to ruin her. She'd got it all worked out! Nearly.

"Quite certainly foolish," George said, looking quite nearly grim.

"Quite," Iveston echoed, straightening his cuff. The mist was gone now as well, though the sky was still heavy with cloud, not a star in sight, nor the moon either. As he didn't respond more fully to George, she had the time to take in the general weather conditions, but as she did so, she did begin to suspect that Iveston was stalling for time.

He was trying to think of some reasonable excuse!

Impossible, as there could be no reasonable excuse for dragging her outside to kiss her in the rain. To kiss her repeatedly and heatedly in the rain. She might as well be precise about it. Though being precise, the words and the images that flooded her upon saying them even in her own thoughts, brought forth such a rush of heat and longing and . . . no, some things were better off left in vague and hazy terms. Particularly when facing one's brother with a savage Indian at his back.

Things were looking rather hopeless for Iveston. It was rather funny, as long as she didn't end up married to him.

As she very definitely did not want to lose Edenham, she decided to help him. Iveston could be thrashed for some other thing. She could wait for that, a short amount of time anyway.

"It's quite simple, George," she said. "I can't even begin to remember how it started, though I'm nearly certain it was a scientific inquiry, but Lord Iveston and I got into a mild debate about . . . my hair."

George Grey's black eyebrows raised fractionally and he crossed his arms over his chest. Her George lowered his black eyebrows and took a step nearer to her. Clearly, more explanation was required. As Iveston was looking at her in some interest and curiosity, she was going to have to invent an explanation.

Oh, dear.

"I assure you, nothing happened beyond us both getting a bit damp and uncomfortable," she said.

To judge by the looks in the eyes of the men, that had not come out quite right.

"I think we should go back inside," Iveston said, which was most reasonable of him as it was not at all comfortable out of doors now that her clothing was damp and her hair a ruin.

"I think explanations are due first," George said, which did not strike her as particularly chivalrous so much as particularly inconvenient.

"I do think it is entirely possible to have explanations while comfortably out of the mist!" she said, a bit loudly, it must be admitted.

"Yet you did not think so with Lord Iveston," George responded, "or was it his idea, Pen? Did he force you out here?"

Iveston bristled; she could see that clearly even in the dark. If George made one more inconvenient comment, she might well see herself married to Iveston! It was not to be borne, not after so much effort on her part to snag Edenham. George's foolish display of what she did not know was not going to ruin her marriage prospects.

"George, that's completely ridiculous," she snapped. "I told you that we were engaging in a minor and utterly innocent conversation about my hair. Lord Iveston remarked that he thought that my hair, which put him in mind of a cousin of his or some such, would not curl when damp. I wagered that he was wrong and we set out to prove the point. Nothing more complicated than that."

"Why would you wager upon that?" George said suspiciously.

"Why do you wager on anything?" she snapped. "It was a chance to make two pounds. I never turn aside from making a simple profit."

"But why would *he* wager on it?"

She had no idea.

She didn't know what to say to that and looked at Iveston, who was watching her with a gleam in his eyes that sent a shiver down her spine. She shivered. George took note of it and frowned. George Grey, the Indian, smiled.

"Because, Mr. Prestwick," Iveston said, "I never turn aside from an opportunity to engage Miss Prestwick. She is endlessly fascinating, as I suspect you must know."

What a lovely thing to say. She almost believed he meant it.

George was silent for longer than he should have been. A simple grunt of satisfaction would have been sufficient. They should all now return to the soiree and make as little of this as possible, not as much as possible. Couldn't he see that?

Men, especially brothers, were so stupid about matters of decorum and social necessity.

"Your hair curls when wet," George Grey said softly, staring at her. She didn't like it in the least.

"Yes, I know, which is why I've won two pounds," she said. "I expect you to pay me promptly, Lord Iveston. I'm quite determined to not be given short shrift just because I'm a woman."

"I shall drop round tomorrow, shall I, and pay you your due," Iveston said, staring at her very much like the Indian was doing. She didn't mind it half as much.

"That explains, somewhat, what you are doing out, alone, in Lady Lanreath's back garden," George said. He was like a dog with a rat about the entire event, which was perfectly horrid of him. Couldn't he see he was making it all worse and worse with every word he uttered? "But it does not explain the condition of your dress, Pen. You look a proper disaster."

She looked down. Her dress was in a muddle. As it was of tissue-thin silk, it did show every mark of being handled. And it looked most decidedly handled. She was particularly rumpled around her waist, where Iveston had not resisted in the least the impulse to grab her to him. A wet fluttering made itself felt behind her knees and elbows at the thought. With determination, and her brother's stare upon her, she ignored it as best she could. She thought she did a good job of it, actually.

"Miss Prestwick had a bit of a shock and is still clearly suffering the aftereffects of it," Iveston said.

Well, perhaps she could have done a better job at her fluttering. She wasn't used to dealing with flutters, that was all.

"A shock? Of what type?" George asked.

If she were going to be questioned like a common criminal, she did think someone might offer her a chair, and out of the rain, at that.

"I saw a rat, if you must know," she said crisply, looking at George, her inspiration for the idea. "You know how I am about rats, George. Well, I saw one running straight at my ankles and without any forethought or hesitation, I must admit, I threw myself into Lord Iveston's arms. I even believe I screamed."

"She most definitely screamed," Iveston said. "Clamped her knees around one of my thighs, wrapped her arms around my neck, and screamed. And screamed. I'm surprised you did not hear her."

"I didn't scream that much or that loudly, Lord Iveston," she said in some annoyance.

There was no need to make her look a complete fool. George was her brother, after all, and would make good use of this story for many years to come. Iveston, who had brothers of his own, was clearly tormenting her, but for what cause? All she'd done was kiss him with as much passion as she had in her to win a wager. Was that anything to be annoyed about?

"My left ear is still ringing," Iveston said with a pleasant smile upon his face.

Who had ever determined that Lord Iveston was an innocent, awkward man? He was deviousness itself.

"Naturally, I'm not complaining," Iveston continued, looking at George. "I understand irrational fears. I do have four younger brothers, after all."

"It's not irrational," she said hotly. "Rats bite. And this rat was the size of a cat."

"Perhaps it was a cat?" George said. "It is rather dark out here."

"It was a rat," she gritted out.

Why couldn't George leave well enough alone? Did he want to see her ruined by Lord Iveston when it was Edenham who was the one who was supposed to ruin her? Not that he knew that of course. She loved George, usually, but she wasn't such a fool as to tell him she was planning to arrange for Edenham to ruin her. George was a man, after all, and they tended to bristle at that sort of arrangement.

Men were such romantics.

"Of course," Iveston said in a perfectly patronizing tone. "Still, I did feel that, as she was clinging to me, I should endeavor to hold her up and so I, with great care, held her about the waist. The wrinkles will attest to it, I trust. But all perfectly innocent, Mr. Prestwick, though not very wise, I willingly admit."

George Grey had said not a word for many minutes. He had his arms crossed over his chest, his shoulders leaning against the brick wall of the house, and was obviously amused. Oh, he was silent, but he was laughing. She could feel it.

"I can't think why you are here, Mr. Grey," she said. The rain had stopped completely, but she was most tired of having to stand about, damp, required to explain every little thing. It was bad enough to do it for George, but did this Indian have to be involved?

"I have a sister, Miss Prestwick," he said, as if that answered anything at all.

"You do?" Iveston said, his attention off of her for the first time that evening. She did have to admit that she didn't enjoy the change in the slightest. Was Iveston now going to seek out Mr. Grey's sister to kiss? "Is she in Town?"

Apparently, he was. What a flighty man. She couldn't think how she'd ever thought him amusing. Of course, she hadn't thought a thing of him yesterday, but since meeting him today, he was more . . . something or other than she had expected him to be. Very much more.

"She is not even in the country, Lord Iveston," Mr. Grey said.

"A child, then?" Iveston asked.

Well, really. He was suddenly more interested in this mysterious Indian woman than he was in her. How very like a man. They were so changeable as a rule. It was quite annoying of them.

"My twin," Mr. Grey said, which she did have to admit, was the slightest bit interesting.

"Really?" George said. Bother it all. Now he was fascinated by this nameless Indian princess, for she had heard some small rumor, which had captured her attention completely, that Sophia's father, an Iroquois, was something quite like royalty within that nation, which explained quite a lot about Sophia, now that she thought about it. "Do you share a strong resemblance?"

"No," Mr. Grey answered.

It must have been a relief to his sister as Mr. George Grey, while attractive in a primitive sort of way, was positively savage-looking with quite a dangerous cast to his features. Not at all the sort of looks that a woman would want to possess, although perhaps Iroquois women were different in that.

She considered it thoroughly for a few seconds and made her decision. No, it was highly unlikely that any woman, no matter her race or nation, would want to look either savage or dangerous.

"How nice for her," she said crisply.

Iveston chuckled, and then he coughed into his hand. Most peculiar, even for him.

"Pen," George said, shaking his head at her.

Oh, bother, what had she said now?

"I'm cold and damp, George. Do you suppose we could go in now? My hair curls in the wet. I have won two pounds off the ever-obliging Lord Iveston, and now I should like to enjoy this soiree beyond the padding of my purse."

Let it be noted that she was not asking anyone's permission. The question, and it had been a stupid question to begin with as George should know that she was well able to protect her good name better than anyone else as she had the most to lose by losing it, had been answered satisfactorily. She was done with kissing Lord Iveston, done with pretending she had not been kissing Lord Iveston, and done with answering questions about her activities. Let George find her when she was being seduced by the Duke of Edenham, that would be something worth his time and trouble. In fact, she was counting on him doing just that.

"Well spoken," Iveston said. "Now, Mr. Grey, tell me about your sister. Why didn't she come to England with you? What is her name? Is she affianced?"

Penelope was walking from the damp darkness into the light of Lanreath House when she pulled up short at Iveston's words and turned to face Iveston, who did not even have the grace to look abashed. "I suppose you'll be asking next if her hair curls in the rain?"

Iveston, blue eyes shining like a summer day, replied, "Not until I meet her, no, Miss Prestwick, though it is not a question I have ever asked before now."

"And if you ever meet my sister, which I don't think you ever will," George Grey said, "I don't think you'll ask it of her."

Mr. George Grey did not look at all offended. In fact, he looked amused.

"Why ever not?" Iveston asked.

"Because Elizabeth's hair curls wet or dry," Mr. Grey answered.

"I should like to meet her, I think," George said. Her own brother! If this wasn't turning into the worst evening of her Season, but then again, the Season had just begun.

Penelope swallowed a curt retort, which she was certain would be turned back upon her somehow, and walked with all her dignity intact into the noise and light of Lanreath House. No more dark gardens for her. Unless Edenham had a fascination for dark gardens, then all would be reassessed to suit his urges.

And she did so hope he had urges.

❧

IVESTON resisted every urge he had, and they were considerable, to pull Penelope into his arms and kiss her into limp-kneed submission. Although, even limp-kneed, she was hardly submissive. No, the girl had the most unique talent for standing and delivering, even when flushed with desire and roiling passion.

At least, he assumed it was roiling passion. That she was so silent about her feelings and so loud about her intentions did make her something of a puzzle. A delightful puzzle.

He'd never known a woman like her.

He wanted to know her better, in every sense of the word.

What sort of woman arranged to be kissed by a groom? For he did now believe her. Penelope was too forthright and too lacking in the normal levels of tact to lie about it. She clearly saw nothing wrong with arranging for her own needs to be met.

There was something scandalous about that, and he liked it.

There was also something very frustrating about her flat

refusal to pursue him. She was interested in him. He knew she was, but she was too fixated on Edenham to notice it. Well then, the obvious course was to force her attention onto him.

He didn't anticipate much trouble there. Look how jealous she was even now at the mere mention of Elizabeth Grey. He would have her exactly where he wanted her, Penelope, not Elizabeth, in a matter of hours. He wasn't at all certain how he was going to accomplish this, but he knew one thing absolutely: he was going to enjoy himself immensely.

Eighteen

"Darling, I thought you'd never arrive," Sophia said to the Duke of Edenham. "Lady Richard, you are looking quite as beautiful as ever. I do think London agrees with you completely. You must get up to Town more often."

The Duke of Edenham and Lady Richard were perhaps the two most beautiful people England had ever produced. Their features were elegantly cut, their eyes expressive, their forms exquisitely shaped. They were each intensely lovely and intensely miserable, marriage having not met their expectations in the slightest.

Darling Edenham had been scarred by death, each of his three wives very nearly literally dying beneath him, and Katherine had been scarred by betrayal. She had married for love, and disreputable, though charming, Lord Richard had strayed. More than once and never with discretion. That he had strayed into Lady Paignton's bed made this evening a very important one for Lady Richard. It was time to put old ghosts to rest, not at all literally speaking as Sophia had no real desire to see Lady Paignton murdered, and certainly not by the delightful Lady Richard.

That would be a very poor end to what should have been a very remarkable life.

"I think it is the children who agree with me, Lady Dalby," Katherine, Lady Richard, answered, giving Sophia a breathy kiss on the cheek in greeting.

"I can quite understand that," Sophia said, studying Katherine. "You might have children populating your nursery one day. If you married again."

"I am content with the children in my brother's nursery, Sophia," Katherine said softly. "Very well content."

"Are you?" Sophia said, and with a smile, she added, "How wonderful for you. No one in London is ever content. You may begin a new fashion. I do hope so. There is nothing more stimulating than a new fashion taking hold."

"I do feel hugely insulted and I shan't stand here and listen for another moment," Edenham said, grinning. "I was under the firm impression that I was the most stimulating man in Town, and it was you who gave me that impression, Sophia. You seem quite mercurial of a sudden. I can't think what to do about it."

Edenham was positively joyous. He was clearly delighted to see his sister out in Society, and well he should be. It did Katherine no good at all to hibernate. It only led to all sorts of unflattering speculation, which was the worst kind of all.

"But darling, you must stand and listen for there is so much I must tell you," Sophia said, drawing the two of them to a spot along the back wall of the reception room, a wall simply dripping with large mirrors, to have a private chat. Private? With mirrors? Oh, she knew precisely what she was about. "You know of the wager, naturally."

"Wager? I'm afraid I do not," Edenham said.

"Does it concern Edenham?" Katherine asked in a worried undertone, casting a glance about the room. The occupants of the room glanced back at her. Many, if not most of them had not seen her since her husband's very timely death.

Katherine was wearing white muslin of the most pristine lines with flawlessly cut white kid gloves. As was her practice, and which she was becoming quite famous for, which would likely annoy her completely, Katherine was wearing no jewelry whatsoever. As a consequence, and in direct conflict with every other woman in the room, she looked as classically beautiful and pure as a vestal virgin of old. Her dark chestnut hair was done up in a loose pile and her hazel brown eyes looked enormous in her delicately structured face. She was, as far as it was possible to be, the direct physical and emotional opposite of Bernadette, Lady Paignton, and it was a mystery to half the population of London, the female half, how Lord Richard could possibly have fallen from his wife's bed into Bernadette's. The male half understood it completely.

Sophia, because of her unique experience of the world, understood it as well, though she thought Lord Richard a complete fool and didn't shed a tear when he'd been killed in that duel. She'd wager Katherine hadn't cried either. She did hope not.

"But of course it does, darling, which is why the room is full to bursting," Sophia answered. "Now Edenham, I do want you to prepare yourself, but it seems that not only has a wager been placed on White's book that you shall marry Miss Prestwick, but someone, I leave you to guess it, has made a wager that Lord Iveston will be the man for Penelope. Darling, you have competition. And everyone in Town is here to see who shall win the delightful Miss Prestwick. Are you quite prepared for that?"

Edenham, to his immense credit, which did so much to demonstrate why she found him so attractive, did not so much as blink.

"It's not to be lances on horseback, I presume? Then I am hardly alarmed. A wager. What is that? Wagers are made every day. I do not fear being on White's book. Is not Miss Prestwick alarmed that this episode will tarnish her good name?"

"I can see you have not spent much time in conversation with Miss Prestwick," Sophia said blandly.

"Is she a ribald sort?" Katherine asked.

"No, not at all," Sophia said. "Miss Prestwick is . . . practical."

"Practical. That doesn't sound terribly amiss," Katherine said. "Hugh, are you planning to marry again?"

"Not exactly planning," Edenham answered.

"But if you stumbled into it, you wouldn't cry for help?" Sophia said, chuckling.

"That's about it," Edenham said.

"Oh, Hugh," Katherine said on a sigh. It was perfectly obvious she felt that her brother had enjoyed as many wives as he ought.

"As you have arrived far later than Lord Iveston," Sophia said, ignoring Katherine for the moment, "he has far outpaced you in his courtship of Miss Prestwick. You shall have much to do to catch him up, darling. I suggest you start as soon as you are able to find her."

"To find her? Where is she?"

"Lord Iveston dragged her out of the room a half hour ago, which did change the odds in his favor, which I'm certain you will see the logic of. Why, he may have won the wager, and the girl, already. I do, do wish you had arrived earlier, Edenham. I can't possibly help you if you're not here to be helped."

"You've wagered on me, I take it?" Edenham said.

"Ten pounds," Sophia said, and then added, "but I'm desperate to get fifteen on Iveston. He does look good for it, doesn't he?"

It was at that moment that Penelope and her brother entered the reception room, Iveston and George bringing up the rear. Penelope looked utterly disheveled.

"Oh, dear," Sophia said. "I do think I should make it twenty on Iveston. I can't see how I could lose, do you, darling Edenham?"

He didn't answer. She had hardly expected him to.

∞∾

LORD George Blakesley, just back from placing his wager on White's book and looking forward to a bite to eat at Lady Lanreath's famously well-laid table, was accosted by two things almost immediately; one was the sight of Iveston looking a bit bedraggled about the cravat trailing behind a very bedraggled Penelope Prestwick, and the other was Lord Penrith grabbing him by the arm and pulling him off into a corner, far away from the food, it should be added.

"What are the odds now?" Penrith asked.

"They were in Edenham's favor," Lord George answered. "What's happened?"

"No one knows. But something. Edenham's just here. And he's talking to Sophia. Things should perk up quite a bit now. I can't see that Iveston has much chance, truthfully. If Sophia is aiding him in acquiring Miss Prestwick, the matter is as good as settled."

George, as he was Iveston's brother, did not care for that statement in the least. What to do but rally to Iveston's standard?

"I don't believe you know Iveston well at all, Penrith. My money is on my brother. He is more determined and more charming than is generally credited."

"I don't mean to insult you and yours, Lord George, but it is not so much that Edenham is the better man here but that Sophia Dalby is clearly backing him. I wonder if you understand how fully that changes things."

They were both standing quite stiffly now, their chins tucked down and their brows lowered. If there was one thing a man was prepared to tussle over, and of course there were many, many things any man would tussle over, it was his success at making the right wager.

"What do you mean, Edenham is the better man?" George asked, shifting his weight to the balls of his feet.

"It is not about the man, George," Penrith said impatiently, "it is about the woman, and the woman is Sophia Dalby!"

"You discount Miss Prestwick entirely? Her preferences? Her opinions?"

"Entirely," Penrith said. "If she doesn't realize it yet, she soon will. Sophia will pair her with whomever she thinks best. The girls in these cases give every appearance of being delighted with Sophia's choice."

"And why should Sophia choose Edenham over Iveston?" George bit out.

"I have no idea and I couldn't possibly care," Penrith snapped. "As long as I'm not the man she has slated for the altar, I'm completely indifferent. Aside from my wager, that is."

"And what is your wager?"

"Fifteen pounds that Miss Prestwick will not marry Edenham, her brother placing fifteen pounds that she will. Now it seems I must wager that she will marry Edenham."

"I will wager you forty pounds that she will not marry Edenham."

"That she will marry Iveston, instead?" Penrith prompted.

George took a moment to consider it. Sophia was still chatting up Edenham. Iveston's cravat was still a disaster. Miss Prestwick was ignoring Iveston thoroughly while eyeing Edenham like a cordial.

It did not look good for Iveston. Still, a brother was a brother. And there was the matter of that crumpled cravat. Miss Prestwick's gown looked slightly the worse for wear as well. That settled it.

"Done," Lord George Blakesley said, hand out.

"And done," Lord Penrith said, clasping his hand and shaking it firmly.

❧

"SHE'S doing it again," Lord Ruan said under his breath, staring at Sophia across the wide reception room.

She looked bloody marvelous, as was to be expected. Her black hair was piled high upon her head, her gown was white silk with some sort of clever pleating at the back, and her jewels were emeralds set in Spanish gold. She had them dripping from her ears and a matching hair ornament tucked into the soft black of her hair. She looked a goddess, a pagan goddess from the New World, which was apt, wasn't it?

"I beg your pardon?" Lord Dutton said.

"Good evening, Dutton. I was just remarking that Lady Dalby seems to be matchmaking again. I can't think why."

"Can't you? I've heard she receives a priceless Chinese porcelain for each match she manages."

"And she requires porcelains? I don't think so. I think there is something else which drives her, though perhaps it is only that it entertains her, moving people about on a chessboard of sorts, playing at a game only she understands."

Dutton was staring at him as if he'd lost his mind. Perhaps he had.

"What game could that be?" Dutton asked.

"I have no idea," Ruan answered, chuckling softly. "I only know that she does nothing without purpose. You understand that, don't you, Dutton? Why else has she been tormenting you by way of Anne Warren? You know of the satire, I assume?"

Dutton, who was by all appearances sober, which was somewhat remarkable of him given his general drunkenness of the past month, looked at him in surprise. "The satire of

Cranleigh and Amelia Caversham? Of course I know of it. Everyone knows of it."

"No, Dutton, not that satire. The satire that shows your father, among others, attacking Sophia in a less than cordial manner."

Dutton gave every appearance of having been delivered of a rude shock. And so it was. Ruan, hearing of the decades-old satire, had hunted it down. It had not made pleasant viewing.

"The Lords Westlin, Melverley, Dutton, Cumberland, and Aldreth were pictured in a wood in hot pursuit of Sophia, though Aldreth was drawn to the side and not an active participant. I think that must be significant, don't you? Can you not see, Dutton, the lines of connection? Sophia marries her daughter to Westlin's heir, a tidy revenge if ever there was one."

"And she aids both Melverley and Aldreth's daughters into fine marriages? What revenge there, Ruan? No, you are seeing bears under bed frames. I believe none of it."

"You have not seen the satire," Ruan said softly. "It is chilling in its depiction, yet salacious for all that. Sophia is portrayed as being naked, ripe, the Indian showing very strongly in her. Yet it was twenty years ago. How old is she now? She must have been scarcely more than a child when it happened."

"When what happened?" Dutton said sharply. "It's a satire. A fiction."

"How many satires do you know that are pure fiction? No, the artist requires something from which to build his art."

Ruan could not stop staring at Sophia. She glittered in her finery, her skin flawless, her hair thick and glossy, her manner assured, and her gaze sharp. She was more than she seemed, more than she let them see, yet what he saw was completely compelling. He wanted her. She knew it. If all went well, he would have her. If she allowed it. He knew with utmost certainty that no one ever touched Sophia without her express and considered permission. One look at the satire explained the why of that.

"I think you overstate it," Dutton said.

"Do I?" Ruan said quietly, shifting his gaze to Dutton briefly. "You think that Sophia did not arrange for both Aldreth's and Melverley's daughters to be ruined? Have you forgotten that so quickly? Yes, they were married well, but not before they were well ruined. And what of Anne Warren, who is under Sophia's protection? Do you think that all that has happened to you is an accident?"

"Nothing has happened to me."

"Certainly Anne Warren has not happened to you, no, nor upon you, nor will she. Not with Sophia guarding the gate. You are being punished, Dutton, for the crimes of your father."

"Crimes? Against a whore?" Dutton said hotly.

"She is a whore no longer. I am not certain she ever was," Ruan said, his gaze returning to Sophia. She was talking privately with Lady Richard now, Edenham having wandered off.

"Oh, there is no doubt that she was."

"There is always doubt, Dutton," Ruan said quietly, "or there should be."

⌘

"THERE is no doubt of it," Lord Raithby said. "It's Edenham, all the way. I only wish I'd put more money on him while at White's."

"It's my sister you're talking about. You do realize that?" George Prestwick said.

Things had gone from a mere muddle to a full-blown disaster. His sister was the subject of two wagers, something had happened in the Lanreath back garden and he would have wagered one hundred pounds it had nothing to do with a rat, and he could think of no way to stop the momentum. The thing was, Pen didn't seem to think anything was wrong. Not a muddle and not a disaster. No, she seemed quite as on point as she ever was. Of course, Pen on point was normally very off point, but even that wasn't the problem. No, the problem, one of many, was that Iveston and Edenham seemed to find nothing at all wrong with Pen and the situation as it now stood.

And, of course, that was a problem of huge proportion. It indicated something very nearly sinister, for it was impossible for anyone of any sense to think that the situation, by which he meant the wagers, was at all normal, right, and good.

Pen was not a normal sort of girl. He liked her that way, but he was not so dull as to not realize that he was alone in that. He'd had a lifetime with her, understood her, loved her in an appropriately brotherly fashion. The same could not be said of Iveston. There was nothing appropriate or brotherly about the look in Iveston's eyes or the sluggard appearance of his cravat.

A rat, indeed.

The problem, again, one of many, was that Pen seemed very happy about the situation. He wanted her happiness, brotherly love and all that, and so if things were progressing in any sort of direction she found favorable, he was hesitant to put the brakes on.

But he would not see her ruined. There had been quite enough of that this Season and he was not at all willing to add his sister to the pile of ruined girls, no matter how happily they were hitched now.

"Sorry," Raithby said. "I do seem to have forgotten that. All these marriage wagers over the past month, it's quite stunning, isn't it? I do wonder why now, and why not ever before? What's changed, Prestwick?"

"I can't think what. It all started with Lady Dalby's daughter, though why anyone should have wagered on her is a mystery still unsolved. The point is, though I can make no sense of it, is that since then, there have been nothing but wagers about who will snare whom, and when, and how. I've lost sixty pounds since it started. I have no knack for these seduction wagers, I can tell you. Less so when they involve Penelope."

"But here, Prestwick, there's your answer. There's no need to take it so hard about Penelope. She can't possibly be damaged by it as it's being done to all the girls this Season. A fashion, if you will, that will likely die out when the Season ends."

"And until the Season ends?" George said, turning his dark eyes upon Raithby's face. "I'm to do nothing?"

Raithby shrugged. "They all end up married, don't they? And well married. I shouldn't let it bother you."

"You don't have a sister, do you, Raithby?"

"No. Why?"

"What do you think of Iveston's cravat?" George said, looking across the room to where Iveston stood talking pleasantly with Mrs. Warren.

"It's a disaster. I can't think why he left Hyde House in such a state."

"He didn't," George answered. "My sister did that to him, and to his cravat."

"Oh."

A stilted silence followed that remark. It was only after a footman brought them each a glass of port wine that George said, "You're going to wager on Iveston now, aren't you?"

Raithby, a quite accomplished gambler, said, "I am. You wouldn't care to take me up, would you? Ten pounds that Iveston becomes your brother-in-law?"

"No, Raithby," George said evenly, "I wouldn't care to make that wager."

∽◈∾

"I don't suppose you know the status of the wagers, Mrs. Warren?" Iveston asked.

"Lord Iveston, I can assure you that I have made no wagers of any kind whatsoever."

"Which is not actually what I asked, Mrs. Warren," he said with a half smile.

They stood in the drawing room, beside a beautifully carved chest in walnut with some minor gilding on its face. Whoever had designed Lanreath House had indulged in an obvious passion for gilding. There was hardly a surface free of it.

"Lord Iveston," Mrs. Warren said, her fan moving languidly about her face, "I begin to wonder if you actually do want to marry Miss Prestwick. You certainly are behaving like a man determined."

"Determined to win a wager, Mrs. Warren," he said. "I can hardly think I am unusual in that."

"But the wager itself, and the method, Lord Iveston, are quite unusual, are they not?"

"Perhaps a year ago they would have been, but now I find myself in the thick of fashion. It is most comfortable, I assure you."

Mrs. Warren laughed. She appeared to do it reluctantly, yet she did laugh.

"Fashions change, my lord, yet wives do not."

"And a wager made, such a wager as this, is never forgotten. Where do I stand?"

"Lord Staverton, who does not approve in the slightest, has told me that, as of a half hour ago, the odds were distinctly in the Duke of Edenham's favor. I am sorry, Lord Iveston. Or should I congratulate you?"

"To be discounted by one's peers is not a subject for congratulation, Mrs. Warren. I must see what can be done to raise my esteem among them. The situation as it now stands is intolerable."

"And if you find yourself married to Miss Prestwick? Would that also not be intolerable?"

Iveston looked down at her, at her flawlessly white skin and her pewter green eyes, her dark red hair a coiling mass upon her head. She was wearing white muslin and a silver cross dangled above her breasts, small diamonds at her ears. She looked as pure as ice.

No one was as pure as ice.

"You will soon find yourself married to Lord Staverton. Will you find it intolerable?"

She flushed. In anger, not embarrassment. "Hardly. He is a wonderful man. I am fortunate to have his regard."

"I am pleased to hear it. He is a good man. He deserves a good wife."

Mrs. Warren took a deep breath and regained her composure. "Lord Staverton needs no protection from me, if that was your intent, Lord Iveston. Yet who will protect Miss Prestwick from you?"

"Mrs. Warren," he said, dipping his head in a bow, "the question is who will protect the male population from Miss Prestwick?"

Nineteen

It seemed to Penelope that the entire population of London, or at least those sheltered within the stone walls of Lanreath House, was trying to keep Edenham from her. All she wanted to do was ruin the man! How much protection did he need from that? Certainly she'd do everything in her power to entice him to enjoy it. She had every expectation that he would.

Just look at how Lord Iveston had enjoyed his brief moment in her arms, his lips upon hers, his hands wrapped around her waist . . . and her gown truly was a disaster as a result of his manhandling. She didn't suppose he could help it. He was a man.

Actually, he was far more a man than she had supposed, not that she'd given him much thought once she'd discounted him. And she still was discounting him. The Duke of Edenham was the man for her. If only she could get him alone and encourage him to toy with her. Why, she might be a duchess by next week!

He had come with his sister, Lady Richard, she knew that, though by hearsay only. Still, it was reliable. Where he was now was a mystery. Lady Richard was in the reception room speaking with Sophia, about what she couldn't imagine. A stirring of suspicion wound into her thoughts. Was it possible that Sophia would, in a fit of pique at not being paid, speak ill of her to Edenham's sister, poisoning the well, so to speak?

All the more reason to get Edenham ruined at the first opportunity.

It was just then, when every thought she possessed was directed and consumed by the Duke of Edenham, that Lord Iveston appeared at the other side of the room. The room hushed.

Oh, bother it all.

Penelope enjoyed a good gossip as much as the next person, but there was absolutely nothing worth gossiping about concerning her and Iveston. Certainly anyone should be able to see that.

Iveston, looking quite as tall and elegant as was his habit, looked directly at her with his bold blue eyes, and then, without any hesitation whatsoever, which did not look good, or at least innocent, to the witnesses in the room, made a resolute path to her.

Her heart fluttered quite wildly in her breast. It was with mortification, obviously.

He did move quite well, almost languidly. She could not quite decide if it was the result of superior tailoring or that he truly was as perfectly proportioned as he appeared. If she ever had the chance again, she just might delve into that. Certainly, if he found cause to remove his coat and waistcoat, she could get a better look at . . . his true proportions. All for science, or nearly so, and certainly not for any lurid intention. Not at all. This was Iveston, after all. She did not want him.

And then he was before her and Edenham, whom she had not seen for hours, let it be remembered, flickered and faded from her thoughts. Iveston was right in front of her. It was all perfectly logical.

Of course it was. Everything she did was perfectly logical. She'd made a firm habit of it.

"Miss Prestwick," he said, bowing slightly, his blond head gleaming in the candlelight.

"Lord Iveston," she said, dipping into a shallow curtsey.

Lady Paignton was watching her without any subtlety whatsoever from not fifteen feet away. She had executed the most innocent and bored curtsey that had ever been imagined. Let Lady Paignton find something scandalous in that.

"You're not engaged at present?"

Only in looking at him, but there was no need to be that honest, particularly with a man.

"No, not at present. I expect my brother to join me at cards at any moment."

Another lie. She hated cards and George barely tolerated them. They were not very adept at the idle games of the ton, a fact that must be concealed, naturally.

"I should so hate to drag you off from a spirited competition, yet I do find that I should like more proof."

"I beg your . . . what? More proof? More proof of what, Lord Iveston?"

But of course she knew. The hammering of her heart and the watery feeling rushing into her knees and elbows proclaimed it.

"More. Proof," he said, looking down at her with complete composure. Actually, he looked almost bored.

Her glance skittered about the room, noticing with no trouble at all that Lady Paignton was smirking at her, that Edenham had his back to her, that George was frowning at her, that Penrith and Raithby were staring at her expectantly, and that Sophia Dalby was looking daggers at her.

She hardly needed more inducement than all of that.

"Whatever you require, Lord Iveston, shall be supplied," she said politely, her composure quite firm, even resolute. Oh, definitely resolute. She was not going to show any reaction at all, not to him and not to them. "What did you have in mind?"

"Nothing spectacular, I assure you," Iveston said. "It is only that the odds are most markedly in favor of Edenham, which is a blow to my pride."

"What a terrible pity," she said crisply.

"Isn't it," he said blandly, eyeing her casually. "I would very much like to shorten the odds, Miss Prestwick. I do think we can manage that between us, don't you?"

"As I do feel this is somewhat beyond the bounds of our original agreement, Lord Iveston," she said softly, "I do think that I may expect something in return."

"Besides your most obviously displayed pleasure?"

"Yes. Besides that," she said, a bit more sharply than was wise. She got hold of herself immediately. Iveston seemed to take note of it and smile. Bloody sot. Did he think he could get the best of her? Not likely.

"What would you have of me?"

"Only that, if the odds do change in your favor, that would logically mean that Edenham will think himself out of my favor. I want you to make certain he knows he still has a chance to win me. Can you do that, Lord Iveston?"

He smiled, a tight little smile that thrilled her. He was angry. How perfect. He deserved every bit of it. The only thing that could be better was if he developed those little white marks on his neck. Did he know he gave his emotions away on his very skin? She did hope not. It was a wonderful advantage in dealing with him, those telltales. Why, he must be the most abysmal gambler imaginable.

"I have no doubt of it," he said.

"Yet I do," she said.

They were speaking quietly, in a secluded quarter of the

room, the wall nearly at her back, her gaze encompassing the entire room. It was not to be imagined that they were overheard, and certainly no one would ever guess by their demeanor that anything untoward was occurring between them.

She would never have supposed Iveston to be such a superb liar.

She had, however, always known that she was very good at it.

"You require some test of my ability?"

"No. Only a test of your results," she said. "If I am to subject myself to your unnecessary exercise, then I do think it only fair that you subject yourself to some proof of my own devising."

"I think you have got far ahead of yourself here, Miss Prestwick. I have required no proof of you; no screams of passion, no heaving bosom, no quivering—"

"Lord Iveston," she interrupted, her breathing having gone quite annoyingly shallow, "I only suggest that there is no way for me to know what you say to Edenham, let alone what affect your words may have."

"You could take my word for it."

"I could, but I won't. I am a far more savvy negotiator than you seem to think."

"Miss Prestwick, you are entirely incorrect. I put absolutely nothing beyond you."

"Lord Iveston, I am hardly insulted by such an observation."

"Miss Prestwick, I would do nothing to insult you."

"Nothing but require me to endure your . . . experiment again."

"And again," he whispered, his blue eyes gone quite molten.

She was not alarmed; it was what men did when an attractive woman was around. She was a bit surprised, however; she had never expected the mild Lord Iveston of the day before to have anything molten at all going on beneath the skin.

She seemed to have quite an effect on him. It was a quite pleasurable state of affairs, truth be told.

"Again, Lord Iveston? Isn't that a bit . . . greedy?" she asked softly.

"Entirely. But then, I am most accustomed to having all my needs filled nearly upon the wish. I see no reason to change that now, do you?"

"Of course not. I wish for the same accommodation myself. It sounds a perfectly lovely way to live out a life. Is it?"

"Yes," he said, moving a half step closer and turning slightly so that he could see more of the room.

Penrith and Raithby were whispering furiously. Penrith held out his hand, showing two fingers. Raithby seemed to respond by producing three fingers. They nodded in agreement and then turned in unison to stare at her again.

Wagering? Over her, obviously. It was nearly scandalous as everyone knew that Raithby was entirely horse mad and never gave a thought to anything else. Until now. She nearly preened.

"I think you'll enjoy it," Iveston said.

But he wasn't speaking of his well-accommodated life. No, by the look in his flagrant blue eyes, he was speaking of . . . it. What they were about to do. Although, as he hadn't actually spelled it out, what were they about to do? She was all for keeping to the terms of a bargain freely made, but she was no fool. There would be no blindly walking into what could easily become her ruination. No, not that. Not with this man.

Still, it wouldn't hurt to have a bit more practice, would it? After all, a groom was just a groom. She probably should get more experience with a man closer to Edenham's station in life. There were likely differences, perhaps even vast differences in technique and preferences. It was very nearly her wifely duty to Edenham to come into his bed with as much innocent practice as she could manage.

How convenient that Iveston stood at the ready, so eager to tutor her.

Of course, being a man, he had no intention of being of service to her. No, he was in this for his own reasons, but that didn't mean that she couldn't get her needs met as well, did it?

Naturally not.

Poor Iveston. He truly did not know what an utterly essential service he was doing for her.

Ah well, she would send him a nice note later, after she was the Duchess of Edenham.

"Enjoy it or not, Lord Iveston, I do require some sort of evidence that you will convey what I want you to convey to Edenham precisely when I want you to convey it."

"I'll confess to being slightly confused, Miss Prestwick. If you could elaborate?"

Actually, she was a bit confused herself. He was standing very close to her and the urge to reach out and touch him was strangely strong. Because she had kissed him? He was familiar to her now, in a vague way. Perhaps that was all there was to it. Most certainly, as she was determined to marry Edenham, that is all there was to it. But it would be more convenient if he moved away from her a step or two.

"Perhaps later, Lord Iveston. Now, I do believe that we should proceed, before the evening's activities become more focused."

"Certainly, Miss Prestwick. How pleasant it is to converse with a woman of such a practical bent. It is quite beyond the ordinary, I assure you."

"Actually, Lord Iveston, I had not thought you had much experience with women of any type, practical or not."

"I have every hope of convincing you otherwise," he said softly as they walked through the room, nodding pleasantly at the guests they passed, their mutual manner both so casual and so calm that, if not for her wrinkled dress, there should be nothing to murmur about at all.

But her dress was wrinkled, as was Iveston's cravat, and that did lead to the smallest of speculations. She only hoped Edenham was paying attention. As it happened, he did turn to look at her as they passed not ten feet from him on their way out of the drawing room and into the stair hall. He looked curious and not a little bewildered. Perfect. There was nothing worse than a man who was too sure of himself in affairs of the heart. They behaved very negligently, very quickly and she would have none of it, most especially not from her future husband.

The stair hall at Lanreath House was not exceptionally large, though it was exceptionally well-appointed. The walls had been faced with white marble, the stair treads of pale stone, and the stair rail was of nicely wrought iron. The candlelight from the massive candelabra at the base of the stairs created a very appealing glow. More importantly, there was no one, not even a servant, using the stair hall at the moment. The moment the door to the drawing room closed behind Lord Iveston, he placed both of his hands around her waist, pushed her up against the closest wall, and kissed her savagely.

Well. He seemed to have no control at all when it came to her. It was very nearly comical.

In fact, she felt like laughing. The only thing keeping her from it was his mouth pressed firmly against hers, doing hot and tantalizing things with his tongue that the groom had never managed. As to that, Lord Iveston seemed to be using every opportunity to do more. This kiss was very much more than the last one.

It was so nice when a man made every effort to surpass himself.

She really ought to push him away from her. Or at the very least she should take a step back so that her breasts were not rubbing against his chest. Yes, she really ought to do that. And she would. Eventually. Certainly there was no rush about it, was there?

"You do this very well," he said, nearly echoing her own thoughts about him. She sometimes had the strange sensation that Iveston could read her mind. She didn't like it in the least. "You think I do it very well. We get on, don't we, Pen?"

"Miss Prestwick," she said against his mouth. "You are too familiar."

"Yes, I am that," he said, grinning. She could feel the movement of his mouth against hers, his breath nuzzling against her skin, the vibration of his words tickling along her spine. "You don't mind, do you, Pen? You like what I do. You like the way I do it. You would like more of it. You–"

"You talk rather a lot, don't you?" she said, pushing at his cravat, putting her mouth on his neck and biting him gently.

"Only to you. There seems so very much to say," he said, moving his hands so that they pressed beneath her breasts. Her nipples tingled in invitation.

"Does there? I hadn't noticed," she whispered, licking his ear.

He shivered. He also, perhaps in retaliation of sorts, flicked his thumbs over her nipples. She moaned and bit his earlobe.

"How much more can you stand?" he said softly, pulling her against his hips, his leg pressing between her knees.

"I was about to ask you the same," she said, running her hands around and under his waistcoat, nipping at his throat. He had the most tantalizing throat. Someone should be paid to write a sonnet about it.

"I'm a half step from taking you on these stairs," he groaned, his mouth at her neck, her throat, the swells of her breasts.

"That sounds miserably uncomfortable. I shouldn't like it in the slightest."

"Oh, yes, you would," he said, chuckling.

She giggled in reply, which truly wasn't much of a reply, was it? But it was all she could think of, being that thinking was becoming increasingly difficult and the reason for engaging with Lord Iveston all but forgotten in the mist of desire and longing he created whenever, and she would never admit this to him, naturally, but whenever he looked at her.

The door to the drawing room opened suddenly, throwing noise and reason all over them. Iveston pulled away from her instantly, so sudden a movement that she lost her balance and nearly fell to her knees. He put a hand on her elbow, steadying her, all the fun of the situation completely gone, and looked with the most bland demeanor at the intruder to their . . . experiment.

It was Sophia. Penelope found she was not a bit surprised. Sophia was just the sort of person who intruded into the most private of situations, and she did it without a hint of reluctance.

"Can you sing?" Sophia said, looking at them without any degree of censure or even curiosity that Penelope could detect. As her vision was a bit clouded by remnant passion, she was not entirely certain of her conclusion.

"Are you speaking to me?" Penelope asked.

"I am. Can you sing?" Sophia said, the door having been firmly closed behind her.

"Passably well," Penelope said a bit curtly. "Why? Do you think I should sing now?"

She was more than a little frustrated. She and Iveston had been having such a pleasant time and truly got on better than she would have believed twelve hours ago, if she had bothered to think of him at all, which she nearly hadn't. Oh, a passing thought, a speculation, but nothing serious.

And still, it was nothing serious. Edenham took all her serious thoughts. But perhaps Iveston could have whatever was left over.

"I should say it's essential that you do," Sophia said, walking over to them. "Iveston, you shall play for Miss Prestwick. That is why you have sequestered yourselves, to choose your music and your key."

And with that, the doors burst open and Lady Lanreath beckoned them in with a cautious smile and the beginnings of a frown. It might have been possible that Lady Lanreath did not care to have a girl ruined at her house, not when she entertained so rarely. But of course, if Penelope could arrange for Edenham to ruin her tonight, then Lady Lanreath would just have to live with the results. As would Penelope.

The thought was not as cheering as it had been just an hour previous. She couldn't think why, except that it must have something to do with her impending performance.

Yes, that was logical, wasn't it?

Twenty

"WHAT song can you sing passably well?" Iveston murmured as they walked with as much innocence as was possible given that their clothing was horribly mussed.

"What can you play?" she countered, smiling at her brother, who did not smile in return.

Oh, bother. If she weren't careful, George would make a fuss over the wrong man entirely and botch the whole thing. She simply had to get him alone and explain things, though she could not but wonder if George was perhaps beyond the point of explanations. Brothers did have a notoriously short leash when it came to their sisters. What they felt about other women was entirely different, which did seem the worst sort of illogic. Did they really believe that their own sisters were any different from any other woman? How was a sister supposed to do all that was required to catch a man if her brother put all sorts of hindrances in her way? Hindrances of the *no touching before marriage* variety? How could a woman get a man if she wasn't allowed to touch him? Innocently, of course.

Or nearly so.

"I play beautifully," Iveston said.

"I suppose you think you do everything beautifully."

Iveston smiled and said, "Only because I actually do."

She couldn't help it. She chuckled.

Lady Paignton looked at her in distinct disapproval. As if she had the right! Lady Paignton was a scandal and should be more tolerant of others, a definite *judge not lest ye be judged* approach. Of course, there was nothing about Lady Paignton that suggested one whit of intelligence so Penelope was forced to allow her a great degree of latitude. But she did not like her.

She could ignore Lady Paignton: who was she but the sister of the hostess? She could not as easily discount Lady Richard, Edenham's sister. Lady Richard, a remarkably beautiful woman, was looking at her with a great degree of scrutiny. That never boded well. No one, especially a woman on the marriage mart, could well tolerate scrutiny. Why, Society would crumble into ruin if anyone actually looked very hard at it.

The pianoforte was in the front corner of the room, near one of the windows that faced Berkeley Square. Iveston walked to it with an easy stride, displaying no hesitation or discomfort that she could detect. She did so hope she was matching him in that. What to sing? She couldn't think of a thing. Every song she had ever learned, and she'd learned upwards of one hundred as she did enjoy singing very much, had run out of her head like a pack of braying dogs. Not a single song.

Iveston sat with singular elegance, looked up at her with a pleasantly bland expression, and began to play "Of Plighted Faith," an air from the opera *The Siege of Belgrade*. She knew it. Of course she knew it. Everyone knew it.

And with the melody lifting her, she opened her mouth and began to sing.

❧

"I didn't think it was possible, but his cravat looks even worse. He should sack his valet," Lord Raithby said.

"It's not the fault of his valet," Lord George Blakesley said, his gaze fastened on Miss Prestwick.

"Ah, the girl then," Raithby said. "I shouldn't have thought she had it in her, though I can't say that I know her even slightly. However, she does give one the impression of severe respectability, doesn't she?"

"I hadn't given it a bit of thought," George answered.

"Well, I had," Lord Penrith said, entering their number without qualm, which really was very bold of him given George's state of mind, "and I, while finding Miss Prestwick pleasant enough, also thought her a bit unusual. Perhaps it is only that Lord Iveston magnifies the unusual bits in her, though how or why remains a mystery."

"I should think it all remains a mystery, wouldn't you?" Raithby said. "The wagers are all over the field, though Edenham is still quite the favorite."

"As he hasn't even approached her yet this evening, I find that inexplicable," George said, not at all wanting his brother to appear lacking, yet not wanting him to be married just to win a bet. It was a most uncomfortable state of affairs.

"Perhaps that is the answer. Get Edenham with her, let us observe them together, and the wagers will likely level off. Iveston may even pull ahead," Raithby said.

Penrith said nothing more, but he did appear to be watching Sophia Dalby with pointed interest. That was not an unusual occurrence on the most ordinary of days, but George did not think in this instance that Penrith's interest was amorous.

"Ten pounds more on my brother," George said abruptly.

"That's family loyalty, I must say," Raithby said.

"Not at all. It's his cravat, Raithby. One simply cannot ignore the evidence revealed upon his crumpled cravat."

❧

"It looks to me as if she attempted to pull his cravat off with her teeth," Lady Richard said, looking quite severe. But then, Katherine had developed the knack or perhaps the need of looking severe upon her marriage to Lord Richard, her completely irrepressible late husband.

"She may have done," Sophia said mildly, nodding a greeting to Anne Warren, wordlessly encouraging her to join them.

Katherine, more than ever, was sunk into an abyss of misery that hadn't got a bit better, and indeed, may have actually got worse since her husband's death. Completely understandable, even with a husband such as Richard Becklin had been. Handsome, charming, dangerous, and dead. That was the usual order of things. The problem was that Katherine had married for love and love, in the form of Richard Becklin, had betrayed her. It wouldn't do Katherine a bit of harm to spend a little more time out of her own thoughts and into the light of the world, as dirty and spoilt as it sometimes appeared. Why, look at Anne, and she did hope Katherine would look hard at Anne. Anne Warren had suffered more in her life than Katherine had in her brief marriage. Surely some resiliency was expected. She was the daughter of duke, after all. Did these delineations mean nothing anymore?

But of course they didn't, which was the entire point, wasn't it?

"And you say she would very much like to marry my brother?" Katherine said. "She has an interesting way of going about gaining his attention."

"And yet she has it. Fully," Sophia said, taking a glass of Madeira as a footman passed them.

"They do sound lovely together," Anne said, staring at Iveston and Penelope. "Almost as if they had practiced before tonight, but that's not possible, is it?"

The three women looked at the pair, and what a pair they made. Iveston so tall and fair, Penelope so dark and petite, yet they looked a match for all their mismatched looks. There was something in the air between them, some deeply rooted comfort, a certain sense of play that, unless they were more careful, would send Edenham out the door and into the gloom of rejection.

"Hardly," Sophia said. "They met just this week, I believe, at the Prestwick ball, though I don't think they exchanged even ten words between them. Then. Of course, now they seem to get on very well together."

"They certainly do," Katherine said, looking at her brother. Edenham looked frigidly composed and gave every appearance of enjoying the music. What a performance. Edenham's, of course. "I can't think why a girl should be so bold as to proclaim her desire to marry a particular man. It's quite scandalous, I'm sure."

"It's in her nature to be bold, I believe, and she is utterly determined to marry well, for which she can scarcely be faulted. Actually, I find there to be a sort of blunt charm about her, and clearly Iveston appreciates her in precisely the same way."

"The charm or the bluntness?" Katherine said, casting a glance at Sophia.

Ah, it was so good to see a little fire in Lady Richard's eyes again. She looked better already.

"Perhaps in the way she chews on his cravat," Sophia said, laughing lightly. "But no, can't you see, darling, that Miss Prestwick, so young and so inexperienced, is using Iveston to capture Edenham? It is quite an old game, nearly instinctive, but as it is so boldly performed by her the effect is certainly dulled, wouldn't you say? Edenham doesn't look alarmed in the slightest. After three wives, he certainly knows his way around any trap a female is likely to set."

"I spoke to Lord Iveston at the Prestwick ball," Anne said, "and he seemed a delightful man, though one with absolutely no interest in marriage, at least not at present. I think this might be all for show, though I can't see what Lord Iveston would have to gain from it."

"Can't you?" Sophia said with a smile, putting her empty glass on a table behind her. "There are many wagers in play regarding the delightfully bold Miss Prestwick. I should think Lord Iveston's behavior rests very firmly on a financial foundation."

"That makes perfect sense," Katherine said, sighing and looking at her brother again.

"Yes," Sophia said softly, watching the pair at their musical outpouring, "it does, doesn't it?"

❧

"I can't make sense of any of this," George Prestwick said as he watched his sister singing, and very prettily, too, in perfect time with Lord Iveston's playing. Anyone watching them would think they'd been practicing together for a month. It wasn't possible that they had, was it?

No, ridiculous. He would have known.

Wouldn't he?

"Tell me, didn't Miss Prestwick meet Iveston for the first time just this week?" Lord George Blakesley asked.

It should have been something of a relief to know that he wasn't the only brother caught unawares. It wasn't.

"Last week, in fact," George Prestwick answered. "At our ball. I don't even think I saw them speak."

"Things can happen that no one sees," George Grey said from his slouch against the wall. "Especially where women are concerned."

"She's not a woman. She's my sister," George Prestwick said.

"It's even worse with sisters," George Grey said.

"That's true, isn't it?" George Prestwick asked, glancing at him.

Grey nodded.

"Only boys in the Blakesley nursery," Lord George said. "I suddenly find I am thankful for my brothers."

"You seem very observant," George Prestwick said to George Grey. "Have you noticed anything? Anything I should know about?"

Grey shook his head. "Only the wagers. You know about those."

"I think the wagers might have more to do with this than anyone supposes," Lord George said. "Certainly Iveston has barely shown an interest in leaving the house before this week. I begin to wonder if, the wagers nullified, all this would evaporate."

The three men nodded, considering it. They looked nothing alike, behaved nothing like, and as far as Mr. George Grey was concerned, their life experiences had been nothing alike. Yet they each understood two things to varying degrees: women and wagers. Combined, those two separate and disparate elements could produce anything, absolutely anything. If men had any sort of sense at all, they should avoid putting women and wagers together as a life principle as women and wagers were rather like fire and oil. Yet, without fire and oil coming together, there could be no light.

Pity that women could not produce something as practical as light. All they seemed able to produce was trouble. Oh, and heirs. Must have heirs, after all. Society would falter rather quickly without them, but it did seem a high price to pay, didn't it? All that combustion just for a few heirs.

"The only way," George Prestwick said, "for a wager to evaporate is for it to be won or lost. The thing settled, as it were."

Lord George nodded. George Grey crossed his arms and put his foot against the wall, which was really not at all polite of him, but one did not go about telling an Indian that he was not being polite. It seemed entirely beside the point.

"Which means," George Prestwick continued, "that either my sister marries Iveston or Edenham."

"Or she marries no one at all," Lord George said. "The wager, on all parts, will be lost."

"Small loss, to save a sister from an unwelcome marriage," Grey said.

But was it unwelcome? George Prestwick looked at his sister and could not see an answer to that.

Women and wagers. What a colossal mess.

⁓

EDENHAM didn't know what he had been thinking, letting Sophia convince him that Penelope was his for the taking. Taking? She gave every appearance of being an hour away from a betrothal with Iveston. Wagers flying all over Town, on White's book, recorded for all time, and he with no woman to show for it.

He didn't precisely want a woman, at least not this one, certainly not at present, but his name was on White's book! Preposterous mess. He couldn't think how his life could have been so pleasant yesterday and such a muddle today.

Oh, yes he could.

His gaze moved from the happy couple at the pianoforte to Sophia Dalby, standing and talking to his sister and Anne Warren. She caught his gaze and smiled at him, looking as innocent as a spring lamb. If he'd been in a better frame of mind, he would have laughed outright.

Penelope and Iveston gave every appearance of having practiced this piece for a month. What sort of fairly made wager was that? As to appearances, there was something very specific about the mess that was Iveston's cravat. He'd heard the rumor about what had happened to Penelope's dress, the rain, the rat, the rescue, and he was willing to accept it, but a man's cravat only looked like that after some serious effort. He was no stranger to either cravats or women, after all. If he was not entirely mistaken, it looked as if Iveston had a love bite on his neck.

Truthfully, he would never have supposed Miss Prestwick had it in her. She looked so very proper and her manner of speech was quite irregular for a woman. Bold, actually, though there was certainly nothing amiss with a woman being bold, depending entirely upon to what she turned her efforts.

Was it a love bite? For all that Iveston's cravat looked as though it had been nested in by rats, it was still too well-placed to reveal much.

"I can't think what she has against his cravat," Lord Dutton said. "He looked quite presentable when he arrived."

Edenham looked askance at Dutton. He was his usual well-turned out, polished self. Not at all cut that he could see. Dutton, quite out of his usual manner, had been lolling about Town three sheets to the wind more often than not the past month, and over a woman, too. The right woman, which is to say, the wrong one, could do that to a man. It was good to see that Dutton had got hold of himself and his pride and was shaking off the shackles of melancholy.

"He's out to win a wager. I think he can't care that his cravat was sacrificed."

Dutton continued to stare at Miss Prestwick and Iveston; they did sound well together. "What of your wager? What will you sacrifice to win it?"

The question acted as a spur, shaking him out of his muddled thoughts. He had the answer and it was the perfect answer.

"I made no wager, Lord Dutton," Edenham said calmly. "A wager was made without my knowledge or direction. Certainly whomever Miss Prestwick agrees to marry is of no concern to me. Why should you think otherwise?"

And without waiting for an answer, Edenham walked off and rejoined his sister, leaving Dutton with his mouth open and apparently nothing to say, which was ideal, wasn't it?

Twenty-one

"THEY certainly appear as if they'd spent much time together," Katherine was saying to Sophia as Edenham joined them. "Their timing on the piece is nearly perfect."

"No, not at all," Sophia said. "I'm certain I would have heard of it. This is their first pairing, I assure you."

It was at that moment that Penelope came to a particularly pretty run of notes, and that Iveston joined her. Their harmony was perfect.

"Nearly miraculous, isn't it?" Edenham said, staring at Sophia.

"I should say so," she said. "It's quite startling, isn't it?"

"Is it?" Lord Ruan said, coming up behind Sophia.

He looked quite as dashing as usual, which was so convivial of him. There was very little Sophia enjoyed more than a man who knew what he was doing and enjoyed himself while doing it.

"Quite," Sophia said.

"I can't think that much startles you, Lady Dalby," Ruan said.

"An astute observation," Edenham said, "and one I quite agree with."

"I'm flattered," Sophia said. "I shouldn't like to be thought of as a woman who starts at nothing."

"Is this nothing?" Edenham asked, turning slightly to face Miss Prestwick and the pianoforte. "Before today, no one had heard of this girl and now she is the subject of wagers."

"That's hardly to her credit, Hugh," Katherine said. "I don't think it kind of you to point it out."

"I make no judgments, only observations," Edenham responded.

"I couldn't disagree more," Sophia said, facing Penelope. The song was just ending. "It is to her credit, and you should judge her well for doing such a splendid job in a single day of that which every girl of every Season wishes for; she has made a name for herself. She, this darling girl, has grabbed everyone's attention and is determined to keep it for as long as she requires it. Such a girl should be applauded."

As the song was done, the room did applaud. It was nicely timed.

"As long as she requires it? What the devil does that mean?" Edenham asked Sophia. But it was not Sophia who answered him.

"Until she gets a husband," Katherine said, looking at Sophia with the barest of smiles.

"Precisely," said Sophia.

"And when is that to be?" Edenham asked.

"Darling," Sophia said softly, laying her fan on his arm, "don't be so coy."

Lord Ruan laughed.

∞

"I can't think what you're being so coy about," Penelope said. "All I'm asking is that you escort me over to Edenham. I should think you'd be glad to be done with your part in my . . ."

Well, what to call it? Of course, there were words to describe what she was doing, but they were not the sort of words one said in front of a man.

"Your pursuit of a husband?" Iveston said pleasantly, his turquoise blue eyes twinkling almost dangerously. Dangerous? What could possibly be dangerous about Lord Iveston?

His kisses?

Perish the thought.

Oh, of course he kissed quite splendidly; she was not the type of woman to lie about something like that. No, a man had to have his skills, his areas of expertise, and Iveston had clearly found his. He could kiss. He could kiss very well. Well, what of it? A woman did not choose a husband based upon something as inconsequential as that. Why, if that were so, she might as well have married the groom. Though, to be honest, the groom's kisses, what she could remember of them, quite paled in comparison to Iveston's.

He *could* kiss.

He could also play the pianoforte and she wasn't about to marry him for his musical skills either.

Marriage? Why ever had marriage entered her mind when cataloging Iveston's scant list of skills? She nearly blushed in shame at the wayward nature of her thoughts. A woman did not make the most ideal marriage by becoming distracted by incidentals.

"You're blushing," Iveston said, standing up from the bench.

He was quite tall, nearly towering over her. She supposed she should find it extremely unattractive, it was only that he looked so very well, even with his cravat a tatter. He was a very handsome man. There was little point in denying that. There was little reason to deny it either. So, he could kiss well and he was handsome. What was that? Nothing to build a marriage upon.

"I don't think so," she said. "I never blush. I never find the need."

She sounded like a prig. She knew it. She couldn't seem to stop herself. The problem was that Lord Iveston didn't seem to mind. *All* the men minded. Why didn't he?

"Can't you feel it?" he said softly, taking a step nearer to her. They were quite close enough. It was entirely unnecessary. He did it anyway. "Can't you feel the heat of it?"

"No."

She wasn't going to count the little lies. If she did, she would be overwhelmed with counting in a half hour's time.

"You never blush," he said, looking at her mouth, "yet you are blushing now, for me. I like that."

"I don't care what you like."

"Did you know," he said, ignoring her completely, still staring at her mouth, "that your mouth goes quite rosy when you blush? Nearly like a berry stain. It's quite compelling. I do think you should stop, if at all possible, or I shall be hard put to refrain from kissing you again."

It was a horrible truth to admit that she didn't mind the idea in the least.

Whatever was wrong with her? She needed to plant herself at Edenham's side immediately or Lord Iveston would distract her past all reckoning. And that couldn't happen, no, couldn't be allowed to happen. She had her plan and she was not going to be waylaid by a few kisses of superior quality.

How did Edenham kiss, as long as she was thinking of it? Certainly, after three wives, he must have developed some talent for kissing. Pity that she couldn't ask one of them how he . . . performed. She did like to have all her facts in hand before making a decision. Of course, she could simply arrange to kiss him herself. There was nothing like firsthand exposure. It was so much more reliable than hearsay.

"I do hope Edenham likes the color of my lips," she said. "Do you think he will?"

Her words had the desired effect. Iveston pulled back from her and considered her from beneath his pale brows.

"Let's ask him, shall we?" Iveston said. And without another word, he escorted her across the floor to where Edenham stood with Sophia and Lady Richard.

Penelope braced herself. She was more than certain that this was not going to be pleasant. If there weren't already so many wagers flying about the room, she would have wagered on it.

❧

"With so many wagers placed on Miss Prestwick's marital prospects, I haven't been able to get a man's attention all evening," Bernadette, Lady Paignton, said. "I can't even find that Indian, and I did think he'd be an interesting experience."

"You have too many interesting experiences," Antoinette, Lady Lanreath, said. "It's becoming something of a problem, don't you agree?"

"No, actually, I don't," Bernadette said.

"I should like it very much if you would change your mind," Antoinette said softly, looking out over her room full of guests, at how perfect it all looked, and how empty it was of all meaning. It wasn't even her house anymore, having been passed to her husband's son. The moment he married she would likely be thrown out on her bonnet. "I may want to marry again, and it will be a bit difficult to arrange if you continue on as you are doing."

Bernadette turned her green eyes upon her sister, looking quite obviously stunned. "I had no idea. Why didn't you tell me?"

"I had no idea myself," Antoinette answered. "I think watching Miss Prestwick has inspired me. This girl, nothing stops her, does it? She is arranging her own match, on her own terms. Did you or I do the same? We did not. We married where we were told. She is barely younger than we are now, yet so much stronger in resolve. Yes," Antoinette said, lifting her chin, "she has most assuredly inspired me."

"To marriage," Bernadette said skeptically.

"Yes, to marriage. I do not aspire to be any man's whore, Bernie. I should think that you would want more for yourself. Certainly I want more for you."

Bernadette smiled. It was a smile without joy and without warmth.

"We want different things, Toni. However, I will do whatever I must to aid you. I only want your happiness, nearly as much as I want my own." And then she smiled, a most genuine smile.

"Very well. For now. Don't think I shan't try to convince you of my wisdom and brilliance upon this topic, however. I shall return to it at some future date."

"I shall look forward to it."

"You are an appalling liar."

"Yes, but I'm so good at everything else."

And at that, both sisters laughed, causing Lady Richard to look over at them, and frown.

❧

"Now, darling, don't frown," Sophia said. "Miss Prestwick will think you don't approve of her."

"I'm nearly certain I don't," Katherine said, and then smiled. "But as she may become my sister, I don't wish to start off on the wrong foot with her."

"Oh, come now," Edenham said, frowning at both women. "I'm hardly likely to marry Miss Prestwick and you both know it."

"I certainly do not know any such thing," Sophia said. "I've wagered that you will. Don't disappoint me, darling. Ah, Lord Iveston, you've escorted the lamb to the wolves. How cordial of you."

Miss Prestwick, for perfectly obvious reasons, did not care for the metaphor in the slightest, and who could expect her to? She was a woman of resolve and action, yet still a lamb in the ways of men, for all that. Although, as Iveston turned his head to greet Lady Richard, it became clear that the lamb had sharp teeth: Lord Iveston had a love bite on his neck, and quite a nice one, too.

Darling Penelope grew more interesting by the hour. It was to be expected that Iveston had come to the same conclusion. Would Edenham? That was the question, and an entertaining one it was.

"What a lovely concert," Sophia continued, studying Penelope and Iveston. "Such harmony and what can only be assumed a natural fluidity of timing and instinctive musicality. No one can believe that you have not been practicing together, in seclusion, for weeks."

"As I've only just met Lord Iveston, that would have been impossible," Penelope said.

"Which is precisely what I've been saying, darling, but of course, no one will believe me," Sophia said. "I do think you should lend your voice to the choir, as it were, Lord Iveston. You are certain to be trusted far more than I."

"And I?" Penelope said, her gaze quite as blunt as a hammer. "I am not to be trusted?"

As there was another woman at the pianoforte, both singing and playing, and as she was sharp one note out of every three, it did not look at all hopeful that anyone was prepared to believe that Penelope and Iveston had come together so beautifully as a result of mere chance. But Sophia was not going to be the one to say that to her. No, there was a better source entirely.

"Certainly the duke has expressed doubts," Sophia said, casually fanning her face.

Miss Prestwick gave Sophia a look she clearly hoped would wilt her—it didn't—and then turned to face Edenham. To her credit, she faced him squarely. To his credit, he gave every appearance of gentleness.

To Iveston's credit, he did not hold his tongue, but stepped in and settled the issue instantly. Or tried to, poor darling.

"We've just met," Iveston said. "Last week, in fact. I was under the impression that you met Miss Prestwick the same night that I did, at a ball in her home."

"I did," Edenham said, "though I do think that, between then and now, you have become better acquainted with her than I have done."

"I daresay that's true," Iveston said, nodding pleasantly. "As I understand it, Edenham, there is a wager on White's book, the odds quite heavily in your favor, that you will marry Miss Prestwick."

"So I've been told," Edenham said calmly.

Penelope was scarcely breathing. Katherine was clearly uncomfortable at the boldness of the conversation. Sophia could not have been more delighted than if she'd written the script herself, and she nearly had.

"You may be unaware of it," Iveston continued, moving so that he stood nearer to Edenham and almost directly facing Penelope, "but I placed a wager of my own, that I would marry Miss Prestwick."

"Having known her for less than a week?" Edenham asked.

"Quite right," Iveston said, smiling. "Ridiculous bit of nonsense, isn't it? I did it to win a bet, of course, an entirely different wager with Cranleigh, and of course, I have won it."

"What?" Penelope said sharply. "A wager? You . . . it was nothing but a wager?"

Iveston turned the full force of his blue gaze upon Penelope. She gasped on a whispered intake of breath. Katherine murmured some unintelligible bit of comfort. Sophia smiled behind her fan. Penelope needed no comfort; she was the sort who came out fighting, which truly was so clever of her.

"The first wager, Miss Prestwick, which I am quite certain you can have known nothing of. I shan't be so crass as to discuss the particulars with you, but I have won it many times over."

Penelope did not fire up in her anger and outrage, no, nothing so pedestrian as that. She looked quite icily calm and held herself as still as a marble statue.

"You shan't be crass enough to discuss it, yet you show no hesitation to perform in calculated fashion to win this mysterious wager? How perfectly like a man you are, how hopelessly illogical in your thoughts and actions."

"Thank you," he said, bowing crisply in her direction. "I am pleased that you have, finally, noticed that I am a man and will ever behave as one, Miss Prestwick."

It was as if a cold wind blew through the room at that exchange of observations, a wind that began at the epicenter of Penelope and Iveston and rushed out to encompass the room. Sophia was certain she was not imagining that the drawing room grew quite quiet, the girl at the pianoforte sounding louder and more discordant as a result. Poor girl. But then, she couldn't help them all, could she?

"The wager on White's book, what of that?" Edenham asked into the awkward silence.

"Oh, yes, you must explain about that," Sophia said. "It's the key to the whole thing, isn't it, Miss Prestwick?"

"No, I–" Penelope began. She looked nearly flushed. It quite agreed with her.

"Miss Prestwick," Iveston said, cutting her off, his glance to her as slicing as his tone, "asked me to place a wager on the book that she and I would marry. Her idea was that it would intrigue you enough to want to pursue an alliance with her. My idea was that it could only aid me in my wager with Cranleigh."

"An odd way of getting a man's attention," Edenham said.

"Yet did it not work?" Penelope asked a trifle angrily. Not

very wise of her to be angry now, but that was part of the charm of youth. How else to explain it?

"Yes, I confess that it did," Edenham said. "But the wager that she and I would marry? Who is responsible for that?"

And here is where Miss Penelope Prestwick lived up to every one of Sophia's expectations of her.

Lifting her delightful little chin and staring both men in the face from her very diminutive position, she said clearly, "I am. I am responsible for both wagers."

"I do hope you can afford to lose your wagers, Miss Prestwick, for you have lost them both," Iveston said calmly. And with that, he walked away from her.

She followed him with her eyes until he was lost from view.

"Were you prepared to lose, Miss Prestwick?" Sophia asked.

She turned back to face them, looking fully at Sophia, ignoring Edenham and Lady Richard entirely. That told the entire tale most explicitly.

"No, I don't believe I was," Penelope said in a hushed voice.

"Then I think it's past time I talked to your father, don't you?"

Twenty-two

VISCOUNT Prestwick was a man who enjoyed a social outing as well as the next man, but as he was far more interested in maintaining his fortune and, indeed, increasing it, he kept hours that did not suit the ton. He was up at first light, working, and he was therefore not at all disposed to attend a soiree such as the one Lady Lanreath had hosted last night where dinner was served at half past midnight. Being a man who wanted all that a title implied and yet being a man who understood the cost of maintaining all that a title implied, he was eager to know everything that happened in the upper branches of Society and yet able to witness very little of it firsthand. So it was that he was taken completely by surprise when Lady Dalby presented her card to Hamilton, his butler.

Was he *in* for Lady Dalby?

He most assuredly was.

Lady Dalby knew everything that happened in Society for the simple reason that she instigated much of it.

Prestwick instructed Hamilton to make Lady Dalby welcome in the red drawing room, a quite sumptuous room that should show her the proper respect; he was no fool. He had not got himself a viscountcy by alienating the wrong people, and even the right people took great care not to insult Sophia Dalby. It was for that reason that he hurried into his bedchamber, throwing off his coat and waistcoat, alarming his valet exceedingly. He didn't care a whit about his valet. It was only completely necessary that he wear a waistcoat that was the first pitch of fashion. The green silk ought to be just the thing.

When Harold Prestwick, the first Viscount Prestwick, entered the red drawing room, he was as puffed up and polished as it was possible for a man to be. Sophia Dalby, in a white muslin gown with fitted sleeves, a pair of pearl earrings, and a straw bonnet crisscrossed with red ribbons, looked at him admiringly. He was quite certain it was a gaze of admiration. What else? He was a very fit man and still in the very pink of health, and she was a famously lovely woman. He had not heard that she was quite so forward in choosing her companions, but he was more than willing to be pursued by so noteworthy a woman.

She rose to her feet in a fluid motion that was quite wonderful to behold and greeted him with a curtsey and a flirtatious smile. He was utterly certain it was flirtatious. What else? She was Sophia Dalby; she dealt in flirtation the way a baker dealt in bread.

"Lord Prestwick, how kind of you to see me," she said. "Are you quite recovered?"

His smile froze on his face. Recovered? Didn't he look as fit as he was certain he was? Perhaps the green silk did not suit his complexion. His valet had made some comment in that direction, but he had ignored him. The green silk waistcoat had cost him twice as much as any other waistcoat he possessed; he was certain it must look wonderful for that reason alone.

"Lady Dalby, I could not fail to be in top form for a woman as exalted as you. I am honored that you came to see me. What refreshment may I offer you?"

"Only the refreshment of your charming company, Lord Prestwick," she answered, taking her seat again. The chairs were covered in the same red silk damask as the walls, making it quite a warm and welcoming room. To say that Lady Dalby looked like a pearl set in a red box would have been redundant. Lady Dalby always looked remarkably beautiful. She was famous for it. "By your manner, I must suppose that you have not spoken with Miss Prestwick yet? Nor Mr. Prestwick?"

"No. They are still abed."

Why should the whereabouts of his children, his grown children as to that, matter to her? Certainly she couldn't want George for a paramour; he was far too young at twenty-three to be of any interest to a woman of her mature years. Though she still looked quite young herself. How old was Sophia Dalby? She'd been famous for fully twenty years and yet she didn't look to be anywhere near forty. He couldn't think how she was keeping youth clustered about her white shoulders, unless it were in taking young men for lovers. Well, she couldn't have George.

Unless there was some measurable benefit to either George or himself.

He was not an unreasonable man, after all.

"Oh, this does put me in an awkward position, Lord Prestwick. I do not know quite how to proceed from this point. What would you advise?"

And she looked directly into his eyes, her dark brown eyes as provocative and mysterious as every rumor of them, and her mouth tilted up in the smallest of smiles.

He said what any man would have said. "Proceed directly, Lady Dalby. I promise that you will be well cared for, your every need met, if I may be so honored."

"How gracious you are," she said, leaning forward slightly to adjust her skirt. There was the slightest shadow, just a suggestion really, of the sweep of her bosom. He felt himself harden just below his green silk waistcoat. "It is certainly quite clear how well served the viscountcy will be under your firm hand and wise counsel."

He lifted his chest and grinned. The buttons of his waistcoat felt a bit tight across his chest, but he didn't suppose that was unusual in such a regularly fed man of his years. He looked, he was quite certain, as prosperous as he was.

"What would you have of me, Lady Dalby. I am entirely at your disposal."

"Again, so gracious, but I do not require you to be at my disposal, Lord Prestwick. Only your daughter. And perhaps that lovely stretch of land you own on Stretton Street?"

All thoughts of Sophia Dalby's beauty and charm evaporated like mist. Prestwick was, first and foremost, a man of numbers and accounts, and he was not going to give away anything to anyone, no matter how pretty her bosom happened to be.

"I can't think why you're asking, Lady Dalby. I wouldn't give my mother, if she lived, such a gift."

"Would you give it for your daughter?" she said, leaning back upon her chair, the picture of composure.

"To her or for her?" he asked.

Sophia laughed lightly and nodded her head at him in an entirely pleasant manner. "She is very like you, Lord Prestwick. I do like that about you both. There is something so soothing about a direct answer. One finds so few in Society who are capable of it."

If they hadn't been talking about money and property, he might have taken the time to find offense in the comment. As things stood, he felt the sting of criticism, but not the throb of poisonous libel. After all, it was likely true.

"Miss Prestwick approached me yesterday with a request, Lord Prestwick," Sophia continued. "She asked that I help her find a duke for a husband. I answered that I would, for a price.

As she has nothing I want, she offered you up to me, and quite without hesitation, I might add. I do think it showed such spirit on her part, don't you? A fearless negotiator, your daughter. I do think she should be commended for it."

"She made no arrangement with me," he said, forcibly ignoring the fact that his daughter had been bold enough to offer him, bodily, one assumed, to a beautiful and dangerous woman in the form of payment. Aside from the shock, he was almost flattered. But that was not the point at the moment, more's the pity.

A duke? It was a splendid idea, and if there was one woman in ten thousand who could arrange it, it was Sophia Dalby. Penelope wanted the proper husband and had gone to the proper person to see it done. What she should not have done was left the contract, as it were, open. One did not proceed in any business dealings without all the particulars agreed to, and signed, before the first breath of the first step was taken. A sloppy bit of work, that.

"No, she made it with me, and as we are two adult females, I can't think but that it's binding, no matter the results."

"The results? What do you mean?"

"I mean, Lord Prestwick, that your daughter, all eagerness, made her bargain with me without arranging for payment, and then before I could arrange anything at all for her made a bit of a muck of it with both the Duke of Edenham and the Marquis of Iveston. I can't think what's to become of her marital prospects now, and I did warn her against being precipitous all the while doing what I could to aid her. Still, I did my part and, no matter that her prospects on the marriage mart are exceedingly dim at present, I do think a bargain made must be a bargain kept, don't you?"

"Dim? Why dim? What's happened?"

"Darling Lord Prestwick," she said, smiling gently at him. It was singularly horrifying. "Miss Prestwick has made quite a spectacle of herself, wagers all over the book at White's, first for one man and then the other, and then both together. It's all anyone who has nothing but time in which to idle can speak of. Naturally, as I am quite good friends with Edenham"—and here Prestwick felt a pang of actual pain in the region where he supposed his heart must be, for Edenham, rich as a king and in possession of his title, would have been the perfect husband for Penelope, and Sophia would have been the ideal person to arrange it—"I was able to keep him out of the worst of the fray, for lack of a better word, but Iveston, whom as you must know, is not often out in Society and is very much more inexperienced at dealing with women, fell fully into the thick of it. He and Miss Prestwick have . . ." and she shrugged in a female gesture of helplessness.

He had heard many things about Sophia, but helplessness was not one of them. He didn't quite know what to make of it.

"Have what?" he prompted. "My daughter's reputation is intact, I trust? Penelope has always been a very practical girl, not given to fits of any sort."

"Yes, well, she hasn't always been trying to arrange for a husband, has she?"

"You don't mean to tell me she's been ruined?"

He felt slightly cold and wet across the brow. If he fainted it would be the end of everything. He refused to faint, simply refused.

"No, Lord Prestwick, she is not ruined. Not *quite* ruined."

That didn't sound encouraging at all. How could a woman make *not ruined* sound like the worst possible situation?

"You are proposing something, aren't you? You're here to help."

"I'm here, Lord Prestwick, to be paid." She smiled. "As Penelope is your daughter, I have made the assumption that a bold, straightforward approach would be most welcomed by you. As I told her, I do nothing for nothing and while I am prepared to help her gain her duke, I am not prepared to do so as a public charity. I am quite confident that you understand completely."

He did. He had not got where he was, being a very wealthy viscount, by doing things for nothing. One only did things for nothing for the right person, a person who could eventually, if events fell into a lively order, do something for you. As Sophia was far higher than he on the ladder of privilege and influence, she was not in a position to be required to do something for nothing, and he knew enough about her history to know that she had worked tirelessly to get where she was. He had nothing but admiration for her. Indeed, he only thought it was a very fortunate arrangement of events that Sophia herself did not feel the need for a duke, for surely, as she and Edenham were friends, she could have married him without any effort at all.

What could Penelope have been thinking?

❧

PENELOPE had been thinking all night, not able to sleep in anything more than fits and starts until dawn finally broke and she tumbled into a deep sleep that lasted for three hours. It was going to have to be enough. She simply had to work it out, make everything fall into place.

It was all a hopeless muddle and seemed quite impossible. Things had looked so hopeful yesterday. She had made her arrangement with Sophia, which was hardly an arrangement at all, pursued Edenham with a very logical plan that had somehow landed her all over Iveston for the better part of the day, and now had been made a laughingstock who could not win a man on a bet.

It was simply not to be borne. She was not the sort of girl to tolerate being a laughingstock. Simply not. There was no negotiation about it whatsoever. Things must, from that specific point, be remedied.

She was going to win a man. One of those wagers on White's book was going to be won. But which one?

Penelope paced her bedchamber, her brow furrowed, her feet scuffing across the carpet. Her cat, Peacock, was chasing the train on her dressing gown, batting at her ankles. She was too upset to be either annoyed or amused. She had to marry! Actually, it was more complicated than that. She had to pick a man to marry and then force him into it.

Of course, truly, wasn't that always the way of it? She was very disposed to believe, particularly now, that most men had to be forced into it one way or another, and as long as that was how it worked, why should she feel any shame about what she was being compelled to do? Certainly he would be happy enough once the deed was done and there was no undoing it. There was nothing observable in Society that disputed that notion and, so, it might as well be a fact.

Very well then. It was a fact.

Now, which man must she force and how was she going to go about it?

Her initial plan, to arrange for Edenham to ruin her, seemed the most logical, as well as being the most impractical. She had barely spoken to Edenham. How was she going to get him to ruin her today? For it must be today. She simply could not wait another week, what with all this wagering nonsense, which would only grow worse as the hours passed, the whole of Society watching, waiting to see who, if anyone, would do anything.

And they wouldn't. No, no one, and by that she meant Edenham and Iveston, who had proved himself, hadn't he? He was very nearly a rake, toying with her as he had done, and clearly so proud of himself and not one whit repentant that he had kissed her passionately and done it all for a wager. It had been one thing when they had both been doing it for a wager, and known it, too, but to do it behind her back, that was the worst sort of behavior. She would not have thought he had it in him. How on earth had a man as backward and peculiar as Iveston was reputed to be ever learned how to kiss like that?

Oh, bother, not kiss, but maneuver and manipulate, that's what he was so very good at. Kissing, well, kissing was not so very difficult, was it? One simply put some effort into it and there you were, being kissed.

Being kissed.

Penelope felt her nipples tighten just thinking of it.

She did not have time for tingling nipples now. Now, she had to think how to get herself married. To Iveston.

To Iveston?

She shook her head violently and just barely missed kicking Peacock a glancing blow. Peacock, being a very agile and experienced cat, jumped onto the bed, glared at her, and then jumped down and scooted under the chinoiserie chest where she took up licking her left foot.

Practical cat, Peacock. Get out of the way and then get on with life, which in her case meant a bath.

Peacock's example before her, though she would deny it if anyone ever accused her of taking advice from her cat, Penelope made her choice. It would be Iveston. It had to be. He simply had a leg up on Edenham, what with all their private moments because of the wagers. If only Edenham had been around more, but he hadn't, and that left Iveston.

Penelope felt immeasurably better, that decision made. Now the only thing left to do was to somehow arrange for him to ruin her, and the sooner the better. She grinned and hugged herself just thinking of it.

❧

"THEN we are agreed," Sophia said, eyeing Lord Prestwick appreciatively. She did so enjoy doing business with a man who had a business frame of mind. Penelope became more easily understood after communicating with her father.

Penelope and George looked very much like each other, dark of hair and eye, of slim frame and a sort of quickness of manner that was nothing like Lord Prestwick. Prestwick was barrel-chested and of ruddy complexion. His hair, what he had left of it, was dark blond and frizzy. His eyes were of grayish blue. Still, at heart, Penelope, while she clearly looked like her late mother, was very much like her father.

"Agreed," he said. "You seem very confident, Lady Dalby."

"I am always confident, Lord Prestwick. It is why I succeed so regularly."

Prestwick chuckled and nodded his head. "That is very true. Now, when will you begin it?"

"Now, I should think. It only requires that you summon Lord Iveston to you. He will come and things will proceed from there."

"You will want to speak to Penelope, naturally."

"No," she said slowly, "I should think not. Your daughter is quite able to manage Lord Iveston and, once she is certain who it is that she wants, will get him."

"How can you be certain it is Iveston she wants?"

Sophia smiled. "Lord Iveston will convince her of it, of course. Isn't that how it's usually done, Lord Prestwick?"

Lord Prestwick puffed out his chest and grinned. Sophia smiled encouragingly at him. He was a dear man, wasn't he, and so very agreeable about giving up a lovely bit of land to aid his daughter's matrimonial aspirations. What better thing could be said of a father?

"But if you're not going to speak to Penelope, then what is it that you are going to do to ensure her marriage to Iveston, Lady Dalby?" he asked, which was perfectly right of him as he surely did not want to pay something for nothing.

"I will drop in at Hyde House now, Lord Prestwick, where everything will be managed beautifully. You need not deliver the deed to the land until the day of their wedding. I am that confident."

"Of course, Lady Dalby," he said, bowing.

"A pleasure, Lord Prestwick," she said, dipping her head, her bonnet concealing the very satisfied expression on her face.

Twenty-three

"You won it," Cranleigh said. "I can't think how you managed it, but you definitely won."

"Of course you can," Iveston said almost sullenly. "You can imagine very well how I did it."

"You don't look the worse for wear. I trust you left Miss Prestwick in good condition."

"I suppose you're trying to be amusing?" Iveston said stiffly, looking at Cranleigh a bit severely.

Cranleigh, who had not been smiling, looked even less as if he were smiling. Not quite grim, but close. "Not at all, Iveston."

"Good."

They were sitting in the music room, Iveston at the pianoforte, picking out a tune that began nowhere and went nowhere. It was entirely appropriate to his mood.

He'd won his wager with Cranleigh. There were not words to express how little that meant to him. It had all stopped being about Cranleigh and that meaningless wager from the moment he'd first kissed Penelope, likely a few minutes before. She was an astonishingly forthright little thing, so full of ideas and plans, so blunt in her opinions. Having been hunted by every mama with a bland daughter in tow for the past ten years, conservatively, he could say without qualification that Miss Penelope Prestwick was the only honest woman he'd ever met.

It was nearly thrilling. Certainly it was shocking, at least at first, but once one found one's footing, and he had, it was quite a pleasant experience. No, pleasant wasn't quite the word. Refreshing. Yes, Penelope was refreshing. And exasperating. And impossible. And irresistible.

His tune turned quite melancholy, his fingers finding their own way upon the keys, reflecting accurately, too accurately his private thoughts. He knew this to be so because of the very odd look on Cranleigh's face.

"You don't look at all happy to have won this particular wager."

"It wasn't for very much, was it?" Iveston replied.

"Perhaps for more than you yet realize."

Iveston looked up at Cranleigh and said, "I do realize it, Cranleigh. Don't be absurd."

It was at that moment that Amelia, Cranleigh's bride, entered the music room looking as fresh as sunshine in white muslin with some sort of pattern in blue thread around the hem of her skirts. She smiled upon seeing her husband. Cranleigh grinned. Iveston sighed and let the keys reveal his condition.

"Lady Dalby's just arrived. She'd very much like to see you, Iveston," Amelia said.

"I'm not in to Lady Dalby," Iveston said.

"You should see her," Cranleigh said, which was a shock.

Cranleigh, for the most part, hated Sophia Dalby, though no one could quite understand why. If Cranleigh understood why, he was not forthright about his reasons. Forthright. Only Penelope was reliably forthright. Of course, she was also a woman who had only used him to get another man. That was unforgivable, wasn't it? Obviously. He was no such man to be used that way. Ridiculous of her not to realize that.

"I'm not in," Iveston repeated, his gaze on the keyboard, watching idly as his fingers moved over the keys, the music rising to the high ceiling where it was forever trapped until wasting away to whispers of sound, and then nothing at all.

He heard a few hushed words between Cranleigh and Amelia, ignored them, and then the door opened and Sophia Dalby was admitted, his mother at her side. Words could not express how profoundly miserable he was at this moment.

"Iveston, do stop that dreadful business at the pianoforte," Molly, his mother, said crisply. "I should want to jump into the Thames if I hear one more melancholy note."

Iveston left his seat at the pianoforte, lifted his chin, and faced his mother. As Lady Dalby was smiling at her side, he did not expect mercy. No, nor did he deserve it.

They sat. The music room had recently been done up in a rather stunning shade of aqua green silk damask. The instruments, golden wood and a bit of gilt here and there, mostly upon the harp, looked quite good against the pale green. So, too, did the occupants of the room. Of course, Sophia Dalby looked good in any room.

"Lady Dalby, what delicious *on dit* do you have for us today?" Molly asked as Ponsonby, the butler, supervised the bringing in of tea and cakes.

Cranleigh groaned, and quite audibly, too.

"Cranleigh," Molly said, a scowl forming between her brows that was almost an exact match to Cranleigh's rather famous scowl, "I do think you should get over this horror you have of gossip. How is anyone to know anything without someone having talked about it? Certainly I don't wish anyone ill, but I must know what is going on in Society. How else am I to avoid offending someone if I step into a posthole of my own ignorance?"

"Quite right," Cranleigh said, nodding fractionally. "It would be entirely possible for you to insult, why, even our dear Iveston."

"Oh, don't be absurd. Iveston never does anything," Molly said on a bark of annoyance. It was perfectly clear that she had meant her statement as a compliment.

"I do think you can't have heard of his latest adventure into Society, Molly," Sophia said, pulling off a glove to take a cup of tea from Molly's hand. On her right hand she wore a ruby ring of impressive size surrounded by seed pearls. It made a stunning statement against her white gown and white kid gloves. "Lord Iveston has won quite a wager. Everyone in Town had a pound or two in it. It's all anyone is talking about. You hadn't heard?"

"No," Molly said, staring first at Iveston and then at Cranleigh. "I had not heard the first word."

Molly, born and bred in Boston, of petite frame and iron spine, was not a woman to cross. A mother of six sons, five living, she had the temperament and the inclination to deal with any infraction as fully as she saw fit. She often saw fit. Not a one of her five sons cared to find himself on the wrong side of her; as to that, neither did her husband, the fourth Duke of Hyde.

"It was a small matter, mostly between myself and Cranleigh," Iveston said, refusing a cup of tea with a wave of his hand.

"Mostly? How modest you are, Lord Iveston," Sophia said pleasantly. "Surely you are fully aware that White's book is nearly in tatters because of this small wager."

"Did you wager on it?" Cranleigh asked her.

Sophia smiled, her dark eyes twinkling. "I'm the better by twenty-six pounds, Lord Cranleigh. And you? How much did you lose?"

"Perhaps I won. Did you consider that?" Cranleigh said.

"Of course I considered it, but as the wager, at least the report I had of it, was that you wagered that Lord Iveston should not be able to win any sort of attention from the lovely Miss Prest-wick, and as he has done so much more than that with her, I did think you must have lost. Was I wrong?"

Cranleigh was silent and glaring.

Iveston was silent and sullen.

Neither one of them dared a look at their mother.

"Who did you hear this from, Sophia?" Molly asked.

"Why, from Lord Iveston. He confessed it freely to both the Duke of Edenham and Miss Prestwick. I was standing right there. As was Lady Richard. The poor girl was taken quite by shock, if I am any judge."

"*Oh!*" Amelia said, her blue eyes looking quite accusatory. Cranleigh looked like he wanted to crawl under the rug. Little doubt Molly would beat them both with a broom if they attempted any sort of escape now. "In front of Edenham? And Lady Richard rarely goes out. It could hardly have been comfortable for her, let alone poor Miss Prestwick."

"*Poor* Miss Prestwick can take care of herself," Iveston burst out.

"Quite obviously she cannot!" Molly said, bristling, her eyes gone quite steely grey. "I did think my sons had better manners than to engage in wagers concerning virginal young girls in Society. I would have thought that, with your natural advantages, you would have seen fit to treat others, particularly the *weaker vessel*, with far more care than I have seen witnessed here this Season!" Molly was working herself into quite a rage. Iveston and Cranleigh closed their mouths and endured it. It was not wrong to state that they believed they had it coming. "First Blakes pulls Louisa into a closet in my own house, with half of London pressed against the door, ruining a girl of good lineage, though her father is a lout. Then you, Cranleigh"—Cranleigh's ears turned a bit red along the outer edge—"abscond with poor Amelia into a conservatory and do something entirely dreadful to her dress, ruining her gown and very nearly the girl, and now you, Iveston, of whom I never would have believed it, have done something scandalous to Miss Prestwick, who I am quite certain did nothing whatsoever to you!"

Nothing whatsoever?

No, that was wrong. That was most assuredly wrong.

She had done everything to him. Everything. Nothing was the same now. And never would be again.

"But of course, the wager at White's was entirely different, Molly," Sophia said. "The wager there, one of them, was that Iveston would marry Miss Prestwick. Of course, I don't suppose he should mind losing that wager as it wasn't for much."

"How do you know what is on White's book?" Iveston asked, his voice nearly hoarse with frustrated . . . what? Rage? Longing?

Longing?

No, not longing. Longing for what?

Or for whom?

Sophia simply shrugged, her expression entirely unconcerned. "I find a way to always be aware of what is happening at White's, as well as most of the other clubs. How else is a woman to know what is happening in the world of men and protect herself accordingly?"

Cranleigh laughed, a short bark of abrupt male laughter.

Iveston felt absolutely no desire to laugh, abruptly or not.

"I should think so," Molly said, eyeing her sons most severely. "Why, Miss Prestwick is a perfect example of that. I should say she had no idea that there was a wager with her name on it, poor girl. She was clearly defenseless against you, Iveston. What *did* you do to that dear girl?"

"I wasn't aware that you knew Miss Prestwick," Iveston said in reply. Anyone who referred to Penelope as *dear* and *poor* had clearly never met her.

"I don't," Molly said. "But I am quite certain that she can have done nothing to earn such treatment from my sons. Is that not a true statement?"

Cranleigh looked at Iveston, most suitably abashed.

Iveston took a deep breath and answered, "It is most assuredly true. Miss Prestwick did nothing. And nothing was done to her. Nothing . . . alarming."

"Is that what Miss Prestwick thinks, or is that just wishful thinking on your part, Lord Iveston?" Sophia said just before she took a sip of tea, her black eyes shining merrily at him over the rim of her cup. It was becoming increasingly clear to Iveston why Cranleigh had such violent thoughts about Sophia Dalby so often. She could drive a man to anything. Even marriage. Most especially marriage.

Marriage. He'd thought of it before now, naturally, always in terms of how to avoid it. Now, Penelope dragged into something slightly sordid because of a stupid wager, he found he didn't have quite the same determination to avoid it.

He might have to marry her. Just to save her reputation, of course. She did have a sterling reputation, or had, until the wager, which had got a bit out of hand, actually.

The poor girl shouldn't be made to suffer a lifetime on the shelf simply because of a wager, should she?

Of course not.

He should do the right thing, the honorable thing, and marry the girl.

If she'd have him.

There was that. She didn't seem to want him, not in that way.

Of course, she did want him very much in the other way; there was no hiding that fact, was there?

Iveston found himself smiling for the first time in hours. He simply had to marry her, didn't he? Of course he did. He'd explain to her that it was for her own good, to protect her name, and she would see reason, she was rather famous for that, by her own reckoning, and she would marry him. He was the most logical choice, wasn't he?

Of course he was.

"I do think I should ask her, Lady Dalby," Iveston answered. "That would be the wisest course. When I return, I shall know precisely what Miss Prestwick thinks. About everything."

"I have no doubt of it, Lord Iveston," Sophia said, taking another sip of tea.

Molly sniffed in annoyance and said nothing.

Cranleigh laughed again, quite ruefully, too, which was excessively odd, wasn't it?

Twenty-four

PENELOPE was dressed beautifully in white muslin. The bodice was cut modestly, but flatteringly, the sleeves fitted snugly and ending at the elbow. A silk ribbon in scarlet, quite wide, was tied beneath her bosom, and she was wearing diamond earrings that resembled Spanish fans. She looked, she was utterly certain, enchanting. Quite more than enough beauty and allure to tempt Iveston into ruining her. He seemed on the cusp of it already, didn't he?

He certainly did.

Why, given his past experience, all it should take was a single moment alone and he would be kissing her without restraint.

She could hardly wait. The thing to do, naturally, was to hunt him down, wherever he might be hiding himself. He was either at home or at White's. She did so hope he was at Hyde House for then she could call on Lady Amelia on the pretext of worrying about the return of the torn shawl. That would do nicely. It would give the appearance of courtesy and solicitation when all she was after was the delicious Lord Iveston's mouth and hands upon her person.

Not that she'd changed her mind regarding Edenham at all. Certainly not. He would have made the ideal husband, but as Iveston, for reasons she could still not work out, had been quicker off the mark, then Iveston would simply have to do. She did think he might do rather well.

It was as she was arranging her hair in the hall mirror, arranging a wave to fall just so, that she heard Iveston's voice and Hamilton's reply. With an audible gasp, Penelope hurried to waylay Hamilton before he could announce Iveston to her father. She was perfectly capable of driving a man to ruin, but it would be so much easier and quicker without her father watching on. Obviously.

Hamilton, with a most odd expression on his normally pleasant face, nodded and gave every indication that he would allow her to see to Lord Iveston. With considerable grace, if she did say so herself, Penelope greeted Lord Iveston with a deep curtsey, giving him more than enough time to study her décolleté, and smiling, waited for him to bow. He did. She then waited for him to say something. He did not.

Penelope had a very difficult time not rolling her eyes at Iveston's obvious backwardness, but she did it. Just. She, clearly, was going to have to manage this ruination all on her own. Iveston was, for whatever peculiar reason, going to be obstinate about it. And of all things! One did think, as one had been taught certain truths about men from a most early age, that the one thing a man could manage with almost no thought at all was a simple ruination of an innocent girl. As she wasn't precisely or perfectly innocent, that ought to have made it all simpler. With Lord Iveston, nothing, not even getting his hand upon her breast or a finger under her hemline, was going to be simple.

Penelope nearly sighed in frustration.

In fact, she did. She was frustrated. Most urgently frustrated. She could feel it building in her like a flickering wave of burning water, even though she was nearly certain that there was no such thing as burning water. Certainly she had been more sure of that yesterday, before Iveston and his silly wager and all those nearly innocent kisses.

Iveston looked wonderful today. His eyes very blue, his skin very fair, his hair shining blond. He wore his hair quite short, but arranged forward, and it did set off his brow, which might have been the finest brow of the present Season.

It was as she was admiring his face that he spoke, quite jerking her out of her reflections. "Miss Prestwick, I fear I may have caused you some difficulty. I wagered intemperately. I would not see you hurt by it."

Oh, yes. Quite fully jerked out of her reflections.

"Lord Iveston, I should have thought you would have reasoned it all out before you began. Did you not foresee some difficulty?"

"No, not really," he said.

As the wager, as she gathered, was to make her want him in some obvious fashion, she could not but find it in excessively poor taste that he should say such a thing to her face.

"How predictably odd of you," she said, throwing back her shoulders just a bit. Of course it did wonderful things for her bosom, but it also did wonderful things for her resolve. Perhaps Edenham was not completely out of reach. Perhaps she did not want Iveston to seduce her.

Iveston also straightened and seemed to nearly glare at her. It was nearly funny.

"You have forgotten your own wager? Your double wagers, Miss Prestwick. How could you have hoped to win them both?"

"It should be quite obvious, even to you, that I did not intend to win them both. I have been entirely honest with you from the first, Lord Iveston, which you can certainly not say to me. You were to be a spur, that is all. If I may say so, you did not do an adequate job at all. If you had been paid in coin for such a shoddy performance, I should very much have demanded a full refund."

Iveston was breathing a bit more heavily than she thought was usual for him. His eyes were cobalt blue, and most importantly of all, he had two white spots on his neck, just below his very nicely shaped ears. Really, he had quite a cunningly shaped head and it was quite right of him to keep his hair short, the better to show it off. It also allowed her to notice whenever she had said just the precise thing to bring him to white-hot frustration. Suddenly, she was enjoying herself immensely.

"Perhaps I can do better," he said quietly.

She had learned that, even though Iveston was usually quiet, it did not mean he did not experience the full range of emotional responses. Not at all. In fact, she did begin to think that, at his most quiet, he was the most fully engaged. Perhaps a bit more experimentation was due?

Why not?

"To what purpose? The wager is done, the damage as well," she said, prodding him. She did think she might have a talent for it. And she did so love to acquire new talents.

"To prove myself, Pen," he whispered, taking her arm and leading her into the closest room, which just happened to be the conservatory. She would have chosen better, if there had been a way to do it and still look reluctant. The conservatory didn't even have a chair! It was all roses and stone floors and miles and miles of windows. Hardly a place for a seduction. It wasn't even dark. Everyone knew that the best seductions happened in the dark. "Or, if that does not serve, so that you may prove yourself to me."

"I beg your pardon? Prove myself to you? Whatever for, and as what, I should like to know. I don't have anything to prove to you, Lord Iveston."

"No?" he said, closing the doors of the conservatory behind him, standing in front of them almost menacingly. Ridiculous. Lord Iveston could not menace a small dog, let alone a fully grown woman who had some small history of kissing experience beneath her sash, as it were. Not that any man had ever gotten beneath her sash. In fact, no man had even tried. It was almost, when pondering it on some dreary dead of nights, insulting. "Not the degree to which you have been previously seduced? I confess to having had my curiosity aroused upon that topic. I should like satisfaction, Pen, and I should very much like for you to provide it."

Well, perhaps a small dog. Even a small child. Even, in this rare instance, a small woman, which she happened to be. Iveston was tall and built precisely as a man should be, and the hot blue look in his eyes was just the tiniest bit menacing, in the most delightful manner imaginable. He wanted satisfaction?

Very well, then. So did she.

"You presume quite a lot, Lord Iveston," she said, backing away from him. "Yet, I do find I have my own curiosity about you."

"Have you? Regarding?"

"If you have questions regarding my innocence, it is equally true that I have questions regarding yours. Can you complete a seduction, Lord Iveston? Can you woo? Can you pet? Can you seduce? At all?"

"This is not the sort of thing one discusses with a lady."

"I'm not asking you to discuss it. I'm asking you to prove it."

Iveston looked at her from beneath his golden brows, studying her quite seriously. She stood her ground and met his stare.

"Very well then," he said softly, his eyes as bright as turquoise stones. "I shall prove it upon your body. Will you stand still or will you require me to run you to ground?"

Her heart hammered and the beat echoed between her legs, causing her knees to go all wet and wobbly again.

"I have not yet decided," she answered in a conversational tone. "Must you be forewarned, my lord? Are you afraid I will outpace you?"

Iveston shook his head at her, the smallest smile tugging at the corner of his mouth. "Shall we put it to the test?"

And then her heart trembled within her breast and she tingled in all the right places, and, with a smile, she turned and ran through the roses.

He had her in three steps. Three of her steps. She had no idea how many steps he had taken, likely one large one would have done the job. He had very long, well-turned legs. The thought was enough to make her head swim.

He wrapped one long arm around her from behind, pulling her hard against his length. And he was hard. With the other hand, he tucked his fingers beneath the neckline of her dress and pulled it down as far as he could without tearing the fabric, and then he kissed the top of her shoulder. Her neck. Her back.

His mouth moved slowly, leisurely, deliberately over her skin leaving the whisper of moist heat and carnal hunger in its wake. He ground his hips against her bottom. She pressed back against him. He groaned softly and the hand at her waist moved upward, upward. Her nipples tingled in anticipation and her bosoms ached heavily. He did not disappoint. With unerring accuracy, Iveston untied her bodice. It fell loosely down, a muslin crumple, and caught on the crests of her nipples in an exquisite agony of sensation.

Iveston, that imbecile, did not remedy the situation in the slightest. No, Iveston, backward as ever, turned her in his arms and kissed her fully on the mouth, her breasts and her turgid nipples apparently forgotten. The only thing he was doing right was that he had his leg pressed between hers, which was quite delightful, and he had his hands firmly on her waist, truly encompassing her, and he had his delicious mouth deeply and fully on hers.

Oh, very well. He did have most of it right, but what about her slack bodice and her tempting breasts? Didn't he find them tempting in the slightest? How was it that he was able to resist a quick fondle? Or a slow one, as to that.

What sort of seduction was it when the woman wondered what was wrong with the man, with her, and with the moment?

"Touch me," she commanded as his mouth lifted from hers, working at his cravat with her hands. She wanted the thing off him; she wanted everything off him, to see his naked body, to feel his heat. How white was his skin? Did he have hidden freckles? Was there blond hair on his chest? Did it curl or was it as straight as his hair? "Can't you touch me?"

"What do you think I'm doing," he snarled, grabbing her to him even tighter, her bosoms flattened against his coat. She pulled his cravat off with a growl, tugging it across his neck, holding it in her hands, fighting the urge to strangle him with it.

"Not enough," she snapped. "It's not enough!"

And with that, she grabbed his lapels and yanked his mouth down to hers again, eating him alive. His mouth was hot and wet and furious. She was equally so, everywhere. Hot. Wet. Furious. This man, this mild, wild man, did things to her, made her think things and feel things that she hadn't thought she was capable of. That she hadn't wanted to do or feel until meeting him. Tasting him. Touching him.

"It will never be enough," he said, grinding his hips into hers. "Don't you know that yet?"

"Ridiculous," she said. "It would be enough if you did it right." She punctuated her quite valid critique with bites to his neck, his throat, pushing past the tie of his shirt to open it up, to taste the skin of his chest. She had at least one answer; his chest was nearly hairless, just a light sprinkling of pale golden hair.

"And you know how to do it right?" he said, pressing his thumbs against her nipples and flicking them. She groaned and almost fell to her knees. "Just what did you do with that groom? And where is he now? I think I must kill him."

"Shut up. Shut up, shut up, shut up," she said, her head thrown back, her eyes closed tightly against the sharp pleasure of his hands at her breasts, his thumbs rubbing hard circles on her nipples, his mouth at her throat, lower, moving lower, excruciatingly and slowly lower.

"Did your groom do this?" he whispered, and then he took her nipple into his mouth and bit down, his hand strumming hard at her other nipple.

She cried out and, her knees being all of water, would have fallen at his feet if he had not been holding her so tightly around the waist.

"I truly will kill him if he did this to you, Pen," Iveston said, his breath warm against her skin.

"You don't even know where he is," she said, for truly, someone had to point the truth out to him as he seemed ever to lose the important bits. And, she did suspect it would drive him to distraction.

She was right. It did.

"You love to torment me," he said, moving his mouth to her other bosom. She tried to appear nonchalant about it. She was not at all confident of her performance. "You have an appetite for torment. Shall we test that as well?"

"Oh, no, not at all necessary," she began, and then his hands pushed her bosoms together and he laved them both, nipping and licking and utterly, utterly tormenting her.

She didn't know how she kept her feet. She was trembling all over and her legs were shaking like branches in a winter wind.

"Not necessary? Very well, then," he said, and abruptly stood away from her. Whereupon, she promptly fell to the hard floor, her bodice a complete disaster around her waist.

"You truly are the most peculiar man I've yet to meet," she said.

"And you've met so many men," he countered, not even offering her a hand, but standing well back from her with his arms crossed over his chest. There was something suspicious about that. Something quite important. For all that Iveston was an imbecile and exceedingly peculiar, he had never been impolite.

"Enough to have an opinion on the matter," she said, pulling up her bodice and retying it before making any effort to stand. When she did stand, his cravat still twisted in her hands, she said, "I do think that this would have gone better in the dark, don't you? I can't but think that all this light can't have helped you in your efforts."

"You think I need help?"

"Well," she said with a negligent shrug, "you do seem to have petered out rather quickly, and I was under the impression, my past experience with the groom notwithstanding, that men were able to keep at it a bit longer than you have done. Are you feeling quite the thing, Lord Iveston? Maybe you'd do better after a lie down?"

Iveston stared at her, nodding, with the smallest and most unfriendly smile upon his face. He walked over to her, the roses no hindrance, their blooms full and fragrant, seeming almost to bow as he passed.

Nonsense. He walked through the rose shrubs. There was no more to it than that.

When he reached her, he took the cravat from her hands and said, "Better in the dark? Let's try that, shall we?" And without waiting for a word of permission from her, he took his cravat, that long length of smooth linen, and, standing behind her, tied it around her eyes.

She was instantly, and provocatively, in the dark.

She stood as still as stone, and waited. All her senses, save sight, were quivering in heightened expectation. She could hear his breathing, slow and steady, the frantic thudding of her heart, the faint sounds coming from the kitchen below their feet.

He did not move. She could feel that, feel his nearness and his restraint. It came to her like the humming of harp strings, a thrum of tension that he wouldn't unleash. Not yet. Perhaps not ever. No, surely not that. She wouldn't allow that.

"Is it better in the dark, Pen?" he asked, his voice soft against her ear.

She shivered at the sound of his voice, and suppressed it. "Talking? Is talking better in the dark? I shouldn't say so, Lord Iveston. Not at all. Not a bit of difference."

She heard the quick intake of his breath, a laugh suppressed.

"Not talking," he said. "Right then, we'll make a list and you shall keep the memory of it. Not talking. But then, what of this?"

His hands rested on her shoulders, moved down caressingly, firmly, purposefully to her bosoms, cupping them through the muslin, fingering her nipples. The sensation pulsed through her like an arrow shot and she gasped into the darkness that surrounded her and only her. She was alone in the dark. Iveston watching her in the soft light of late afternoon, the sounds of the street coming softly through the windowpanes, the sound of a door closing somewhere in the house, footsteps distantly . . . and Iveston's hands. His scent surrounded her in the dark. He smelled of cologne, the faint scent of cloves undercutting a musky odor. Or was that the roses?

He undid her bodice ties, an unhurried motion, and pulled the muslin down, exposing her fully to the suddenly chill air of the conservatory. She felt wicked, was certain she looked the worst sort of jade, and she didn't care. No, worse. She liked it.

He ran his hands over her bare breasts, a fingertip inspection, trailing down and around, a man at his leisure exploring a woman designed for his pleasure. He toyed with her, avoiding her nipples while she arched into his evasive touch, flicking her lightly now and again. She moaned and bit her lip, her hands clenched in her skirts, submitting to his touch and the blatant willfulness of his choices over her body.

"Better?" he whispered, his voice magically felt against her bosom, his tongue flicking a nipple almost negligently.

"Marginally," she said softly, lying with the skill of a diplomat.

"Can you measure the difference? I do know how you treasure precision in all things."

And so saying, he kissed each nipple tenderly before suckling deeply, taking her fully into his hands and nipping her. She flinched and groaned. He braced his hands on the sides of her ribs and held her upright.

"What say you, Pen? Are you a woman who requires darkness or will you burn in sunlight with just as hot a fire?"

"I think, Lord Iveston," she said, "that it must depend upon who is wielding the torch."

"And who wields the torch that lights you up?"

She could not see him. But she knew. She knew he was staring at her with all the heat of a hundred suns lighting his eyes to blue fire.

She took off her blindfold and held it in one hand, its ends tumbling onto the floor, and stared at him. He was on his knees looking up at her, at her naked breasts, at her naked eyes.

"Lord Iveston," she said softly, dropping to her knees in front of him. "Lord Iveston," she repeated in a whisper.

He took her in his arms and lifted her dress back up over her back to cover her, kissing the top of her head, her cheeks, her mouth.

"I'm in love with you, aren't I?" she asked, looking deeply into his eyes.

"Yes, Pen," he murmured, kissing her mouth, sealing the thought.

"How long have I loved you, Iveston?"

"From the first kiss, Penelope, which is just as long as I've loved you."

"I shouldn't have thought that possible," she said, wrapping her arms around him and burying her face against his chest. "Of course, you will marry me, won't you? I'm quite completely ruined."

"I would have married you anyway, Pen, with or without ruination."

"Would you? I have my doubts about that, Iveston, but I shan't blacken the moment with discussing it."

"I would appreciate that, Pen, I truly would."

They held each other for many more minutes, the light going quite lavender grey, the roses all around them slowly losing their color in the fading light.

"Iveston?"

"Yes?"

"Now that I'm completely ruined, have you given any thought to finishing the job?"

Iveston pulled back from her, studied her face, stood, offered her his hand, and then when they were both standing and their clothing in good repair, turned his back on her.

"No. I have not."

If that wasn't just like a man.

"I can't see what's to be lost now. There's no need to get sentimental about it, is there?"

"Sentimental?" Iveston said, turning to face her again, his features flatly aghast.

"Certainly sentimental. I have needs, Iveston. I should think that, as my future husband, you should be the one to meet them. In point of fact, I should think you'd want to."

"I shall meet all your needs, and happily. Once I am indeed your husband."

He looked a proper prig, truth be told. She wouldn't have thought it possible that the same man who'd tied his cravat around her eyes and stripped her half bare would turn prudish now that they'd come to an agreement. A man as changeable as that was not to be fully trusted, that was plain. He might, if the occasion presented itself, seek a way out. After all, he hadn't loved her even two days ago, had he? He might be the sort who fell in and out of love like a monkey on a chain.

Certainly she couldn't let him escape now, now that she had discovered she loved him. She knew herself very well and knew she was not one to fall into love often or easily. No, it was Iveston for her. Now she had to make certain that it was Penelope for Iveston.

There was only one thing to do. She had to ruin him fully. He would thank her later, she was certain.

"Now, Iveston," she said, walking up to him. She must have had some look in her eye for he backed away from her. She wasn't too worried. The windows were behind him. Where could he go? "Why so skittish? I only want to kiss you."

"Penelope," he said, trying to sound stern, no doubt. Poor Iveston.

"Yes?"

"We should go find your father."

"We will."

She was stalking him through the roses, poor Iveston backing away from her, tipping over a pot or two, the roses tumbling together, falling in a quiet sprawl. The conservatory, her conservatory, the room that was supposed to win her a husband, was in shambles and getting worse by the moment. All to a good cause, though, wasn't it?

"He could have reservations, be reluctant to give you to me," Iveston said. She could see his eyes, his beautiful blue eyes, sparkling in the light coming from the glass doors to the hall. He looked both alarmed and charmed. As well he should.

"He won't," she said. "Who could possibly be reluctant about you? You're Hyde's heir."

"You were reluctant."

"I'm not now," she said, laughing.

"You thought me peculiar. Don't deny it."

"I certainly did. When you act peculiar, you should not be surprised when you are found peculiar. Rather how you are behaving now, Iveston. Am I to be required to tear the coat from off your very lovely body?"

Iveston stopped. Of course, his back was to the window, the light all but gone now, the lights in the houses across the street illuminating the windows in flickering golden rectangles. He had nowhere to go. Nowhere but into her arms.

"You couldn't. What would you say to your father?"

"I would say," she said, standing up against him, her hands wrapped around his back, her mouth kissing his neck, "that you were blind with love for me, ruined me completely, and that your coat was torn as I struggled to resist you."

"An interesting telling of events. Quite imaginative," he said, kissing her face, running his hands down her back.

"Well, he is my father. I can hardly tell him the truth."

"And the truth is?"

"That I quite thoroughly ravaged you, Iveston. Haven't you guessed?"

And with the words, she ripped his coat very nearly off his body. The rose thorns did help some, but she had done the best work of it, let there be no doubt about that.

∞

LORD Prestwick and Lady Dalby sat staring at each other in the red drawing room, listening to the sounds of tumbling pots coming from the conservatory on the other side of the wall. Lord Prestwick looked uncomfortable. Sophia did not.

"I think that certainly enough time has passed for Lord Iveston to make his presence known to me," Prestwick said, pulling at his waistcoat.

"Darling Lord Prestwick, you simply must trust your daughter on this. I have no doubt at all that she is managing Lord Iveston quite beautifully and will do most of your work for you. She does have that way about her, which you've certainly noticed. I know I have."

"You're certain that he'll offer for her," Prestwick said.

"Completely," she answered. "What's more, so is Miss Prestwick. If she were in any doubt as to her eventual success she would seek help. As she has not, I know things are well in hand." And by *things*, she meant men, but there was no good reason to inform Prestwick of that. He was Penelope's father, after all, and fathers did require a great deal of protection from knowing what their daughters did when hunting upon the marriage mart.

"And if he doesn't?" Prestwick asked, fussing with his sleeve, until the sound of a pot breaking and shattering upon the floor of the conservatory echoed through the house. Then he turned a bit white, then flushed, then stood up to walk about the room.

"Then you shall insist upon it," she said, "and he will agree as Lord Iveston is a most honorable man."

"Honorable?" Prestwick said, staring at the wall that separated the red drawing room from the conservatory. Sophia was completely certain he was not staring at the very nice landscape painting hanging there. "You can say that? Now?"

Sophia smiled and said as gently as she could, "Darling, do you know your daughter at all? I am quite certain she is managing Lord Iveston beautifully and indeed, will achieve everything she wants from him. What's more, she will manage it so that Iveston wants to give her everything she wants from him. What more is there to it than that?"

What more, indeed?

Twenty-five

Four weeks later

THE wedding was an intimate affair, but the wedding breakfast, held at Hyde House, was a complete crush. One could hardly blame Lord Prestwick for wanting to rejoice extremely publicly in his daughter's profoundly good match to Hyde's heir, and as to that, the Duke and Duchess of Hyde, who had seen three of their five sons married in a single Season, were glowing in satisfaction.

Of course, George and Josiah Blakesley, the two remaining sons without wife, were planning to leave the country on the first available ship.

As if running ever did any good.

Sophia surveyed the red drawing room of Hyde House with a very contented gaze. As all of Society and certainly all of the Blakesley family saw this as a very important marriage, Lord Henry and Lady Louisa had returned from wherever they had been to attend, and poor Lord Cranleigh and Lady Amelia had never even got to leave on their wedding trip, Lord Iveston's marriage to Miss Prestwick having been announced before they could make their departure. As Hyde House was quite large and possessed of very many bedrooms, Sophia did not think either couple was suffering, although as to that, neither couple was in the habit of confining themselves to bedrooms. Miss Prestwick was clearly of the same mold. One did begin to wonder if it was a family trait, which did cause her to look at the Duke and Duchess of Hyde with new eyes. What a charming family.

Penelope, their newest member, made her way through the throng very purposefully until she stood directly in front of her.

"Lady Dalby, I wanted to thank you. You were an invaluable help to me, which I'm certain you must know."

Sophia smiled. Charming girl, she did so thoroughly enjoy Penelope. The girl was a complete original. "Darling, you did it all yourself. Certainly you must know that."

"I know nothing of the sort, Lady Dalby," she answered stoutly. "In fact, I know you must have done a considerable amount on my behalf for the simple reason that I made no forward progress at all until sitting myself down in your white salon and begging for you help."

"Were you begging? I had no idea," Sophia answered, swallowing a laugh.

"I certainly felt as if I were begging," Penelope said, smiling a bit reluctantly. "I don't know quite how I find myself with Iveston, even now, though I do love him deeply, which is also a bit of a surprise, isn't it?"

"Is it?" Sophia responded.

Penelope, her black hair up in quite a becoming manner, just a few curls trailing across her shoulders, looked quite happily confused by the whole manner of her marriage. Well, she was young yet. She'd work it out in time.

"I suppose I may confess that I did think Edenham would be the best choice," Penelope said softly, but by no means in a whisper. As it was her wedding breakfast to Iveston that was being celebrated, and as at least four people could possibly have heard her confession, Sophia raised an eyebrow and waited. "Oh,

Iveston knows all about it," Penelope continued in response to the eyebrow. "I don't have any secrets from him. What would be the point?"

Yes, very young. And clearly unscarred by life's little adventures. Sophia had a great many secrets from a great many people, and could not see anything to be gained by vomiting them up all over Town. But then, she was no longer young, and even when young, she had never been as young as Penelope was now.

"I understand completely," Sophia said, and she did. "I don't think you'll be surprised to hear that I always believed Iveston to be an ideal choice for you. I'm so pleased that you saw that for yourself and managed to deliver him to the altar."

"It was like that, wasn't it?" Penelope asked on a whisper, laughing. "It was an awful bit of work, let me tell you, and he was most obstinate for far longer than made any sense at all, but I did manage it."

"You most certainly did, and managed it quite well. You are content, darling? Truly content?"

"I am," she said, her dark eyes glowing, smiling devilishly. "But Iveston and I have discussed it fully and we have decided that we are each going to give you a gift, because we both know, no matter what you may say to the contrary, that without you we should not have found each other. We are quite firm about it, Lady Dalby. We are going to give you a gift."

"Well, if you've decided quite firmly, then I simply must graciously accept, mustn't I?" Sophia said with as straight a face as she could manage. "May I enquire what it is to be?"

"Oh, but you must have guessed," Penelope said. "It's something of a family tradition now, and we shouldn't like to break form with tradition. Iveston is to give you a lovely Chinese porcelain, and I, because practicality must rule the day, even in gifts, have arranged for a spectacular black lacquer cabinet in which the porcelains may be displayed. You approve?"

Sophia grinned and took Penelope's charming chin in her hand and said softly, "I quite approve. And you are so right. If I'm to receive porcelains every week, I must have a proper place for them, mustn't I? Trust you to think of it, Penelope. But where are all these porcelains and black lacquer cabinets coming from? Not the shops?"

"Oh, no," Penelope said. "From the Elliots, the American branch of the family, though Lord Cranleigh did have a store of exotic items packed away, a legacy of his travels abroad. But two Elliot ships have come in, just two days ago from New York and six days ago en route from China. You can imagine the joy in the house, having such an impromptu reunion, and just in time for the wedding."

"Yes, I can imagine," Sophia said, searching the room with her eyes. "And what did you think of the Elliots?"

"Not at all what I should have expected," Penelope said, toying with the end of a black curl. "I have little experience of Americans, none really outside of your nephews."

"Which would not be at all the same, would it?" Sophia said lightly.

"No, I don't suppose it would," Penelope said, nodding, considering. "But where are the men of your family? I know they were invited."

"Gone off to France, darling, along with all the rest. My brother, my son, my nephews, even Lord Hawksworth. Didn't Amelia tell you?"

"I don't think she knows," Penelope whispered, looking across the vast room to where Amelia stood with Louisa, her cousin and sister-in-law by marriage. "They don't get on very well, from what I understand. My brother George is so reasonable and so affable compared to hers, from what I gather."

"Oh, don't believe everything you hear, darling. I think that once you've become closely acquainted with Lord Hawksworth you will find him a most affable man. Sometimes sisters do not see their brothers in the most flattering light."

"Perhaps because they so seldom stand in one," Penelope said abruptly, and then laughed. "Oh, but there are the Elliots. Have you met them? I'll introduce you, shall I? I do think you'll get on well together, both being Americans as you are."

Sophia could only look at Penelope, convinced she meant her words and wondering how she could be so uninformed. Youth again, she supposed. Youth was a vast excuse and covered so many sins; it was extremely unfortunate that it did not last a lifetime.

"Before I must share you," Penelope said, "I did want to make certain that you received proper payment in agreement of our bargain. My father did make mention of it, telling me that he was taking care of it all, but I did want to make certain. You did make it all possible, Lady Dalby. I shall never forget it, or you."

Sophia looked deeply into Penelope's black eyes, eyes so like her own, yet sheltered in a way that Sophia had never been. There was a loveliness to innocence, to shelter and protection and ignorance as to how difficult life could become so very quickly. Perhaps the loveliness of innocence was rooted in its very fragility. Certainly, it was to be treasured for as long as it lasted.

"That is most kind of you to say, Penelope. I shall never forget you and this moment either. Rest assured, I have been compensated. Lord Prestwick is as honorable and forthright as his daughter."

Prestwick, true to their bargain, had sent his man round with the deed to the land on Stretton Street that morning. The plot on Stretton Street was partly in answer to the very last remnant of her innocence being stripped from her so long ago.

That land was now hers. Lord Westlin had wanted it, and she had it. Delicious. But truly, annoying Westlin was merely a side issue, a pleasurable one, but still a side issue. The plot bordered the entire length of Devonshire House, which was a lovely and well-deserved irony. She had boxed them in, quite as fully as she had been boxed in when she'd arrived in London those many years ago, young and alone and in need of family.

Family by way of the Spencers had been denied her.

As Georgiana Spencer had married the Duke of Devonshire, and as the duke was not at all pleased with his wife for her deficiency in producing an heir, taking in a young half-breed from America had been deemed a risk the Spencers were not willing to take. The duke must be appeased, however and whenever possible. Sophia had been refused admittance, and so she had been thrown back upon the streets of London to make her way as best she could.

And so she had made her way as best she could, and she had done very well at it.

She was having her revenge in well-managed bites, and there was nothing anyone could do to stop her.

It was as Penelope was leading her through the throng toward where the Elliots were standing, looking quite definitely American in their stance and general bearing, that Lord Ruan caught her eye from across the room and began to move in the same general direction.

Lord Ruan, quite unexpectedly, had not parked himself upon her doorstep in the past four weeks, but had been scarcely seen. She had wondered at it initially, having thought they were surely on their way to a most pleasant dalliance, and then she had put him from her mind. Seeing him now thrust him very forcibly back into her thoughts and into her path. She could not quite decide how she felt about that, though she did feel a slight quickening in her breathing and a single, weak flutter in her heart.

He was a most stellar-looking man with quite a unique air about him. There was that. That alone would have been enough, but that he had another more mysterious quality about him, something of immense strength and perhaps even sorrow shading his piercing green eyes. Well. It was enough to intrigue any woman.

And then the Elliots were before her and Penelope was managing the introductions quite nicely, until things skipped slightly out of her hands, as things were wont to do when one did not quite know the players in the game as well as one might have done.

"Lady Dalby," Captain Jedidiah Elliot said, his grey blue eyes sparkling. "Sophia. It is good to see you again."

"You know each other?" Penelope said just as Iveston came up behind her and put a hand upon her waist. She leaned into the pressure of his hand slightly. It was utterly charming.

"I've heard stories about Sophia, Lady Dalby, all my life," Jedidiah replied.

"Darling, I can't possibly be that old," Sophia said serenely. "We met briefly two years ago, when Captain Elliot was on his return from his first trip to China. But I have not had the pleasure of meeting the other Elliots. Mr. Joel Elliot, is it?"

"It is, ma'am," he answered, bowing curtly, a huge smile on his face. "Though it's captain as well. My first ship, my first time in a London port, my first meeting of the famous Sophia Dalby."

Whereas Jedidiah, older than his brother by a year, was tall and of angular frame, Joel was more muscular and broader of shoulder. Jedidiah was possessed of straight brown hair that had a clear tendency to be shot with blond streaks, whilst his brother had dark brown curling hair. Jedidiah had grey blue eyes, quite like the seas off Ireland, and Joel a darkly rich brown. One would suppose that they were not of the same mother and father, yet they were. It was merely that Jedidiah had his mother's coloring, very much in keeping with Molly, the Duchess of Hyde's coloring, and as Sally Elliot was Molly's sister, the situation was well explained. Joel looked very much like his father. But it was the third Elliot who had captured Sophia's full attention. She had not expected her.

"My sister, Miss Jane Elliot," Joel said with a cocking of his head. "She insisted that as I was coming to London she be allowed to grab a ride across. I'm going to leave her here while I go on to China. She was going to spend a few months with Aunt Molly, perhaps see a bit of England, and then return to New York on the first Elliot ship. Now that Jed's here, she'll be going back sooner than any of us thought."

"And I'm to suffer for it," Miss Jane Elliot said. She was quite stunningly beautiful with softly curling dark brown hair and huge dark brown eyes. There was something quite poetic about her brow and the angle of her nose was an artist's dream. "I thought I might be here for at least part of the Season, but we had a leak below decks on the larboard and had to stop at Nantucket for repairs. Then we spent two weeks in the Azores, and now I've come to find the Season is nearly over and Jed ready to ferry me off. Arriving for Iveston and Penelope's wedding has been a wonderful thrill, but it seems that it's all that's allowed me."

"How absurd," Sophia said. "I know Molly would love to have you for a year. There is no need to rush off simply because your brothers must."

"We promised our father," Jedidiah said. He was the more serious of the two, that much was obvious.

"And your mother, too, I should expect," Sophia said, "but they could hardly have known that Miss Elliot would not have any time at all to experience the joys and intrigues of London Society."

"Intrigues?" Miss Elliot asked.

"Joys?" Captain Joel asked.

"Father?" Captain Jedidiah reminded.

"There isn't much use in mentioning fathers to Lady Dalby," Iveston said. "She simply ignores their existence when there is an intrigue at her fingertips."

"Lord Iveston, you are utterly wrong," Sophia said, smiling. "I never ignore fathers. I give them most careful and most studious attention, and then I do what I want with their tacit approval, even if their knowledge of what they are approving is a bit faulty."

Penelope coughed lightly and looked at the floor.

"I could never achieve Father's approval," Miss Elliot said. "He's not here and Jed won't move from his promise. I've tried."

"I haven't tried," Sophia said softly, smiling at Jedidiah.

Jedidiah shook his head repeatedly, but he smiled slightly in return.

It was all but settled. Jane would stay in England, and her brothers would sail across the seas without her.

❧

THE Duke of Edenham had escorted his sister Katherine to the wedding. Katherine, he was pleased to see, was chatting happily with Molly, the Duchess of Hyde, who was glowing with happiness. Small wonder with Iveston finally married. He wasn't sure what had happened there, but he knew Sophia Dalby had been at the heart of it. Good for her. If managing to get the difficult ones married entertained her, there were worse things. Certainly everyone seemed happy enough with the outcome. He could hardly quibble with happiness.

Edenham strolled the edges of the red reception room, exchanging a word or two with everyone there, knowing he was doing exactly what Sophia would want him to do and not able to stop himself. She was correct. He had spent too much time in mourning, as had Katherine. It was unhealthy, and it bred gossip.

He'd had far too much of gossip. Being a duke at a young age, he'd been gossiped about, naturally. And the gossip had been of the natural type. He'd barely noticed it. But upon the death of wife after wife, and even his child with his last wife, both dying in the same bed, in the same hour, the gossip had grown teeth and horns.

He did not like being talked of. He did not like being stared at. He did not like being thought of as the duke who killed his wives.

He had not killed his wives. They had died. People died every day. It was only that more of his people died than any other, and on more days.

Katherine's situation hardly helped matters. Her husband had been profligate and had, as these things went, been killed in a duel. And so they found themselves.

Hiding away did nothing to stop it. Very well, then. He and Katherine would face it. And by facing it, they would kill it.

Let the gossips talk of that, of how they, between them, killed every rumor circling their family name.

"Lord Dutton, how good to see you," Edenham said pleasantly.

"Edenham," Dutton said, his eyes slightly glassy. The rumor of Dutton was that he was again becoming a five-bottle-a-day man with energetic ambition. It looked to be entirely true. "A sprawling affair, isn't it? Not at all like the backstreet intimacy of Staverton's marriage to Mrs. Warren Tuesday last."

"I suppose not. As this is a first marriage for both, and as Iveston is the heir apparent, I think that must explain it."

"I suppose it must," Dutton said, taking a long drink from his glass. Port wine.

"You attended the Staverton wedding?"

Dutton snorted, a most unattractive sound. "Hardly."

"You know very much of it, having not attended."

"Rumor only, which I find most usually reliable, don't you?"

"I couldn't say," Edenham said, not at all impressed. Dutton hadn't always been such a sot, had he? It didn't seem so. But then, he and Dutton had never run in the same circles beyond the boundaries of White's.

"If Sophia starts the rumor, then it's solid, is what I've found," Dutton continued, staring across the room to where Sophia stood. "She might make it up, but she makes it true. Eventually."

Nonsense, most assuredly.

"Who's she caught in her net, now? Who's that girl? Do you know her?" Dutton asked, drinking again.

Edenham looked again and saw a girl. The girl.

She was exquisite.

He had never seen her before.

She was remarkable.

He took a step in her direction. And then another. And another.

Iveston and Penelope moved off to another group, making their rounds of the room, spending time with each of their guests. Quite right. Most hospitable of them.

Edenham stood where Iveston had stood, Lord Ruan suddenly at his side, two Americans before him, cousins to the Blakesleys, that's all he got of the connection, but it was a good one, wasn't it? It would be a good match, though it was a bit surprising to find that she was an American.

Miss Jane Elliot.

He would marry Miss Jane Elliot of New York.

He couldn't make a bit of sense of the conversation, was vaguely aware that the men were captains of merchant ships, that Miss Elliot might or might not be staying in Town, that Sophia wanted Miss Elliot to stay.

Yes. Stay.

I'm going to marry you.

It would not be difficult. He was a duke, after all, and he could marry anyone he chose, within reason. Miss Elliot was most definitely within reason. She was related to the Duke of Hyde, and that was good enough for him.

He stood, murmuring the right words at the right moment, aware somewhat dimly that Miss Jane Elliot did not seem at all impressed by him. She had not heard of him, surely, which was to his benefit, wasn't it? No gossip to soil her ears, turning her against him before she even got to know him. She would not be afraid. There would be no hesitation.

Miss Elliot and her brothers were snatched up by Cranleigh, and they walked across the room to some distant spot. Miss Elliot had not seemed at all unhappy to walk away from him. No, she had gone readily enough, no lingering looks at him, no shy smiles, no virginal blushes as she endured his stare.

It must be the American strain. Certainly Sophia was very similar in her responses to men. Odd behavior for a woman when she held a duke's attention, but he was prepared to discount it as a result of her early environment and certainly nothing so serious as a flaw in her nature.

Somehow, and it seemed to take an age, he got rid of Ruan and got Sophia alone in one of the corners of the room. There were still too many guests to have his conversation with her freely, and it was not wise in the least particular, but he could not seem to stop his tongue.

"I want your help, Sophia," he said.

"Of course. Anything at all, Edenham," she answered promptly.

"I want to marry again."

"But how lovely! And of course you should. Do you know whom yet?"

Edenham blinked. He could actually feel himself blink. He

hesitated only a moment and then he said, "Miss Jane Elliot. I will marry Miss Elliot."

Sophia held herself very still, and then she nodded once, slightly, and said, "But darling, haven't you only just met her?"

Of course, it sounded ridiculous when said outright that way. But it happened every day, didn't it? A man saw a woman he admired or even merely desired, and he took her. There was nothing especially complicated about it, was there?

Naturally not.

"I have. And I have decided. She would make me an ideal wife, I believe. I am, you will be forced to admit, a good judge of women. Haven't my three previous wives been exemplary?"

"They have," Sophia said solemnly, but her eyes were shining mysteriously. He was entirely suspicious of anything mysterious. "Yet I must point out that you were not married for any great length of time to any of them. Through no fault of your own, naturally."

"Thank you," he said, gazing across the room at Miss Elliot. She radiated beauty and sound breeding, her skin and hair and eyes . . . well, he could go on and on, but what was the point? He would marry her, that was all. "Since you agree with me, and since it is clear to me that you have some warmth of acquaintance with the Elliot family, I would ask you to help me present my suit to her."

Sophia nodded, looking at some middle distance between himself and Miss Elliot, plotting, no doubt. He was entirely approving of plotting, as long as it got him Jane Elliot.

"That may prove difficult," Sophia said, looking up at him.

"Why, if I may ask? I am in the pink of health and possessed of every attribute a woman seeks in a husband. I am a duke, after all."

Sophia nodded again, this time her smile escaping her compressed lips. "Yes, darling, and that is precisely the problem.

What does an American girl want with a duke? They have no use for them, you see, not you personally, you understand, but as a concept, as an ideal. To her, you are simply a man far older than she, living in a country that is foreign to her, with three dead wives and two small children to his credit. Why, my darling Edenham, would Miss Elliot want to marry you?"

To his absolute horror, he could not think of any reason that did not involve his being a duke of England.

Claudia Dain is an award-winning author and two-time RITA finalist. She lives in the Southeast and is at work on Sophia's next highly successful attempt at matchmaking.